Half-way There

Based on a True Story

By
Martha Harris

www.bookmanmarketing.com

© Copyright 2000, 2004, Martha Harris

All Rights Reserved.

No part of this book may be reproduced, stored in a
retrieval system, or transmitted by any means,
electronic, mechanical, photocopying, recording,
or otherwise, without written permission
from the author.

Reviewers may quote brief passages.

ISBN: 1-59453-151-X

Cover Story

The sun tilted its spout to pour out more beauty of its radiant color, on and on as far as one could see. I was a child again—all new and free of life's empty shell of wanting to be filled.

Green grass sprouted from the banks of Cold Branch Creek. Four-leaf clovers and daisies blanketed the foreground of our resting place beyond its edge. Nature divided and gave out its shares of beauty to wild flowers of many colors. Even the clouds beyond the hills were waiting their turn to douse the creek and its surroundings.

A visionary part of me reached out to touch what I'd missed in earlier life. Even the poison ivy, clinging to the trunk of a cherry tree, had set me free. It didn't hurt me then or ever again.

The top of the hill was in sight. I visualized the green, rolling meadows just beyond. Yellow, golden daffodils on both sides of the path led me into the valley of truth.

A smile lit up my face, and I was skipping again.

This is only a dream, a resting place on my way to *A Place Called There*. As for now, I realized I'm only *Half-Way There*. My dreams are my foundation, the inner core of my personality. They will not exceed the main structure of my being.

About the Artists

Rudine Taggart is a self-taught artist, living in Rainier, Oregon. She enjoys working with ink and watercolor. With thirty-five years of experience, she has perfected her artwork in pictures such as the fall scene following Chapter 2, titled Conditioned. I'd like to call it "Color My Mind."

Other scenes in this book done by Rudine are the cover picture, titled "Half-Way There"; "The Blizzard," renamed "Let's Press On," following Chapter 11, Fugitive From the South; "Angel Form," following Chapter 26, MySher; and the Dogwood tree named "Hope," following Chapter 34, My Religion of Reality.

Virginia Rainey of Longview, Washington, specializes in portraits. There were no pictures of Tommy available when he was young. Virginia took him back in time to when he was a young boy, even younger than what he looked like when most of this book took place.

Acknowledgements

Johan Lindblad, my son-in-law, sent me the taped recording of *I Will Always Love You* from Sweden and granted me permission to use it in this book. He was a member of the band "Sin City" who dedicated the song to my daughter, Sherry, at their wedding. The band composed and played hard rock music, but this one was soft rock. The lead guitarist, Johan's distinctive feature was his long, beautiful hair, even longer than "MySher's."

Jan (pronounced Jaun) Svensson, keyboard player in the band, wrote it. Shortly afterwards, he died at the age of 21. In the early 1990s, he fell from the top of a building during a party in Los Angeles. The band was beginning to see great advancement until then. Their relationship dissolved after his death. Peter Sandberg of Norway sang it. Other members were from Sweden. Sebastian Hagar, the drummer, was their "front man." Under the Scorpion Zodiac sign, Sebastian was an entertainer who sold the band.

The poem "Methamphetamine" I took from my daughter's journal with her permission. I changed only a couple words. According to Sherry, she and a few of her male friends wrote it.

Ronnie Monroe, pictured with Sherry after the poem "Methamphetamine" and before Chapter 29, was the lead singer of a band that performed in the Seattle-Longview areas. Occasionally, I went out with Sherry where he sang. Ronnie called me his "Sweetheart," but no one ever took him seriously. Some nights, I had more fun than they did. Sherry dressed me in red leathers once to enter a dance contest. I didn't win, but the group wanted to start a dance and name it after me. I don't think they were ever serious about that either, but I loved all the attention, even the videos Sherry took of me just having fun. Sometimes Ronnie came to parties at my house. At one of those parties—I don't remember Ronnie being at this one—there were members from five different bands who showed up, including Alabama. That was when Alabama was singing at the Attic in Longview, Washington, and when the group was just beginning. Those were the good old days and definitely happier times.

I would also like to thank Desiree Hellegers of the Washington State University in Vancouver, Washington, for her advice. She is in the creative writing department there.

Others who helped with this book are Shirley Johnson of Hayesville, N.C., who helped me with the proofreading and my piano teacher in Longview, Washington, who helped me compose the song *We Thank Thee*. It's been many years since this was first done—1972. I don't remember her name.

Contents

Chapter 1
Man or Beast..1
When I was a young girl I accidentally caught my brother, Tommy, and a large group of teeneage boys engaged in sexual intercourse with the family cow. "That's life on the farm."

Chapter 2
Conditioned...9
The conditioned life learned in the foothills of the beautiful Blue Ridge Mountains of North Carolina.

Chapter 3
"Cap it, damn it!"..15
An unusual character teaches Tommy how to survive in the wilderness.

Chapter 4
As Strong as Death..17
A German Shepherd goes mad and still displays love beyond expectation.

Chapter 5
A Way Out...23
After running away from responsibilities and life itself, I came home. My father said, "Toots, don't ever leave me again. I would have been dead a long time ago, if it hadn't been for you." I could never leave him after that, but sometimes I prayed for his death.

Chapter 6
Unmarked Angel...27
A human being represents an angel with godly deeds.

Chapter 7
Fading Away...37
My father's new destination with death diminishes his pain, his history, his sanity, and his life.

Chapter 8
Dead and Buried...45
The way a child sometimes handles a parent's death.

Chapter 9
Clouded Future...49
Formally meeting my future sister-in-law who had previously tried to kill me.

Chapter 10
Thelma and Louise and Me Too..53
A ghost indirectly brings me to live with my brother, Jimmy, and my sister-in-law, Thelma.

Chapter 11
Fugitive from the South...59
In one of Tommy's escapes from prison, he meets a woman of prestige.

Chapter 12
Thunder Row..69
Stories about Tommy being imprisoned with "The Birdman of Alcatraz" told beside a campfire while an "albino" mountain lion prowls in the dark.

Chapter 13
Stage of Never Ending Dramas..75
Being lost or virtually lost and finding a way home.

Chapter 14
Two Dresses for a Blue Lady..81
A lost love that can never be regained, but it can never be forgotten. "Will love come back for me?" I ask myself.

Chapter 15
Ride the Wave..87
Feeling emerged in someone's path so much that you can't control what happens. A giant wave wraps around you and takes you to wherever.

Chapter 16
Words of Hope...93
Getting an education the hard way.

Chapter 17
Ups and Downs..99
The "highs" and the "lows" of a relationship.

Chapter 18
Friends and Neighbors...103
A person could do without some friends and neighbors, one might think.

Chapter 19
I Was Once There..109
A love that only comes once in a life-time.

Chapter 20
The Storm..111
The fun loving personality of my second husband left me with no room for improvement until I said goodbye.

Chapter 21
Angel on Her Shoulder..115
Linda Carter, a friend, tells me about the comforting hands of a spirit and shows me a letter from God, which mysteriously appears on her coffee table.

Chapter 22
I Want to Believe in Cinderella...121
The real personality of my brother, Jimmy, is revealed.

Chapter 23
When I Think of Tony..131
Recollections of my youngest brother, Tony, after his accident. He was burned beyond recognition and died about two weeks later. His death and the death of two other relatives, who had also died mysteriously, left puzzlement somehow connected to a calico cat.

Chapter 24
"Poppy"..137
My grandfather, they called him "Poppy." He wasn't the "Grandpa" we all would like to have.

Chapter 25
What Keeps It Alive?...147
The love of a man that goes beyond "till death do us part."

Chapter 26
MySher...153
My beautiful daughter recognizes help from "The Old Man" who lives in our dreams, in our hearts, in the sky, and all around us. He takes the place of her adopted father for awhile.

Chapter 27
The Presence of Good and Evil...167
The inviting feeling of good can only come when we face the evasion of bad and discard it.

Chapter 28
Evasive Goodbye..175
The power drugs holds over a person, to the point it destroys everything of value in just one short moment.

Chapter 29
Live in Hell and Die and Go To Hell...183
The combination of a daughter's addiction to drugs and a boyfriend's addiction to alcohol brought back an old phrase—"Live in hell and die and go to hell."

Chapter 30
My Prayers...187
Hopelessness brings prayer and prayer brings relief and healing, regardless of the scares.

Chapter 31
Father and Daughter 191
Shameful secrets I let go of.

Chapter 32
Under "L" for Heart Doctor 195
An unusual description of love gives warmth.

Chapter 33
Dreams 199
Curiosity leads to predictions of catastrophes in dreams.

Chapter 34
My Religion of Reality 205
Sorting out truths in my mind may lead to a more meaningful life, but it's sometimes hard to face.

Chapter 35
"Beasty" and "Big Red" 211
A trip to Montana confirms some people who live elsewhere are only *Half-way There* too.

Chapter 36
"Honey, I'm Home" 217
Woman's work in a man's world has been tough, but it's getting better.

Chapter 37
Ravenous 225
Some insight into what made Tommy have a ravenous thirst for blood and how he overcame it. This was a part of himself that he didn't want me to see.

Introduction

Remember how nervous you were when you first started driving a car? That's how I felt writing this book. When our abilities don't match up with the task, that's how we become. But, just like a phobia, if we face it a little at a time we will eventually overcome.

To me, a book is like a big word or a big picture puzzle. Each time another syllable is added the word becomes larger. Each time another chapter is added the book becomes larger. Not just any syllable will work; neither does any chapter work. If a few pieces are missing from the puzzle, the picture is no good, and one's efforts are all in vain. The person putting it together may have learned something, but the picture is still incomplete. However, with this style of writing the picture can go on and on—indefinitely. A new experience waits around every corner. It connects into a large picture, with nothing more than a leaf missing here and there. The picture is still whole and may be even more beautiful without the extra leaf, just as a dress might be more beautiful without an extra sequin. The unfolding of each page leads the mind to travel in realms of its own.

As a child in school, I used to write book reviews by reading as little as three paragraphs, one at the beginning and two at the end, out of an entire book. I could basically guess what was in the middle. No way will anyone be able to do that with this one, at least not with the physics I've experienced. It includes many different kinds of art and should be kept on a shelf to refer to again and again. Because its meanings run so deeply, one might read it many times and still get something new from its pages.

So many people have asked, "What is it about?" If I briefly described it, I would say it's a self-healing book. It has been a great therapy to me to write it. A broader picture would have to include an autobiography, a biography, a comedy, a mystery, and the list goes on. Most of all, it includes drama because it includes life. Life doesn't move smoothly on a straight line, it ticks back and forth like a pendulum of a clock, or moves like a Ferris wheel. One moment you're on top, the next moment you're not. Regardless of its ups and downs, it includes hope.

One important part of hope is the truth. How can one hope for a better tomorrow until present circumstances are acknowledged? We can hope for awhile. Eventually, we get worn down like a rock washed away by the ocean. Then by accepting things the way they are, failure becomes a set pattern. Every person has his/her limits.

If I had to categorize it, it would be a memoir. Somewhat like a personal journal, it includes thoughts, feelings, dreams, and conjectures. Following a short story format, one can read only one chapter to get a sense of a story, just like a word with one syllable still has meaning. Yet, it connects into a book like a word with added syllables, and one can not get the full picture without reading all of it.

The story's based on truth; only some names have been changed to protect the person's privacy or their last name may have been forgotten with time. These names appear only once with asterisks at the beginning of each chapter. The order in which some things appear may not follow true to life. In other words, it is not written in chronological order. Ralph Waldo Emerson, an American poet, essayist and philosopher who lived between 1803 to 1882, confessed he did not know the truth. "The truth is as hard to capture and bottle up as light." I have come as close to the truth as I possibly could, in this attempt to stumble upon clues that might reveal only specks of the riddle of the universe and still make an interesting story.

It portrays only part of my life, my brother Tommy's, and my daughter Sherry's. Naturally, since Tommy is my brother and Sherry is my daughter, my life would include parts of theirs.

Parts of it might make you laugh until you cry, and other parts might be too sad to handle. Don't be afraid if you read something bad within these pages. Jesus wasn't afraid to put devil or demon in the Bible; neither did he expect you to be afraid to read it.

It includes sex scenes of the oddest kind and should be rated all the way from "G" to at least an "R" rating, if you have an old-fashioned way of thinking. Yet, it could even be considered spiritual, and by some it may be considered religious. It tells about life—yours, mine, and the boy's next door—and the good and bad in it pulling against each other to make a whole.

The main word in this description is "self-healing." Yes, regardless of what you've gone through or how you've felt, it should offer some kind of help. It should also offer some kind of help to the people who have "all their ducks in a row," or think they do. Much is left to the imagination, requiring the reader to read in between the lines. I also believe that regardless of what your age is this also applies; it applies to anyone from eight to eighty — blind, crippled, or crazy. I hope that counselors, psychologists and psychiatrists, all, recommend their patients read it as part of their therapy. The truth is no one is ever totally healed mentally by a doctor…or by reading just one piece of material. It requires some self-help just to get to the "half-way" point. That's where the title comes in. It's apparent we all are imperfect. Because of our imperfections, we need a lot of help. Hopefully, these pages will offer both the carrot and the stick to help us get started on a wonderful recovery. Maybe, with time we will be *Half-Way There*. And it will have served a good purpose, which I intended. It won't, if you don't let it; it won't, if you don't read it. An interesting, new journey awaits with each additional page. You'll just have to read it.

Everyone and everything is going somewhere. A fruit falls to the ground, uneaten or partially eaten. It goes back to the earth as part of the earth's nourishment. Rain drops fall and eventually combine with other raindrops on its long journey back to the sea. All things work together for a good purpose: The good keeps the bad in check. The bad strengthens the good with exercise of the soul. In Romans 8:28, it reads: "And we know that all things work together for good to them that love God, to them who are the called according to His purpose." When we reach the point of walking in the right light, we will reach *A Place Called There*. Then, we can accomplish anything according to His purpose. After that, we can go to a better home when it's time. Otherwise, we stay at the *Half-way* point, struggling to reach a higher rung when it may never be ours.

Dedication

They called him "Tommy." His real name, given at birth, was James Nolan Parker. He was my oldest brother. I also had a brother by the name of Jimmy. There was great difficulty in getting a separate birth certificate for them. Mom didn't realize that James and Jimmy were the same names.

Through experiences of the "hard life," Tommy passed on to me one important key to success—perseverance. He has always been my favorite brother. I dedicate this book in his honor.

Tommy Parker

Chapter 1

Man or Beast

In a speech on Charles Darwin's *Origins of Species,* he said, "The question is this: Is man an ape or an angel? Now, I am on the side of angels." I tend to agree. It's true: we all have both good and bad in us, but as long as we can improve, regardless of the circumstances and however little it might be, we're still going in the right direction. We are given our own experiences. With our brains, we see, hear, feel, and think, accepting some kind of guiding force deep within us, like a submerged submarine's propeller that drives us to press on.

Even though I've had plenty of psychic experiences, my angels…and devils…have come in the form of people. My oldest brother, Tommy, was no angel. He made many mistakes during his life. But he was one propelling force I learned to accept early in life. Neither was he all bad. In some instances, he was the instigator and leader among men…or boys, whichever the case may be. Jimmy Rogers, a minister of that area in southwest North Carolina, told him: "If you ever become a preacher, you'll become the best. If you ever become a drunk, you'll become the worst."

Tommy's time for looking like a young boy had past. He was beginning to look like a young man and was extremely handsome. His hairstyle had recently changed to copy James Dean. Tommy's real name at birth was also James. There was great difficulty in getting my two older brothers separate birth certificates because the other one was named Jimmy. Mom didn't realize that James and Jimmy were considered the same names. Through experiences of the "hard life," Tommy passed on to me one important key to success: perseverance. One thing that showed up in his character was self-assurance, much like that of James Dean, and he carried himself very much in the same manner.

Tommy wasn't the only boy around who harbored a mean streak. This was the mid-fifties—a time when people thought differently. Maybe they were just backward during those days. In church one Sunday evening, I just happened to be sitting directly behind one boy that got my attention. In fact, he got everyone's attention. He was a complete stranger in our church. Rumors ran wild about him.

The preacher always had an altar call at the evening meetings. He picked out various people in the group whom he tried to persuade to be "saved." Here in the Church of God, people who accepted Jesus Christ as their Savior went to the altar to be "saved." This wasn't the only place to be delivered from the power and consequences of sin, but it was the main place where one had the support of other church members to help them in their endeavors. Since this boy was a stranger, it was an obvious choice for him to be singled out. The preacher believed that strangers hadn't yet come to God because that was the only church within miles.

Everyone stood up for the altar call. The soft music in the background—*Oh Sinner, Come Home*—wasn't quite enough to cover up what was spoken, especially since I was close enough to hear every word.

"Are you lost?" The preacher started his persuasion.

"Nope," the boy answered, "I just live down the road a-piece."

"You, you didn't get my meaning…Would…would you like to be born again?" The preacher came back with a slight stutter in his voice.

"Nope," the stranger responded in a coarse voice, as if trying to sound like a man. "I'm afraid I might be a little girl." The young, light-brown hair boy looked serious enough. He didn't crack a smile during the entire conversation. That's what made everything seem so funny.

Biting our lips and the tips of our tongues, the entire congregation could hardly hold back roars of laughter. Whispers about him were overheard; yet, everyone was putting a finger to their lips, reminding each other to be quiet. The little white church at the fork of the road where Cold Branch and Tusquittee met held a humorous note that Sunday evening, in an otherwise rigid setting. The people there were inflexible with raising their children, much less being tolerant of any kind of misbehavior—and especially in church.

The congregation just couldn't keep their mouths shut, including me. Two incidents, which I overheard from their whispers, were he had eaten a skunk…and climbed a cliff. From that description, it sounded like he was a cliff dweller from way back the mountains somewhere—somewhere back in these North Carolina hills.

"What's a cliff dweller," I heard myself whisper loud enough to interrupt the preacher's questions. He looked at me a little strange and continued with his questions. Needless to say, I didn't get the answer right then and there.

I'm sure the preacher didn't think it was so funny. Regardless of what he said, this boy always had a "come-back." He sure was witty, but a complete "smart-ass." Or *was he just plain stupid?* The people thought so. Whether he was just answering the preacher's questions in his own way or just trying to be a smart-aleck is beyond me: I definitely couldn't see into this boy's mind. Eventually the preacher gave up and worked his way back to the pulpit. A blank look on his face told everyone he could not protect the young man from himself.

After church everyone let go of their laughter. They "cranked up the gossip mill." I wanted to hear more about him, especially the incident about him eating a skunk, and the answer to my previous question. The grown-ups ignored me somewhat because I was a child in their eyes. Even though I was only eleven years old and weighed forty-one pounds, I didn't look at myself like I was a child. I'd taken over the responsibility of an adult since Mom had left, and I felt I should be treated as one. They believed that children shouldn't talk unless an adult spoke to them first. Someone—I didn't see because so many people were standing around talking and listening in a huddle—assured the rest of the folks that the boy eating a skunk was a definite fact and added: "He stunk like a polecat for two months." From his appearance, the gangly stranger looked like he hadn't taken a bath or washed his clothes in a long time, but he no longer stunk like a polecat.

It was natural for the stranger to be the topic of gossip in this small, but spread out, community. When the question was asked by someone other than me where he was from, one church member just said, "Over yonder," pointing toward a far off mountain. All I could see was an arm and a finger pointing toward the east. No one seemed to know exactly where.

Now was a chance to get an answer to my previous question: "What's a cliff dweller?"

"It's a person who lives in a cliff in the side of a mountain," a heavy-set lady, dressed in a neatly starched floral patterned dress that looked very much like my own flour-sack dress, snapped back in a sharp tone, as if I wasn't supposed to interrupt their conversation.

"Where is this cliff? I didn't know there were any cliffs around here. He must have come from a long way off. If he wasn't serious about going to church, why did he come?" I asked.

"You're too full of questions, little girl," the lady stammered.

I resented that remark, but I shut up to let the adults get a few words in.

"The cliff he climbed was straight up," another one in the group related with awe in her voice. "And he did it with his bar hands!" This lady seemed to be as amazed as I was. She was dressed in a dull-brown gabardine skirt and a snow-white blouse with ruffles around the collar and sleeves. In the church lights, I could see that her eyes matched her skirt.

"How did he do it?" I wanted to know.

"No one knows fur sure," an answer came back from another lady in the group, who was definitely more understanding of children butting into conversations. She was standing behind another, preventing me from seeing what she looked like.

"We don't have time to figure it out now. I haf-ta go home," the heavy-set lady concluded with a blunt ending and in the same tone as before. Obviously, the conversation was over before I could get my curiosity satisfied. I wondered why they had to act that way, but I had to accept the situation as it was.

—It was a pitch-black night. No stars or moon could be seen at all. The laughter had died down. All of a sudden, all the people were gone—except for me. They had walked on ahead of me, leaving me to walk home alone in the dark. There was no traffic out here on this country road miles from town. I seemed to be the last to depart, mainly because of wondering about the boy in church. *Why would any one want to climb a cliff? Did he do it just to see if he could? Why would he eat a skunk? Was he that short of food? Surely he could've killed some other kind of animal.* The woods were full of squirrels. They made the best dumplings I'd ever tasted. I knew some people like opossum and there were plenty of them around. One of my sweethearts, Drew Cothern, had taken me opossum hunting once. I never helped him eat it, but I sure enjoyed the hunt as well as carrying it home by the tail. He said they tasted good. After being lost in thought, I realized it was time to go home. The mystery of the stranger was left in the churchyard.

Quietness surrounded me like I was the only one left on earth. Darkness was all around. Somehow I knew I wasn't completely alone. Someone or some kind of animal was waiting up the road a-piece. There were plenty of wild animals, such as coyotes and cougars in these hills, but I knew it wasn't an animal. My sixth sense told me it was a person: a male. Whoever it was, he had most likely seen me approach from the light through the opened doorway of the church, which had just closed. The preacher was turning out the lights in the church. The person waiting in the dark must have been listening to my footsteps on the pavement. He was just ahead, and I had to pass.

Suddenly, out of the black night he grabbed me, covering my mouth. I could tell he was young, probably in his mid-teens, from the touch of his body. His presence developed a knowledge in me indescribable to all five senses, except feel and the power of just knowing—it had to be my six sense.

He must have thought I was too little to do anything to prevent him raping me and that he would never be identified. I glanced around as I was falling in the darkness and could see only faint outlines of a person's body. He didn't seem to be the "funny boy" in church. He was huskier. The stranger had been taller and skinner.

His attempt to rape me was overwhelming at first; then I decided no way was I going to let this happen. *I can overcome a teenager. The people in this area would never believe the girl wasn't at fault anyway.* My reasoning told me, *to overcome this incident, there'll be one less scar on my mind I'll have to deal with later.* My mind had always given me strength when my body had failed me. Tommy had taught me if I wanted to do something, all I had to do is believe and take action; then expect results. My physical strength came from my mind. After some wrestling with him in the dark I was able to jerk loose and run away.

Even though I never learned his identity for sure, I believe he was the deacon's son. He had been standing a few rows ahead of me in church when we stood up for the altar call. I briefly noticed him looking at me then, but I didn't think much about it until now. If that was the case—and I felt sure that it was—*he's too good looking to resort to rape.* My thoughts concluded, then broke, *there should be at least one girl around that would oblige him.*

The boys of this area dropped out of school at an early age. While they were in school, their ignorance ran high. For instance, Jimmy, my own brother who was almost four years older than me and almost four years younger than Tommy, was only one grade ahead of me and in the same classroom. Each teacher taught two grades, alternately in the same room. She'd caught him copying more than once and told him he should be in my place and I should be in his.

My classmates' ignorance really showed through when a student from Ohio was hanged in that same school. "Oh, my God," the teacher screamed out. I was too short to see it through the classroom windows. The other students were trying to see him too, some even jumping up to see through a window. Apparently the teacher saw him hanging from a tree. She ran out to rescue him. Everyone thought it would be too late. Because the rope was tied incorrectly, she was able to save him.

I never dreamed that something bad—the lack of not knowing how to tie a knot correctly in this case—would turn out to be something good. People had always told me "two wrongs don't make a right." Maybe so, but here was something to think about. In the constant battle between good and evil, good will always prevail in what seems like an endless tug-of-war.

Calling the Ohio boy strange because he was in their eyes, the students said he went around with a mirror on his toe trying to see up the girls' dresses. "He acted like a know-it-all," the students said in whispers among themselves later at recess. They never said anything about him being an outsider, but I'm sure this was at least part of the reason for the other boys hanging him. In this area the Confederate Flag flew in the people's minds, if not on their front porch, and resentment toward the North still existed. There's not much doubt in my mind that he ever acted like a "smart-ass" again. They cured him of that.

Before the incident, a large group of boys had formed a circle during recess to hide their actions. Everyone thought they were just playing some kind of game and didn't pay much attention to who was involved. Most likely, the ones that did see the hanging were afraid to talk. The school never found out who did it because no one would admit to seeing anything. It was a "hush-hush" type of situation, so the students were coaxed into keeping their mouths shut.

The subject still came up at recess among the students long afterwards. "I don't know now…and I'll probably never find out for sure…but there's a strong possibility that Jimmy was somehow involved in that attempted hanging," I told my best friend, Lois Killian, and a few others shortly after the incident. Someone mentioned he wasn't in school that day. There was so much commotion involved that I didn't notice. By that time Jimmy was skipping school two or three days a week. Shortly afterwards he quit while he was still in the sixth grade.

Growing up is hard to do. No set of instructions is given to us. Most kids learn the hard way, but Tommy was determined that I learn with his help, if at all possible. Tommy, Jimmy, and I were coming home across the mountain from Atlanta one day. A good portion of the 100-mile trip was switchback after switchback. Tommy told us about the time when he'd hitchhiked across a nearby mountain. He said he thumbed the same man three times. "How is it possible to thumb the same person three times?" I asked. "I jumped off the bank and got ahead of him. On the third try, he stopped," Tommy answered.

Home was to the north across the Appalachian Mountains. We got behind a slow-moving car with five good-looking, young, mountain boys in it. They were rowdy and persistent, and flirted with me for miles. I didn't think there was any harm in just waving at one of them. When I did they tried to run us off the road. Tommy said they wanted us to stop so they could beat him and Jimmy up and take me with them. Since Tommy was an excellent driver, he didn't wreck, nor stop; he managed to go around them. Although the road was extremely curvy, they were soon left behind.

In my memory of the incident, Tommy cautioned me, "Don't ever do that again! You could get us killed!" He knew the ways of North Carolina and Georgia boys and tried to teach me this in his own fashion.

"I'm only a little girl. What would they want with a little girl?" I didn't realize I was flirting until Tommy pointed it out.

"They can't see how little you are," he answered. "Besides that doesn't mean much to them anyway."

In my innocence, I couldn't understand why. "It was only a wave," I told him. *Were they crazy too...like the boy in church? Did all the boys in this area have something wrong with them?*

"Boys are just plain mean in this part of the country," Tommy explained. "They don't care about how young you are...or how small. They don't care about anything. And maybe small is better to them."

There were various ways the boys I grew up with acted like smart-alecks. They generally treated me with respect, probably due to Tommy's protection. Occasionally two walked me home from church, one on each arm. They were nice boys!

Sometimes the girls became involved too...with the dark, devious pranks that kids play. Especially on Halloween; then, we did everything we could think of —cut down large trees across the road so the school bus would be delayed on its next trip, tip over outhouses, burst pumpkins, and all kinds of destruction. The boys had to move all the debris out of the road the next day for the bus to pass, but they didn't seem to mind. They were just physically minded and wanted to stay clear of anything that developed their thinking for as long as they could. This was one day out of the year we could release all our growing-up-pains—the wrong way, of course—and the girls would turn into nice little angels the following day. "Sh...sh...be quiet!" someone in the group whispered loudly one Halloween night during our escapade. A neighbor had caught us destroying his property. He would shoot us on sight and not think twice about it.

All of us—about thirty—started running for cover. We were afraid we'd get killed. He had a gun. In the process I was knocked down, very likely due to me being the smallest in the group. Everyone ran over me, stepping on me as they scattered. Ending up with some scrapes and bruises, but not seriously hurt, I played it to the hilt. One of the boys that usually walked me home from church came back, picked me up in his arms and carried me almost all the way home. "Man"—his nickname suitable to the fact that he was big and tall like a man—treated me very gently. He was the brother of Bernell Mosteller, one of my friends. I never heard him called by any other name, except "Man." From his caring nature came a sweetness I'd never before tasted. I was glad our escapades were over for the night. A sweet, loving kiss—my first kiss—told me that this was more my style of having fun. When I finally came around to telling him I was okay and it was all right for him to put me down, he gently placed me on the ground. We walked hand-in-hand the rest of the way home in conversation and friendly loving contentment. A bright, full moon added to the night's brilliance. On the way home, I wondered why he gave me so much attention—because of me being so little. My best friend, Lois Killian, was a full head, or more, taller than I was. "Man's" sister, Bernell, was about the same height as Lois, but she wasn't as slim. Both Bernell and Lois had accepted me as a friend, so why shouldn't a boy accept me as his sweetheart. *It should be okay,* I thought.

"Tommy would disapprove of everything I've done tonight," I told him. Just walking home alone with "Man" would have been enough to make his eyebrows raise much like Dad's—the right eyebrow would raise higher than the left. This must have been an inherited expression, because I sometimes had that same expression too. The situation wouldn't have mattered to Dad, but it would have mattered to Tommy. We had done more than hold hands; we'd kissed, and I liked it.

"Yeah, but he's not here," he said in a low tone.

When that night ended he seemed to be afraid of me. I suppose it had something to do with his male hormones. And he didn't want to lose respect for me. When I saw him again we spoke only on a casual basis. He acted "stand-offish" and shy. "Well, he's just come to his senses and decided he didn't want any part of a little girl like me," I said to myself.

That Halloween night I decided never to willfully cause destruction again. It was well embedded in my mind that this was doing wrong to others...and to ourselves. *How would I feel if someone came along some day and destroyed something of mine that I'd worked so hard for?* An immediate change in me came about.

I walked away from that type of bad conduct with pleasure in my mind knowing I'd done the right thing. I must have had some type of leadership ability then. Because of the change in me, some of the other kids—at least the ones I was with—changed too. Thinking back, I'm sure the reason they changed was because of my determined nature.

If "Man" were here today, he'd be paying attention to me, instead of running around with a bunch of boys, I thought. Even though, I wondered *how could any person give me so much attention in one sense and turn around and be "stand-offish" and shy in another?* Even the teenager who tried to rape me chose a different outlet. All these boys seemed to be backwards, but they had plenty of self-confidence.

In Montana, people have a saying: "Where the men are men and the sheep quiver." This wasn't Montana; it was North Carolina; a difference in scenery, but no difference in men. It was a hot summer day during our break from school. About fifteen or twenty boys gathered around in a "hush-hush" fashion again, like so many had done the day of the hanging. Something was about to happen, but I was too young to know exactly what. Excitement clouded the air as the boys scattered here and there, running around in circles preparing for *the event*. If one didn't know better, they would have thought they were preparing for fireworks at a fourth of July picnic. I was just that naive…a tip to the other end of the scale. Even though, my curiosity scored high.

"One more thing to do," I heard Tommy call out to the rest of the group. "Hold it! Don't do a thing until I get back!" he shouted.

Running down the slightly slopped hill to the house and rounding the corner, he called, "Tootsie, where are you?"

I was discreetly trying to stay out of sight and didn't answer on the first call. "Toots," he called again in a more stern fashion, "get here!"

As my eyes met his on the next corner, I asked, "Where's the fireworks?"

"What fireworks?" Tommy questioned. "This isn't the fourth.

"Yeah, but it's close. It's only a few days away. Where did you get the money to buy firecrackers?" I continued prodding. I couldn't see where he could have possibly gotten the money to buy any more than firecrackers. And *why would firecrackers cause so much unusual behavior*?

"Firecrackers…what are you talking about? How about you going to the spring to get us a bucket of water?"

"What? Just when the fun's going to start? Can't I wait until it's over? I'd like to see them too, you know. I won't get in the way."

"We need some water. Come on now!" he said impatiently.

"What do you need water for? You won't set anything a-fire out in that field," I blurted. "We already have water to drink. What do you need more water for?"

Handing me the bucket, he wasn't going to shut up until I went after the water. "Oh, okay," I said, taking the bucket from his outstretched hand. That appeased him.

"No," I stubbornly fought back after he was out of sight. "I always do what I'm told. This time, I'm not going to." I wanted to see what was going on…and what was so secretive. By not answering my questions, it had to be something he didn't want me to know. I knew Tommy was very protective of me, but *fireworks couldn't be that dangerous.*

The spring was located about a quarter of a mile straight down hill and on the way back it would be straight up hill, with a bucket full of water…so it was easy to procrastinate. The pain of going to get the water and the pleasure of finding out their secret was too hard to resist. Both the carrot and the stick had been placed. The decision to sneak a peek came naturally.

Since I didn't want them to catch me watching, I carefully peeked around the corner of the house. It was obvious the boys were distracted and wouldn't notice me. They lined up behind a big block of wood—our chopping block—after carrying it to the center of the field. Our cow, which Dad hadn't got around to selling yet, was coerced into backing up to the right position in front of it. Dad was an alcoholic and sold everything of value—a new electric cook-stove, a four-acre cornfield, and a few other things of lesser value—to support his habit after Mom left.

"What's a cow doing in this scene?" I thought out loud. *A block of wood seems okay…but a cow?* This picture was becoming more interesting with each passing moment. The first teenager, a dark-haired boy, dressed in a torn checkered shirt tied around his waist and faded blue jeans with bare feet, stepped onto the chopping block. Then down came his pants. I didn't see their faces; my eyes went straight toward their actions, leaving my own face full of shocking expressions.

"Oh boy, what have I got myself into by choosing to stay here to watch?" To put it bluntly, he carried carnal knowledge to heights I'd only read about before. The rest of the boys were going to do the same. *Okay*, I thought. *I've seen enough. I'd better get away from here fast. Tommy will kill me if he knew I'd stuck around here to watch.* Leaving that scene behind, I took off running.

Slipping and sliding down the red clay path to the spring, I couldn't get away fast enough. I knew Tommy would whip my ass if he caught me spying on him. I even forgot the bucket and ran back to get it. My thoughts rambled on and on. *How could they do such a thing? There's a huge difference between girls and boys, including their minds.*

As I ran down the hill to the spring a book that I'd recently read, but couldn't remember exactly where I'd gotten it, helped spark my imagination. Our school had no such books. Most young boys read books like these with a bunch of friends. Since us girls were afraid to even discuss subjects like these, someone I knew had offered me a couple of books to read for myself. They were on sexual behavior. I suppose I was just trying to make excuses, to reason why my brother would do something so outrageous. One of the books was called *Sexual Behavior in the Human Male*, written in 1948 by Alfred Kinsey, a mid-western zoology professor. "Many traditionally forbidden sexual activities were common place," he wrote, "forty to fifty percent of boys raised on farms had had sexual contact with animals." According to the other book, "Many of Kinsey's findings may have been based on flawed methods and some were false." I didn't know what to make of these things.

Our upbringing had been very strict, strictly forbidding this type of conduct. Mom had left a few weeks earlier. Since she'd left, Dad had stayed in bed past out from so much drinking. I was the only one around to care about the well being of the entire family. I wondered *why were these boys disregarding their values? And why did I read material on this subject only a short time earlier?*

Arriving at the spring, I relieved all the evil thoughts inside my mind with a long sigh. A long-handle dipper hung from a forked stob on the bank of the spring. Cool, fresh water from the spring seemed like the ideal thing to replace the bad feelings within me; so I drank. While drinking the cool water, I noticed the beauty that surrounded the spring and made a comparison of it to the hill I'd just come down. A dogwood tree stood not more than a few feet away. Its blooming time had passed. Still, my mind didn't suffer from lack of imagination; I could picture its blossoms in my mind. The blossoms resemble a cross with bloodstains. I'd been told that Jesus was crucified on a cross, made from a dogwood tree, and that's why its blossoms looked like that. A honeysuckle over-lapped some of its branches. Not yet fully in bloom, it still brought a honeysuckle-sweet smell to the area. Maybe some of the beauty here was all in my mind, reaching out in an attempt to capture something sweet. In another direction, wild blueberry bushes of unripe fruit and bunches of poke salad large enough to seed itself were sparsely spread throughout the woods. The trail I'd just come down was hard clay dirt. Dirt around the spring looked darker and richer. A world of difference, yet they were so close. Some of the clay dirt had to be mixed with the other soil surrounding it.

Life was flourishing here, and on both sides of the trail as well. A thought came to mind: *This area must represent the good and bad on earth.* It seemed like it should somehow offer some kind of connection to the situation now, but I was too young to know exactly what those answers might be.

Not quite filling the bucket to the brim, I headed back up the trail to the house. Mumbling to myself much like a child, I said out loud, "I can handle Tommy's actions a lot better than I can handle this hill." Even though I didn't look at myself like a child, it was the first time in many years that I had reminded myself of one. When I was four years old, I'd set our wall paper a-fire just to see what it looked like. Then again, at about the same age, I'd stuffed a bullet up my nose. I can't remember why I did that—maybe lack of anything better to do. Mom had to take me to a doctor to get it out. Even the doctor used great care in removing it because he didn't want it to go off. Another time of acting stupid happened when I was about six. We'd just come back from Washington State after living there for awhile. Our family had made several trips across the United States. Dad had worked there before his retirement setting chokers for a lumber company. We'd just gotten back to North Carolina and were visiting Aunt Lillie. Noticing three beehives, my curiosity got the best of me. I thought they were bugs, and even bugs needed some attention. Still in my little robe, which I was so proud of, I walked up to the hives and started petting them. Slowly and gently rubbing my fingers across their wings, I talked to the bees as if they were pets. They didn't seem to mind too much at first, but it didn't take long to find out they didn't want me there. I ended up with about four bee stings. Considering the situation, that wasn't very many stings, but it was enough to send me running and crying to Mom. Now, the child was coming out again.

Along the trail to the house, I became tired and stopped for a rest. Sitting at the edge of the trail, my thoughts were briefly interrupted. Two ground squirrels were rustling in the leaves. They seemed to be gathering something: maybe it was acorns, left over from last year. I looked down and saw some scattered here and there, picking up a few. As I turned around to notice their playful gestures, they reminded me of the two squirrels Jimmy had on our front porch in a cage.

Again—my thoughts went back to my brother and his friends.

I wanted to be on the winning side, spiritually and morally, regardless of my brothers' actions. No matter how much I thought, I couldn't possibly see anything good in seducing a cow. Regardless of the reason, I couldn't see anything good in hanging a person either. *Did boys all over the world think so differently from girls…and why?* It didn't seem sensible to me. *Why do we violate our inner values with destruction of ourselves, as well as destruction of so many other things, leading to a scarred soul?* I thought, as the preacher of our church had suggested in his sermons. We were also taught by our elders not to destroy anything, steal, lie, or do any kind of mischief, as well follow the Golden Rule. It never occurred to me then that we were just trying to make our lives more fulfilling by adding surprise, one need that belongs to every human being. *We are more apt to violate our values to meet a need*, I later reasoned.

Tommy had a determined nature too, much more than mine. He was a role model—a teacher. *How many lives would he change from this incident alone, not accounting for others I'm not aware of? Is this how the world becomes so sinful, as the preacher had told us? Why is my thinking so different from his? He has two sets of rules: one for me and one for himself. Our society is responsible for that. They approve of almost anything for boys…and disapprove of almost everything for girls. How many mistakes has our grown-up society made? How many more will they continue to make?*

Approaching the top of the hill and close to the house, I noticed all the commotion had ceased. The boys had scattered. Some had started to go home. Going to the porch where Jimmy kept his squirrels, I pulled out a few old acorns, which I'd picked up on the trail, from my pedal-pusher pockets. They looked so old, I didn't know if they were any good. I just wanted to give the squirrels something to eat. As I started to feed them, one bit me. "Oh well, nothing in this life is perfect," I concluded. "I'll figure all this out some day. But now…I have to get to work on today."

Chapter 2

Conditioned

Tommy was a great philosopher in spirit, if not in words. His experience outweighed his education by far. It didn't take much formal education to know about life. He had experienced most of it the hard way. I asked him what grade did he go through and he answered, "The seventh." "You still don't know how to read or write, do you?" I asked. "Not much," he said, unashamed. The last time I remembered him going to school was when we lived in the cove—I was four years old then.

Lack of education didn't seem to stop him from teaching me the best way he knew how. The more experience he got the more he wanted to pass on to me, but he was careful not to tell me some of the things he didn't want me to know, such as the incident with the cow or the meanness in him. Sometimes he was demanding or bossy. I usually followed his instructions to a tee, wanting to please him, because I loved him very much. Most of the time, especially when I got a little older, I thought I knew better than he did about what he was trying to say. At times when I was alone, just sitting in a wooded area and looking around at what nature had to give us, I often wondered why he gave me so much information so early in life, and I reasoned over the details. As it turned out, I needed that information early. I seemed to know that he wanted me to do what I was told rather than what I saw. His advice seldom skipped a beat in forming my inner thoughts in one way or another. He wanted me to touch great heights in reasoning or just be able to sit down and think about some of the things he, himself, must have known would never be able to reach. He gave me the seeds for a beautiful garden; then nourished them with the only love he knew how to give: his advice.

It was unusual for him to give me lengthy talks in forming the personality he wanted me to have. One side of him was the secretive ways of his actions and the other side was kindness and compassion when he talked to me. The conversations were usually brief. Sometimes they started like this:

"We don't have to run like water…over a woman, or man, or anything…regardless of the circumstances, and we don't have to be conditioned to failure like animals." I knew he was talking about Dad when he said that. Dad had deteriorated since Mom left. It was obvious he used her as a crutch. I added my own thoughts to his comments, trying hard to reach only the good and letting go of the rest: *We are people, made in God's own image.*

"I know you've never been to a zoo. Someday…when you go, you'll probably see a huge elephant chained to a stake and wonder why. He could free himself with one slight pull, if he decided? He doesn't break free, because he's been conditioned to failure. He was chained when he was smaller and had less strength. Because of failing so many times, he quit trying.

"It's important for you to see how to improve yourself, regardless of the circumstances, and to keep trying. I want things to be a lot easier for you than they have been for me." Then, he continued by telling me a little story that related to what he wanted me to over-come: "Animals that hate each other have been put in a cage with a glass partition between them. They would jump at each other over and over again, but failed again…and again. After they quit trying the partition was taken away. The animals went to where the partition had been and never tried to cross that point again. They had been conditioned. I don't want you to be conditioned like those animals or like some of the people around here." I wondered where he'd gotten that bit of information and thought to myself, *he's been to places I've never been and talked to a lot of different people. He must have gotten it from them.*

Actually, a lot of people in this part of the United States where we lived, Southwest North Carolina, reminded us of these animals in spirit—they quit trying. Tommy just loved me enough to instill in me a never-quit-trying attitude. And I believe this is "an idea from God," which makes him an angel. He offered the best he had to me.

I once tried to present an idea to a lady who lived there and she said, "You make me nervous. I don't wan-a listen." This is definitely a sign of a person who has quit trying. Southern people, especially my mother, who still had some spunk left didn't call these people odd; they called them "quare." I'd noticed her strong personality in her comments and actions before she left. It was much like Tommy's, more than she had wanted to believe.

I wanted to have real meaning to my life and strength that was sure to overcome. When I looked up "try" in my Bible concordance it said: "see also 'test'." In Luke 8:13, it reads: "They on the rock are they who, when they hear, receive the word with joy; and these have no root, who for a while believe, and in time of testing fall away." *This is where real strength lies, and this is where it is built—in testing, trying, and overcoming.*

Real meanings to this scripture and others slowly came into focus. Tommy's philosophy and what I'd heard from the preacher of our church all played some important parts, as well as what I got from books. Later a new friend came into my life, adding growth. Her name was Fannie Parker—the same last name as ours because she'd been married to a Parker but was now divorced. Fannie added much more than she'll ever know to the good side of me. She was a lot like Tommy in a way, because she added little bits of information along the way—throughout the days, weeks, months, and years I knew her. It was up to me to put the pieces together like a giant picture puzzle. I don't think either one of them knew how to express themselves very well. Sometimes their sentences would be incomplete, or they would word them differently. I felt their love so strong that I could finish their sentences with my mind. More often than not, I changed the way they said something to fit my own thinking. The idea was still there, and it was meant to be nourished.

In my point of view, that scripture meant to build your spiritual strength like a rock and you will succeed because you have exercised this part of your being, just like exercising your muscles or your mind. "What you don't use, you lose." If a person doesn't exercise this part of themselves—a part that has been given only to humans by God—their spiritual strength becomes so weak they fall away when the going gets rough. So it stands to reason if a person quits trying, he is more apt to fall away from God because he will not have enough spiritual strength left to overcome. It just could be he has put trials in our lives for this reason: exercise of our spiritual selves to urge us on to action, out of desperation. A kick in the seat of the pants, yes! Maybe that's what it takes to get us to move. His divine influence should be welcomed into the hearts of all men.

I know Mom had it hard raising us, even to this point. She did get help from Dad outside the household in the form of support and outside chores.

The memory of Mom still took me back in time: Mom had told us that "Root Hog or Die" was imprinted on Hayesville's city seal. I found out later that it was just an old saying, dated back to the early 1900's. Mom often repeated this statement to us because it applied to our lives. "A long, hard row to hoe," was another expression used by North Carolina Tar Heals.

Tarpaper covered the outside walls and roof of the one-room house, built of planks where we lived when I was born—"a far cry" from our present home. Mom covered the hard clay dirt floor with tarpaper as well. She said it helped prevent moisture and coldness and it was easier to keep clean. This was the average home in this "neck of the woods" during those times—1943.

The longing for her opened the door to memories—the only thing of her that remained. I saw things again as if she were here…and as a little girl: Very little had changed with time—except the place where we lived—including God's perfect landscaping. Colors of green, yellow, and orange leaves covered the trees in the valley as far as one could see on this bright sun-lit morning. My eyes lifted toward it, scoping everything in sight. Occasional cornfields spread out here and there among the wooded area. Cattle grazed in the open fields. Landscaping was no problem here; it all was quite beautiful, lying in the arms of God. A winding graveled road, hardly wide enough for two A-Model cars to pass, curved around the slopped hills. Cold Branch Road led to a beautiful creek of the same name where tree limbs hung over both sides, often touching in the middle. It bridged to the other side, making a curve around a neighbor's corn field which had pumpkins in it, and to the Church of God; then met with Tusquittee Road and another creek, also bridging to another area just as beautiful, in a fork of the road. This fork was where all the people got together for fun on the weekends—to play craps or card games, to have cock fights or dog fights, to have turkey shoots, to have fights with each other, and to do anything else they might dream up—and yes, to go to church too.

The crackle of a fire in an open hearth where my mother cooked all the meals was a nice warm awakening sound on a cool autumn morning. In my vivid memory, I could still smell the bacon cooking and the smoke from the open fireplace. And I could still smell the earth of this place. It was all the good Mother Nature had to offer. I accepted it into my subconsciousness.

A very clean woman, Mom pushed us kids outside to play—if we were old enough—right after breakfast. She didn't want us messing up her house. She didn't want any help cleaning it either. We weren't "old enough to do a good job," she would say. In the winter when it was too cold for us to be outside, we either contained ourselves or she would tie us in a chair to keep us out of things and to give her more freedom to do her chores.

This wasn't just a mean, cruel thing she dreamed up to do to us kids. She had learned to keep us out of things for our own safety. The responsibilities of women doing things without all the modern conveniences made it difficult to handle young children too.

At six months old I had crawled near the open fireplace and a red, hot coal went down my high-top shoe. That was something I can never remember: being without shoes. What we did have we learned to appreciate and take good care of, so it lasted a long time. Some of the kids in other families went to school with no shoes at all, even during the wintertime when frost was on the ground. All of Aunt Lillie's children seldom owned a pair of shoes. The high tops on my shoes held the coal close to my ankle, making it difficult for Mom to remove. As a result of the burn, my leg almost rotted off. Doctors told her it would have to be removed. She refused to accept this answer and fortunately my mother never gave up when it really mattered to her. Mom took me to doctor after doctor, and eventually her efforts paid off. The incident left a big scar on my left ankle but it eventually healed without amputation.

In another manner, my mother did give up. When she left her very words to Dad were: "I'm leaving you and your damn kids with you." She threw her clothes, wrapped in a sheet and tied in a knot, over her shoulder and went down the graveled road. When I asked where she was going, she answered in an upset, angry tone, "Somewhere, nowhere, anywhere…as long as I'm away from here." She didn't add any other words. She just turned and walked away, never looking back.

I couldn't understand why she was so angry. Dad hadn't touched a drop of booze for five years and he had drunk only two sups the day before. We—my younger brother, Tony, Mom, Dad, and I—had went to a Sunday dinner at a neighbor's house when it happened. I hid behind their house and listened to my father and Bruce Mosteller talk, while Mom was in the kitchen helping his wife, Tennie, prepare the evening meal.

Bruce was quite a drinker himself. Most men of the area were big drinkers. One could often see a ten-quart water bucket of white lightening setting on a blank which had been nailed between posts about four feet above the porch floor with a dipper in it. The drinking water set beside it. Bruce kept his booze in a cool mountain spring a few paces from the house.

Bruce continued for a long period of time to persuade Dad to take a drink with him, but Dad kept saying, "no." Eventually he gave in and went with Bruce down to the spring for a sup of the deadly brew, which took only a few years to kill him.

Tony took Mom's leaving extremely hard. He leaned up against a big old maple tree in the yard and cried for days. I tried to comfort him, but apparently he needed time to forget.

Besides being young, age seven at the time, she petted him beyond belief. It made me sick to my stomach the way she babied him sometimes. After school she would say to him, "Come here sugar-lump, come sit on mamma's lap." Then all of a sudden her actions and words changed. "To hell with you," she said.

All of us had many inner wounds, which healed over with scars, because of many different reasons. We were not a family that hugged each other or talked about anything. We just ignored all feelings, especially bad ones, like a huge elephant trampling down our home.

"Bad feelings should be looked at like a gauge," Tommy would say, associating the subject with the cars he worked on. Whenever he was home, most of his time was spent working on old cars. He could put a motor together, piece by piece, even when he was a teenager. When he got through with it, which seemed to be never because he always had something extra to do to it to make it run better or look prettier, it gave that special roar he wanted it to have and it could out-run anything on the road. He'd run off and left the cops like they were standing still a few times. In one instance he out-ran the cop and waited on him to catch up; then did the same thing again and again. He cleared a six-foot fence, without turning the car over, and drove off through a field. They put up roadblocks to catch him but that didn't work either. He drove the car up a steep clay bank to go around the roadblock. Up the bank and around the cops, he was gone in a flash. After that he figured he'd better get lost for awhile. So he went out west to Portland, Oregon, and entered a national race. It looked like the average car: they told him he was wasting his time. But not Tommy, he entered anyway and came in fifth place. I knew he wanted to take first but that was "pretty good" considering all the others had racecars and he didn't. "We wouldn't ignore our car if the gauge said it was low on fuel or oil. Would we?" The rest of the story was usually left for me to figure out. I learned how to be a deep thinker because of him leaving parts of the story out.

With my mind, I reasoned right along with his conversation: *So why do we have to ignore people? But again, maybe this is part of our testing. Grief, anger, fear, and anxiety are all natural emotions because we are imperfect. By knowing our weaknesses, we gain strengths. If an alcoholic acknowledges what he is, he can make the situation less by staying away from people who drink.* The only trouble was it was practically impossible to do that in this area where almost all men were big drinkers.

Rather than ignoring our spiritual self—our feelings which acts like a gauge—what we really need to ignore is our self-centeredness. "How shall a man gain his life except he lose it?" *God must put those negatives in our lives to tell us something is wrong, and we should put those negatives in their proper place, just like a red light that says "stop"—let's do this differently. At that point, there's no need to keep noticing the gauge, just take action,* I thought. Once we have noticed our emotional gauge, steps should be in order to correct those negatives, just as a person would stop for gas.

Tommy must have learned something from his many experiences and from his own words, because I never again saw him repeat some of the bad actions of earlier times.

I'd read somewhere that "Codependents are usually obsessed with their need for sex or love because of past wounds. They're trying to recapture that which was lost or never given." This was my father—obsessed with the loss of my mother. "Unhealed or scarred-over inner wounds are the powerful hidden reasons for all self-defeating, self-destructive patterns in our lives."

My father must have had plenty of inner wounds and didn't know how to heal them, except with the presence of his wife, his crutch, which left only a scar. *Accepting people ahead of God causes this action,* I thought. Just as he sent Tommy to guide me in earlier years, he later sent others, some I thought were advocates of the devil, to teach me other lessons. Whether good or bad, testing or not, I hoped I would use those stumbling blocks for stepping stones, as Tommy had taught me. This must have been the reason he was a little rough on me at times.

I don't really remember Tommy being around too often. He spent more than five years of his early adulthood in prison. Whenever he was around—and he wasn't working on old cars—I felt he was continually bossing. It sort of reminded me of the *Boy Named Sue*, Johnny Cash's country song; his father named him Sue so he would be able to overcome. As I remember the song, he wasn't around very much either.

Our lives, Tommy's and mine, have been an obstacle course of stumbling blocks, partially caused from helping the wrong kind of people. But, we have been angels to each other.

Martha Harris

Colors of green, yellow and orange leaves covered the trees in the valley as far as one could see. Cold Branch Road led to a beautiful creek of the same name where tree limbs hung over both sides, often touching in the middle.

Chapter 3

"Cap it, damn it!"

Tommy started going with Betty Mull when he was just a young boy. She was a pretty little thing with long dark hair and brown eyes. Their relationship lasted for about five years.

On the way to see her, he would often run into Sam Dowell, her uncle. The turn-off to his place was one road up from hers. A lot of times Tommy spotted him first and would hide. He was afraid of Sam. There was only one way in, and more often than not Sam was out roaming the countryside and would catch him.

Wearing a full beard, Sam was a muscular, mountain man with long ash-blond hair who looked and acted like Davy Crockett or Daniel Boone. He stood about six feet or better, weighing about 250 pounds and nothing but muscles. Always fitted in old blue jeans, with a wide belt and suspenders, a checkered shirt and high boots, he carried a holstered knife on one side and a hatchet on the other. Even in the summer time, he wore a coon skin hat. Sometimes he wore his special shirt. It had buttons all over it. There wasn't room for another button anywhere on it, even on the sleeves. He must have made it. I'd never seen anything like it in my entire life.

Sam had plenty of money, because he made moonshine. The 180 proof corn whiskey was distilled above his house, high upon a ridge where he could see revenuers if any came near. Most likely they never did, because everyone thought he was crazy. Even in the church yard, people would sometimes whisper, "Ya better stay away from him. He'll kill you." When asked why, they would answer, "He's crazy."

Beginning with a high, shrill voice and ending with a deep, course voice, he hollered out across the hills—apparently to himself—"Cap it, damn it! If you can't cap it, comb it." These words echoed down over the hills and into the hollows. He was talking about his still when he said "Cap it." No one ever knew what he meant by "comb it." And they were too afraid of him to ask.

He wallpapered his house with money, ranging from one to one hundred dollar bills. A large cedar chest, stashed full of money, was in the living room area of his small, mountain home. Metal straps crossed it in two places, with a metal hasp for a lock. Occasionally he hung his money out on a clothesline. *Maybe he washed it. Or maybe he was just sunning it.* I wanted to know why. So I asked Bernell Mosteller, who was a friend of mine and a relative of his, why. She said, "He washed it, because he said it was dirty."

Paul Trull, Roy Trull's father (Roy was Tommy's best friend), and Arnold Trull, Paul's brother, got some of the money while it was still hanging on the line one day. The young men snuck up to his house that bright sunny afternoon while Sam was away and snatched a few bills off the line. Sam returned about that time with fire and brimstone in his eyes, scaring them to death. They said it was only fifteen dollars, but Sam got furious with them. They never did it again.

Sam sometimes threw his knife at his own shadow. He dug small holes in the ground, about three feet by three feet, for what seemed like no reason at all. Tommy helped him dig these holes. He said he was scared to death of him. He didn't ask any questions; he just dug.

Over time Tommy got to know him and became less afraid. Even when he was afraid of him, he tried hard not to let it show. He also helped Sam build a playhouse, out of rail fencing, in the middle of the road. It was an old, backcountry road that nobody traveled. He had cokes (cola), eggs, whiskey, candy, cake, or almost anything in the playhouse a person would want to eat. Sam allowed Tommy to come around his place because he trusted him and shared his food and drink with him readily. Very few people were allowed to come around. He protected his area in the mountains like a bear or some other animal. Tommy and Sam became good friends. They would actually play, or act like they were playing, in the playhouse they built, even though Tommy was a teenager and Sam was much older, at least middle-aged.

Apparently he liked Tommy a lot, for he didn't want him to leave once he came around. Or maybe he was just lonely. He trusted so few people and scared them so badly that they didn't want to be around him.

He taught Tommy how to survive out in the wilderness. The first thing they did on a camping trip would be to start a fire to heat rocks all day for their beds. Together, they killed a wild hog and gutted and cleaned it. Its belly was filled with fresh corn on the cob, carrots, potatoes, onions, and any other vegetable they happened to have. The hog was wrapped in corn shucks and laurel leaves and laid on a gunnysack—they called it a "toe-sack." They lifted it by the ends of the gunnysack and put it into a hole in the ground, which they dug. The ends of the sack were neatly tucked in. About one to one and a-half inches of dirt was used to cover the hog. Big rocks were laid across the dirt and a fire was built on top. This process took about an hour. The meal was left under the burning coals sometimes for two days. They later lifted it out in the same way that it was put in and feasted on its tender morsels for several days.

Betty and other members of her family would build a lean-to. A lean-to offered shelter, replacing a tent, which they didn't have. Short birch limbs, with the leaves still on, were gathered to build it. These branches were turned up side down. Starting from the bottom, they laid them over small poplar poles. "The back should always go toward the wind," one instructed the others that didn't know. There were never any leaks.

Sometimes they built a cabin, depending on how long they wanted to stay out in the mountains. From yellow poplar trees, they peeled bark to use as shakes (shingles). The bark would flatten out when laid up side down on the ground. Poplar trees were straighter, so they used the peeled trees for poles to build the framework. String, stripped from the inside of the bark of the hickory tree, furnished tie-downs to bind the body structure together and tie the shakes that covered it in place. The shakes over lapped each other on rows of poles; then rows of poles were laid over the shakes to help hold everything in place. The second layer of poles alternated positions with the first. Once done, the oatmeal colored house would be so camouflaged that anybody could walk right past it and not even see it, if they weren't looking for it. There was no maintenance and it lasted a lifetime. (Today some rich people use these same kind of shakes to go on the outside of their homes.)

Before nightfall they made their beds. First, they dug a hole in the ground and laid the hot rocks in it. They placed a thin layer of fallen leaves and dirt on top of the rocks and about six inches of moss on top of the leaves and dirt. Making their beds on top of this, they stayed warm even in the "dead of winter."

Tommy got to know this big man. But he never lost his fear of him—or respect of him. "He wasn't as dumb as people thought," Tommy shared his belief. "He acted like that to divert revenuers." (Wayne "Cutworm" Phillips, who owned a store in Hayesville, spent a lifetime capturing his life style and even made movies of him.)

Sam was very odd indeed. He even cleaned his gun in church. Paul Parker, a deacon of the little church at the fork of the road at that time, told him to take his gun outside to clean. He told Paul he had as much right as any of the other damn hypocrites there. They just left him alone after that. "That was when the Church of God at Tusquittee was first built—sometime in the mid '40's (1945 was the actual year it was recorded at the assessor's office). It didn't have windows in it yet," Tommy related at a campfire one night as he taught us how to build a lean-to like Sam had taught him.

Chapter 4

As Strong as Death

A longing for my mother kept returning, again and again. Or, was it a hurt? With it, my mind overflowed with memories—memories I thought had faded with time. These memories helped me reach for something in the past that might help me with the present. They seemed like the only knowledge I had to draw from. School didn't teach me how to survive in this world. There was no one left at home to answer my questions. Dad was almost completely helpless because of his drinking. His blindness wasn't nearly as bad as his habit. Tommy and Jimmy were gone most of the time. They'd be gone for days. Who knows where they'd gone or when they'd return. Tony was too young. He couldn't tell me anything. He just added to my burdens of overwhelming responsibilities. The mothering feelings I had for Tony were welcomed though. I was happy to be there for him; even though I felt inadequate, that's probably where the frustrations and sense of doubts came in. I felt completely empty, just a hollow shell with needs. The needs went much deeper than a hungry belly or feeling a great need to take care of my youngest brother. Somehow, they had to be met. Even God seemed to be at a distance. *Why did these needs exist? Who could I depend on now?* Tommy had taught me to depend on myself. The church had taught me to depend on God. Now, even God seemed to say, "You must try." Along with the tears I cried each day, my body sometimes had a deep quivering sensation. I wanted to know what was going to happen next. The security of my life—my mother—had been taken away. I'd been left alone to take care of Tony's life as well as my own. "How could I measure up?" I often asked myself. *I can't get anything done with all these doubts. I have to pull out of it.* With these thoughts in mind, one of Tommy's sayings kept repeating itself: "Trying is not good enough!" He would say. "You have to do it!" "But how?" I asked myself. The memories of the past offered some quiet relief. Maybe they would show me how to get over another stumbling block, which I had to face—now. So I let them creep in and flood my mind.

It wasn't all that hard to think of an incident concerning Bruce Mosteller, because he was the one that encouraged my father to take his first drink of whiskey after being off the stuff for five years.

Bruce had a brother, named Peck. Bruce lived on Cold Branch, and Peck lived on Tusquittee. I came to know them early in life, because my parents were neighbors of Bruce and his family when I was born. At that time, we lived in a small one-room house at the gap of the mountain on Cold Branch. The house was built of planks and covered with tarpaper. Tarpaper also covered the roof of the house and even the dirt floor. Mom said it helped keep the place cleaner and helped prevent moisture. When I was four years old, we moved to Tusquittee, which was closer to Peck. Our place in the cove on Tusquittee was also built of planks, but it had a wooden floor. It was built on a slope, the front porch being the highest off the ground.

Mom would sometimes put Tony, since he was the baby, on the high porch and tell our German Shepherd to watch him. Since Dad was off working most of the time, he'd gotten us the well-trained dog for protection. He understood and obeyed ever command. Tommy named him Old Joe. Mom had almost complete freedom when Old Joe was around. He guarded Tony's every move, making him go back to the center of the porch whenever he got too close to the edge. This gave Mom a lot of security. It was like having a giant playpen for him, with a playmate to boot. Joe would gently nudge Tony in a different direction when he got too close to the edge of the porch. I thought he was the smartest dog in the world. Most of the time, Tony would turn around and crawl the other way, just from Joe's gentle nudging. Very few times did he ever need Mom's help to make Tony turn. The occasional times he did, he would stand in between Tony and the edge of the porch and bark to let Mom know that Tony was in danger. Joe never did use force, but he never gave up.

Mom didn't seem to like animals at all, except for eating purposes, especially in her house; but she liked this one. "He kept his place," she said.

Joe had saved my life at least a couple times from Oscar Ash's old bull. The first time it happened I was bawling, because Mom had insisted I go outside to play in mud pies. I hated mud pies with a passion, even at four years old. If only she could look at me like a helpmate. I might have been small, but I felt very reliable. I wanted to do something useful. I wanted to help her with her work, but she thought I was too little. Slapping the pies with anger, I wished I would die. I must have sat there crying for hours. Dusk was approaching fast and I could see Oscar herding his cattle down the path toward me. "Good," I said. "Maybe Oscar's old mean bull will kill me; then she won't have me in her way anymore." As the cattle came closer and closer, I knew what the old bull would do; so I just sat there for as long as I could, waiting for it to happen. When the bull lowered his head and dug his hoofs into the ground, I knew he meant business, so I chickened-out and started to run. Joe was right there in a nick of time to cut in between us and save my life. I ran under the high porch, feeling very safe for Joe took over and herded the old bull and the rest of the cattle down the road.

The second time, Joe had saved Tommy's life as well as mine. Mom had sent Tommy and me to the store for a sack of flour. It's a good thing Joe went along too. For on the way back, we had to pass a high cliff. The rocky bed of the creek below looked tiny. It just happened that Oscar was herding his cattle home that day too. We somehow got pinned in between the cliff and the old bull. Tommy hit the bull on the head with the 25-pound sack of flour, which he'd been carrying on his shoulder. This barely fazed him. Joe came running to our rescue, directing him out of our way so we could escape a long fall to our deaths.

Joe always kept as close to us kids as possible, mainly for our protection. Never did he demand anymore attention from us than we were willing to give. He especially stayed out of Mom's way and her things; he seemed to know she didn't like dog hairs all over everything. If she placed a pot of freshly strung green beans on the porch, he would go around it. When he wanted to come into the house, he would always wait until someone in the family said, "Come in!" His behavior was strictly obedient.

On Tommy's and Jimmy's two-mile trip out of the cove to catch the school bus each weekday morning, Joe sometimes watched them until they were out of sight, rounding a bend in the road. Other times he would follow them all the way to the bus stop, depending on what they wanted him to do.

Our Joe was not just another dog. He had become Tommy's constant companion, when he wasn't babysitting Tony or fulfilling Mom's commands. Both Tommy and Mom thought the world of him.

One day Bruce and Peck came by to take Old Joe hunting. Joe wasn't a hunting dog, but they wanted him to go anyway. Maybe they thought he would protect them if they ran into danger. Peck followed Bruce on their trip into the woods, with Old Joe out front and the hunting dogs in hand. While the two were walking through the woods, Peck said to Bruce, "There's a tick on your back, Bruce." Bruce answered, "Help it off, Peck." Both men talked extremely slow, much slower than the average Tarheel. Not one bit of excitement was ever heard in their voices, probably because they didn't experience much. As they got deeper into the woods, Old Joe was the first to face the danger. He was just ahead fighting furiously with a coyote. Once they got close enough, Peck was able to shoot the coyote. Then, they went on about their business of hunting, as if nothing had happened. That evening, they brought back several squirrels, giving Mom a couple, of which she made dumplings. I'll never forget the taste of squirrel and dumplings. They were the best tasting dumplings I've ever had. Not much was said about Joe getting into a fight with the coyote. Whatever was going to show, it would do so in time. So, there was no need to worry about it.

Mom briefly mentioned to Tommy that maybe he should tie him up, but he didn't. There was a chance that Joe had contacted rabies from the coyote he had fought with, she thought. She usually insisted on things like this, but she was feeling poorly at the time and didn't. She had the measles.

It might have been an old wife's tale, but Mom said people with the measles shouldn't let the light hit them. So blankets were hung over the windows of our small home in the cove. It was during the hottest part of summer. The big maple, locust and oak shade trees surrounding the house didn't provide enough protection from the sweltering heat.

The rest of us caught the measles too, but it didn't affect us very much. Mom was in and out of bed during the day, which was unusual for her. As for me, I wanted to go outside. We had been cooped up for several days because of being sick with the measles. The next day, all of us kids arose early, wanting to go outside. Tommy wanted to take Old Joe over to Aunt Lillie's. Mom reluctantly agreed to let him go, telling him to be careful. "It's been about four days since the hunting trip. If Joe's got rabies, it'll show up anytime," she reminded him.

When Tommy returned, he told us what had happened on the way to Aunt Lillie's. As they passed Tom Casedy's old place, Old Joe fell in a branch and took a fit when he drank water from it. He ran around in circles, stumbling in and out of the creek, casing his tail until he fell over. Afterwards, he had a hard time getting on his feet again. When he finally did get up, he started snapping at a bawling calf and bit it on the nose through the wide cracks of a log barn. He then made a dive at a couple of cars that drove by. Tommy walked beside Joe the entire trip. He didn't know what saved him from being bitten—a guardian angel maybe, or maybe the love of a pet that sometimes lingers on beyond expectation…or maybe both. At Lillie's, Old Joe walked away from Tommy. He seemed to know it was time to go before he bit his loving friend. Tommy called repeatedly for him to come back. This was the first time Tommy couldn't get him to obey commands. Joe turned around and took what he must have thought was one last look at Tommy, as if to say "goodbye" the best he could and walked away.

Later that day, we noticed Old Joe wobbling into the yard. We didn't know how or why he'd returned home. Mom told Tommy he would have to try to tie him up until Dad got home, which was several hours away. Tommy had made a metal link-chain, which he used to tie Joe. It was too weak to do much good, but we couldn't let him wander away to spread the phobia anymore than he already had.

Barely holding back the blankets, I watched Tommy tie Old Joe to a maple tree at the edge of the yard. Saliva dripped from his mouth and his tongue hung out. His tail dragged between his legs. His eyes looked wild and crazy. Our friendly, protective German Shepherd had gone mad. I felt very afraid for Tommy. Since Dad was off working and came home only on the weekends, Tommy, being the oldest, took on his responsibilities while he was away.

Mom quietly told us not to make too much noise. He might become vicious and bite Tommy. We became as quiet as possible. Our voices tuned down to a whisper. We tiptoed through the house. "The dog might hear us and come through the window," she added. Being enclosed in the house, we were left with very few things to do except talk, which we did quietly.

As soon as Tommy returned to the house after tying Joe up, Mom started with a little story about mad dogs. She wanted us to use extreme caution around them. "Mad dogs go blind; the madder they get the blinder they are. They still have good hearing though. They are thirsty all the time, but when they drink they get worse. It takes them about nine days to go through the final stage," she explained and went on to tell us a story about Tommy and Geraldine Stamey, Tommy's friend, who were playing in the barn when a mad dog lunged at them. "They climbed up in the barn loft to get away from him. The dog jumped as high as he could to get at them. He was in about his fifth day of madness only, and it took five bullets to kill him," Mom said.

After much persuasion, Mom finally agreed to let me go outside to go potty—do number two. We'd been peeing in a three-pound coffee can all day, afraid to go to the outhouse. The house was in between the dog and the outhouse. As I opened the front door, I faced Joe who was no more than thirty feet away. With his head bowed, he seemed quiet enough. I needed to go potty —bad! No way could I hold it until Dad got home. Mom repeatedly told me to be careful, even after I was already in the yard at the edge of the house. I thought, if she didn't be quiet, she would cause the dog to take notice.

Apparently Joe hadn't yet lost enough of his eyesight to let me sneak past him, or maybe his hearing was sharper than I thought. At this point, it didn't matter whether he heard my footsteps or Mom trying to give me quiet instruction from the doorway. He started growling and jumping. I knew better than to get too sure of my safety, because Mom had cautioned me thoroughly that the chain wouldn't be strong enough to hold him. His jumps became stronger when I started to run; the noise under my feet seemed like thunder, as I tried to hurry without making too much noise. As I rounded the house and neared the upper end of the yard, Joe broke the chain and came after me.

Tommy came out of the house to draw his attention, but Old Joe seemed to know I was easier game. There was no time left to stop and think about what I was going to do. The outhouse was probably another twenty feet from where I was. The top of the outhouse came to mind but to get up there…how? As small as I was, how was it going to be possible to get out of his way in time? Even at age four, I knew I still wouldn't be safe inside the outhouse. Mom had warned us of mad dogs plenty of times. The door was too flimsy, and the dog was too fierce. *My feet wouldn't even touch the edge of a car seat if I sat up straight in one*, my mind unveiled as I quickly looked down at my body. *The door, I could somehow climb up the door. I have to, not only does my life depend on it, but being bitten by a mad dog is worse than death*, I thought. *And I have to do it now.* These thoughts seemed more like feelings than actual thinking, racing across my mind like falling stars.

"Please God, help me," I begged out-loud. Scrambling up the door anyway I could, I just barely escaped…but I don't know how. Possibly an angel lifted me there.

Breathing a sigh of relief, I lay flat down on top of the roof, becoming as still and as quiet as possible. Mom still screamed out instructions from the doorway. Slightly raising up from my position, I put my finger to my mouth, telling her to be quiet.

My urge to go potty was still there, but it had to take second place to the situation now. *Maybe I can go off the edge of the outhouse once the dog has quietened down*, I thought. *That might make too much noise and rouse him again, so I'd better try to hold it.*

In the hot afternoon sun, I lay flat on my stomach for some time. The tarpaper, which covered the roof of the outhouse, was so hot it burned my skin. Sweating was surely the only thing that prevented the melting tar on the roof from sticking to my body, wherever I didn't have clothes to cover it. Sitting up, I bent my knees and pulled my clothes tightly around my body, hoping to cover more skin.

Dad came in just before dusk. He knew exactly what was wrong with Joe. Mad dogs in this part of the country during those times—1948—were common. They didn't get their shots. It was easy for Dad to recognize the signs of madness. He went into the house to get his gun. Then he went outside to unchain Joe. Tommy had managed to tie him up again while I was still on top of the outhouse, but I was still too scared to move. Dad took him to the nearby woods to kill, because he didn't want to do it in front of us kids. It was amazing to watch my father handle this dog with so much ease. Tommy had handled him with ease too. It's strange, Joe acted much calmer, almost like a normal dog, with both of them. *Why did he act so vicious with me?* I couldn't figure it out—it must have been just one of those questions that was never meant to be answered. I admired both my father and my brother for being able to handle such problems. My father was an adult, making it foreseeable for him to manage such obstacles; Tommy was a growing boy, only twelve. He reconfirmed my feelings toward him that day. He was my hero. Afterwards, I looked at him as if he was grown up too.

As I watched my father lead Joe into the woods, I climbed down from the top of the outhouse. My dress was a little damp from so much sweat. Now that the time was right, the urge to go potty had left me. *Did I want to go potty just because I wanted to be troublesome to my mother?* I must have been a lot more trouble to her than I wanted to believe—one of those ways I got on her nerves. Thinking of myself, I rushed into the house, hungry. I knew I'd have to wait for that too.

Soon after that, it became a law to give dogs their shots in North Carolina. They were offered free during the late '40's, too late to do Joe any good.

Even though it hurt to see Joe die, I knew it was something we all had to face. My brother needed Old Joe to hold together his memories, to hold together his world of connection with something he loved. I loved him, but not nearly as much as Tommy. Even as young as I was, I still felt for him and mourned his loss. I felt for Old Joe too. He was more like a person than a dog.

Old Joe had always tolerated us, even with our faults, but had made no mistakes himself that I could see, until now which wasn't his fault. *How did this happen?*

A thousand memories filled my heart and my mind. They weren't replacing this big ache. They weren't easing this lump in my throat. They weren't quieting this feeling of shakiness I had inside—the feelings I had then because of Joe's madness and the feelings I have now because of inadequacies and insecurities. Things will never quite be the same without him, especially for Mom and Tommy. Joe seemed to be some type of connection between Mom and Tommy. This friendly link had been broken. By now, all other ties had been broken too.

Not even an animal's love is totally unconditional, but sometimes it is carried beyond what we expect and provides a closeness not easily replaced. For "love is as strong as death" and with it we will overcome all obstacles.

Remembering Old Joe was not only a brief time away from thinking about Mom being gone, it was a sweet awakening. I had come up with a few answers: *If a dog can keep trying, so can I.* Another answer was love. *I loved Tony enough to keep trying.* So, what's next? *Waiting or doing!*

My mind returned to the circumstances at hand. The sound of katydids could be heard this time of year, especially in the early evening, and lightening bugs were beautiful to watch. *Those huckleberries I saw in the woods are probably ripe by now. It's awfully late in the summer; maybe they're gone. That won't be enough to live on. Apples are plentiful.* I'd seen some trees on the way to school. *Surely there was some poke salad left, or had it all gone to seed. And walnuts—there should be some walnut trees around. There's a few things left in the garden. We don't need much, just a few staples such as salt, sugar, flour and some kind of seasoning to cook with.* I mostly needed knowledge, which I had very little. *We can't live on just thoughts. Actions have to come sometime.*

Chapter 5

A Way Out

Yesterday had now caught up with today. I must have spent months going over the past as if it held some special secrets—even while I worked. *I'm living in the now world. How can the past help me with the situation now?*

Tommy's words of wisdom and comfort seemed so distant. Even his bossiness was missed. I had to face the coming days alone. With no one to help me, I wondered how I was ever going to make it. I felt afraid, a feeling I didn't have when he was around. I hadn't felt the security of his presence in many months now.

I sat on the front steps, crying and thinking about the incident at Bruce and Tennie's. My spirit didn't reflect the day's beauty with all its sunshine; but instead, the hurts of the passed months deep within.

Four acres of corn, a nice, big, potato patch, a large garden, and furniture above normal standards disappeared within weeks. Even our nice, new, electric cook-stove was sold to help Dad buy booze. Yet to come, our above-average house would go too.

Staring at the freshly hand-washed clothes hanging on the line, I wondered what was going to happen next. I knew if I left, the clothes would still be there when I returned and the colored ones would be all faded out.

Dad was passed out. Every since Mom left he no longer wanted to live. I had already gone through hell or what I believed to be hell because of his condition.

How I managed to get by this far was beyond me. Days stretched into weeks and weeks into months. Still Tommy and Jimmy had returned just once in awhile; then, only for brief moments. To pick up some clothes and take out the door again, they hardly gave me enough time to ask a few questions. Tommy was probably staying at Roy Trull's, a friend of his since I was nine or younger. Roy had practically lived at our house before Mom left. I didn't have the least notion where Jimmy was.

I continued to function by scrounging around the house to find pennies, nickels, anything to buy Tony something for school lunches. We both went to school without breakfast many times. I occasionally managed to find a nickel to buy Tony a fudge bar for lunch. After school I mopped up three-quarters of a wash tub full of puke before I would even let myself think about from where the food was going to come. With this being the scene day after day, it was hard to keep self-pity and bitterness out of my life. I tried replacing the bad thoughts with some of Tommy's words but wondered how would they ever fit into the situation now.

I had to do something. Maybe Aunt Lillie would know what to do. Her family had always been dirt poor, but she had more experience than I did. So off I went to her place.

"Lillie," I said, crying, as I stepped into her yard. "We have no food in the house." She was sitting on the porch, stringing green beans. The "table had turned"; our family used to have the most, but now we had the least. We'd exchanged places in what seemed like over-night. I found myself silently wanting her to share what little she had with me and Tony. "What am I going to do about Tony? Tommy and Jimmy are gone. They are old enough to take care of themselves. Dad is passed out. I don't care about myself, but I have to take care of Tony. He's only a little boy."

This responsibility, along with many other heavy responsibilities given to me at such a young age, turned me into one of the biggest enablers the world has ever known. I've been told more than once, "Martha, you never do anything for yourself." I never quit trying but it always seems to be for someone else. I actually thought to do for others was to do for God. This is not necessarily true and this is how we sometimes put people before God; these lessons were yet to come. Maybe my ignorance was the reason God loved me enough to teach me how to cope with the situation. It's just pathetic he had to go to such extremes.

"Let's sit down and think about it," Lillie helpfully suggested. "We can come up with something if we put our heads together."

Lillie and her family of ten kids lived in a house with cracks between the planks up to a quarter of an inch or more in places. They had a fireplace to heat their small three-room house with two beds in one room and one bed in the living room. During the day, everyone gathered around a roaring fire to stay warm in the wintertime and covered up with many quilts at night. Several children grouped together, sleeping in double beds. Her entire family shared a couple of old dressers, used for folding clothes. One was placed in the bedroom and one in the living room. Other clothing items were hung on a few long nails, just as the pots and pans were hung on long nails in the kitchen. Several acres of corn, a garden, and a small wage of practically nothing that Bill, her husband, earned supplied their large family with the bare essentials. Even part of those wages went to supply him with booze. Yet, Bill was considered to be a good provider. They simply didn't have enough to provide another family with food. I had seen them eat corn meal gravy over corn bread for breakfast many times. Even that was so scarce that Lillie often wondered how she could feed one extra person as small as me. Homemade cream corn, fresh out of the garden, was a special treat any time of day for their large family of many unfulfilled needs.

"Let's think about what you do have," she continued, "salt, sugar, lard (shortening made from hog renderings), or anything like that? I'd share with you, but you know we barely have enough to live on."

"No," I answered, "I don't want your food. I'd like to do something to make things better."

"Well, what do you have? Think about it."

Shaking my head, I said, "We're completely out of everything."

"Do you have anything left in the garden?" she asked.

"Let me think a minute." After some hesitation I said, "Potatoes…that's all. The rest is all gone."

Mom even had a new Buick every year, I thought. *Why can't I manage any better than this? Martha, this is a child's way of thinking. You can't think like this any more*, I reminded myself. *If you do, we'll all die*. Admitting the facts, Dad's drinking was the reason I couldn't manage any better. He seldom gave me any money at all—for school lunches, for food in the house, or for anything.

Lillie simply advised, "Go back and cook some potatoes with the skins on. You'll have to make do with that until your dad comes out of it."

We ate just potatoes with no salt or butter for what seemed like weeks. When help finally did arrive it came in the form of a stranger who offered one pound of lard, a box of Morton salt, and a can of evaporated milk. *Or was that stranger an angel?* I thought he was Dad's friend.

That's when I learned to make biscuits and gravy. "We have a small amount of flour left; maybe that will be enough," I told myself. "Fried potatoes would be a nice change too." It seemed like a delicious meal after all those long months with practically nothing. The skill of cooking came easy, as if I had an angel by my side telling what to do. I learned enough skills to get by with a bare minimum of coaching which was very useful in developing self-discipline. Pretty soon, the staples I had would be gone, and the potatoes would be gone as well. "What will I do then?" I asked myself.

If anyone was going to do anything about the situation, I knew it had to be me. *Mom left Dad in the past to get him to straighten out. Maybe I can do the same,* I reasoned. Very similar to my mother's actions, I crammed some clothes into a box and took off down the road, trying very hard not to think about Tony. Thoughts and feelings about him periodically found their way back into my mind anyway, only to be pushed out again—and again—with another thought. I had to think about myself…but mainly, I thought about the changes, I wanted it to bring. That was how I rationalized to cope with the situation.

Trigger, our friendly Collie dog who had replaced Old Joe, insisted on going with me. Nothing I could do would persuade him otherwise.

Skipping and singing along the way kept my spirits high. After a time my energy level wore down. But I didn't stop walking, not even for a moment's rest. Before the eight-mile journey ended, I was thankful Trigger had come along. Whenever I felt so tired I thought I would drop in my tracks, I set the box on Trigger's back and held onto it with one hand. I felt he was happy to oblige. *It's amazing how things turn out for the better,* I thought. *At least, it turned out for the better by Trigger coming along.* He had never wanted to go anywhere with me before. This time, he insisted, and I wondered why, as I did about most other things. He must have somehow known I would need him.

My concentration was steadfast on my long journey. I felt like Little Red Riding Hood going to Grandma's house. This time, the big bad wolf wouldn't be waiting. Anything was worth a try. Just maybe Dad would see his whole family breaking apart and do something to change.

My mind was more on positive things now, because I had quit procrastinating and was doing something constructive. Indecisiveness that came before my decision and my inadequacies of fulfilling all the responsibilities alone were really the hell. I did learn to make decisions more rapidly, even if they were wrong. The more I made decisions, the easier they became.

The morning dew soon wore off and the bright afternoon sun became prominent. I tried to tell the time of day by the sun just to occupy my mind. The important thing was to get to Grandma's before the sun went down.

By late afternoon the sky began to cloud over. I always enjoyed a good thunderstorm. In this area, the air cooled down just the right amount to really feel good. It felt like the whole earth had just been cleansed. The excitement was better than fireworks during the Fourth of July, excitement that left peace from God instead of man-made. The rain felt warm, and I enjoyed it.

Grandma and "Poppy" were not very happy to see me. They were cold and empty of feelings. Mom was not there as she had been in the past. It was totally different from what I expected. They had few words for my welcoming, and even those words were sharp and disappointing. They mainly asked me a few questions about my trip, but their real feelings, which were left unspoken, showed up in their expressions and gestures. "Okay," Grandma said, with a coolness in her voice. "We can't do nothing to change things now. We don't know when your mother will be back to take you with her. She may not even want to take you with her." The sopping wet dress I was wearing went practically unnoticed. It seemed immaterial now. At least, it left cleanliness untouched by the indignities of the human world.

A week past and I was just sitting in Grandma's yard thinking about the possible mistake I had made when three strangers drove up and started talking to me. "Your dad hired us to come and get you," the driver said.

"He figured it would take three men to handle you, if you didn't want to come. We are here to force you, if you don't come willingly," the stranger in the back seat added.

I was really happy about this. It was what I wanted. *Was this enough time for Dad to change?* I asked myself. "Let me think on it awhile," I replied. Dad had tried to kill me twice because I refused to drink his awful tasting whisky. Regardless of what he was like, he did love or need me more than my grandparents. They just barely showed their heads out of curiosity from the strangers being there. The day I arrived flashed through my mind. Apparently they didn't care. My heart went back to Tony as it had done so many times before. I could feel tears starting to wet my cheeks just from the thoughts. I didn't want the strangers seeing this. Tears showed weakness, so I thought. Sitting with my knees up against my chest, I pulled my dress around my legs. Hoping to hide the tears, I slightly bent my head to the right away from them, drying my eyes with my dress tail. "Okay, I'll go with you," I said. "Just let me get my clothes."

I left Trigger there because he was off somewhere; besides, I could barely take care of myself, much less a dog. It never occurred to me that Trigger might have to take care of me. I'd been taking care of other people and things for so long I was dead toward the feeling of having something take care of me. As it turned out, Trigger wasn't needed. I was concerned about how he was going to make it back home without me, but the stranger sitting in front on the passenger side kindly reassured me that animals have a homing instinct. That made me feel better.

Dad was sitting on the front porch crying when I returned. This was the only time in my entire life I ever saw my father cry. "Tootsie (a nickname he'd given me at the age of two)," he said, "don't ever leave me again. I would have been dead a long time ago, if it hadn't been for you." I could never leave him after that; even though, I sometimes prayed for his death.

Tony had managed to stay alive during the time I was gone. His clothes looked like they hadn't been changed since I left. The clothes on the clothesline were still there, some almost faded out completely from too much sun. I suppose I was afraid to ask him how he survived. I was afraid of what he might say. He probably went without food or just eat scraps until Dad came out of it—or, maybe he ate at a friend's house. A pitiful way to be. It was something I didn't want to face.

Chapter 6

Unmarked Angel

Tommy was not only my oldest brother. Although he spent most of his early adulthood in prison, he was my father, my mother, and my friend too. Whatever I did, whether it be artwork or cooking, he demanded utmost perfection whenever he was around. I drew a hula girl on his arm to make his first tattoo when I was nine years old. The girl had to dance with each flex of his muscles. The same type of perfection was required from him in everything I did, including driving a car which he taught me the same year. It was a 1930 Model A Ford coupe which he had "souped up." Even though it was more than twenty years old, it purred like a kitten because of all the work he'd done on it.

Just like a good soldier, I performed all the duties of the household, seldom missing a day of school with honors for years. That old saying "hungry children can't learn" didn't apply where I was concerned; or at least, I thought it didn't. I defied some rules of Mother Nature, some rules of society, and a lot of other rules set up to lower one's ability to achieve because of Tommy. In some cases, I added other people's advice too. They were older than I was, so I should learn from them, accepting the good and discarding the bad, as Tommy had taught me.

At least one of those rules caught up with me though; it had to do with my size. I weighed forty-one pounds at age eleven and didn't reach sixty until I entered high school at fourteen. Tommy told me I'd better go to school and get a good education. When I asked him why, he answered: "You'll never get married. You're too little."

I went to bed hungry many nights, learning to take care of the people around me and trying to meet their needs, especially Tony's. As for my own needs, they always came later. I got to the point of finding it hard even to recognize them, especially when I was hungry. That must have been why I sometimes couldn't sleep at night.

Mom would never allow us to stay inside and watch her prepare meals or do anything. From the earliest time I could remember She'd always said, "You get in my way." The first cake I ever made, I asked a neighbor lady what went into it. "Just tell me the ingredients, and not how much, since I don't have anything to write with." It makes one want to believe in reincarnation… or angels. I want to believe it was angels. Even though I didn't see one, one of these celestial beings must have been there to guide me every step of the way, because it turned out great.

Three brothers, our father, and I lived in a small two-room house with three full-sized beds, less than a foot from each other, and a wood stove in one room. The boys slept together and I slept alone. The house we lived in when Mom left home was now gone. Altogether, we'd lived in four different places since she'd left. We moved into the little house closer to the fork of the road to buy food items on credit. Aunt Marie and her husband, Arb Martin, owned a small grocery store there. We could buy groceries there, and Dad would have to pay for them with his disability check. I knew he would pay the grocery bill first, and buy whiskey with whatever was left. It was part of his upbringing, a value he had kept all his life. It was very important to everyone in these hills to pay their bills, even if they had to go hungry later. The move here provided a lot of security for me. I wouldn't have to wonder from where our next meal was going to come. I could get groceries from Aunt Marie's store, but I'd have to be saving about it. It was just automatically understood that we shouldn't be wasteful. It might take away from a needful person or a needful time. Whenever circumstances permitted we made a garden and canned food for the winter. These were times when Tommy and Jimmy were around to help with the chores. Those times were becoming less and less. They had other people to see and other things to do. Jimmy was gone most of the time. The time I spent with him was so little that I didn't even get to know him. Tommy was going in that direction too. They were much like the leaves falling to the ground in the fall, deteriorating with winter frost, sprouting in the spring, then coming back again to make a full circle with summer's forest green. Both of my older brothers would come home often for clean clothes and a bite to eat; then take down the road again.

An automatic alarm clock in my brain—the only clock we owned—awoke me each weekday morning at four o'clock or earlier. In the winter months, I first built a fire in the heating and cooking stoves. On days when I had a dry bed, I'd jump back in bed until the house warmed up. I was a bed wetter. Tommy had tried to break me of it. He'd even stuck my nose in it a few times, but nothing seemed to help. On the backside of our house, a beautiful creek separated us from a neighbor who arose early each morning to take care of his animals. I could tell what time it was by the activity of this family. With buckets in hand, they'd be slopping the hogs or starting to milk the cows or feed the chickens.

When the school bus drove up Tusquittee Road, I knew I had only about thirty minutes to be up at the road to catch the bus when it returned. By that time the family was fed—usually biscuits and gravy—the dishes washed, the beds made, and the floor swept. The remaining time was spent getting ready for school.

Occasionally adults dropped by after church, and they would be amazed at how tidy and clean our little house was. Even though I was very young and tiny—a child in their eyes—I didn't feel like a child very often, except for wetting the bed. I reached to the out-skirts of my abilities, stretching its capacity to the limits. I used every speck of knowledge I could muster because I knew it was needed to survive. I learned to overcome most things, but bed-wetting was one of those things I thought I had to learn to live with because I didn't know how to stop. Tommy helped me in many ways. He said things to make me think and try harder. Wondering about everything became a good habit. It added wisdom. I knew the day would come when I'd have to overcome the bad habits, like bedwetting. These church ladies would say, "Why, this is better than any adult. How do you accomplish it?" It was apparent they accepted tobacco use. I didn't hide it. Although dipping snuff, chewing tobacco and smoking cigarettes seemed to be a part of life, I had a weak notion that someday I'd have to give that up too. They saw only the exterior; never the inner feelings, never the things that went on behind closed doors, such as Tommy rubbing my nose in my own pee and telling me, "I'll break you from this, if it's the last thing I do." They never saw all the effort I put forth. As for the wet bed, it was definitely out of sight when they came by.

I briefly answered with a shy nod, "I just do it," and kept the secret to myself. My real experience in later years told me some other reasons why I tried so hard: I had never seen anything different. My mother, as a model, would never allow cluttering around the outside or inside of our home. She was a spotless housekeeper. I had taken on where she had left off, and I had to be as capable as well. This was so much a part of me that I thought I was born that way.

Tommy added his teaching after she left home earlier in the spring. He must have thought it was his responsibility since he was the oldest, just like he'd done years ago when Dad was away. I'm sure he wanted me to be more perfect than he was. He expected perfection, and I gave the best I had. Whenever the highest quality, according to him, wasn't reached he made me do it over again, a hundred times if necessary.

I thought it was awfully strange to expect so much from me and expect so little from Dad. Eventually, I came to the conclusion that was the way of the south. Not much was expected from men here. Our father was the worst alcoholic I've ever seen. He could drink three gallons of white lightening and still walk in a straight line, or maybe that's what it took to make him pass out. The only way one could tell he'd been drinking was his blood-shot eyes and an empty bottle. His speech and walk remained the same. I remember going to a friend's house once for one hour; upon returning, I found he had drunk a pint of pure rubbing alcohol. The empty bottle was in the garbage, and it was apparent he hadn't used it for anything else. Other times I'd come back home to find my vanilla flavoring, which I used to make cakes, was missing. Since he was legally blind and going through the separation from Mom, we excused him. Furthermore, he was excused because he was a man. No woman would have been permitted to do such, regardless of the reason, without complete destruction of her reputation.

As a powder monkey, he had an accident when I was about six. Dynamite blew up in his face because of too short a fuse. His head swelled as big as a half-a-bushel. The accident left him with no eyesight at all. Everyone who saw him—his family, friends, and co-workers—thought he would remain in total darkness. Since he had good insurance where he worked, specialists were brought in from various parts of the world to bring back the small amount of eyesight he was eventually left with. He received insurance money monthly to compensate him for the accident. This support was later transferred to us kids after his death; or should I say, transferred to my mother. It was used mainly to supply him with booze prior to that.

After Mom left he never told any of us when to come home, what to do or not to do. He just survived. Most of the time, like the incident with Tommy and the cow, he was too drunk to even notice. They should have carved him a tombstone that said: "Died when my wife left me and buried when I couldn't stand the pain any longer."

Tommy told Dad he was being too lenient with me, that I needed more supervision. He expected him to whip me for spending an evening with some friends. Dad returned his comment with: "She does much better than you do, so just leave her alone." It was important to be trusted, and trust he offered. This goes to show some major contributions to life are often overlooked. I didn't necessarily need his guidance, but we all could have stood a little more affection.

Mom was in charge of disciplining us or telling Dad to do it. Now that she was gone, my father let us do almost anything. Once when Tony, my youngest brother, and I fought on the school bus he was ready to whip me then. Tony came in from school looking like a stuck pig. He had about a quart of dried blood on the front of his jacket from a nosebleed. I told Dad, it was unfair, that I had only tried to hold Tony to keep him from hurting me. When we rolled over in the floorboard of the bus he hit his nose on the base of a seat. It seemed like he'd started the fight for no reason at all. Just penned up emotions that had to be released one way or another, I reasoned.

"Okay," he warned, "if it ever happens again."

That was all he said. The incident was closed, but it drilled values in me that reached clear to the soul. I could never willfully hurt my brothers again.

My thoughts were *Tony hit me in the head with a hammer before Mom left, and he never received any punishment for it. The situation hasn't changed where Tony's concerned; he's still the baby.* So after that, I just stood and took it when we got into fights. I felt sure that Tony wouldn't start another fight with me prior to Dad disciplining me. That justified his actions, so he would do it again. I couldn't see why adults didn't think like I did.

Every Saturday I hand-washed a bed full of clothing in the creek. The clothes were thrown over bushes to dry and ironed to perfection with a smoothing iron, an old-fashioned iron heated on a wood stove. Tommy had to have his jeans creased to perfection. Not one wrinkle, other than the crease, was permitted, and he changed clothes every day. If they weren't according to his standards, I did it again and again until it came out right.

A neighbor lady felt sorry for me, inviting me into her home to use her old-fashioned wringer washer, electric iron and ironing board. At her place I boiled water in wash tubs and sometime used a scrub board. The clothes were often put into boiling water to get them cleaner. To keep from putting our hands into the boiling water, the clothes were dipped out with a stick and twirled around it to remove excess water. I later learned an easier way to get them cleaner with very little effort: tie them off in a swift stream, leaving them there for several hours. The swiftness of the water cleansed them better than any bleach and soap wasn't needed.

This gracious lady, Fannie Parker, who is also considered an angel in my eyes, will always be remembered for her kindness. I overcame my pride and welcomed her offer to help with open arms. A petite dark-haired woman, she must have had a lot of Indian blood in her. She was a quiet person, soft spoken and warm hearted. She had unbelievable wisdom, which seemed to escape most humans. Also unlike other people, she never seemed to age. She retained her looks for years, changing very little. A special kind of peacefulness, which made me feel secure, surrounded her. Even though she never went to church, she gave me the love of an angel without wings or a halo.

Fannie's youngest daughter, Judy, became one of my best friends. Her oldest daughter, Joyce, and I never did get along. Even though Joyce and I sometimes fought like cats and dogs, Fannie always remained my friend and treated me like one of her own children. She listened to me often, possibly more so than her own. Maybe it was because she somehow felt connected with me in a different way. She seemed to think more sensible, more like I thought. This must have been why Joyce didn't like me. She was jealous of the way Fannie treated me, another flip of the coin where tails were turned face-up. I hoped that someday she would see the goodness Fannie brought, rather than remain jealous of our relationship.

Following church one Sunday afternoon I threw a rock at Joyce, hitting her on the forehead. She was saying some nasty things about me for what seemed like no reason at all, just like Tony had done. I truly think I meant to miss her, but she stepped in the way. I thought it was just a clod of red clay dirt. She said a stone was in the middle of it. Joyce jumped off the clay bank, mad as a hornet and started fighting like her life depended on it. I couldn't see why she was trying so hard, since she was almost twice my size until I whipped her.

Her paternal grandmother, Modene Parker, jumped on me the following day while my best friend, Lois Killian, and I were just walking home from Frannie's. Modene was married to Cliff Parker, a relative of Dad's. It seemed like most of the people around here were related in some way. Modene went out of her way to meet me. Weighing more than 150 pounds and being an adult, she whipped me. I weighed only 51 pounds and was taught all my life to respect my elders and not to fight them back. She bent my fingers back until my hands were solid blue and threatened to throw me off the Tusquittee Bridge onto the rocks below. Mad as a wet hen, she said, "You're coming with me," and practically dragged me inside her living room. Pointing to a kitchen table chair setting in the living room, she blurted out, "I'm going to tie you up in this chair and beat you to an inch of your life."

"Here's where I draw the line. You're not going to do that," I told her. "I let you whip me because you are an adult, but I won't let you do that. That's carrying things a little too far."

"You don't have much of a choice, little girl," she stammered. "How are you going to stop it?"

"Oh yes, I do have a choice. You'll see how I stop it, if you try to tie me up in that chair," I calmly answered.

This treatment lasted several hours. "I'll teach you to jump on my granddaughter," Modene snarled back angrily. Grabbing me by the top of my dress, she slung me around.

"You can't get very much accomplished like that," I told her.

"Everybody knows what kind of reputation you have. Why can't you be like other kids?"

"What do you mean, like other kids?" I asked. I didn't think I should have the reputation they gave me for fighting. "I fight back only to protect myself."

"Other kids do what they are told and don't get into fights," she said.

"Other kids do fight when the situation calls for it, and sometimes even when it doesn't," I quickly replied.

By this time she was getting worn down. She was tired of bending back my fingers and slinging me around. I had more stamina than she did, and she knew it. "I can go on like this until you're ready to drop," I told her. "So you might as well stop." Her voice slowed down, and she became calmer. The fight was over. In a way, I had won. I'd worn her down and refused to let her see me cry with pain. I left her house with my head held high with stubbornness and pride. She was worn down to a frazzle.

I told Fannie the entire story a couple days later. She noticed my hands were still blue from Modene bending back my fingers. "Even though I was scared, I refused to show it," I added. Crying was out of the question until she was out of sight. Even then, Lois called me weak for not being able to take it without tears. *They weren't in my position.* "Why does everyone expect so much from me, yet give so little of themselves in return?" I wanted to know.

"Why don't you try asking yourself what could you learn from this incident? Don't you think that would be more beneficial?" Fannie slowly replied.

"You're right. I'll give it more thought," I told her. I was born with a stubbornness to lead me to greater heights. Might as well put it to good use. Tommy's coaching always played an important role in making it so too. Now I had an additional helper, someone who listened to me as well as giving me advice, and someone who understood me better. Besides, Tommy had his own things to do these days and was giving me less and less attention. Fannie didn't boss me like Tommy did. She didn't expect so much from me either. She expected as much from herself as she expected from me. The statement of people giving so little didn't apply where Fannie was concerned. She gave me what I needed at the time.

There wasn't much in these hills to keep us occupied other than hard work and these petty fights. Hoeing in cornfields and gardens were just part of our lives, even as children. I didn't mind the work. I liked it, because I was at least accomplishing something that way.

Realizing that I was mortal, the search for a deeper meaning to life was implanted in my mind. I went back to its source, to my memories. I reached ahead into the future—anywhere to gain knowledge—and the future let out its secrets. One of my favorite recreational pass-times was connected with times to come. The Bible, I did not fully understand, but in its chapters came a means of perceiving certainty for telling fortunes. A Bible could be found in almost everybody's house, even when no other books were around. I placed a pair of opened scissors in chapter one of Ruth and tied a headscarf or some type of rag around the Bible and in between the scissors to hold them in place. I held one part of the scissors with my forefinger and another person held the other side of the handle the same way to tell their future. After each question I read the sixteenth verse in that book. The Bible would turn if the answer was yes, and it would not turn if the answer was no. Later—I can't remember if its beginnings came in a dream where I also got a lot of my predictions, or just through a psychic experience—I learned that this form of predicting was not in accordance with God's wishes. An inborn conversation with myself, so I thought—or was it a conversation with my guardian angel? Afterwards, every time I did it, uneasiness crept into my soul, giving me an eerie reminder that this was wrong. I suppose, both Fannie and the preacher had something to do with it being instilled into my brain.

During the hot summer months swimming was a special treat and a way to add variety. Even though the creeks had poisonous snakes in them, we came back to earth in a likable way. Us kids loved these times. We could forget just about everything, except having a good time. Jimmy usually carried it to extremes though. He threw me in an eight-foot hole and told me to swim or drown. That's how he taught me to swim. The temporary fear was soon forgotten. Cool, mountain water wrapped itself around our bodies and into the crevices of our consciousness, allowing our minds to move on a hot summer day. It generally moved in a direction of appreciation for everything around us. Green grass sprouted from the banks of the water. Nature divided and gave out its shares of beauty to wild flowers of many colors and trees of various shapes and sizes. Even the clouds just beyond the hills were waiting their turn to douse the creek and its surroundings. The feeling it gave us was clean and peaceful. At least, it was that way until Jimmy took after us with a waterdog. Judy and Lois screamed and hollered to the top of their lungs. Nobody ever heard them, except for the ones nearby, because we were too far away. We were told that the mudpuppy, sometimes also called the hellbender, would clamp onto a person with its jaws and not let go until it thundered. Jimmy was as mean as they come, loving every minute of it with his mischievous ways. After awhile he would get bored and give up the chase.

The relaxing mode took over again, leaving things more peaceful. Climbing out of the water, somewhat exhausted, I noticed a patch of four-leaf clover and some scattered daisies. I lay down with my head resting on one hand. Reaching down with the other hand, I started picking the clover. Finding a four-leaf clover meant good luck, we thought. Now that Jimmy was gone, we already had all the luck we needed. "How about trying our luck out on these daisies?" I coached Lois and Judy, my constant companions as well as my best friends, into joining me. One by one, the petals dropped to the ground. "He loves me. He loves me not." We repeated with each petal, all the while thinking of some special beau and hoping the last petal on the stem would end with "he loves me."

A butterfly soon caught my attention. Its beautifully colored wings left our resting-place and settled on a nearby cherry tree. Such large, red, ripe cherries; they made my mouth water. At the base of the tree, poison ivy twined around the trunk of the tree and onto the branches. "Oh no, why does everything good have to have something bad clinging to it?" I wondered.

"I don't know," Lois mumbled. "But you know how you are."

"I want some of those cherries so bad I can taste them," I returned in conversation.

Both Judy and Lois reminded me about the bad effects of poison oak, poison ivy and a weed-like plant, which grows to be about eighteen inches to two feet high, called sumac. A milky substance comes out of the sumac's milky-green stem when broken. Every time I'd ever been around it, I'd end up with my throat swelled level. Jumping up and down, I cried from all the pain it gave me. It usually took three penicillin shots to get rid of it. Nevertheless, I came back day after day and sat under that cherry tree, hoping I'd eventually think of a way to get at the cherries without the poison ivy getting to me. We didn't have a ladder or a board to lean against the tree. Even if I could find a suitable board to climb, the poison ivy extended beyond the trunk onto the branches of the tree.

"Where do I go from here: just sit here and hope, until they're all gone; stay away and try to forget about the cherries; or climb the tree regardless? I have to make a decision soon," I told my friends. "The season is almost gone. Am I going to be here still wishing when they're all gone?" With that thought in mind, I stood up and started walking toward the tree. "I'm going to climb that tree."

"You can't, you know what will happen," Lois firmly reminded me.

"Well…so be it. I'm climbing it anyway," I sounded back.

I threw some cherries down for Lois and Judy. Then I ate to my heart's content.

"Aren't you afraid of getting poison ivy?" Judy now prodded.

The girls knew I hated needles with a passion and to somehow pay for the penicillin shots was another question. "How are you going to pay for all those shots?" Lois asked.

"I did it, so now I'll just have to face the consequences." Starting my descent down the tree and over poison leaves, I regretted facing tomorrow. It would take that much time before feeling the full effects. I hoped I wouldn't wake up screaming. "Now to take my medicine. It seems shameful to have to pay such a high price for something God put on this earth for us to enjoy."

I didn't get poison ivy then…or ever again. God must have known I was talking more to him than to my friends. He spared me the agony. Neither did I test the Lord by deliberately walking into it again. *That would be the same as taking advantage of him.*

Later I did have the opportunity to find out that God's healing extended into the future. I went on a fast river-rafting trip with a large group. Three of us were bounced out of the raft. I went down in a deep hollow pool of water and felt glad to surface without touching bottom. *Oh my God*, I thought, *another deliverance*. Then, I snapped out of it. There was no way out at that particular point: high, rocky banks and the water was too swift. Having no other choice, the river carried me down stream to a semi-still part. Poison ivy covered the only way out there. I again chose the poison ivy over the alternative. Not having much time to think things through, I acted and thought at the same time. What choice do I want: *this river or poison ivy*? The answer was clear. I climbed out onto the poisonous vines. One of the guys jumped out of the raft, once it was stationary along side the riverbank. Running over the rocks and ivy to reach me, he threw me across his shoulder and carried me back. Back in the raft, the group told me they had seen a dreadful look on my face when I first surfaced—a look that made them think I was near death.

Another form of entertainment was to swing from a grapevine across a canyon in the deep woods. Oh, what a thrill it was to feel like Tarzan or Jane where our imaginations ran loose to explore a mighty jungle.

"A good portion of our spare time is spent fighting," I told Fannie one day, answering her question as to how we spent most of our time. *A piece of the human world*, my mind accepted. "My teacher told me the other day she was going to rope me off in a ten-square-foot area at recess to stop my conflicts with other students. She must have seen us when we were just playing around. I took on six girls all at once just for fun. While all six took a spill I stood back laughing, waiting to see which one was going to make it off the ground first.

"One of the boys at school hit me in the stomach with his fist. I doubled him in pain. He later warned another guy who was trying to start a fight with me, 'You don't want to fight with her,' and mentioned the incident. I kept it to myself about how badly he hurt me. I was afraid if they knew how I really felt they'd whipped me every day.

"In the church yard the other day about dusk, I took on two girls and one boy all at once," I told Fannie. "They were all bigger than me. Tony ran to get Jimmy to help me, but by that time the fight was almost over. I was on top of the boy beating him up."

"How'd you whip all three?" Fannie asked.

"I grabbed both girls by the hair of the head and smashed their heads together. Then I grabbed the boy by the neck and swung him to the ground. Whatever you do, you have to do it fast so they don't have enough time to think."

After Jimmy pulled me off, he took me by the hand and led me toward home. He said, "It looked like he needed more help than you did."

"Yeah, I heard about that," Fannie said. She added very little to the conversation, as if she trusted me to somehow pull the right solutions out of my own mind from merely talking about it.

Most fights happened close to the church. "A girl about the same built and weight as Modene drew a knife on me after church just last week. They won't leave me alone."

"Didn't that scare you?" Fannie asked.

"Yeah, but I wouldn't let it show. If you do that, you're a goner. She held a knife, but she didn't seem too anxious to use it. It must have been a scare tactic. Some time ago I made her get on her knees and beg me to let her go. She wanted to get back at me for that."

"How'd you do that?" Fannie asked. "That must have been awful hard."

"I jumped up and grabbed her hair, and swung her to the ground. I had to. It was the only way I could whip her.

"Why does fighting have to be part of our lives?" I asked. "Why do the bad things have to happen?"

"Good questions," Fannie stated, hesitating between sentences. "Maybe they happen for the benefit of somebody. Can we have a top without a bottom…or a front without a back? It doesn't seem possible. The situation might be worse, if we didn't have both good and bad. I think they're put in our lives to learn something. We definitely become stronger with exercise. Don't you agree?"

"Yeah, but that's really hard to understand," I said. "Tommy's said some similar things to me before. I understand more now than I did then."

"You'll understand better in time. Just look for the answers," she added.

"Let's get back to the story," she said. "What happened next?"

"I walked away from her. I caught myself wanting to walk back and fight her when Lois called me chicken. Stopping in the middle of the road, I reminded myself, 'It's stupid to continue with these fights. It'll go on forever, if one of us doesn't stop first.' Chicken or not, I knew it had to be me."

Something I didn't tell Fannie was that I felt as if I had an angel beside me—one I couldn't see—some kind of super power or something I didn't know how to describe who helped me with these fights. Whatever it was, it gave me strength. I could lift three times my weight an unlimited number of times to my shoulders. I never did put the weights any higher, because I was afraid I'd drop them on my head. We lifted them during gym at Hayesville School. Elf School didn't have a gym class. Sometimes I went to Hayesville and sometimes I went to Elf. The fork in the road where we lived gave me the opportunity to go to whichever school I preferred. We lived a little below the intersection of where Cold Branch and Tusquittee met. Kids on Cold Branch Road went to Elf and the ones on Tusquittee went to Hayesville. The boys at Hayesville could just barely lift the weights off the floor. I wondered why did I have so much strength and they didn't. Most of the time, that something inside me was gently nudging me to notice how wrong the fighting was. *Fannie would think I'm crazy if I told her I had some kind of super power,* I thought. This feeling—or whatever it was—was writing on the blackboard of my heart to develop my character and enhance my moral and ethical qualities. I was becoming a better person, hardly noticing the change. I could feel the words in my heart. Fannie was the angel I could see.

I continued on with the rest of the story: "After church that night the moon dressed the sky in blood red," I changed the subject somewhat. "The preacher had just finished a sermon about the world coming to an end. In his sermon, he said the moon would turn to blood. We thought it was the end of time. A bunch of us kids sat on the warm paved road above the church and cried and prayed for forgiveness until dawn. I was glad I'd walked away from the fight earlier, because I had less to be forgiven for." When the sun began to rise and the moon disappeared in its brightness our fears were released and we all went home.

"So, that's where you kids were."

"We didn't do anything wrong. We really did pray all night," I repeated slowly. "We thought that was a definite sign of the end of time."

Fannie smiled. "No, I didn't think you did. I was just worried about you all. I'm glad to know that bad turned out good. You see, things have a way of turning out right."

The true wisdom was not in knowing the world had not yet ended but in a deep heart-felt appreciation "for hope of future life and Thee." The earth is full of God's riches when something is gained in his behalf.

Fannie was truly an unmarked angel. She came into my life at a time when Tommy was slowly fading out. She helped me make a connection between this world and God's riches above. *That's mighty important,* I told myself.

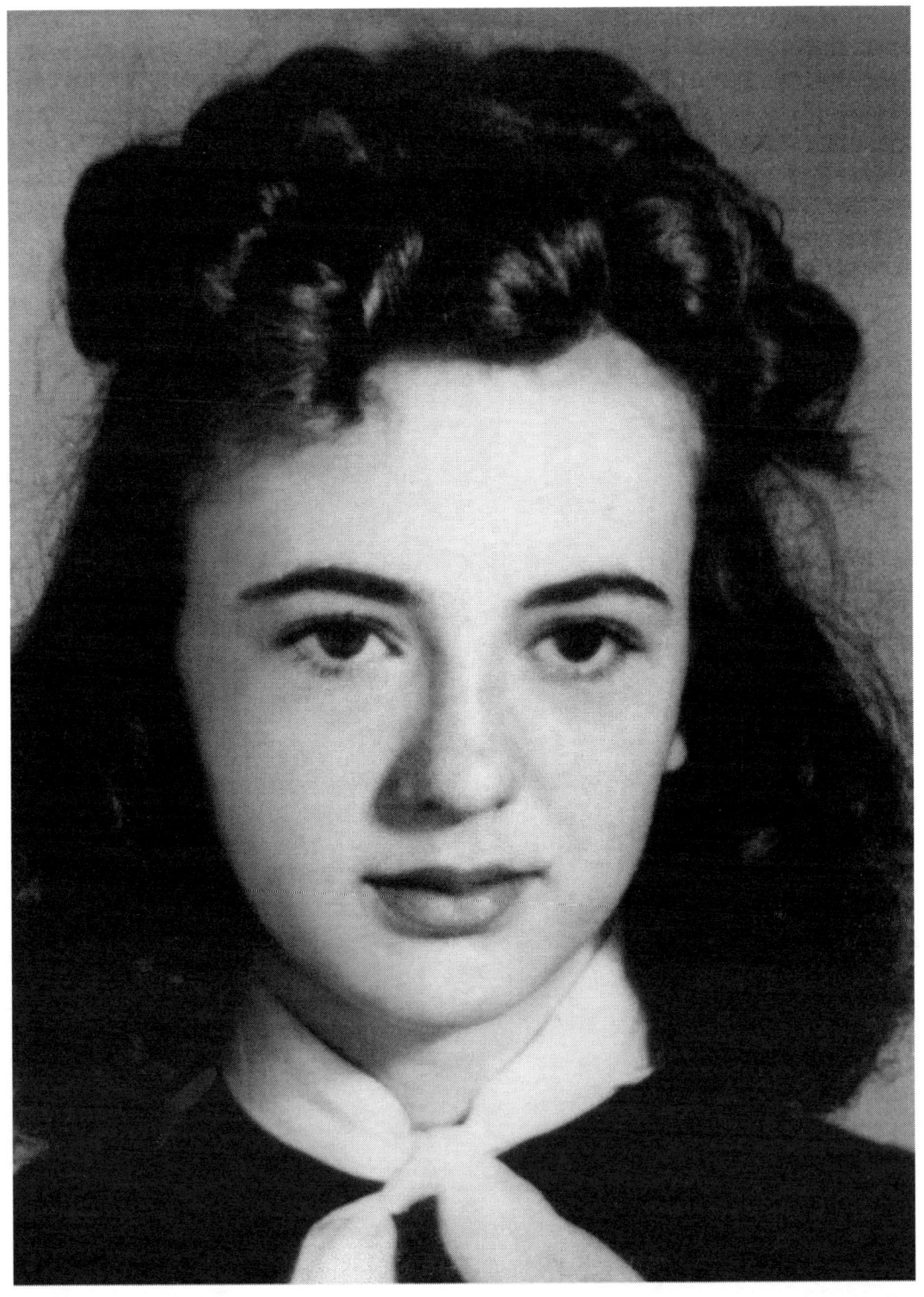

Looking through these eyes at 14, I stood strong, willing to endure and overcome. Face reading books have told me that a person with white showing at the bottom of their eyes will let nothing stand in their way. They can be dangerous because these kind of people tend to be headstrong as well as volatile. I could look like dessert; but if crossed, someone could be the "barbecue."

Martha Harris

Chapter 7

Fading Away

My father never did change, like I thought he might …and hoped he would. *This must be why the Bible says a drunkard will not enter the Kingdom of Heaven*, I thought. *Some never change. Death comes before a change can take place.*

It didn't take long for him to get back into his old ways. I found myself running through an ice-cold creek to get away from him, and he came right after me. I didn't really think. I just acted. When I came to my senses, I was sitting in the middle of a thick briar patch. Looking down at my legs, they really should have been torn all to pieces. They weren't bad, just a few scratches.

He will never get me in here, I thought. Even I didn't know how I got in here; there was no opening of where I came through. After he gave up looking for me, I began to think about how I was going to get out. Looking around at my surroundings, I said out-loud, "I could starve to death before I could get out of this place. Not even a rabbit could get in here. How did I manage it?" Somehow I got in; now, I must somehow get out. It was late in the day when I finally managed to make my way out with a few more scratches. I looked back to see what kind of a dent I'd left in the briar patch, but there didn't seem to be any. There was no way of knowing how I got out either. Maybe an angel made the right opening at the right time to free me. I had to wait for the right time and know when that moment would be. I believe the reason it took me so long to get out was Dad needed that time to preoccupy himself with something else and forget about me. He did exactly that; he was gone when I returned.

Lois and Judy asked how I got scratched up. I tried to brush them off, making the answer as simple as possible and never telling them the full story. I felt ashamed for the way things really were.

From a well, a well we didn't use, just outside the kitchen window, I could hear Dad's voice while washing the supper dishes the next day. Yet, he wasn't there. The voice moved onto the porch and became clearer. I went to the porch to answer his call, but the voice had no substance. "Dad!" I wanted to know: "Where are you?"

He just kept calling my name: "Tootsie, Tootsie, help me," over and over again. Apparently he was in some kind of trouble, and his spirit was calling me for help. His body didn't exist. Yet I stood only a couple of feet from the sound. With the voice still repeating my name, I turned and walked away. Feeling no fear, because it was my dad's voice, I felt an uneasiness, which left a cold, empty hole in my heart. I didn't know how to help him. I didn't even know where he was. Tears came to my eyes, because I wanted so desperately to help him, but I didn't know how. He wasn't there, only his voice came from that spot. The sound getting lower and lower, it kept calling and followed me back into the kitchen. With tears streaming down my face and my back turned to the voice, I said, "Dad, I'd like to help you, but I can't."

About a week later, Tommy brought him home. Dad said he'd been recuperating from food poisoning. He had almost died the same time that I'd heard his voice. His voice had come to me from approximately ten miles away but sounded like it was only a few feet. I suspected it was something a lot more serious than food poisoning. Both Tommy and Dad left out all the details. *Were they just trying to cover it up, because they didn't want to worry me? Or could it be they looked at me like a child, a lesser being. Did they think I didn't know the difference between truth and fantasy?* The truth would have been more appreciated, regardless of how much it hurt. They didn't know these thoughts in my mind. I accepted all the answers they gave me without full explanation. I had to. Maybe they told me all they knew. *Well, it must be pretty important to learn how to read minds*, I thought sarcastically. *It's very strange: they want my help, but they don't want to give me something as small as an explanation.*

Lacking answers, my mind began to wonder about the previous times that Dad had been given another chance. There were many. My father had met death, head on, several times. Once a long time ago, when Mom had left Dad, he went after her at Grandma and Poppy's. Poppy shot my father through the neck. The bullet went through his body at a slant. Doctors at a hospital in Hiawassee, Georgia, took the bullet out of his back. He just barely escaped death. Dad developed a slight speech defect because of it. The bullet affected his vocal cords. Poppy wasn't even taken to jail, since the incident occurred on his property.

As Dad walked up the slightly sloped yard to the porch of their home, Poppy was on the porch with a gun. "Don't come one step closer, or I'll kill you," my grandfather warned Dad.

"I've come here to get my wife," Dad replied, and kept on walking. He wasn't afraid of the old devil himself.

My grandfather was very similar to the old devil himself. When he got mad his light blue eyes would turn glassy white like a snake's. Just this alone gave most people the scare of their life. Even the milkiness of a snake's eyes tinged his.

He had threatened me once with a stick we hung hogs with—a stick about three to four inches in diameter, strong enough to hold a hog weighing approximately three to five hundred pounds in the air. This type of stick is about four feet long and is easily recognized by its pointed ends.

Poppy called me a whore for wearing pedal pushers to the table, while we were eating the evening meal. I was the only one other than one son out of eleven of his own children, plus numerous grandchildren, who stood up to him.

I told him: "I don't tell you how to wear your overalls, so just lay off of me."

His eyes turned glassy white, which scared me to the point of turning my stomach. All these feelings I kept under cover and stood my ground.

He went outside to get the stick. With his eyes looking wild and crazy, he slowly walked through the kitchen door, holding up the stick. His walk didn't show much anger, but his eyes and his voice did. His threats to beat me to death came through loud and clear.

"I'm waiting for you to do just that," I said. "Someone is apt to die today. One of us is liable to end up in prison. I'm ready to go. Are you?" I gathered that my inner strength was just as strong as his was, maybe stronger. I had intentions of putting all the mental powers I had to the task—and to the test. *There's no backing down now.*

My grandfather must have realized the kind of person I was and decided to reconsider. He calmed down. We continued eating our dinner without me changing clothes.

He had called me a whore a few times other than that because of me dancing to music on the radio, even when no one else was around. I tried hard not to let him see me, but a few times he'd caught me by surprise. *The person doing wrong here is him,* I concluded.

Another time when I'd seen his anger against me: I'd used some of his shaving soap to wash my hands because there was no other soap in the house. There was no way of knowing he didn't want anyone to use it prior to his outburst of rage. Even though, I apologized. We seemed to know how far to push one another. We were both headstrong, but we respected each other and used common sense.

My grandfather didn't like backing down. The seriousness of his eyes told that. When he made threats he usually carried them out, even if for no other reason than to show an example.

In another incident when my father had been delivered from death's door, some men had cut him all to pieces with a knife. Foot-long scars were permanently embedded into his back. His limp body was wrapped in sheets and left for dead.

He should have learned something from the many near-death experiences, but that's what he wanted. Tommy had saved his life a few times, which was caused from his drinking. It looked like he'd saved it again this time.

The last chance he will have to change will soon come to pass—I could feel it. Two days before Dad died, I went to Fannie's house to spend the night. Lois, Judy and I all slept together in a big bed (a full size bed). Thoughts about my father dwelled in my mind. Telling my friends how I felt, I cried myself to sleep. When I finally drifted off to a restless slumber near dawn, he evaporated into my dreams. Even my dreams told me he was going to die soon.

My last memory of him alive, which I talked to Lois and Judy about that night, displayed the many hurts of previous times. He was sitting in the middle of a bed, twirling a loaded gun. Naturally he was drunk. "Even a six-year-old would know better than that," I told them. No one could take the gun away from him. It was as if his mind didn't have any more room for the pain inside; he was waiting to relinquish his soul to eternal rest. To fade away in this world would mean peace, and this alone brought a smile to his lips. His pain had reached its limits; eliminating his history, his memories, and his sanity.

Somehow, I knew he wouldn't die from a bullet wound from that gun either, but his time was very near. Neither Lois, nor Judy believed me when I told them that he was going to die soon.

A bunch of us girls were just sitting in a parked car talking the next day, when thoughts of my father's death wouldn't subside. Instead, the feelings became stronger. Out of shear frustration, I wished he would die and get it over with. "No," I told the girls, "I don't wish that either. I just wish he would straighten up… but I know he won't."

I got out of the car and started walking toward home, knowing I had to try once more to save him if I could. As I got to the corner of the old dilapidated barn just above our house, something that felt like a glass partition stopped me dead in my tracks. Nothing was there to be seen, but I could sure feel it. I walked back from it about ten to fifteen steps and ran at the invisible wall. Several times I did this. Each time the same thing happened at the same place. No way was I going to save my father from his infected search for death this time.

Eventually I gave up and went back to where the girls were, telling them what had happened. "Lois, it looks like I'm going to have to spend the night with you. I can't go home."

Crying myself to sleep as I'd done the night before, I told Lois, "The first words that I hear tomorrow morning will be 'Roy is dead.' Those words will wake me." She tried to sluff it off by saying I was just imagining this. Her real concern was to ease my grief.

Reaching out of the bedroom window, I wanted to touch something more comforting. I remembered a touch-me-not flower being there during the summer. It was soft, sweet and beautiful…but it was gone now. At that time it seemed to glow in the bright moonlight, but I no longer remembered its color. With one soft touch, its pedals folded. We shared the conversation of its remembrance. Lois reminded me then, "If you touch it, it will fold up and hide its beauty. It's only to look at." There was nothing here now that was comforting to my senses. It had faded away with the bitter coldness of winter and the bitter coldness of real life.

That was a better time, now passed. I closed the window and dozed off to sleep, with tears still in my eyes. What seemed like moments afterwards, those words woke me. Judy brought the Christmas-day message.

I never shed a tear during that walk home with Judy. There were no tears left. I felt cold and empty inside. He had faded away in the world and I, only for a brief moment, had faded away too…but only in my thoughts. The numbness lingered with each passing curve of the road, as if I was leaving part of myself behind.

As I walked into the house, I noticed the cedar Christmas tree through the open door to the kitchen. Lois and I had decorated it with strings of popcorn and glued-together circles of construction paper. We'd gotten the colored paper and some glue from school. I wanted to put more decorations on the tree, but I didn't know what it would be. We didn't have anything else. "We can think about it and add some more decorations later," I'd told Lois. Now I was glad we didn't add anymore. A cold, but accepting, thought entered my mind: *It would have been just more to clean up.* Then, I added to myself: *This is the wrong way to think, especially at a time like this. This type of thinking is a sign of bitterness...but it's a fact.* Two presents lay underneath the tree. I had put them there myself—one for Tony and one for me. When us kids needed a little money, we caught spring lizards during the summer time for fishermen. We sold them to a man who picked them up weekly in his van. I didn't have enough of that saved-up money left to buy a stocking hat for me and a pair of gloves for Tony, so I'd decided to get them at Aunt Marie's store on credit. Lois and I had wrapped them two days earlier.

With a numb feeling, I pulled back the covers from my dead dad's naked body. He was on his left side, facing the door to the kitchen. Sopping wet, an imprint of wetness was left on the covers in the shape of his body. His body was curled, with his knees up against his chest, as if he was cold. I slightly brushed my fingers over his right cheek and shoulder. The coldness of his body was the same as I felt inside, and probably just as empty. I felt as if I still had a body to move with and a brain to think with, but they were just there, with no spirit: a total hollowness. Movement of my body was more like a machine. *I cared. I cared too much. Just the same, he was better off dead.* With what seemed like a none-caring attitude to others, I asked Aunt Marie, who was sitting by the stove crying, "How did he get this way?" It didn't feel like a none-caring attitude to me. I had just given up hoping that he would ever change.

Through her sobs she answered, "Someone said him and Ralph Ledford (my first cousin on Mom's side, Lillie's oldest son) got into a fight and Ralph drown him in the creek.

"Who are the people who said that?" I asked sternly, "I'd like to talk to them, and..." I stammered. "How did he end up in bed with no clothes on?"

"Whoever put him in bed must have took his clothes off, or maybe he was able to take them off himself. His body's wet. That would explain how the bed got wet. I don't really know. I just got here a short time before you did."

It then dawned on Marie that I wasn't crying. "You're the one who loved him the most. Why aren't you showing any respect for the dead?" Marie demanded angrily through her tears. She continued raking me over the coals. "You could have saved him, if you'd been home," she said. "I thought you were more responsible than that."

It's funny (meaning strange) how a child can be expected to show more responsibility than an adult. I didn't feel like a child, but *they thought of me as one, except for expecting too much from me.* These thoughts were never said. They should've been understood without me saying them, but they weren't. "He should have felt an equal amount of responsibility as I did. He should have changed. It (his death) was something he wanted. I couldn't babysit him all the time," I told her.

Even with the responsibility I faced and accepted, it still wasn't enough. I didn't know where Tony was. I let him go where he wanted and do what he wanted. Although I was in between three and four years older than him, I wasn't any bigger. If I had told him what he could or couldn't do, we would have been fighting all the time. I just filled his basic needs of food and clothing, by cooking the meals and making sure that what he wore was clean, and he had a clean place to live in and a clean bed to sleep in.

Eventually someone else butted in and answered some questions for me, explaining that I'd been crying for days—it must have been Judy. She recaptured the past couple of days, telling Marie about the partition that I couldn't see.

My numb spirit heard only mumbles, yet I knew what they were talking about. Partially in a daze, I finally told her in a solemn voice, "I couldn't come home because an invisible wall wouldn't let me."

I never received the straight answers that I wanted then. I couldn't ask Tommy or Jimmy; they were gone. Marie told me as much as she knew. No one knew for sure how he died or why such an odd barricade stood in my path. It was just his time to go. Apparently God didn't want anyone to save him either, not even me. His opposition told me that. I accepted the information that was given as part of life. "No need to worry over spilled milk," I told Marie. Naturally, she thought that was a cold way of putting it and said so. "But it's a fact," I added. "What's done is done. Now, it's time to accept it."

History had declared him dead. It had eliminated both the good and bad from his memories. Of the time when he was just a young man, he'd chopped down his own mother's bed. This time carries its own story. Tommy was only four or five then. Dad had wanted some money to buy a car. Elihu (pronounced Li-hue), Dad's father, had put $100 in an old money belt and hid the belt in a pillowcase full of down feathers, which hung on the wall. When chickens or ducks were killed, the feathers were put up to save until they got enough to make pillows. Mom knew about the money and told him. Naturally, Dad's parents found out about the missing money, and they knew who took it. He became defensive when Elihu asked about the money. One thing just led to another. They quarreled and wrestled in the yard. Pretty soon, Dad had Elihu's head laying on a chopping block, and he was fixing to chop it off with a double-bitted axe when two men came along and butted in to save Elihu. Dad was still furious, so he chopped down his mother's bed instead. Everyone, especially Mom, knew Dad was very mean when he was young. Mom said he even tried to kill Tommy several times when he was growing up. He borrowed a shotgun from Bill Ledford, Aunt Lillie's husband, to kill Tommy. Mom said she went to Neal Kitchen, who was the sheriff, to get help. He wouldn't help her. Neal told her that if he had a son like Tommy, he would have killed him a long time ago. By the time she got home after going to see Neal that day—they didn't have phones in those days—Dad's temper had settled down, and everything had returned to its normal pattern. After that she never voted for Neal again. Neal came to Poppy and Grandma's, Mom's parents, to talk to Grandma about Mom not voting for him. Mom told Grandma she wouldn't vote for the damn son-of-a-bitch again if her life depended on it, because of what he'd said and because he wouldn't help her when she needed it. Tommy and Dad were quite a bit alike; they both had bad tempers. At least, they were people you didn't want-a mess with. It could get pretty serious. Later, when Tommy grew up he put a stop to Dad treating him mean. Tommy put him down in a ditch, wanting to kill him with his bare hands, when someone happened along and broke up the fight. Dad left him alone after that.

Of the time when he'd first started calling me "Tootsie", he'd eliminated that too. It took me back as far as my own memory would take me. I was sitting propped up in bed when he came home from work. "My little girl is getting better," he said. I stared that memory in the face and recalled the sweetness of his voice, as he lavished me with attention…"We'll call you Tootsie."

I must have been about three years old, or even younger, when he first gave me the nickname Tootsie. That has always remained my earliest and my fondest memory of him, and I can remember almost every thing since I was four, so I thought. Mom told me I was about two.

I also recalled my mother telling him it wasn't right for men to give their daughters attention like that. That was the last time he gave it, other than when he got drunk out of his mind and forced me to drink his booze. Then he would start by wanting me to sit on his lap. Talking softly in a kind voice, he would ask me to have a drink. When I made an awful face and shook my head no, the beatings would replace his kindness. Jimmy would get him off me by making him angry and telling me to run, whenever he was around. That's how it'd started the day I found myself in the middle of the briar patch.

As for Mom telling Dad not to lavish me with attention, it apparently had something to do with sex. Incest was definitely unacceptable in my family. I'm glad I didn't have to live through that too, but my father's attentions didn't represent incest either. My mother just had an over-active imagination when it came to men around girls.

It seemed like Mom was even paranoid when it concerned sex. When I was about six I overheard her and Aunt Lillie talking. When I rounded the corner of the house Lillie was telling her that I probably knew as much about sex as she did. Mom said, "She'd better not, or I'll whip her."

Even at age six, this seemed strange. I don't remember how I learned these feelings. I knew about sex—I thought I always knew. Adults seemed to make mountains out of molehills. To me, it was no big deal. It was just another need we were born with; yet, we were taught we had to disregard it, like it didn't exist. Well, it does exist. Children have sexual feelings too; they're just not as strong, and that's another truth adults don't like to deal with. What children don't know is how to deal with those feelings. If it was talked about more openly and if the whole truth was known, there would most likely be a lot fewer mistakes and less confusion. Here's where the adults could tell us kids what the Bible says about sex. Apparently, God wanted us to have one mate, so we wouldn't end up hurting each other. He was very precise in stating what He wanted, and that was to love Him with all our might and to love others as ourselves. If we love our neighbor as ourselves, we don't steal from him or covet his wife. The Bible doesn't say not to talk about sex; it points out that if you do certain things, then you will hurt others. But you can't tell grown-ups anything. They think they already know everything. So pretty soon—along about the same time sexual feelings get stronger—you start believing like the adults do, but because it wasn't talked about you don't know how to deal with it. Especially when I was young, some things were written on the blackboard of my heart…or on the blackboard of my mind. I seemed to just know some things without being told. Maybe it was my higher self. All my life, I've had this little voice inside me trying to get me to listen. It told me right from wrong. The older I got the less I heard it. As time passed, I could have been too busy to listen, but I think the gap between God and I just got a little wider. *What is it that adults fear in children? Is it fearing the inadequacies of our memories…or the truth of them?* "A child will lead them." At this rate, I could understand why. Hating deception came to the foreground: *If the devil is the "father of deception," then which is better: deceiving your children or wanting them to know the truth?* I thought it was my own knowledge that led me toward truth. But who's to say, maybe it was spirits who led the way. "For he shall give his angels charge over thee, to keep thee in all thy ways." I take *"all thy ways" to mean talking to us too.*

Most people search for life everywhere. You find it in the ground beneath your feet, in the spring waters of the valleys, in the whippoorwill's call following a fresh spring rain, in the lighting bug's flash as dusk turns to night, in the stars lighting up the sky so brightly at night, and even in the clouds just over the hills that may never come by. My mother had poured life into my father's veins. Now that she was gone, his new destination was death. It came early. He was forty-eight years old, eleven months, and thirteen days. It was a Christmas I'll remember until I die.

Remembering wasn't sweet…as should be. Yet, how could I forget his fading away?

Half-way There

*My Mother had poured life
into my father's veins.
Now that she was gone,
his new destination was death.*

*It came early.
He was forty-eight years,
eleven months, and thirteen days.*

*Remembering wasn't sweet,
as it should be.*

*Yet, how could I forget
his fading away.*

Chapter 8

Dead and Buried

Not until I saw Dad's casket brought into Aunt "Monaree" (actually spelled Montree) Parker's home did I cry again. The thought of never being able to see my father alive, even once more, suddenly struck home, breaking my heart into a million pieces. The feelings of a spirit had returned. I was human again. Human thoughts and emotions rushed over me like a river rushes over all the rocks on its bed.

I sat down side-ways on a kitchen table chair, which happened to be in the living room. Leaning my head up against the back of the chair, I opened up with tears and the sound of crying louder than I had ever cried before. My mind moving swiftly to touch the past, present, and future; somehow, they collided with force in the middle. It was overwhelming. It hurt. At the same time it was a relief. That phase of my life was over, and I was glad about it.

Some time later, I followed the path of the coffin and its attendants to the bedroom. I gently placed my right hand on his cheek, saying quietly to myself, "I never want to be buried in one of these boxes." Yet, the coffin looked like a normal coffin, and he was dressed accordingly.

Now that you're an empty shell, you must be contented. Your pain is gone. So is your awareness. His earthly life had finally left him…his longing for death was over. *Maybe you're at peace now. I hope so.*

Dazed, I retraced my footsteps to the living room and to the chair. There I continued connecting the jigsaw pieces of my life in my mind: He was my father, and I honored, even respected him with great delight—yes, delight. It pleased me to please him. I seldom went against him. When I did it was for not eating. Most of the whippings he gave me were for not eating. I figured that was my personal right. There had to be something on this earth that didn't belong to men.

I didn't like people to talk to me during the mornings. Some of my thoughts, particularly during this time, were *I am the one who has to get up early every morning and do everything. Why should I have to listen to my brothers tell me what to do when they have everything served to them? I am the one who worries about where their next meal is going to come from, their cleanliness and the cleanliness of their household, their teachings, and their general well-being. They don't seem to give a damn. I don't need or want their discipline; they haven't earned the right. They could very easily help me instead of telling me what to do. I have plenty of self-discipline without their bossiness. Besides, if they truly cared about me not eating they would have helped earn the food by paying for it, by cooking it, or by serving it or cleaning up the mess. They wouldn't have left most of the responsibility up to me. They would have shared it.* Sometimes the words came out vocally, in a low whisper.

This was my way of rebelling. I felt contented that it was my decision…and my decision only; it offered me the satisfaction of being in control. At the same time, I felt uncertain about how Dad and my brothers were going to handle my rebellion, and what the outcome was going to be. Just like all the other people of this world who tries to form their own importance, I decided the wrong way to get what I wanted or the wrong way to make them understand how I felt. I tried to form my own significance by having my own way in at least one thing, which was not eating. It was a type of pouting to punish my family for what they put me through. They expected too much. It's next to impossible to obey all the requests made by people—request from your parents, requests from your grandparents, requests from your elders—even to the point of not speaking until you're spoken to. Yet, you're expected to serve their every need. They all wanted us children to listen and do what they said. We weren't supposed to have very much to say except agree and do it. All the time you don't mean any harm in your rebellion, you're just trying to meet a need that seems to belong only to adults…and sometimes only to men. I wanted them to know that I was a human being too, that I wasn't put here on this earth just to serve and meet their needs. I had a few needs of my own. Now, for the first time in my life, I realized what I was doing and knew it wasn't hurting anyone except me. Prior to the day they brought Dad through Monaree's door in his casket I hadn't thought very much about it. It must have been another step in growing up.

At the times when Dad had been trying to kill me, I'd always managed to get out of his way. I'd even drunk his awful tasting whiskey once, which I had to hold my nose to get down. I figured from his persistence he wanted me to drink it; so I managed. Even though it was only about a half-of-an-inch of corn whiskey in a pint jar, I got so drunk I could hardly raise my head off of a pillow to puke. With my Dad's help, I lie on one bed and let my forehead rest on another, vomiting between them in a wash pan, which he'd placed there.

Regardless of the type of love he offered, it was all he had to give. In one sense I hated him for his weakness, and in another sense I loved him because of his need. His need had included me, but I felt deprived and cheated. It seemed to me that Dad and my brothers thought only about themselves. I wanted only a little consideration. It would have been very nice if they would have done to me as they wanted me to do to them. A need wasn't really the kind of love I wanted, but it was all I'd gotten from him since the first time he'd called me Tootsie. *This is being very selfish,* I concluded, and managed to reason these feelings away for awhile. Thinking these thoughts must be normal during a time like this, I tried to improve on them by saying to myself: "It was what he wanted." It didn't stop me from feeling the cold and lonely emptiness. *Why do I miss him so much? He was more of a burden than anything else. Have I grown to enjoy pain? I thought I was prepared for this.* No one can ever prepare themselves for the hurts resting in their unconsciousness. The best alternative is to face it, to feel it, and eventually, with time, heal it.

After the funeral services Tony and I went to live with Uncle James and his family. We left our little place at the fork of the road on Cold Branch without even taking down the Christmas tree. I wanted to go back to clean it up, but I didn't have a way. Tommy was in prison, I thought, and Jimmy had gone to live with whomever, or maybe he was in prison too. They were old enough to go where they wanted and do what they wanted to do. I'd heard about some of the mischief they got into, but the comments were usually too brief to even consider. I don't remember either of them being at the funeral.

James's wife, Laurel*, was *the laziest woman I've ever laid my eyes on.* These thoughts occurred to me as I first entered her presence. She didn't keep a very clean house. Nothing seemed to be in order, and she didn't cook very much. I really hadn't seen very many lazy women. Aunt Marie was the laziest one before I met Laurel, and she took care of a small grocery store and a gas station most of the time while her husband, Arb, played craps or gambled in some form. Marie read a lot or did what she wanted to do, leaving her house to clean whenever she got ready. Sometimes she paid me a small amount of money to clean up her house, and sometimes I cleaned it up without pay. Marie didn't like housework, but that woman could sure cook. She always left quite a mess to clean up afterwards. I tried hard to learn from her and duplicate some of her cooking but never succeeded. Never have I ever tasted food as good as Marie's cooking; it was unbeatable. When I came in from school while staying at James's place, the beds were never made, the kitchen seldom if ever touched. I thought Laurel must have been gone all day. Nothing was done to show me any proof that she was there since I'd left for school. She didn't have an outside job.

I got tuberculoses from Uncle James, I suppose. James's health wasn't all that good. (Years later I heard he had TB, but that was only hearsay.) I didn't know I had it at the time or from whom; I just know how I felt. (It showed up years later on x-rays.) I'd felt tired plenty of times before, even before Mom left, but nothing like this. Most schools gave physicals each year. Every time they did, they'd sent me home with a note saying I wasn't able to go to school. I was anemic, they said. Teachers wanted my parents to do something about my health. I thought being anemic caused my tiredness, and the situation was getting worse. Not eating very much had become a habit, which didn't help either. As time past, so did the proof of ever having TB. At least one of the doctors read the x-rays wrong: One said that it was obvious I'd had TB and pointed it out on the x-rays, and a few years later another doctor said the scar tissue wasn't there. Maybe it was because I prayed a lot. No matter how much I rested, it didn't seem to be enough. I was too young to die, but I felt like I was going to. Each day after school I lay in bed crying and praying for God to give me strength and heal me. "Please God, help me make it through another day," I begged. My aunt and uncle didn't even notice. They were gone most of the time, and I tried to hide the way I felt as much as possible. I knew they couldn't afford to take me to the doctor, and I didn't want to be a burden to them. I wanted to be a benefit.

I'd been smoking for two years or more and had used tobacco in some form or another since I was able to crawl. I knew I was very sick, because I was too tired to smoke a cigarette after school. I was too tired to eat…or even sleep. During those earlier years, I could chew "baccer" and spit with the best of them, even though I was just a little tyke. We used to see which one of us could spit the farthest off a high bank. We thought about tobacco just like the rest of the world thought about food: it was part of our lives and a necessary item. I was actually born with the craving. Every time Mom took a dip of snuff, I had to have one too. If she didn't give it to me, I took a fit. Aunt Lucy and Mom took me to town once when I was very small. My feet didn't touch the edge of the car seat then. Mom made the mistake of leaving her purse behind the front seat on the floor. I knew there was some snuff in it. I crawled off the seat to get the purse and climbed back up. Opening the purse, there it was. *Now to get the box open.* It was a struggle, but I managed to open it. The whole box seemed to explode all over me. "Uh, oh!" Choking, Mom and Lucy coughed to get their breath. They had to get out of the car for some air, then clean up the mess. Not even once did I cough. And I don't see how it's possible to think the way I did, being so young, but I thought they were just weak females. Mom had bribed me with three store-bought dresses for Easter to quit chewing tobacco and dipping snuff at the age of nine. By that time I'd already been using it at least seven years. I managed to give it up because of the bribe and because I changed my way of thinking: I chose to look at it with disgust. It worked, even to the point that it no longer satisfied my craving. I also looked at the over-use of alcohol with disgust because of my dad, and knew I'd never become an excessive drinker because of it. But, I never learned to think about smoking in the same way. At the age of eleven, I let my friend, Lois, coax me into having my first cigarette. It's strange how people manage to acquire a taste for something that serves their cravings. It must be something we put into our minds. Whatever is put there, it takes another form of brain washing to get it out. Most of the time I smoked Prince Albert tobacco and rolled my own. There were even times when I got Rabbit Tobacco, a tobacco that grows wild on the landscape of these hills and valleys, when no other form was available.

It was all I could do to make it through a school day. The teacher caught me copying on a test. It was the first time in my life I'd ever done that, because I was too tired to do my homework. He didn't say anything about it until the end of the school year when he passed me with honors. I asked him why he gave me a "B," knowing that I'd copied on the test. He said he understood some of what I was going through, losing my dad and all. "You were always a good student and put lots of effort into your work," he said. "Beside you copied only two answers." This was shocking: He even knew how many answers I'd copied.

He apparently didn't realize how much effort I was putting into my life just to sustain, and I didn't tell him. He didn't know I had tuberculoses, and he didn't know the mess that Laurel left for me to clean everyday. The house was generally empty of everyone when I came home from school; I could see why, they didn't want to face it. I went through the house mumbling to myself: "Maybe if I just lie down for a little while, I will gain enough strength to clean up this mess later."

My teacher, Mr. Woods, also served in an angel's shoes, another thing which he wasn't aware of. It offered great comfort by letting me know that somebody cared. It instilled in me the first awareness since Tommy's caring that men could also be out for someone else's benefit, rather than their own.

As I look back at the disappointing scenes behind me in my exhausted state, I still recall the pictures clearly and feel the pain that goes with each. It's hard to say what should be forgotten and why. I always thought it was better to face something, rather than to run away. The thoughts at Dad's funeral reinforced that. Regardless of where I might run, the pain would still be there. It would always be with me, deeply embedded in my unconsciousness, until I somehow learned to deal with it.

Slowly the distressing sensations were replaced with good ones. The memories, they still linger, sometimes into the early morning hours—the smell of a warm rain, the touch when there was one, the sight of disgust or pleasure, and the realities which aren't sucked away by too much pain. The scent of where we lived was still vivid in my mind. It was one of Mother Nature's happy gifts. I didn't try to forget. I remembered. And the blank spaces in my body were filled with happy feelings of moonlight wrapped around it. I'd crossed another bridge to a brighter side of life. My father was dead and buried, but my memories weren't. It went back to the truth…and hopefully, a healing that would enrich the future. They say everything happens for a reason: Maybe my resting time in bed not only allowed me enough time to heal, but it gave me enough time to think of better times to come—a time to heal my spiritual self, as well as my physical.

Chapter 9

Clouded Future

One day when I was visiting with my first cousin, Aisilee, Aunt Monaree's daughter, Jimmy showed up in a brand-new Mercury. He was with his future wife, Thelma. "The car's Aunt Lucille's," he said. They were just taking a drive and wondered if I'd like to come along.

I was appalled to see my brother with Thelma. *He's a big boy now,* I thought, *he should know what he wants.* My experience with Thelma hadn't been very good. I was extremely happy to see my brother after so long a time, so I went with them.

The story of how I first met Thelma came back to me. I had just changed schools from Elf, a small elementary school, to Hayesville, a much larger school, which taught all twelve grades. Living at the fork of the road where Cold Branch Road and Tusquittee met allowed me that choice. I could change back and forth from Hayesville School to Elf. Judy went to Hayesville, along with a few of my friends, and Lois went to Elf, as well as a few of my other friends. I had friends at both schools.

Thelma, a complete stranger then, met me the very first day as I stepped off the Hayesville School bus. She never said one word, just glared at me with her big brown eyes and followed me around every day until the school bell rang. Her cold stare met and followed me for many consecutive days and I wondered why. I didn't even know how she knew my name…or how she knew what I looked like…or how she knew when I was going to be there. Apparently word got around real fast in this spread-out community. I knew she hadn't received a telegram.

One day when Thelma missed school I had time without her hanging around to inquire about her. "What's her name?" I asked someone, describing her in detail. Thelma had long, black, curly hair. She had developed into a womanly figure, unlike me and most of the others. In fact, she was very pretty. "Why is she following me?" I continued with questions.

"She's just that way," one of the girls answered. "She's heard you are a good fighter, and she wants to take that reputation away from you."

I didn't think I had such a reputation and besides, even if I did, her actions seemed crazy to me. The girl answering my questions confirmed this was the reason.

How long is Thelma going to continue with these actions? I wondered. "What should I do about it: confront her or ignore her," I asked myself.

I chose the latter, but a totally unexpected climax finally came. Apparently a lot of the kids at school were afraid of Thelma. She had told some of the girls there if they didn't help her beat me up she would catch them off the school grounds and beat them up. They knew that she had relatives who would help her. That was some of their comments. After gathering the support she must have thought she needed they confronted me, with her leading the pack. About a dozen girls—far too many in my opinion—surrounded me, nudging me closer and closer to the edge of danger as if they had it totally planned. They pushed me into an open hatch leading to a coal bed. The coal bed, used for the school's heating system, was mostly underneath the building, but its opening extended a few feet beyond the edge of the foundation.

I felt like they were trying to kill me. If I've ever imagined what quick sand was like, this was one of those times. Every time I took one step forward, I could feel myself sliding back two. Making things worse, these girls were pushing me back every time I got close enough to gain an edge to help myself.

What was Thelma capable of? *No wonder she's a grade behind me instead of a grade ahead where she belonged,* I judged. *Her helpmates aren't much smarter either,* my mind raced in resentment.

It wouldn't have done me any good to cry out for help; no one would have heard me. Besides, that would have been "sissy." Every feeling I had told me what it was like to be buried alive in a pool of quicksand. *This is just a slower process, to give a person more time to think,* I imagined.

Our recess period lasted just a few minutes, the only time in my entire life I considered it to be too long. With a few tears starting to wet my cheeks, the school bell rang. The girls scattered. "Now to make my way out of this hole," I said out-loud. Since they were gone, I stood a good chance, because I believed in myself.

I was happy to find the teacher preoccupied with something else when I sneaked back into the classroom. My homemade dress of flour sacks was in a mess, but she didn't seem to notice or say anything. Mom had hired a lady to make me ten dresses out of twenty-five pound flour sacks of a floral design before she left. She'd always kept those dresses beautifully starched and ironed. They were still kept in neat order. Since my mother was now gone, I had only myself to answer to.

A confrontation was inevitable, I reasoned. Thelma missed school again and never came back after that. Apparently she was at a period in her life when she stayed out of school often.

This was the first time I'd seen her since that incident. She acted like she'd never seen me before in her entire life. Apparently she had blocked out the memory of it. I thought, *how is it possible to forget something like that?*

At the time I had no idea of Jimmy's deceit. I imagined he felt much like I did: just extremely happy to see me, his sister. His real motive was revealed almost immediately. He didn't want to be with me, not even for a short time; he just wanted to take me back to Mom. I'd been kidnapped…and I knew why. "Did she pay him to kidnap me?" I whispered under my breath. The only reason Mom wanted me was to gain the insurance money left for my support, however little it might be. Dad had received a disability check from the company he worked for when he got hurt in the woods. The insurance money Dad got for this accident also provided support for us kids after his death. R.L. Long, my step-dad, was going to a trade school to learn masonry. Since Mom didn't work, they needed the extra money just to supply their basic needs of food and shelter. Apparently, Jimmy was following Mom's instruction to bring me back to her.

My youngest brother, Tony, crossed my mind: *Will he be okay?* I asked myself. *Surely, Uncle James* (and his wife) *will do a better job of taking care of him than Dad,* I told myself.

A deep resentment was instilled inside me toward Mom and R.L. I whipped R.L. every other month. It must have taken that long to build and rebuild the hatred. It was easy to whip R.L. I had developed my physical and mental strengths and he hadn't. Most of the time they were just squabbles, but sometimes he ended up with a few scratches and bruises, which didn't mean much. Whenever I felt like I hadn't done enough harm against him, I would even use a knife as a scare tactic. I loved to see him squirm. I jerked the pillow that he slept on out from under his head when I didn't have one of my own. This made him think I was going to smother him to death with it, which gave me a feeling of superiority. When we first moved to High Point, North Carolina, and lived in a small apartment, I had to sleep on the floor with no pillow. Since he had one and I didn't, I just wanted to take his. R.L. was afraid of his own shadow. *Anyone could whip him*, I thought. It didn't seem right for him to have a bed to sleep on and a pillow to lay his head on, while I had neither. Regardless of how I thought or felt, I was still a bully. Whatever hatred I had for my mother was taken out on R.L. too. Being an enabler, I wanted to give. When I knew I was being taken advantage of, it robbed me of my willingness and became a debt—a debt I didn't owe. I didn't owe my mother and my step-dad a living. I felt like I'd partially raised my mother's family and had done more than my share at my uncle's during the time I stayed there. Now…the responsibility of her second family was starring me in the face, and I wasn't even out of my teens yet.

R.L. called the cops on me a few times. Two policemen entered the door and asked him, "Who is the person trying to kill you?" He pointed me out with his finger. They looked at each other sheepishly. One could tell they were trying to hold back their laughter. Looking around in a hopeless effort, one would say to the other, "I guess we'd better go now." They probably thought if you let that little girl whip you, you deserve it. I weighed only fifty-seven pounds.

That year I ended up with six weeks on my entire report card. Tony and I had changed to Shooting Creek School after Dad died when we went to live with Uncle James. Mom and R.L. were continually moving. I was going back and forth from living with my mother to living with my grandparents. They didn't want me either. Nothing I did seem to please them. I cleared a piece of their land with my bare hands, thinking I might receive some kind of appreciation. I carried the rocks off the field in buckets. The unsettled conditions were partially caused by my rebellious state. During the last two months of the eighth grade I was so discouraged I didn't go to school at all.

Since I had only six weeks to account for in school, it was apparent I wouldn't graduate from grammar into high school. I begged Mom to speak to the principal, who was also my teacher, about it. She finally consented, but her attempt was in vain.

Then I decided to make my own attempt. Facing the principal and looking him strait in the eyes, I reminded him of his requirements: "You have specified that we write seven book reports to pass. Have I not done that? You also said we would have to memorize one hundred lines of poetry. I went past that point and memorized one hundred and twenty-five. You know I was always prompt in every thing I did. And my work was much better than seventy to eighty percent of the class, possibly more. Am I not right in what I say? Why not give me a chance?"

"Okay," he decided. "You can go. But if you fail to be successful in completing high school work, you'll have to come back."

This put a sparkle in my eyes. "Okay!" I said. "Thank you! Thank you very much!" I tried to calm my excitement and not be too prideful. Teachings of the Bible came back to me. In Proverbs 6:16 through 6:19 it reads: "These six things doth the Lord hate; yea, seven are an abomination unto him: A proud look, a lying tongue, and hands that shed innocent blood, An heart that deviseth wicked imaginations, feet that are swift in running to mischief, A false witness that speaketh lies, and he that soweth discord among brethren." Well, that didn't always exclude me, but I was going try this time. My appreciation and thankfulness left me with no other choice.

Before stepping onto the Hayesville High School bus I went into the restroom. A girl I didn't know was there. She spit in my face. Apparently she knew the situation I was in and detested me for it. Doing nothing, I walked away feeling grateful that I was going into the ninth grade.

When I stepped onto the bus one of the kids said, "You can't go, you didn't pass."

"It's okay," I told the bus driver. He let me step aboard.

I told Ruby Dean Bradshaw, a friend of mine who later married my puppy love, about the incident. Every time she met the girl in the hallway, she would deliberately bump into her. Asking her not to do that because it was wrong, I feared karma would return in my direction, if she continued. I didn't mind so much to have to pay for my own misdeeds, but I didn't want to be punished for someone else's deeds. I had enough troubles of my own without getting caught up in someone else's karma.

When I sat down in the classroom, my mind shifted to a girl sitting in the first seat of the next row. She weighed about two hundred pounds. *That girl is going to be my best friend,* my mind predicted. Sure enough, she became my best friend. She made the best grades in our class, and I was second best, just as I predicted the first day there. The teacher separated us. Even though she didn't say what the reason was, I felt sure it was because she thought we were helping each other on tests, mainly her helping me.

My grades continued to remain high. A guy, sitting directly behind me, would always bug me to death for answers on tests. I told him, "How can I get my own answers written down if I'm spending all my time answering yours?"

This heavy-set girl, Net Suller*, didn't believe me when I told her I could predict futures. "Okay!" she demanded, slowly but to the point. "Prove it! "Who am I going to marry?"

She no more than said that, and things started popping into my mind which surprised me. "You're going to marry Paul B Long, my step-dad's brother. You haven't met him yet, and you won't for another two more years," I replied.

My face must have went pale. She noticed the expression it held. Other things—bad things—came forward out of my unconsciousness and stood prominent in my conscious mind, making it probable for me to see the winding road of her destiny.

"What is it? There's more, isn't there?" she asked sharply.

"No," I lied. "There's no more," trying to push the drastic happenings of her future from my thinking. *I could be wrong: If I am, she'll probably never forgive me.*

Her clouded future spread before me as a visible picture in mid-air. I wished I hadn't said anything about it in the first place. We would get into a fight sometime in the future because of Paul B, and she would win. The imaginary fight with her brought stiffness to my body. An unusual feeling: I wondered why. This would somehow eventually lead to her separation and divorce of him. As for the details, I didn't know. *Maybe I'm just going to be a friend of hers then, like I am now,* I thought. The feelings went deeper than that. I was going to be involved more than that, but I didn't know how or why.

What came next curdled by blood. So I pushed these thoughts from my mind, dulling the picture as much as I could. But, I saw Paul B in jail hanging from his own belt, dead because he had killed himself. His little daughter, who wasn't born yet, would be only a few years old when their divorce would happen. He apparently couldn't bare the loneliness it brought.

I was directly or indirectly involved in this scene of her future. I couldn't stand the feelings that came with this prediction. No wonder she bugged me about telling her more. My facial expressions must have been devastating. So I replaced these thoughts with others and tried not to look back.

Very close to two years later she came to visit me at my grandparents. She was with Paul B, and announced they would be married soon. "I just wanted to tell you, your prediction is coming true," she said.

I congratulated them and after visiting for awhile said goodbye, hoping the other part of the prediction would remain "dead and buried." It didn't seem right to tell her the rest of the prediction. Both of them would have enough sadness in the future without my help. Wondering what could I possibly do—or want to do, for that matter—to destroy her relationship with him, I walked away disbelieving my own prediction. I didn't want to spoil her happiness. I wanted her to have all the happiness she could.

I wanted the same for myself: to remember the sweetness of the past—the scent of where we lived, the first green sprouts from a creek bank, the beautiful scenery of God's creation, the lightening bugs that lit up the night, and the warm, fresh air after a rain which could be felt with a mere thought—and, of course, my father's love too.

Chapter 10

Thelma and Louise and Me Too

A burning embarrassment hovered over me that lasted a lifetime upon my arrival in High Point, North Carolina. My mother was already living there with my step-dad, R.L., and my brother, Jimmy, along with his wife, Thelma, whom he had recently married. R.L.'s brother, Paul B, the one's death and marriage to Net Suller* I had predicted for future events, was living there too. All of us would live in the same house to save money on rent.

Upon arriving in town with Uncle Johnny's new wife, Pat, I needed to go to the restroom. I was fifteen and had recently started my period. I didn't know how much protection I would need. Because I didn't have any pads or tampons, I'd torn up an old ragged sheet to use for protection. At that time I don't think I had ever seen a tampon. My life had been so closed that I didn't know what a tampon was; for a different matter, I didn't know what a cooking range was either. I thought a range was a "home on the range" or a "riffle range." After I arrived there, I found out what it was. A stranger later came to our house, and said he'd come to fix the range. I didn't know what he was talking about, but I let him in. He went straight to the electric stove. After that a new entry had been added to my vocabulary. In regards to the protection: The thoughts did occur to me, *If a person has to use this much every month, they'll soon run out of something to use.* Bernell Mosteller, one of my friends who lived on Tusquittee, had told me she washed the rags and reused them. At this rate, I was going to have my hands full of washing. *I never had this many problems with cooking or anything else. Maybe I was a boy in a previous life.* We never talked much about these things, even with close relatives; we were too ashamed. Taking a few, hurried steps toward the service station restroom with my legs held tightly together didn't help at all. The unpinned rag unraveled with each step. I started to run, as if I could get away from it. Its blood-speckled appearance kept up with me all the way there, leaving a long trail behind; it must have been twenty feet or more. I quickly looked around to see how many strangers were staring at me. There was enough!

"This is just as bad or even worse than the tale about one of my great aunts," I told Pat, after we escapèd into the restroom. "You don't know her. When she went to town (Hayesville) for the first time in her life—even though she was quite old at the time—she walked into a hardware store and asked to buy a nickel's worth of candy.

"The proprietor of the store told her, 'We sell only hardware here, lady.'

"She snapped back: 'Well...give me a nickel's worth of that.'

"Apparently she didn't get a nickel's worth of candy, nor did she get a nickel's worth of hardware. But she came out of the store and went into a filling station restroom, just like I've done, but in her case she came out with her dress caught in her panties."

A good time for a joke, even a true one, I thought. I tried to laugh while telling her the story to take away some attention from me. She must have been as embarrassed as I was. "Well, you're out of the line of fire now," Pat said, with a slight laughter in her voice. It was soon forgotten on her part, but not mine.

High Point is well known for its beautiful furniture and has supplied many jobs in the building of it, the reason for us moving there. It's located approximately eight to twelve miles from Winston-Salem, a cigarette-manufacturing town.

Aunt Lucille was living there too with her husband, Roy Trull, Tommy's best friend, and their son, Stanley. Pat and Johnny, lived with them in a small, three room apartment. They lived a few blocks from Mom, closer to the center part of town.

I lived with Mom. Jimmy and I often played like we were fighting. Perhaps that's why I learned to be a good fighter. One day when Jimmy and I were just playing, Thelma seemed to deliberately walk in front of my swing and I grazed her forehead. She quickly turned around, flashing her big brown, devilish stare at me, and sharply said, "I'll knock you under the bed, if you hit me."

That's all it took. Jimmy grabbed my shoulders, since he knew what I'd do. "You little bitch, you can't do it and Jimmy holding me," my anger came out. Since Jimmy hit me, I called her a bitch again. Then, he hit me again. I was too stubborn to give in first. Something instilled into my morals wouldn't let me intentionally hurt my brother, regardless of how much he hurt me. Perhaps it was the time when Dad had disciplined me about hurting Tony, and I was very impressionable. So I didn't fight him back. Neither did I give up. Because of my unsurpassed stubbornness, Jimmy finally gave up and sat down in the corner of the room. "I can't do anything with you," he said. "Do whatever you like." I looked like I was ready to be hauled out in an ambulance, Aunt Lucille who was there at the time, said. I was solid blue from the neck up.

"You little bitch," I continued. "Now I'm ready for you."

Thelma sat down on the foot of the bed and started to cry. "I don't wan-a fight you," she said.

Mom told me, "Toots, you go outside. This is Thelma's home."

Mom threatened Lucille and Roy, saying she would put Roy in prison if he kept me. He was under probation, apparently for doing something illegal with Tommy. And Tommy was in prison.

I slept in a car with no windows in it. Even though it was below freezing, Mom sent Paul B out to take Tommy's coat away from me. I didn't have a coat of my own. Paul B felt sorry for me and gave me the coat off his back.

The next day I wondered where I was going to go. The decision was slow, but I knew I had to do something. Deciding I would risk going to Lucille and Roy's anyway and just take the consequences of whatever would happen, I really didn't think things could get much worse.

They accepted me. Mom's threat was just that: a threat, unfulfilled. While staying there I slept in a six-year-old baby crib that belonged to Stanley. He was two years old. Since Uncle Johnny and his wife, Pat, were living there too, there wasn't enough room for everyone in the small apartment.

The first week at Lucille's the incident regarding Thelma, Jimmy, and Mom repeated itself again and again in my mind, especially after I went to bed. The time when Thelma and her helpmates had pushed me into the coal bed also repeated itself, but it was nothing in comparison with the incident regarding Jimmy and Mom. They were part of my family. They meant more to me than my own life. *This shows how much they care about me,* I thought. The anger was building to the point of being unbearable. I awoke morning after morning, with very little sleep. So I decided to do something about it. I asked Lucille to borrow her coat, which was a man's hand-length below my fingers—but at least it was a girl's coat.

By the time I reached my mother's house my breathing was so loud one could hear it all the way to the other end of the long, narrow house. My body was in a tremble, simply from having so much hate inside. Pushing up my sleeves, I didn't even bother taking off the coat. I swiftly walked to the kitchen where they were sitting and reached and got Thelma. R.L. got in the middle, trying to break us apart.

"R.L.," I said, "I'm mad enough to whip both of you." R.L. backed away and stopped trying to force me to quit. This calmed me somewhat. He apparently knew that force would only make things worse. Thelma backed away and started crying again. "I don't wan-a fight you," she repeated as before.

"Little girl," I called her even though she was much bigger than I was, "You'd better thank your God for not fighting me back. I came down here to send you to the hospital for about four months, and that's the only thing that saved you." Then I turned and walked away, thinking all the angry had gone away. That's all I wanted to do.

Later Thelma's sister, Blonde, came to High Point to live with Jimmy and Thelma, who had moved into their own apartment. I became Blonde's best friend. Blonde and I went to work at one of High Point's in-and-out type restaurants. Most customers were served in their cars, although there was a small space allotted for table customers inside along with a few barstools circling the counter. The wages there were practically nothing, which gave us more of an incentive to appreciate the tips.

I lied about my age to get the job. Even though I was extremely small, the owner hired me anyway because Blonde told him she wouldn't work unless I did. Blonde had gorgeous, jet-back hair, which didn't match her name too well. A beauty in her early twenties, she could twist any man around her finger and the owner was no exception. A few times we'd been just walking down the street, and strangers would stop to ask her to become a prostitute. Even in normal clothing and no make-up, Blonde had a figure like a movie star and her face was just as pretty.

After working there for about a week and with the first pay, I decided I should try to make myself prettier too. So I went shopping for a bra. The following day I hooked the padded form neatly in front before going to work. A brand new bra, it kept unhooking through out the day. Each time as it unfastened, the cups would gradually move out to the sides of my body and disappear under my armpits—or partially disappear. Probably a lot of the customers saw this, for occasionally they looked at me in a funny way. *Oh well, what the hell,* I thought. *Might as well wear it unhooked. Maybe I have smaller boobs this way, but at least I won't have moving tits.* Wasting more time, I went into the bathroom to try to reposition "the humps" so they wouldn't be so noticeable. With a little squirming, I slid the protruding cups closer to my armpits. Larger than my own tits, I squashed the cups with my arms. In this part of the country most people were very serious, but here's where I had to differ again if I ever wanted to live with myself.

The cutest boy was working there. I can't remember his name or what he did. Instead of attracting him, I attracted a lot of others, even rich ones that I wasn't interested in, in the least. One night all of us started drinking on the job. The owner handed us drinks across the counter in paper cups, which we sipped in-between waiting on customers. They were mint gin and 7-Up. I became so happy, I ended up rocking on the barstool while Blonde did all my work for me. I even missed a five-dollar tip, because Blonde took over in the middle of one of my orders. The possibility of missing it anyway existed, because Blonde was prettier than I was. The neatest thing about the whole situation was this cute guy lifted me off the barstool, carried me to the car and took me home at the end of the shift. This wasn't the beginning of a relationship, like I thought it might be. It was the end. Apparently, the owner had told him to take me home. I didn't want these bad things to happen. They just did.

Since Blonde was living with Thelma and Jimmy, we arranged for me to live there also. The previous incidents were never mentioned. Both Blonde and I paid our own way, as well as paying for room and board. Occasionally Thelma would ask to borrow small amounts of money from us but never permitted me to borrow from Jimmy or her. I asked Jimmy to borrow fifty cents once to go to a movie. She showed her discontentment by telling him so. After that I never asked to borrow again.

Blonde and Thelma looked like twins, with the exception of Blonde being a few inches taller and a few years older. She was prettier too, as well as being kinder.

I was curious to know why Thelma was so easily persuaded to allow me to live there. In fact, both her and Blonde wanted me to. After moving in they told me about a ghost, which answered my question. Thelma was afraid and wanted company. She thought I wasn't afraid of anything. With all the situations I'd lived through, I had to agree. I wasn't afraid of much.

It started every night about three in the morning when we came home and went to bed. We worked from six in the evening until two o'clock. The spirit came up the stairs of the two-story apartment where we lived and into the entrance hall. Sometimes taking a few restless steps as if she was wondering who was in her room, but mostly she just stood there looking into our bedroom. We didn't see her; we just felt her presence and heard her movements. Sometimes we saw her shadow in the dim street lights that flashed across the floor.

After standing in the hall a few minutes the ghost would make noises which simulated she was going into the bathroom to clean up and brush her teeth. By this time we knew she had "okayed" us being there. This one particular night I was in a funny mood—everything anyone said or did would make me laugh. I knew the ghost wasn't going to take this lightly. Maybe it was my intuition, but I felt as if I knew what she was thinking, which seemed odd.

With her first steps up the stairs, I started making jokes and laughing. "Here she comes again," I said to Blonde describing her footsteps: "click, click, click." They sounded like she was wearing heels.

With my mind, I could see her, even in the dark: a young, unhappy, dark-haired girl who had something to say. She entered the front door, came into the entrance hall and just stood in front of our doorway as usual. I could tell she liked us, but she didn't like my humorous mood.

"She isn't going into the bathroom to clean up tonight. Maybe she's tired and wants to go to bed…in our bed. Maybe she just wants me to shut up. Blonde, she's coming into our room tonight. She's never done that before."

After each slow step, she hesitated several seconds before taking the next, as if to warn me to stop laughing. "Blonde, she's at the foot of our bed now. Do you hear her?"

Blonde answered, "Yes Martha, shut up and maybe she will go away."

"It's too late now," I kept teasing and laughing. For some reason, I just couldn't shut up, and I didn't feel afraid.

Instead of standing at the center, she moved to my side of the bed and leaned over the foot with one arm outstretched. I could see a faint shadow in the dim light that came from the street. Some fear seeped in by now, but I was still cracking jokes. The next thing I knew an icy cold, bony hand with very long, bony fingers clutched my leg. The human-like touch of her hand around my leg was definitely a physical feeling. I jumped straight up in the middle at the head of the bed.

"Blonde, this isn't funny anymore. I'm ready to behave myself."

The light was straight across from the head of the bed on Blonde's side. She slept in front. "Would you turn on the light?" I practically whispered. "Please Blonde, turn on the light before she…" I stuttered as if out of breath, then continued with my command: "before she comes on the bed to get me," I said half-laughing. "Calm down Martha, don't laugh," I heard myself say.

Both of us edged our way to the light, staying as close as possible to the wall. "Light, precious light," I screamed in a haunting sound that came out funny, more like I was poking fun at her. The light would at least let me know her position in the room, if I could see her. Darkness always represents uncertainty. I wanted to be more comfortable with her presence. Staying clear of an imaginary circle of space around the ghost, we backed our way out of the room.

We barged into my brother and sister-in-law's bedroom and jumped in bed with them. "Enough's enough," I said. "I've had enough." Still cracking jokes to some extent, Jimmy was almost ready to kick us out of bed and force us to go back and sleep with the ghost. Eventually I had to "hang it up." It was becoming daylight. Fortunately we stayed there the remaining part of the night and got some sleep.

The next day we told Blonde's boyfriend, Howard*, about the incident. He'd stayed over night a few times and slept in another room, a small bedroom off the entry, which must have been originally planned for a walk-in closet. He said he was ashamed to tell us before. The ghost had come into the room where he slept, sat down on the half bed beside him and felt of his face. She had brought with her a smothery feeling, causing him to gasp for breath.

After hearing his story, we started making inquiries. We told Jack*, the owner of the little soda fountain restaurant on the corner, next to our apartment, where we visited almost daily. Jack, a chunky type fellow in his mid-forties with a receding gray hairline, told us he'd heard similar stories about the place before and told us why. A young girl, named Louise, who had lived there before had fallen in love with a guy and was jilted. She had killed herself in our bedroom. He told us to check out the mattress where we slept if we didn't believe him. The apartment was still furnished with some the same furniture. The building must have been built originally as a home but was later remodeled into an apartment.

Off we went immediately, to check out his story. We hadn't noticed any bloodstains on the mattress before, but we'd never looked for any either. Taking off the sheets, we saw nothing.

"Blonde, turn the mattress over, it's on the bottom," something was telling me—I thought it was my six-sense. Bloodstains covered probably sixty-to-seventy percent of the bottom of it.

We continued sleeping on that bed until we moved, with the bloody side of the mattress down, of course. After that night we never felt any more fear. We both felt comfortable with Louise's presence.

I felt as if Louise had forgiven me. It seemed strange, but I also felt acquainted with her soul. Sometimes after work while lying in bed Blonde and I discussed how she must have felt and what she must have gone through. Back in the '50's, girls were permitted to sleep together, as Blonde and I did.

These thoughts occasionally lingered in my mind until I drifted off to sleep. *We did have the same name: I'd been called Tootsie for as long as I could remember, but my real name was Martha Louise. Maybe this was why we related so well.* Or maybe she just wanted to tell me about a similar event, which would later happen to me.

My soul sometimes spoke to her spirit and her spirit answered me. I wore a facade, a mask that hides what appears to be strong but is really very weak. The love I'd searched for, for so long, left a hurt clear to the bottom of my stomach. Because of these feelings, I understood why she had killed herself, and I felt she understood me.

It crossed my mind that maybe she was trying to get revenge for me. For many times after that Louise gave Thelma a bad time. She would go into our bedroom, when Blonde and I were away, then into the walk-in closet in that room. Sounds of her throwing hangers all over, even during the day, made one think she was angry with Thelma. Maybe Louise's soul had really touched mine, and she knew how I felt about Thelma—and what Thelma had done to me. When I left the house that day I thought I had gotten it all out of my system. But the anger still lingered. Periodically, thoughts about the previous incidents with Thelma reoccurred, especially during times when I had nothing else to occupy my time. Maybe forgiveness would come someday.

Louise didn't like Blonde's boyfriend either. Blonde married the guy and later found out he was already married, so I heard. It's a strong possibility she related him with the boyfriend that jilted her. Maybe he too was already married.

The spirit of this young girl, I feel, must have realized I would go through such an ordeal in my life, which paralleled to hers…and it was probably undeserving in both cases. How many times have we heard: "She thinks with her heart," or "She sings with her heart"? No way can one actually think or sing with their physical hearts, but we seem to get the deeper meaning that goes along with these statements. We are continually striving to reach higher levels of perfection, whether it be of the body, of the heart, or of the mind. Sometimes just to overcome daily obstacles and survive has to be our first priority, leaving contributions to others or attainment of goals in second place. Maybe it's time to go one step further and think with our souls, the very core of our being.

A ghost has no physical body, no heart that beats, no mind that thinks; it can only have a spirit. Because of this reason, it is natural to assume they know the future better than we do. Just maybe we are using our souls when ESP occurs. To draw a relevant conclusion, we should gain a deeper knowledge of survival, or even understand why people do things against us by using our "spiritual thinking." Understanding is the best way to reach forgiveness, which frees us of unnecessary burdens in this life. Reaching these heights can mean a higher level of spiritual development, an important part of our purpose for living.

Two years later when I moved to Washington State, then at age seventeen, I found myself going through suicide attempts for the same reason. I fell in love with a guy who will always remain a part of my memory, even though he married someone else. In one attempt, I took poison. I didn't notice what kind it was; furthermore, I didn't give a damn. It seemed like an easy way out, and I wanted to take it. This life was past the point of being bearable. I didn't want it anymore. At that time, I wasn't aware of how a person could not die from taking it, but much later I understood why. I slept for at least three days and nights straight, never eating one bite of food or drinking one sip of water. Waking up only to vomit, which I did a lot of, and then returning to bed to sleep some more, my body refused to accept it and threw it up as well as if a doctor had pumped my stomach. No way was I going to tell anyone, and especially my mother, what I'd done. That would have gone to the grave with me.

Now that I'm older with more understanding and wisdom, I think almost everyone has, at least to some extent, thought about suicide. We go through a lot growing up. The more one goes through, the more knowledge we stand to gain, once it's over. No one should be ridiculed because of these feelings. Compassion, understanding, knowledge, and keeping an open mind are the keys to overcoming. No way should these people be considered crazy. Ignorance, ridicule, and evasion of accepting the truth are the true killers of emotional and spiritual development.

By keeping an open mind we learn to connect, just as a slide is connected to a swimming pool. The oddest and simplest things, even a revenant (a ghost) can teach us much, if we're ready to listen with our souls.

My soul tells me it's now time to totally forgive Thelma for what's she done to me.

Chapter 11

Fugitive from the South

Leaving High Point and moving back to the mountains, I got to know my oldest and favorite brother better. Sometimes we would even go on camp-outs like we did when I was younger. I cherished those times with my brother so much that it felt like he was never in prison at all. It felt like he'd only been away for awhile, seeing the rest of the world. It was an accepted part of his life, as so many other things were. If he came in with his feet bleeding, it was obvious that he'd been running from the law. With time, I learned to ask fewer questions. Eventually we would hear as many things about his life as he wanted us to hear. There was too much to cover in such a short time. He generally stayed for awhile, got what he needed, and moved on.

Mom and R.L. were now living in Helen, Georgia, where R.L. could finish his masonry school in Clarkesville, about fifteen miles east of Helen. There were times when I stayed with Grandma and Poppy on Shooting Creek, back in North Carolina. Mainly, I lived with Mom and R.L. at the south end of Helen on the Chattahoochee River. The house we lived in was huge—five bedrooms, an eight-foot wide hallway that went down the center on the bottom floor, a fireplace in every room except the kitchen, and a porch that went around two sides of the old house. Traveling south, it was located on the right side of the road, just before the bridge that crossed the river. After crossing the bridge, a much larger plantation house was on the other side of the road. A tiny house, standing a short distance from the big plantation house, was where people said that slaves were taken and beaten before the Civil War. No one lived in the big house. People said it was haunted. The house where we lived certainly was. One night when I was reading in bed, a ghost that sounded like he had chains around his ankles walked down the long hall and stopped in front of my door. Even with the lights on, I looked up and saw the door open right in front of my eyes. I screamed as loud as I could, covering up my head, so I wouldn't see what walked through the door. It was probably just another ghost with some unfinished business. It was left unfinished, because I slept at the foot of Mom and R.L.'s bed that night. It took a lot to make me afraid of people, but ghost scared the living daylights out of me. A left turn, right after the plantation house, went to Clarksville. After the turn to Clarksville, there was something that looked like an Indian burial ground, a large mound with a gazebo on top. Tommy said it was where plantation owners sold slaves. It looked like it fit this picture, and I believed him. A cliff marked some of the distant landscaping. The story about it goes along with "Lovers' Leap." Two lovers had supposedly jumped off the cliff when their parents wouldn't let them get married. According to the story, the lovers were buried in that Indian mound. The authenticity of that story remains unknown, but it makes for a beautiful, romantic picture. It reminded me of the song "Running Bear," one of the musical tunes of that time. It also reminded me of the song "Patches." Both songs came out in the early 50's. They portrayed a love that would never end and lovers who would rather die than be apart. These stories were brought out more in detail along side the river bank or on one of our camping trips.

Tommy had gotten married, was divorced, and already had a baby girl by that time. She was called Deanna. Her hair color changed four times in two years. One never knew which color she would end up with. He brought her down to Helen to live with us, and I took care of her. Tommy expected a lot from her, even though she was less than two, just like he'd expected a lot from me. I learned to love that child and refused to let him abuse her. Instead of getting angry with him, I handled him with "kid gloves." Talking softly, I made him see that she was only a child—a lot younger than me—and he shouldn't expect so much from her. He said, "Well, Tootsie, she has to learn." I told him there were better ways to teach her, "there has to be." After awhile he seemed to understand that he shouldn't take his angry out on her. Since she was left with me to take care of most of the time, Mom made plans to have me go to Grandma and Poppy's. She wanted me out of the way, so she could take Deanna back to her mother. I told Mom I shouldn't go, because I had Deanna to take care of. She promised she would take care of her for awhile to give me a rest. When they came back after me at Grandma and Poppy's, Deanna wasn't with them. Mom tried to make me understand that I couldn't take care of her, that I was too young. I cried, but accepted these facts. Another change had taken place, most likely for the better.

A stubbornness was born in Tommy beyond compare. This trait brought him out of many life and death situations. It enabled him to work again when doctors said he would never walk again, much less work.

It was also a trait he passed on to me. He tried to instill in me perfection, regardless of how bad circumstances might be. Since I knew and understood he was passing on to me a type of strength he had acquired, his controlling nature was sometimes welcomed. I didn't always like his methods, but I knew his words of advice would benefit me someday, if I learned how to channel the energy into something constructive and not use this same stubbornness in a defensive way. I was in my teens, old enough to understand this.

This part of his personality had its side effects too. It got him into many horrible situations which otherwise would not have existed. *Wouldn't it be wonderful, if only we could learn how to accept the good in each aspect of our personalities and somehow get rid of the bad?*

Never really being the criminal that everyone thought him to be, Tommy's rebellious nature came from serious beatings from Mom as a young boy. Mom always thought he looked and acted like Dad, whom she married only to get away from home and never really loved. She apparently learned this type of abuse from her father who would beat her brothers near death. Girls in those southern family environments usually behaved very well from example—they saw their brothers severely beaten. So their beatings were less frequent and less severe. She would wear out as many as a half a dozen, six-foot hickories, three braided together, up to her hand over him in one beating. Jimmy, our brother, passed the hickories through a cat hole of the small two-room house where we lived at the time. I was only four years old when I first began to notice the serious abuse. I cried and begged Jimmy not to bring her any more hickories. Jimmy would always say: "I have to! If I don't, she'll beat me." The blood would be streaming down Tommy's back once she'd finished. Just like a whipped dog, they'll snap back after they've had so much. He needed time to heal—a time with love, only offered by the women he met.

His spirit clung on noticeably, like a great stallion's. He became kinder instead of meaner as so many people do under these circumstances.

My brothers have told me—and I've seen what I thought was evidence to prove it—that women are mentally strongest of the two sexes. I've learned from Tommy and a host of other men that women only seem mentally stronger: *A man's real deficiency comes by not acknowledging their wrongs in the first place. Women are more apt to admit their wrongs because we think it's okay to be weaker. One cannot change without first admitting it. If you think you're right, why would you want to change? To know your weakness, you gain strength.* In lots of ways, I passed back to Tommy some of the philosophies he'd help pass on to me.

I know he must have many scars left. Every time he tries to forgive Mom, she does something else to cut open the old wounds. The strange thing about the whole situation, she refuses to acknowledge her own wrongs. *How can she possibly heal herself under these circumstances? A psychologist would most likely say she is unable to face her wrongs, because she can't admit to herself that she did something that bad,* like the bad she did to me in High Point. I tend to think that this is one of the reasons we sometimes acquire a split personality.

A subtle calmness was buried deeply within Tommy's spirit, if one only knew how to treat him. Whatever he felt—anger, pain, or distress, as well as happy emotions—I could always see a mixture of kindness and compassion in him as well. His eyes showed plenty of goodness too, like an open deck of cards. They held a beauty, which could melt any girl's heart. His smile enticed every woman he met. With great sincerity, he showed his pearly-white teeth to them.

Much of his early adulthood was spent in prison or running from the law. An eighteen- month sentence was built into eleven years because of escaping prison and fighting with other prisoners.

His beginning sentence of eighteen months started because of selling stolen tires for friends at a service station where he worked on Georgia Avenue in Atlanta. The Clay County sheriff in Hayesville made a deal with "Wild Bill" Ledford, our first cousin, and Terry* and Charles Traud*, a couple of friends, who stole the tires. Sheriff Kitchens caught them with the stolen tires in Tommy's car. Kitchens told the boys their sentence would be less, if they gave him all the answers he was looking for. Tommy had given them specific instructions to jump out of the car and run if they were stopped. The next day he would report it stolen if they didn't return within a certain amount of time. The three, young men told Kitchens the whole story. Even though Tommy wasn't in the car with them, he took the rap for it.

The small one-block town of Hayesville is about five miles north of the Georgia line. It's in the southwest corner of North Carolina, near Tennessee. Residents were sparsely spread out for miles throughout these foothills of the beautiful Blue Ridge Mountains where all the boys called home.

Tommy escaped from prison a total of five times and got into many fights. Each time he escaped or got into a fight, prison officials added more punishment, as well as more time. They put him in a "hole," a small, dark cell where lights were seldom turned on; otherwise, it was pitch-black. Bars surrounded the hole of darkness. Lots of times he stayed in this place with no clothing, no bedding, and a bare minimum of food and water for as long as six months at a time. He soaked toilet paper in water and ate it for a month to stay alive and keep his stomach from collapsing.

At another time, he put himself on a starvation diet, thinking that this might help him get out of the hole. He must have realized he needed to change his methods to make it easier on himself. He figured the prison doctor would take him out in about nine to ten days, but the time elapsed into a cold, hard month.

Sleeping on a cold cement floor, he avoided turning over to his other side, because the coldness was so severe. The warmth from his body would deteriorate if he moved. Guards washed him down with a fire hose and sprayed the mess away from the tiny, four-by- eight-foot room once a week, because the hole had no toilet. The water force was so great it peeled the skin off his body when guards pointed its coldness directly at him. He thought these conditions were the cause of him becoming completely paralyzed from the waist down for six months, which he overcame due to his stubbornness.

This place was indescribable and so were his thoughts. The loneliness and loss of his freedom were the hardest to bare. "You were more apt to make it if you meditated and tried to think of something good," he related. He tried exercise to occupy his time and keep from losing his mind. Two hundred push-ups and two hundred squat jumps at one time, up to one thousand each per day, made up his daily exercise until his body got too weak to respond.

They tried to break his tough spirit, but his stubbornness hung on like glue. A prison doctor finally gave the orders to bring him out. His deteriorated body fell limp into the arms of the guardsmen, but they were surprised to find his condition far better than what they expected it to be.

He was sent to a prison in Indiana at which time his arms and legs were cuffed to bars and he stood on his toes for eleven days. They tied his pant legs with shoestrings and forced Epsom salts down him. He received no food, just water. The guards got a kick out of this. They wanted to know how long he could take it and deliberately passed by, saying smart remarks. Tommy spit in their faces. That's all he could do with his arms and legs bound. He also spent nine days in a straight jacket under similar circumstances.

The experiences I previously had with Jimmy helped me to understand his rebellion. If they'd treated him with kindness, he would have responded more favorably. That's why I knew how to treat him in regards to Deanna.

Under normal circumstances, standard procedure during punishment was to give a prisoner one glass of water and two crackers each day for two days straight; then one meal on the third day. This was repeated for thirty days. After passing a law making this kind of treatment illegal, a 1300 calorie diet was provided. "One would have to be in the hole for four to five days without food before he could stomach this foul smelling dog food. I don't know why it smelled and taste so bad. Its ingredients seemed to be corn meal, tomatoes, chicken liver, and garlic." He poured half of it out and mixed the rest with water, so he could drink it.

He spent eighteen months in a rock hole. Swinging a twenty-one pound hammer, he developed sixteen-inch biceps, a forty-four inch chest, and still wore twenty-eight inch pants. The crew of eight to ten men either kept up with the rock crusher, or they would go to the hole for thirty days; then have to come back to do it all over again. Their hands became so callused they could handle red-hot coals with their bare hands. Sometimes blood would ooze from between their fingers.

"I remember Dad could do the same thing. He used to sit by the fireplace, pick up a red-hot coal and play with it when I was a little girl. I never knew before how he could do it or why. He probably wanted to see if he could. Maybe that's how people learn to walk on red-hot coals. They toughen their skin with calluses?" I interrupted his story.

"I suppose, but I wouldn't suggest it," he answered.

Never once was Tommy pushed to do more work by the gang boss. He always stayed ahead of the production that was expected of him. That was probably the reason he expected so much from others. All his life, people had expected a lot from him—first Mom, then others.

Occasionally, the prisoners could stay off the road gang if they were sick. Whenever Tommy stayed out because of being sick, the gang boss himself would carry around his bush hook, never allowing anyone else to use it, so it would retain its sharpness. The guards may not have liked Tommy, but they respected him as the prisoners did.

A most memorable girl—Angie Louddick* of Romeo, Michigan—picked him up hitchhiking just outside of Detroit approximately three weeks after an escape from Whitakers Prison. She was driving a new 1962 Starfire Oldsmobile convertible. A girl friend was with her.

Tommy had been working on a road-gang, cutting a right-of-way through the Highlands territory, about thirty miles southeast of Whitakers. The mountainous terrain was gorgeous during the day but deadly at night because of the high cliffs and water falls. Poisonous snakes and wild animals made this area their home. He slept in trees at night, thinking it would be safer.

One of the ten-man crew paid another to cut his leg with a bush hook to get relief from the draining and unpleasant task, which distracted the guards, allowing Tommy enough time to escape. The men who were unable to meet the expectations of the gang boss stole morphine from the dentist's office. They arranged to have their feet cut off, their arms broken, or almost anything else to get the doctor to give them a work release.

On his four-day trip out of the Highlands to get to Grandpa Parker's place, he didn't eat at all. His feet were bleeding from so much walking and running from the dogs. A fresh set of dogs was put on his trail several times. At one time he was only about twenty feet from them, but they were confused and didn't pick up his trail. Apparently by crossing the road, he had lost them. Afterwards, he made a stop at Grandma and

Poppy Hogsed's place. A quick rest and some brief conversation, he was soon on his way again running from the law.

Grandpa Parker gave him his first change of clothes and was taking him to Tennessee. Along the way, he slept in an abandon car the first night and inside a cardboard box on a railroad car the second night, which offered some protection from the cold. The next morning when he awoke inside the box, the train he was on was moving too fast to jump off. So he waited to St. Louis to make the jump and hitchhiked back to Chicago, then on to Detroit where he first met Angie. She was another woman in his life and a welcomed one.

Everyone he met on the way somehow knew he was running from the law and offered a lot of help. One guy advised him not to wear Navy shoes: "That's a dead give-away." The stranger mentioned the number of a slow freight and its time schedule out of St. Louis, which could take him all the way to Portland, Oregon.

In the meantime, he ran into two well-to-do women who picked him up just to have sex. They let him out immediately afterwards. They apparently didn't want it known locally. After asking him a few questions, they proceeded with their sexual interlude. Fulfilling at least some of their fantasies, one drove while the incident took place; then they exchanged places. While preoccupied with these women, he missed the slow freight.

Others told him which churches to go to, to get showers and fresh sets of clothing. That night around midnight when Angie picked him up he was wearing a cashmere coat gotten from one of those churches.

Overflowing with questions, Angie asked him how long had it been since he'd eaten.

Even though he hadn't eaten in a couple of days, he answered, "Earlier this evening."

"You're broke and a fugitive from the south," she told him and asked where was he going.

"I'm headed for Alaska," he responded with few words. It was cold and blowing blue snow and not very much traffic. The coat he was wearing was insufficient for the blizzard conditions. She could see when she stopped to pick him up that the wind hurled icy sharp force against his face, as he struggled to press on.

"Since you're not going to be going very far tonight, you can go home with me," Angie helpfully persuaded. Tommy's almost always high-spirited nature escalated even more because of his newly found friend. This was a time of real need. Her helpfulness was greatly appreciated. He went to work for Angie's dad, owner of a Kellogg corn farm. She and her father invited him into their elaborate home, accepting him as one of the family and making him comfortable in every way. "They offered much more than I expected," he said.

The next morning Angie walked softly into his room and neatly laid a dark blue suit, black shoes, black belt, a baby blue shirt, and baby blue socks on the end of the bed for him to wear. Smiling sweetly, Angie told him "The blue brings out the color of your eyes," and left the room.

It didn't take long for her to fall in love with Tommy, possibly because of his beautiful smile and self-assuring eyes. Angie's father offered Tommy a Cadillac and fifty dollars one Saturday evening. The two went out to dinner and a movie. Since her car had bucket seats, her father felt they would be more comfortable in a sedan. The night offered a private part of his life—a sweet memory that lasted.

Tommy never admitted to Angie he was running from the law. He didn't have to; somehow she just knew. While out on a Sunday afternoon drive in her convertible, she pulled up along side a well-dressed gentleman, talked to him for some time, as if she'd known him for years with Tommy in the car beside her. When she pulled out, she turned to him and asked, "Do you know who that man was?"

"No," he answered."

"He's an FBI agent," she calmly remarked. Tommy just smiled and showed a glimmer in his eyes. "You're running from the law," she repeated as she'd done the night they met, but dropped the subject, never waiting for him to answer.

An FBI agent caught him about four months later when he was cashing a check given to him by Angie's dad. The agent was actually looking for someone else, but he recognized Tommy's beautifully descriptive signature when he signed the check. His handwriting during that time was unequalled by millions. They put him in jail under a $15,000 bond, which Angie's dad wanted to pay, but Tommy said, "no." Tommy told him, he would have to go back to prison anyway. Besides, he had his limits on special favors, because he felt it was taking advantage of others.

This being the second time he escaped, they took him back to prison and put him in deadlock, a place where prisoners are kept in one small cell all the time. The guards told him, "We've got you right where we want you now, Parker."

Angie called and demanded to talk to him. Even though prisoners in deadlock were not permitted to receive phone calls, she got her way because of her powerful influence.

She wrote him eight to twelve page letters every day. Guards sometimes held up his mail, because the prison's policy was to accept only two-page letters three times a week. Angie knew his mail was being held when he didn't answer and called Washington D.C. A representative from the Capitol would in turn call the prison officials there, ordering them to release Tommy's mail. When the release came he would get as many as thirty letters or more, all at once.

Again Tommy broke out of prison, this time from deadlock, going through five locks. Possibly this was a type of rebellion against the guards thinking they had him "put."

He made keys out of plastic knives by putting soap on them and inserting the knife into the keyhole; the soap would form a dent where he was to file. Because he had no file, he honed the knives on the sharp corners of the cement base of the toilet. The prisoners made "thumb busters" from rings around ballpoint pens by rubbing it back and forth on concrete to form a gap, so it would fit around the hasp of Master 5 locks. These heavy-duty locks secured the chains that wrapped around the bars. Honed notches on the "thumb busters" also made it possible to release the lock by pushing the tumbler back out of the way when inserted into the lock and twisted.

Three guards were fired over this incident. No one had ever escaped from this prison before, and escaping from deadlock was even more serious. There were eighteen cells in deadlock, all of which had one prisoner in each, but only three chose to break out with him.

Communication among the prisoners was ingenious. They would first tap on a pipe to let others know when a message or item was going to be sent down from the main housing area. The message, tied inside a plastic bag and hooked to a string, was flushed down the toilet. The guys in deadlock put a string with a hook at the end down their toilet; hooked the object and pulled it back to their cell. They trained cockroaches, which made national news, to take objects from one cell to another. One cigarette and one match or some other small item, for example, was tied to the back of a cockroach. They kept "stashes," candy or something sweet, for the large, creepy insects. The cockroaches knew they would get something they liked to eat by crawling into the cells; the guys helped the roach out by catching it and heading it in the right direction. Other times they used Pig Latin, a language only the prisoners knew. All the prisoners worked together, each accomplishing a small task. Timing was of essence. When everything was put together, about eighty or ninety men started a riot to draw attention for the escapees to make their move.

They eventually caught him and sent him to Asheville, N.C. Angie continued to write him and also sent him five dollars a week, maximum of what the prison allowed.

Each time Tommy ran, he was brought back before a judge. The judge told him, "I promised your wife (referring to Angie) I would turn you loose. But after reading your records, the public would ride me out of town on a rail if I turned you loose."

The judges would always follow up with a phone call to Angie, letting her know the results of the trial. Angie told Tommy she could get him out, if he would only stop breaking prison, but she couldn't if he continued.

He was then sent to Atlanta where a prison psychologist pissed him off by asking stupid questions and not really paying attention. The psychologist doodled on a piece of paper and didn't really want to know the answer. He deliberately tried to aggravate Tommy. He asked him how to spell Hayesville, and Tommy told him, "You're the son-of-a-bitch sitting behind the desk. You ought to know how to spell it."

A psychologist should show a more warm and caring nature—they are dealing with the human mind, I tried to add some of my own understanding. *Since it was his job, he was there to get answers, paying no mind as to how he got them.* In my mind, the psychologist gave Tommy the picture of just another person who expected more of him, which he resented.

"Don't chip your teeth at me," the psychologist cracked back. And away Tommy went to the hole to live on crackers and water again for the next thirty days.

After getting out of the hole he was offered a job for when he got out. His fellow cons explained what he was suppose to do: He would be told to go to a certain university on Peach Street in Atlanta; see a particular secretary there who would give him an envelope which included money, car keys, and his orders. Then he would pick up the car; in the glove box would be another envelope with additional orders to go to a specific hotel in Chicago where he would make contact with a certain bellboy. From the bellboy, Tommy would receive another set of keys for another car, which would have further instructions in it. He would receive $1,000 a week and a car for this. There were two reasons why Tommy didn't want to get involved in this. Number one, it was obvious that he would be running something illegal; number two, it was difficult to get out of this type of situation once a person became involved.

On Tommy's next escape, two sheepherders picked him up in Kansas City, Kansas, and took him all the way to Mountain City, Missouri, even though it was out of their way. Most people across the entire United States took him for a fugitive from the south and went out of their way to help him.

Wherever he went, his name always preceded him. An old girlfriend, Francis Dills, back in Hayesville, heard about his whereabouts via radio and contacted him through her relatives. This gave him the indication that the law also knew his approximate location. So he backtracked to Hayesville.

Francis' uncle was a Justice-of-the-Peace in Hayesville. Sometimes she would go down to his house to listen to reports on the radio about locals. She had kept track of Tommy's whereabouts from these reports. Sometimes they were true, for Francis would never have been able to contact him, and sometimes they weren't.

Later, reports came over the radio about Tommy being in Washington, Oregon, Tennessee, Texas, and all over the United States, and all this time he was living in Francis' attic. *They were probably due to mistaken identity,* he thought.

Francis' mother and step-dad, Glenn Martin, who owned the local shoe store, were the first of her relatives to hear the message of Tommy's whereabouts. Glenn himself had received life in prison for killing his first wife, but his time was reduced to twelve years. Prison was where he'd learned his profession, working with leather. Glenn knew how to contact Tommy and did so in Francis' behalf.

Out of wedlock, a child was born to Tommy and Francis, whom she named Michael. Even though Francis was married to another, Tommy stayed in their attic for nine months without her husband knowing anything about the relationship. She took care of him, as if he was her husband too. They had conversations twice a day. She took food up to him in the morning after her husband left for work and then again in the evening after her husband went to bed.

During the day Tommy worked for Hayle Miles*, transporting moonshine. He hauled white lightening across the mountains of North Carolina, Georgia, and Tennessee. Hayle and his wife were people who could be trusted, even with one's life. He trusted them not to report him.

He also hauled the 180 proof corn whiskey for his old friend Sam Dowell. Sam could be trusted too.

He worked for Robert Hogsed, an uncle on Mom's side of the family, when he wasn't hauling moonshine. The law caught up with him when he was gathering eggs and casing them (placing them in large boxes between layers of soft crate type material to be transported to stores) for Robert. Tommy thought Robert must have reported him for no one knew where he was except him and his wife, Madene.

While staying at Francis' place, Tommy sometimes visited with us, his family, on the weekends. There were few televisions and very few things to do for entertainment, so we camped out in the nearby woods and told ghost stories or stories about his life—all of them true—to the wee hours of the morning. I'll never forget Jimmy laying his head on a hard rock and falling asleep when he'd had enough of the story telling.

Francis is dead now but their son, Michael, lives on in Hayesville. These stories have been communicated into the next generation.

At the end of Tommy's sentence, Angie sent him a bus ticket, some spending money and a suit of clothes, along with a "Dear John" letter. The letter came the same day of his release. Apparently Angie had instructed them to hold the letter until the last thing. He was given the letter immediately prior to entering the outside world to freedom.

He wondered about her reasons for doing this. Angie had always been close to him in understanding... and in spirit. "She always stayed with me while I was in prison," Tommy recalled over and over again. "She helped me reduce those eleven years to five years and four months." This was very important to him.

Now, all of a sudden, he didn't know what to think because of this letter. He thought she must have had some kind of contact with other prisoners and treated them the same way.

Why is it that people tend to think the worst about others? I thought. *Is it because of their own insecurities? Or is it because they fail to admit their own wrong?* "It's really very hard to say what she was thinking," I told him. "Maybe she somehow knew about the relationships with other women during your escapes, such as the relationship with Francis. Five years and four months is a long time to wait. Maybe she just got tired of depending on you to do the right thing." Whatever the reason, it was left unknown. She played a part in his life that represented love, freedom, and friendship at a time when it was very much needed. *Maybe she knew that another angel would take her place...tomorrow*, my thoughts continued, but I didn't say it.

"Remember," I said, "the story about the bird that was freed. 'If the bird comes back, it belongs to you. If it doesn't, then it was never yours in the first place.' Maybe she just wanted to know where your heart really was."

That was 1963. Tommy has never gone back to prison since.

Neither has he seen Angie, a farewell that broke his heart...or was it his pride? *Does heart and pride have the same meaning in man's soul? Maybe that's one of the reasons why we are only half-way there. It takes more than winning in an arm wresting match to be "over the top."* This slightly heavy-set girl with long, brunette hair and ocean-blue eyes left a beautiful, yet puzzling, memory in his mind that can never be replaced.

His heart has mended, and he has another girlfriend now...As I thought, another girl would take her place. Regardless of the circumstances, the calling of tomorrow keeps saying, "Let's press on."

Half-way There

The wind was hurling blue snow against his face as he struggled to "press on" in blizzard conditions.

Chapter 12

Thunder Row

Lightening flashed through the over-hanging tree limbs during the night. It was the only light, other than a small campfire. And loud clashes of thunder became the succor of making a terrific setting for the stories about to follow. We'd chosen this beautifully shaded clearing in late afternoon—and in early fall—to make our camp and planned to tell each other stories…and just talk away the night.

Tommy was there after making a trip from the western states. During his time on the western coast a car dealer from Oregon, Frank Wilson*, had heard about Tommy through his reputation. Wilson wanted Tommy to work for him. Tommy towed six of his new cars, one at a time, from Tennessee to Bandon, Oregon. Wilson paid him after each trip and had given him a 1948 Olds convertible at the end of the job.

I thought Tommy had spent all the time he was away in prison. When he came home after each trip, I thought he'd broken out of prison again. That wasn't the case every time; no one had explained anything differently to me before. So, during the time our father had died he was really on the West Coast working, instead of in prison.

Tommy said he sent money back home to take care of the family. He sent it to Violet*, his first wife. She was pregnant with Deanna then. She had left our family a long time ago when we lived on Tusquittee, near the fork of the road, and went back to her own. The money was mailed to her address, but apparently he expected it to go to the entire family. *To our entire family, or to hers? I asked myself. Unbelievable! How could he mail it to her relatives' address and expect it to go to ours? Apparently he didn't feel the need to give to his family, as I did. He felt the need to give only to Violet's. Or maybe he thought Dad should have had that responsibility. That's what I thought too, but Dad didn't accept the responsibility no more than Tommy did. And Violet had her own family, which left me to take care of our family's needs.* When she was around and even when Tommy was there, Violet seemed more like an added responsibility. She could have been helpful, but she was young. She was only fifteen when they got married. We had given them a home during the early stages of their marriage. It wasn't much, but it was all we had to offer. Lots of times I returned from my best friend's house after spending the night to find Violet still in bed, naked, in the early afternoon. This seemed like a person who was ready to take, but seldom ready to give. *Well, she needed the money to support herself, and maybe there wasn't enough to give to us too*, I concluded, and accepted the fact as it was. Besides, by this time it didn't matter anymore. Tony and I had made it through all the ruff spots, and no harm had been done. Possibly we were even better off; we'd learned how to depend on ourselves.

Tommy and Jimmy built a campfire in front of our lean-to. Lois and I spread out quilts and blankets in it to make our beds. The stories began after we cuddled up together, underneath the covers, watching the lightening streak the sky. Tommy had spent some time in prison with the "Birdman of Alcatraz." We were more anxious to hear the story about him, rather than discuss any personal difficulties that we might have had in the past.

Tommy started his story: The warden at Alcatraz asked him how much time did he have left, and Tommy told him eighteen months. "What are you doing here with just eighteen months?" the warden asked. "You mean eighteen Christmases, don't you?" The men in many of the prisons where he served time all had many years, some with several life-sentences. They referred to their prison time as "Christmases." None referred to their sentence in months, except Tommy. The warden couldn't understand why Tommy was sent there with so little time, until he read his records for being able to escape from so many prisons.

"Did you know Robert Franklin Stroud was 'The Birdman's' real name?" Tommy asked.

"No," I said. "How did he get 'Birdman' for a name."

"It started when Stroud found an injured bird on the windowsill of his cell. Apparently he wanted to help the bird and started asking for books from the prison library. One thing just led to another. A lady, who was thought to be in the media, visited the prison during one of their regular tours. She asked him a lot of questions. We heard stories about her boosting his reputation as an expert in canary diseases. I wasn't close enough to know all this as fact. It was something I heard. Word just got around. I think she even wrote a book about him," Tommy answered. "Anyway, he became a legend."

A tall, thin, unattractive man, The Birdman was a pimp of Kitty O'Brien in Alaska. He killed one of her customers, a bartender for refusing to pay a ten-dollar price for the evening. This led to a conviction of manslaughter, and he was sentenced to twelve years in prison. Just before his sentence was completed he killed prison guard Andrew F. Turner on March 26, 1916, before 1200 witnesses in Leavenworth's (Kansas) mess hall which led to a death sentence. His motives for this murder were never adequately explained by Tommy—or by history. I later looked up the information he'd given me that night to confirm it.

President Woodrow Wilson's wife, Elizabeth, who had assumed the President's responsibilities because of her husband's ailing condition, gave The Birdman a commutation just eight days before he was scheduled to die. She was impressed with his work in ornithology. The exchange held a stipulation of solitary confinement where Stroud was allowed to carry on his experiments. A wall separating two adjoining cells was torn down to give him more space. He died in prison in 1963 of old age, just after Tommy was transferred from Alcatraz to Marion, Illinois.

Tommy said, "His reputation of working with canaries was greatly exaggerated through the newspapers. He was a hater of mankind. That's one reason why the prisoners didn't like him. He stuck to himself. The men would have killed him if he'd got out."

"And the guards would have permitted this?" I asked in amazement.

"They couldn't prevent it. Prisoners gave 'blanket parties' when they wanted to kill someone. Ten or twelve men hemmed their victim in a corner and held up blankets in front of the cameras, while someone in the group committed the murder with a 'shank'."

"What's a shank?" I wanted to know.

"A homemade knife," he answered. "Eighteen murders happened while I was in prison. I had no part except as a witness. They were all classified as accidental. The victim's blood sometimes covered the entire walls. The more they tried to escape the messier it got, but their attempt was in vain.

"These men who were murdered were usually punks out to make names for themselves. They might even kill somebody just to gain a reputation, similar to the personality of 'Baby Face' Nelson." Nelson died of seventeen slugs following a shootout with lawmen almost thirty years prior to these incidents. Tommy and I discussed some of his history too, after everyone else had drifted off to sleep.

"How did we get on this subject?" I asked. "Okay, no big deal. Get back to the story. I'd like to hear the rest of it."

"The prisoners didn't like squealers either," Tommy continued. "The long-timers considered the prison to be their homes and protected it as such. These punks, some with characters among the prisoners such as 'The Birdman's', couldn't be trusted. They were usually drug addicts or alcoholics; or they bragged a lot; or they would say, 'I can't,' when asked to do something." Tommy referred to these cons as "the kind of people who have low self-esteem. They don't have any respect for themselves or for anybody else. They were easy to recognize because of being weak-minded." He meant that they could be recognized by their actions and by their eyes. I had learned to read in between the lines somewhat.

"I think that a lot of the other prisoners were also weak-minded, with low self-esteem. The 'blanket parties' is an example of that. I've heard that prisoners also kill others by getting something sharp, putting some shit on it, and cutting their victim with it. It caused them to get infection and die. This sounds awful, but is it true?" I asked.

"No…it's not true," he answered, laughing about what I'd said. "Maybe it was true at a different time and place. But at least, it's not true in the prisons I was in.

"There were many ways they killed someone. With towels, they twisted to choke their victims. In their spare time they might sharpen case knives on cement. I've even had someone crawl over others and me lying in our bunks in the middle of the night to reach a man, who they smothered to death with a pillow.

"Sometimes they gave them the silent treatment, as they did 'The Birdman', and just waited for them to kill themselves. Since they knew all the men were against them, they would get this on their minds and would soon be unable to eat or sleep. Then they would somehow mess up from all the stress and do something stupid.

"A smart-elect newcomer would choose a guy with a bad name, someone the prisoners respected, to pick on." One of these guys chose Tommy as his target to boost his reputation. Since Tommy didn't talk very much, another prisoner spoke up for him. Calling him off to the side, the con told the newcomer that Tommy was getting out in a few months, and he would never live to see the outside yard if he didn't leave him alone.

The guys also saved up lighter fluid until they had about a quart or so. They waited until their victim was asleep and threw the lighter fluid on him, followed by a lighted match. The man in the four-by-eight foot cell didn't stand a chance. All the prisoners, except trustees, were locked in their cells.

"These punks were not of the trustworthy type. A person usually says, 'I can' or 'I'll try' if he's of the trustworthy type. If he says 'I can't,' leave him alone."

In the early 60's, Marion, Illinois, took the place of Alcatraz. Tommy was among the first prisoners to be shipped there. Angie*, his girlfriend, visited him then. It was closer to her home. His own family never visited him while he was in prison. We didn't have enough money to eat properly, much less visit him.

I cuddled up in warm blankets around the campfire, listening to Tommy's story, while something in the nearby woods rustled in the leaves. Lightning flashed, but we couldn't see anything. Then again, and again. The noise was very clear. A small amount of time past, and the others woke up. We all waited silently for the next flash of lightning, hoping to see something. Still, nothing could be seen. Here was my chance to prove to Tommy that ghosts did exist. After some time, the noise drifted off into the woods. We went to the spot where the sound came from and saw evidence of something being drug along a path through the woods. Tommy followed at a safe distance. The rest of us were too chicken, so we stayed by the campfire. About an hour later he returned. "A mountain lion or some other animal that looks like one caused the noise. We couldn't see it, because it was light colored. He had a carcass hidden out there. So much for ghosts," he said. "I was beginning to believe in them."

The following night we watched the sun mark its path to the west in many shades of red. Stories continued beside the campfire as the Bobwhite whistled its name from a lonely hollow far below. A deep loneliness came like a chill in the air. His stories seemed to offer comfort.

His stories continued: In Mountain City, Missouri, Tommy met a girl whose family went "all out" for him. They lived out in the middle of nowhere. Tommy called it a prairie. He stayed there for about a month, before moving on. "They did too much for me," Tommy said. He felt like he was taking advantage of this family, so he waited until they all went to town and left while they were gone.

While there he met Jesse James, a distant relative of the real Jesse James, so he was told. "He was the perfect image of me too," Tommy recalled. "The only difference was he had natural red hair, and my hair was dyed red. He even talked and acted like me." When his newly found girlfriend took him to meet Jesse she introduced him as his twin. They took him to see the genuine Jesse's old homestead in Kearney, Missouri.

After leaving her place he met a good-looking brunette, dressed in men's clothing with a huge handbag full of money. She picked him up in Salt Lake City, Utah. As she stopped the new car, with a Texas license plate, it skidded about the length of a football field. *Maybe she has stolen all her old man's money, and she's running away from him,* Tommy thought. *It doesn't seem likely she'd deliberately drive the car wide-open, if she was running from the law too.* She introduced herself as Marie Salty*.

Tommy didn't ask any questions. He just wanted to get away from her because of her speeding. The best thing he could figure out she was just looking for company. Putting some ease on his mind, she first asked him to make her a sandwich from fixings in a cooler, which set on the back seat. Then she wanted him to drive while she slept. Tommy went to sleep too and went off the road onto a prairie.

"Get this car back on the road before the cops come," she commanded. "We can buy a new car."

Marie brought him all the way to Mom's door on 18th Avenue in Longview, Washington. Mom and my step-dad, R.L., had first moved to Myrtle Creek, Oregon, at a time when I was living with Grandma and Poppy. They later moved to Longview, where Mamie Cochran lived. There was more work in Longview. Mamie was the sister of Ralph Adams, the husband of Hazel (Tooker) Mosteller. "Tooker" was the daughter of Bruce and Tennie Mosteller, who lived on Cold Branch in North Carolina. Mom had been friends with Tennie and Bruce for many years, since before I was born. So when Tooker came back from Oregon to North Carolina to visit her parents, Mom saw it as an opportunity to move west. Tommy ended the trip with $300 in his pocket, money he didn't have before. Every time they stopped for gas or food, Marie would give him a fifty-dollar bill, the smallest she had, and told him to keep the change. The next day after spending the night she left, sending him a postcard from Vancouver, Canada. He never heard from her again.

He thought he would have been better off if he'd stayed with her, because the law caught up with him shortly afterwards. "If I'd thought about it at the time, I would have known she'd pay her way out of a jam," he said, recalling the incident.

On the way back to prison, a riot started in Chicago. The law was bringing him back in chains. Dozens of women beat up security guards and transit people, while the men just stood back and watched. It took about fifteen to twenty policemen to get the women under control. They apparently thought he was being severely abused. In a way, Tommy probably started this riot with a mere look. He was very handsome and conducted himself with warmth, grace, and charm. Just a look and a smile from him would've been all it would've taken, because he had power in his eyes and smile. They gave off a sense of magic that made people believe he could move mountains, and he believed it too. He gave off a sense of goodness too, much unlike the appearance of a hardened criminal. Security guards at the train station helped FBI agents take him into a small room. They stayed there until the women quietened down somewhat. Then they took the chains off Tommy's legs. His hands were still handcuffed to a chain around his waist, connected to an FBI agent. The women were unable to see him, as he was escorted to the next transit. Officials hovered around him in a close circle.

This type of caring was offered to Tommy from almost every woman he met except his own mother. By this time in his life she was beginning to change, but he wasn't close enough to her to notice it. She had married R.L. Long, who was eighteen years younger. She never got a divorce from Dad, so they remarried after his death. They had two children, a boy and a girl, and named them Danny and June. Apparently she loved R.L., because he brought out the good in her. This brought out the realization in me of knowing people who are happy treat others better than those who aren't.

A different type of environment awaited Tommy back in Raleigh, North Carolina, where he was admitted to a new prison. He spent nine months in a sandpit. Eight men averaged sixty-two, two-ton, state dump-truck loads per day, working with Number 9 short-handle scoops. A lot of the men couldn't handle it. They passed out from the hard work. "*Caldonia* and *Ivy Bluff*, movies filmed in North Carolina, were both true and told the real stories of prisoners living in these places."

Pinto beans, canned tomatoes, and biscuits composed their diets. Sometimes the beans and tomatoes were left out in the hot sun to spoil "to the extent of working, as it would in the making of alcohol." Even so, Tommy learned to love canned tomatoes and biscuits. "If I had to live off of just a few things to eat, I'd choose beans, potatoes, tomatoes, milk, onions, and biscuits and gravy," he said.

"It's funny, but I'd choose the same things," I told him. "The only difference is I like corn bread, milk, and onions mixed together. That's my favorite supper."

All our talk came to an end. Raindrops dripped off the outer leaves of the lean-to like a leaky roof. Peace came with the sound of every drop. The small lean-to, made from sticks and tree branches with the leaves still attached, provided us with all the protection we wanted or needed during the storm. His old friend Sam Dowell had taught him how to build a lean-to such as this. The mountain lion had moved out of our way. And the "thunder row" of Tommy's past became a memory. We all went to sleep.

Martha Harris

Chapter 13

Stage of Never Ending Dramas

When I left North Carolina my fighting spirit, in a physical sense, evaporated. Confronted with miles and miles of reality, my mind held onto its memories of anything good and wouldn't let go. Memories of a Bobwhite softly whistling its name in a lonely canyon, fireflies flickering in the dim light just before dark, the smell of a warm rain during a thunderstorm, or the manicured landscaping of rolling hills were not forgotten. Neither were my oldest brother's love and his teachings. City after city loomed always just over the horizon, like an hallucination. I was going to what seemed like a different world and everything of a negative value was left unpacked. Life poured into my spiritual veins. The uplifting memories were sweet and brought contentment with them. The other memories were buried, so I thought with my father, and the scent of a new place was close at hand.

A friend of Mom's, "Tooker", first brought me to Myrtle Creek, Oregon, where she lived. Tooker's parents, Bruce and Tennie Mosteller, lived on Cold Branch Road in North Carolina; they were the same couple that we had the Sunday dinner with when Dad had taken a couple drinks of white lightening for which Mom had left him. Tooker usually visited her parents in North Carolina once a year. She'd been visiting them and was ready to take the trip back to Myrtle Creek. She had lived in the western states for some time since her husband, "Alabam" (Ralph Adams), cut old growth timber in the Oregon territory.

Mom had a place in Myrtle Creek, close by Tooker's, but she was in the process of moving to Washington State. She said I could come to Washington later to live with her there. In the mean time I could stay at her place in Myrtle Creek.

Tommy and his old buddy, Roy Trull, showed up "out of the blue." Tommy brought his second wife with him. Or at least, he said she was his wife. I was always happy to see new faces and especially my favorite brother. His wife, but really his girlfriend, Nancy*, was very beautiful. She had long, jet-black hair with green eyes. Her tall, slender body was very shapely. The only visible flaw she had was a little bit of space between her two front teeth. Otherwise, she was near perfect in physical appearance.

The first night there, Tommy and Roy told the story of their trip across the United States. Nancy must have been sleeping in the front seat on the passenger side. Tommy had fallen asleep, or partially asleep, while driving. Roy was in the back of the four-door car sleeping too. Waking up from a dream, he looked out and was startled with what he saw. Thinking that they were in deep water, Roy jumped out of the fast-moving vehicle. They were actually in a wheat field, which paralleled with the freeway. It led to an old farmhouse.

Roy said he woke up with the wheat slapping against the windows and knew he was "a goner" if he didn't do something—fast. "What in the hell?" Roy stammered. Not waiting for an answer—he thought by that time it would be too late—he opened the car door and jumped flat on his belly in the wheat field. Luckily, he ended up with only a few minor scrapes and bruises. The wheat must have broken his fall. Now they were talking and laughing about it.

Tooker had gotten me a job. It wasn't much, just one dollar a day, babysitting during the summer. I'd completed the ninth grade only at Hayesville High School prior to coming to Oregon. It didn't take much for me to live on since I eat all my meals with the children whom I cooked for as well as taking care of.

Knowing how particular Mom was, I left the house spotless everyday. When I came back home every night it looked like a tornado had swept through it, leaving nothing but destruction in its path. Even the neatly folded clothes in the drawers were dumped upside down, here and there throughout the rooms. The kitchen counters were not only covered with dirty dishes, but they were heaped in unshapely stacks with some food still in them. The table was the same. *How is it possible?* I thought. *It would take at least a month for this to happen; yet, I was only gone for one day. Anyone would have to deliberately try hard to do this much damage.* I knew it wasn't Tommy or Roy. "Did Nancy take the dishes out of the cupboards and smear food on them?" I asked Roy in an angry tone, while Tommy and her were away the next day. "Why would she take the drawers out and turn them upside down, scattering the clothes all over the place? Why is Tommy willing to put up with all this?" I wanted to know. "She's definitely a sick broad.

"Just the thought of Tommy never saying anything about it or doing anything makes me think he's sick too. How much has he changed? I know he's been gone a long time. We saw each other briefly before I left, but not enough to really know what he's like now. How is it possible to change that much?" I continued quizzing Roy, without giving him a chance to answer.

Every day I left a clean house and came back home to find the same mess. Nancy had even taken my neatly pressed, pleated skirt off its hanger and slept in it. While sleeping she'd pissed on it. All I could do was ask myself why. It all seemed so deliberate.

"Why? How could anyone do this?" I continued rambling on with my questions to Roy, outside her presence. "This is much worse than his first wife who stayed in bed, naked, until afternoon. I thought she was bad. Mom isn't this way. Are most other women like this?" Bewilderingly, I went on, trying to get an answer from Roy; any answer. I was very frustrated with Nancy.

Roy was lying on the couch reading a book. "No! You aren't like that…I really don't know," he answered, worriedly. "But what I don't like is Tommy not doing anything about it. I just know some of the stories I've heard about her."

"What are they?" I asked.

"She was baby sitting for your Aunt Ruth's kids in Atlanta when Tommy picked her up." Roy called my Aunt Ruth by her real name; everyone in our family called her "Cuttie." They said they came home one day and found she had deliberately burned Joyce (Ruth's seven-year-old daughter) with cigarettes."

"Who is she, anyway?"

"She's Ruth's husband's daughter by a previous marriage," he answered.

A couple weeks passed and I couldn't get away from there fast enough because of Nancy making so many messes. In a phone conservation, I begged Mom to let me come to Washington. I felt I wouldn't be held responsible for the destruction if I were gone. She said if I came to Longview, Mamie Cockran, Alabam's sister, would meet me at the bus station. Mamie lived only a few blocks away from the bus depot.

When I went to buy a ticket they said they didn't know of a bus stop in Longview and that I would have to take one to Kelso if I wanted to go. "Kelso is a twin city of Longview," the cashier assured me. "Kelso is on the East Side of the Cowlitz River, and Longview is on the West Side."

"Okay, I'll take it. I want to go." I didn't have Mom's address or her phone number. I could only hope she'd call back before I left to tell her about the change in plans, but she didn't.

"I'll take one step at a time," I told myself. When I arrived in Kelso, my first step was to cross the bridge, which was close by. I could see it. Heading straight ahead, I ran into Washington Way, a main street in Longview; then another main street appeared, 15th Avenue, which I didn't take.

I'd been in a situation like this once before, never knowing the address or the direction in which to go; I'd made it then, and I couldn't let myself believe otherwise now either. Its memory took me back in time. I had hitchhiked from Hayesville to Asheville, North Carolina, with Sue Auhoe*, someone I'd got to know while staying on Shooting Creek with Grandma and Poppy. She was itching to get away from Shooting Creek and talked me into making the 100-mile-trip. It seemed more like 200 miles. She wanted to visit her grandmother in Asheville.

Sue had big, brown eyes with dark, reddish-brown hair. Her measurements at age eleven were 42-22-38, and she was nothing less than gorgeous.

At first I thought it was going to be a fun trip. I was too young and naïve to know better. I dressed in a mint-green, chiffon dress—the skirt filled with tiny pleats—and wore low heels, a most ridiculous way to dress for such a trip. *The dress is just not fitting without the heels,* I thought. Never did I have much trouble finding something pretty to wear, since I tailored other people's clothes to fit me. This time I'd gotten the dress from an old smokehouse, near our place on Tusquittee. The smokehouse was filled with beautiful clothes and a cedar chest with furs, high heels, and accessories to match. They were Faye's*, a long-time friend of mine. Faye said she was a hostess down in Georgia, but everyone thought she'd been working as a high-class harlot out of a madam's home somewhere near Atlanta. She stored her clothes there, but seldom came around since she'd started to work. I felt sure it would be okay to take a few items.

As time passed, I changed my mind about the fun part of the trip to Asheville. Sue was over sexed and seduced a complete stranger in the front seat, right in front of me. He was one of the guys that picked us up.

We went to her grandmother's place as soon as we got to Asheville, but she wanted to go out immediately afterwards. I told her I didn't want to go out, but she wouldn't hear of it. Besides, her grandmother was a stranger to me, and I was quiet and reserved. So I went with her, without getting her grandmother's address or phone number in case we got separated. That was a foolish mistake, but not the first one. A person who can be trusted tends to trust others. Going with her in the first place was the first mistake.

I'd always trusted men too, like I trusted my brother, Tommy. *How naïve can you get Martha?* I later asked myself. We did get separated. After leaving the dance hall that night the man, who was suppose to take me back to Sue's grandmother, took advantage of the situation and took me to the outskirts of town, instead. He told me to "put out or get out." After some hesitation, I got out. With Asheville being such a large town, I wasn't at all sure of which direction to go. I stumbled around in the darkness and somehow stepped on a nail. "How did a nail get out here?" I stammered to myself. I was in between a small restaurant and a house in the suburbs of Asheville. I went to the restaurant hoping I could get some help, but I didn't even know whom to call. I was completely broke, which didn't help matters. I just knew I had to try. My foot was bleeding and I was very tired. *Maybe morning will be a better time to try,* I thought. *At least, then I will have some rest.* Smoothing some dried, dead leaves around my body to keep warm in the cool night air, I went to sleep.

Waiting until a reasonable time for someone to be up in the nearby house, I ventured to their front door and knocked. I didn't have the least idea of what I was going to say. Stumbling at my words, as well as stumbling on one foot, I told them I was lost and needed help. They noticed my foot; it had started bleeding again since I was walking on it.

"Yes," I answered, looking down at my foot. "I stepped on a nail a little while ago." I lied; it'd been last night, but I didn't want them to know that. "A friend and I have been staying at her grandmother's place but after going out we got separated before I could get an address or phone number."

"How will you know where to go?" the strangers asked.

"I'll just have to head out in that direction and hope I run into her place." Almost out of breath, I continued. "I'll recognize it, if I see it again." They offered to call the police if I wanted them to. I told them: "No, I wouldn't know what to tell the police either. I'll just have to try, one step at a time."

"We would like to help you," the lady said. "We don't have enough information, so we don't know how."

If it had been Tommy, or some other good-looking man, the lady would have found a way to help him, I told myself. *But for some reason she couldn't help a small 15-year-old girl. This kind of thinking is getting me no where.* So I started out walking in the direction I thought was right.

That day I got a couple of rides and told both drivers the same: "I really don't have an address. I've been there only once and I think it's in that direction," pointing in the direction that I hoped it would be. "If I get close, I'll know. I will recognize the area when I get there." The first person I got a ride with let me out after a couple hours. He realized he could be driving around in circles for a week and still not get there. Both the first and second drivers must have felt sorry for me, because they went out of their way to help me. The second one was more determined. He must have realized how desperate I was. "I'm really ashamed to tell you the truth, but I suppose I should." I started telling him about what'd happened the night before. It made interesting conversation. After telling him the truth about my foot, he mentioned I needed to try to think of some nearby establishments or signs, which he might know; but I couldn't think of any. "A little rest will help," I told him. A little time passed and I could not think of one name. "We have to be close. Just drive over in that direction," I said. Then all of sudden I thought of the name of the apartment complex in which Sue's grandmother lived. It was like a miracle. I didn't remember seeing the name at all—it must have been hidden somewhere in my subconscious mind. I heard a voice inside of me saying what it was and I believed it. My hope was almost completely gone until then. Finally, excitement lit up my face. "I think I know where it's at," he said. Now we had some idea of where to start. The complex was huge. We drove around in it for about an hour. At times I thought he was going to give up too before I could recognized the place, but luckily he didn't.

I was deeply grateful for his help; without it, I wouldn't have made it. *Was he just a decent human being, fulfilling a wonderful part on earth's great stage of never ending dramas? Or was he an angel sent here to help me out?*

My bleeding foot, caused from so much walking before he came along, was left unnoticed by Sue's grandmother and unfelt by me. The glorious realization of knowing I was "over the top" took the place of their pain. I later counted five blisters on my feet; some were busted.

The first thing I did upon entering Sue's grandmother's place was ask if I could use her phone to call Tommy so he could come after me. Since Grandma and Poppy didn't have a phone, I called the grocery store, which was about a mile away. The owner there somehow got word to Tommy to call me back even though he wasn't staying at Grandma and Poppy's. He didn't have to do this for me, but he must have noticed the desperation in my voice. I had to make him realize I needed help, badly. When Tommy called back, I told him the situation. "Tommy, I'll never do this again," I promised. "I've learned my lesson. I wan-a come home. Would you come after me, please?"

Then, I cleaned up, pampering my feet somewhat. They now hurt.

Now, here I was in the same boat again: wanting to go some place and not having much of an idea of how to get there. This time, at least, I had dreamed about Longview and what it looked like two years before. I told Mom's sister, Aunt Lucy, about the dreams. Longview and Kelso were much smaller than Asheville too, which was another plus.

I crossed 15th Avenue and continued on Washington Way. All of a sudden I looked up and saw a sign that said 20th Avenue. I'd gone two blocks too far. I remembered Mom had said something about her living on 18th in our phone conservation. I turned on 20th anyway. I could feel myself being pulled in that direction. Walking down 20th I came to a beautiful lake, Lake Sacajawea, the lake I'd described to Aunt Lucille two years prior to coming here. When I got to the 20th Avenue Grocery, again something was beckoning me to make a decision. Crossing the street, I looked down 20th and could see what looked like a dead-end street. The vision was dim at the end, because it had been dark at least a couple of hours and the streetlights provided only some visibility that far. I realized I should now go back to 18th. This was the direction in which I felt I was being pulled anyway, so *it must be right.* Even though 18th went in both directions, going from east to west and was on both sides of the lake, I felt the strong sensation to turn right onto it. Besides, I'd already passed the lake going down 20th. So I decided to give it a try and see where the sensations led me. Upon turning right at 18th and Beech, I saw a little house on the left, which had a porch light on. Mom had said she would leave the porch light on in an earlier conversation. "That must be it," I said to myself. Suddenly, I just knew that it was, even before Mom opened the door. She'd been keeping a close eye out for anyone who walked by—hoping it would be me.

This wasn't nearly as bad as being lost in Asheville. In my mind, I believed it was because this time I was doing the right thing. It left a clean and calm feeling inside. Some people would probably say I was just using logic. I also felt a strong sensation that something was walking beside me. I accepted it as the angel I couldn't see.

"My God, you made it," Mom poured out her surprise and happiness. "How did you know where to come?" She'd called Tommy in Myrtle Creek after I'd left and he told her the details.

"I felt like I was being pulled in this direction. Every time I needed to turn except one, something told me to and pulled me in that direction. I came down 20th, instead of 18th."

"Well, you're here now and that's all that matters," Mom concluded, leading me to the kitchen to get something to eat. That's how she was with everyone, even strangers: She always thought to feed them.

Later I found out that 18th was not a through street and didn't have a bridge leading to the other side of the lake. An angel did watch over me that day, guiding and protecting me all the way. My perception concluded: *God is more apt to take care of one who does the right thing...and one who never gives up.*

Chapter 14

Two Dresses for a Blue Lady

After staying in Longview with Mom a few days, I went to Toledo to stay with my dad's brother, Uncle Fred, and his wife, Shirley. She was more than twenty years younger than Fred. They needed me. I got up at four o'clock every week day morning to cook Fred's breakfast and fix his lunch before he went off to work and had dinner ready when he came home. I took care of their three boys—changed their diapers, gave them baths, washed their clothes, and made sure they were fed and taken care of just like my own. The first week I was there, I washed down the walls of their house with a hose. Yes, it was that messy. I figured I could pay for my keep that way.

I'd known Shirley prior to coming to Washington and had predicted she would marry Fred a few years before. At the time of her fortune, I thought of it as being odd that she would marry him, since she had the same last name. She had lived just below Uncle James, Fred's brother, on the mountain, northeast of Hayesville, going toward Franklin. Tony and I had lived with Uncle James after Dad died. Shirley and I were basically in the same age group, she was just a few years older. Fred and Shirley met on one of his trips to North Carolina.

Shirley and I got along very well; we even went out together to dances on Saturday nights during my stay with them. It was something I look forward to, and she looked forward to going out once a week too.

"Shirley, Shirley, this is the day," I yelled out from the bedroom.

"This is the day for what?" Before waiting for an answer she continued. "You know we're going out tonight, don't you?"

"Yeah, of course…I remember," I answered. "Remember me telling you I was going to meet someone special? Tonight's the night."

"Yeah," she recalled, waiting anxiously for a thorough explanation. After hesitating a moment, she called back from the kitchen, "How do you know tonight's going to be the night?"

"I'm hemming one bow under on this dress. You remember me telling you I would hem one bow under on a red dress. This is the same dress. Here, look! See what I've done!" I grabbed the dress off the bed, taking it to the kitchen to show her how I was hemming it. In complete amazement, I paced back and forth from the bedroom to the kitchen, rambling on. Unraveling and recalling the story, I started with a dream I'd had two years earlier…still so vivid in my mind.

"There was also another dream," I recaptured. "It's that lavender blue dress." We'd gone shopping at a used clothing store a few days earlier and picked out both the red and blue dresses, which I had intentions of altering. Time had passed so quickly that I needed to take some shortcuts. I'd forgotten about the dreams until I found myself hemming one bow under on the red dress. It was a way to make due until I could do a better job. Since it was lacy and quite elaborate, this was the easiest and fastest way of making myself something to wear.

"I'd better get busy on this, if I ever want to finish in time."

On the way to the dance hall, I was still so excited I couldn't shut up. She drove and listened while I talked. "You know where the YMCA is in Longview?" I asked.

"Yes," she answered.

"And that hole in the ground across from it. It looks like a building once stood there a long time ago. It has something that looks like a human statue at one end. I've never been close enough to examine it completely to see exactly what the statue really is. I think it's a statue of a person. You know where I'm talking about. Don't you?"

"Yes, I know where it's at," she answered. "It's across from the YMCA in Longview, close to Lake Sacajawea," she added.

"Yeah, that's it. Every time I past by the YMCA there I thought of the word Temple*. Afterwards, I always thought of Wanda Gay McClure's old boyfriend. She's my first cousin. You don't know her. She used to have a boyfriend by the name of Hugh*. I never thought of his last name, just his first. It happened so many times that I started asking myself questions to try to fill in the blanks and know the reason why. One day when I was walking by, for about the sixth time and asking those questions, it just dawned on me that I'd meet somebody special by the name of Hugh Temple*. I've never heard of a person with the last name of Temple before. Have you? Can this possibly be true? It looks like this is the night I'm suppose to meet him."

Reverting back to the dreams, I described the dance hall in detail. "I've never been there before in my life. You know that. It has something like a big, round fireplace in the middle of the floor just as you walk through the door. There's a concession counter on the left of a wide entrance hall. It opens up into a large dance floor, with the band in view. You can't see the edges of the dance floor until you get through the entrance hall. There's more space on the right of the dance floor than the left."

"It's exactly like that," she confirmed, slightly laughing in overwhelming surprise. "I'm amazed. How did you know?"

"I just know. I could draw a picture of it. The pieces are fitting together now. At the time of the dreams, I needed something to look forward to. My life was going nowhere. I didn't have anything to keep me hoping. It's terrible to be only fifteen and not have any dreams or hopes to lead you into the future. This was a promise of happier times to come; something to hang onto for awhile—something to tide me over."

We arrived. Through the doors of Plaquato we walked. Just like walking into a better world, I felt as if I glowed with happiness. Maybe it showed. Attention came from all sides. It felt wonderful. Guys were standing in line to dance with me with many interruptions during each dance. Even when I went to the counter to get a pack of cigarettes, there were as many as five guys there, all at once, trying to see which one could get their money out of their pockets the fastest. I sometimes ducked under their arms or in-between them to curb all the attention and go on to dance with someone else I thought was better looking. But no Hugh!

Where could he be? I wondered. The night was almost over. I'd danced with what seemed like fifty or more guys, and I hadn't found him yet. I found Shirley and told her of my concerns. "Shirley, he's not here. I should have found him by now."

She didn't seem to be very concerned. "You still have some time. You'll probably meet him later," she reassured me.

The night of dancing ended. My previous glow vanished too. "Tonight's over and it didn't happen," I told her. "It's strange to build my hopes to this point with no results. It was suppose to happen tonight."

She tried in small ways to comfort me in my disappointment. Then all of a sudden she remembered, "There's a little restaurant I usually stop at when I come up here. Maybe you'll meet him there."

"That's it. That's got-a be it," I said slightly above a whisper. "I wouldn't have all these thoughts and feelings for nothing." I tried not to renew all the hope I previously had for fear of being let down. But this suggestion was all I had. "Maybe," I said in a soft, uplifting voice. "I hope so."

We drove into the parking area, directly in front of the restaurant. Through the large windows we could see three tables pulled together at which all men were seated. "That's him; that's him, Shirley," I repeated with excitement, never taking my eyes off him. "I had doubts it would happen, but here he is." Our eyes met even while I was still in the car. The glow returned and the feeling with it.

The men seem to go somewhat crazy just from us being there. They invited us to sit at their table, and when we didn't accept they rearranged the tables to sit with us. Their friendly, flirting remarks welcomed us with every gesture—except one: Shirley wanted one of the stuffed animals positioned on a shelf above an opening leading to the cooking area. She kept expressing her desires for one, but they kept ignoring her, leaning their attentions toward me. Finally I said, "Which one of you guys is going to buy Shirley a stuffed animal?" Three jumped up, all at once, prepared to buy it for her. Then they argued as to which one was going to do it. "Well, you all three can't buy it," I said.

"Would you like to have one?" one of the guys asked me. From that comment, the rest of the guys were ready to buy one too—except Hugh. He must have been getting enough of my attention without the offer. At this point, I hadn't confirmed his name yet.

"It's very nice of you guys wanting to buy me a stuffed animal, but Shirley was the one who wanted one in the first place. I would have appreciated an offer from you," pointing toward Hugh who was sitting beside me at the end of the table. "You're the only one who didn't offer," I said. "What's your name?"

"Hugh," he answered.

"What?" I asked anxiously, waiting with wide eyes.

"Hugh," he repeated. "Why is it so important?" He must have noticed the astonishment in my face.

"Nothing, it's just something you wouldn't understand," I told him. "What's your last name?"

"Temple," he said.

"You can't be serious," I said amazed.

"That's my name, Hugh Temple," he confirmed. "Is something wrong with it?"

"No," I answered. "Nothing's wrong. Everything is right."

Four o'clock came. I decided it was definitely time to go home. Even though Shirley was older than I was, Fred would still blame me for keeping her out so late. *He will be furious with me for keeping his young wife out,* I thought. Time for parting drew sadness.

The two carloads of men followed us back to Toledo. Shirley said, "We can't go home with them following us. I'll drive down town, so we can stop to tell them they can't follow us home. Fred's going to be mad enough with us for being out so late, even as it is."

After parking in front of one of the closed establishments down town, Shirley told them she was married, and they couldn't follow us home under any circumstances.

Looking toward me, Hugh asked, "How am I going to know where to find you?"

I didn't know how to answer that question: "If it's meant to be, you'll find me. If not, you won't," I answered after some hesitation.

We went home and confronted Fred. His bark was louder than his bite. We said a few words of explanation to calm him down.

There didn't seem to be much hope of ever seeing Hugh again. This brought an overwhelming depression. During the next few days I got into a bottle of codeine that Shirley had stashed away in a medicine cabinet. It brought a high that eased my pain. Sometimes I felt like I was floating on a pink cloud. Realizing that it was becoming addictive with only a few times of using it, I asked myself, "What am I doing? I don't want to become a drug addict. That would be a fate worse than death." Immediately changing my thoughts to disgust for it, I quit.

I was hopelessly in love with Hugh from the very first moment. A few days later, I decided I had to at least try to go on with my life. So I dressed up, put on make-up, and did my hair. "Some fresh air couldn't hurt," I told Shirley. I went to the porch to daydream, if nothing else. Out of the clear blue, he drove by the house. *It is a weekend*, I thought. It had been one week since I'd seen him. "Shirley," I yelled loudly, running back into the house. "Guess whose driving around the block."

"It's Hugh," she guessed on the first try. She noticed my big smile.

"Yes," I responded with deep pleasure. "Yes, yes. I'd better get back out there on the porch, so he can see me. In case he drives by again, I don't wan-a miss him."

Seeing me, he stopped after circling the block again. I couldn't take my eyes off him. I think he was driving a light blue car; it could have been a '56 Ford. The motor purred like one of Tommy's cars. "Your car's real sporty," I told him. About that time, Tommy and Nancy* drove up. They had come from Myrtle Creek to Longview shortly after I did. Tommy being interested in cars, he went over to admire Hugh's car, but I hardly noticed he was there.

That night we went to the Seattle World's Fair. We walked through the fair, hand in hand. I was mesmerized just by his presence. My intensified dreamy look showed sheer delight of life. It was as close as I've ever come to undiluted love on this planet. Even the silence, later that night, was stupendous and satisfying. It seemed to transcend from another world. He asked me did I want to go on any of the rides, but I said "no." I told him I got sick whenever I rode on rides. "Besides, I'm enjoying the pleasure of just being with you."

We got a hotel room in Tacoma, because we hated to give up just a few more moments of pleasure. I undressed, but not entirely. Even though I wanted to let go of all my inhibitions, I settled for a brief goodnight kiss without otherwise touching his body. We both slept on opposite sides of the bed. I felt a little uneasy with guilt, even to go that far.

We faced Fred together around noon the following day. Fred was really worried about me. I was only seventeen and he felt responsible for me. I'd always done anything I wanted without any discipline, except for Tommy's. I couldn't understand his extreme concern, but I honored his wishes by telling him we wouldn't ever do it again.

Hugh and I went out together a few times after that. Then I came back to Longview to live with Mom. Mamie Cochran and I had just returned from Long Beach. I was badly burned from staying out in the sun too long. The next day I was so sick I couldn't even put on a bathing suit to go swimming with Mamie. So I stayed home, dressed in one of Mom's old house dresses. It was a mile to big for me. While watching TV, I wondered if I'd ever see Hugh again. Something in my mind told me it wasn't over yet, but I couldn't see how he could ever find me in a town as big as Longview with no address.

While I was in the kitchen for a glass of water, I heard a knock on the door. Mom and my step-dad were gone, besides *they wouldn't be knocking. Who could it be?* I thought. *I don't expect anyone.* Then another knock. As I opened the door I almost fainted. It was Hugh. "How did you find me?" I asked, almost stuttering because I was so happy, "I thought I'd never see you again."

"I just asked questions," he answered, hugging me.

"Hug me tighter," I enticed. We stood there in the doorway, tightly embracing each other for several minutes. I didn't want to let go.

I told him about Mamie and I going to the beach. "You must think I look awful. I felt so bad I didn't even comb my hair."

"No," he said. "You look fine." We embraced again. I felt fine. It's really strange, but when you feel loved, you feel beautiful no matter what. That day we just stayed home and talked and watched some TV.

Numerous times afterwards we went out—for long walks along the ocean shores of Long Beach, camping, dancing, and double dating with Mamie. Mamie started going out with his best friend, Bruce*. Most of the time she drove. On our camping trips, I crawled in the sleeping bag with Hugh; my frilly dress still on. I was afraid to take it off. When we became tired after riding around too long I lay my head in his lap, or he lay his head in mine. At times we put a blanket over our heads and necked under the covers, while Mamie and Bruce talked in the front seat. Our kisses lasted longer than I thought I had air for. They sent a chilling message to every acupuncture point of my body.

Then one night we went to a dance in Tacoma. Hugh didn't want to go in. I knew something was wrong, but I didn't know what. I wanted to know what it was, so I forced him.

He started, "Mamie, you have a ring, don't you?"

"Yes," she spoke out with astonishment. Mamie was probably fifteen years older than I was, and she'd been married before. He wanted her wedding band, but why?

"I want you to put it on," he said. "We're going to tell everyone we're married."

We all went into the dance hall together. He had the band announce our fake wedding and play us a song. Somehow we got separated for a while. I was dressed in the lavender blue dress, the other dress I'd told Shirley about earlier and the one I'd worn on the trip to the Seattle World's Fair. Mamie took our picture in front of his car earlier that evening. At the dance, it seemed like all the guys were trying to pick me up, all except Hugh. *Where is he?* I wondered.

This night held a deep suspense. I kept waiting for the picture to unfold. Then all of a sudden it happened. A girl approached me on an outside deck where the lights were really bright. There was a large opening to the dance floor. I hoped Hugh would see me there. He did eventually. He saw both of us talking. "You don't know me," she started her introduction, telling me who she was. "I'm five months pregnant, and the baby belongs to Hugh."

"I'm sorry," I told her. "I didn't know."

When Hugh approached he tried to convince her we were married. She walked away. Telling Hugh I felt sorry for her, I added, "Maybe we should tell her the truth."

"No," he said. "That won't accomplish anything."

We left the dance early. I felt uneasy, but I couldn't figure out why. The days that lay ahead told me why. She apparently checked out the story and found out it wasn't true. I didn't see Hugh for some time. Hoping to find him, I went back to Plaquato. I did see him there again. He said she had him put in jail. She was only 17, the same as I. He tried to show me the news clipping to prove he had been under an $1100 bail, but I threw it aside. I was so devastated.

After that he came down to Longview to see me almost every weekend, at least for awhile. He always had on his work clothes when he arrived. They were logger's clothes. He worked in the woods. He said he didn't bother to go home to change clothes. Apparently he hid some clothes in his car or in Bruce's car and changed after he got to Longview. I suspected he was married because of this. Sometimes he would spend the entire weekend with me, making me wonder how could he do that with a new wife. For several months this went on. Then one night Bruce called to say Hugh wasn't coming down. No matter how much I coaxed, he wouldn't say what the reason was. That told me the answer. "Okay," I said, "I'll tell you why. He's married." It was later confirmed when Bruce showed up to take Mamie out.

I couldn't get him out of my mind. The one true love of my life, and I'd lost him. I sometimes woke up in the middle of the night hugging my pillow. Mamie and I slept together. She woke up too because of my restlessness. "As long as you don't hug me," she teased laughingly, hoping to cheer me up.

Mamie was manager of the apartment building where we lived. I stayed with her, taking care of her three sons while she worked during the day. They were school-age boys. One or more of the apartments were often left vacant, allowing me the privacy I wanted. Sometimes I'd sit in a corner of one of the vacant rooms, crying for hours without anybody knowing it. I withdrew more and more. I wanted so badly to end it all. Occasionally, I'd hold a razor blade inches away from my wrist, trying to get enough nerve to do it. It seemed sick, but I couldn't help myself. I went home to Mom's and tried it again, this time with poison, which was easier. Sleeping for three days and nights and never touching one bite of food or drinking one sip of water, I woke up only to throw up. I came to the conclusion that God didn't want me to die. He wouldn't let me. I'd just have to live with the pain.

I kept the picture that Mamie had taken of us for the longest time. Then one day it disappeared without an explanation. No matter how much time past, my feelings for him wouldn't disappear. His face, along with the two dresses, remained part of my memory. So, this is what forever is for: *It doesn't seem right, but it's part of life.*

Chapter 15

Ride the Wave

I was taking care of Mamie's three boys. The oldest was bigger than I was. I lived with them during the week, babysitting and doing all the cooking and housework for two dollars a day. I did all the ironing and sometimes even made pies and canned jelly. I stayed with Mom on the weekends when Mamie and I didn't go out.

One evening Mamie wanted me to help her find a man whom she had recently met. Small apartments faced both sides of the walkway where she wanted me to go alone and knock on one of the doors. Apparently he had told her he lived there. Her friend wasn't home, and I don't think we ever found him.

As I was about to leave the complex, a sticker on the window of a door entered my peripheral vision. I stopped dead in my tracks. It said some smart-alecky remark about being a bachelor, which I don't remember. I just stood there, looking at the sign for several minutes. "Whoever lives there is the guy I'm going to marry," I said out-loud.

Upon returning to the car to let Mamie know that her boyfriend wasn't home, I also told her about the incident with the bachelor sticker. She brushed it off in disbelief.

Six months passed and I was visiting my mother. Dressed in a royal blue tweed suit, which I'd made for myself, with matching purse and heels, I decided to walk up to the St. Helen's Inn. The Inn had a soda fountain and restaurant in one end with games and things for young people to do in the other end. I was feeling restless and had nothing else to do. It was on a weekend.

When I arrived two middle-aged gentlemen and a very stylish, pretty black-haired lady were sitting in a parked car in front of the Inn. Calling me over to their car, one asked, "How about going to a party tonight?"

"Do you have anything planned for tonight?" Another asked.

All three began talking at the same time and so fast I didn't have a chance to say much. "Do you have a car? Would you like us to pick you up? If you don't want to go to a private party, how about a public place?" They continued, thinking that that might persuade me faster.

They looked like they could be trusted, especially the well-dressed lady; they were certainly friendly. "What harm could I do, if I borrowed a friend's car and met you at a public place," I told them. "But I'm only nineteen. I can't get in."

"We'll take care of that. Just go get the car and meet us over at the Midway in West Kelso," they coached.

Both the guys were outside, walking up and down in front of the bar waiting for me when I arrived. *This shows a sense of responsibility*, I thought. *Maybe they are nice people.* "Well, nothing ventured, nothing gained," I recaptured an old phrase and took each guy by the arm, letting them escort me into the place.

Every man there lavished me with attention. I adored it. The ladies in the group decided to phone one of their sons to come down to meet me. He would distract their husbands' attention away from me. They agreed and laughed teasingly.

He was a big man, weighing well over 200 pounds and over six feet tall. His name, Norman Bourne, carried an English background. Although I was only five feet and weighed ninety-five pounds, he attracted my attention with his wonderful personality. He also seemed very intelligent, which I always admired.

Sure enough, when I finally got to see his apartment it was the same place Mamie and I had gone to six months prior. Dreams I had, since that incident, depicted the interior of his apartment exactly. Five sacks of empty vodka bottles set in front of a hide-away bed in the middle of the living room floor of his small, studio apartment. The bed was still out and unmade. I walked around in the small kitchen, checking the cupboards, fridge and even the drawers to see if things matched up with the dreams. They did—even to the dried evaporated milk on a can opener left on the counter. Actually, this wasn't very impressive. I thought he must be very lonely, like I was, to have drunk so much booze. Apparently he didn't stay home very much: the rest of the house was fairly clean. *Men seem to be the type that can't face difficulties very well and need something to camouflage their thoughts and feeling,* I pondered from past images. I always looked for reasons why people did things: *This must be the reason for his heavy drinking.*

I went over to see him periodically. Only occasionally did he come by to see me. Even then, he brought a friend with him. Both of them sat in the kitchen talking to Mom, hardly noticing me. That didn't represent much interest.

In the meantime, I quit staying with Mamie and started living with a cousin, Sue Parker. Sue and I had something more in common than just being distant cousins. Her father, Cliff Parker, and my father, Roy Parker, were like identical twins even though they were only first cousins. Cliff had come to visit us once after Dad's death and I marveled at their resemblance. I sat on the steps, hardly taking my eyes off him, listening to every word he had to say. If I hadn't known my father was dead, even I could have mistaken him to be Dad.

Sue was a gorgeous, sophisticated, black-haired, young woman in her twenties. She started dating Roy Trull, Tommy's friend.

Roy had come to Longview with Tommy and Nancy* soon after I left Myrtle Creek. Tommy and Nancy were now living with Mom. Roy started living with Sue. He soon got connected with another buddy, Randall McAlister, who also started living with Sue. Roy had lived with my family, off and on, since I was eight or nine and had become my protective figure, just like Tommy had been. Since Roy was Sue's boyfriend, Randall just naturally assumed he was mine.

Roy and Randall never did any work. The less I knew about how they got by the better. Sue and I were out driving when I first learned what they'd been doing. The cops stopped us. Before they could walk over to Sue's car to search it, she told me to grab a jar of change, which was hidden under the seat, and hide it under my coat. I did what she told me and asked questions later. The cops didn't find anything, because they didn't search us. By that time, they must have had enough proof without additional evidence, so they came to Sue's place later that day and arrested Roy and Randall. They were hauled off to jail and went into prison for six months for burglarizing phone booths.

During their time in prison I went with Aunt Lucy once to see Roy. She was married to him prior to coming to Washington State, but they had gotten a divorce. Lucy apparently wanted him back. I never asked to see Randall. His ego was hurt because of it. "Randall practically killed himself with exercise to get in shape for when he got out," Roy later commented.

The day of Randall's release came, which I dreaded. He showed up at the door where I was babysitting a nine-year-old girl. I had quit staying with Sue and had another live-in babysitting job, which paid better than the other jobs I'd had. No way did I want to go out with Randall. I had never led him to believe otherwise, except one night I'd slept with him at a friend of Sue's. All of us—Roy, Sue, Tommy, Nancy, another couple, Randall, and I—were having a wild party. There was no where else to sleep, and I was tired. Since Randall respected me, no sex took place. Tommy slapped me the following day, when he got me alone. Both Roy and Randall got mad at him when I told them later. I asked them to drop it, and they did.

"Just for old times sake?" Randall pleaded when he came to see me the first day he was released from prison.

"If I go out with you tonight, will you promise to let it be the last?" I consented after some time.

"I promise," he said, slowly backing off the steps.

"You'll have to come back later. I'd like the chance to get ready."

"Of course," he consented. "I expected that."

He decided to show me off in my royal blue, satin dress. We went bar hopping. I still wasn't twenty-one. That was no problem, especially since I was with Randall. He was actually about twenty years older than I was.

At one place in Vader, five good-looking guys came in and sat down in the booth next to us. While Randall was in the restroom they started talking to me. One in particular was very friendly. I exchanged conversation with him, but I didn't flirt. When Randall came out of the restroom and saw this, he immediately went over to their table and asked all five of them outside for a fight. They just laughed at him. When we got up to leave, the one talking to me followed us outside. He was much bigger than Randall was. I'm sure he thought he could handle him and sublimely called his bluff. The stranger didn't know whom he was messing around with. By the time I could jump out of the car and run about twenty feet to break up the fight, the stranger lay on the ground near death. He couldn't move, and still Randall wouldn't stop.

Butting in to shield the guy, I practically screamed to partially bring him to his senses: "If you hit him again, you'll have to hit me." Firmly I continued, "Randall, he's already ready to go to the hospital. The cops will be here any minute." With that comment, he decided to quit. We ran to the car, and he sped off quickly.

He was leaving town that night, going to Denver, Colorado, and he wanted me to go with him. Naturally I didn't want to go. Even if he had been in my basic age group, he wasn't the type I wanted for a husband. I asked him to take me to Aunt Lucy's. I would spend the night there, since I didn't want Mom to notice anything peculiar.

When we arrived at Lucy's, we both got out of the car. He grabbed my shoulders, shaking them. "I know you're not afraid for yourself," he threatened. "But you'd better be afraid for Stanley (Lucy's small son) and Lucille." They were both home alone and didn't have a phone, which he pointed out.

He took some silver money out of his pocket to show me it still had bloodstains on it from his last murder. He had been staying with a family in Amboy. The man and Randall had gotten into a fight; now the man was dead. The pieces seem to fit right in with the rumors about the death. I asked him why the law didn't put him in jail. He told me everyone in the family was afraid of him, which also seemed to fit in with the stories. Nobody would testify against him or even say he was at fault. There were news articles on it, but I never did read them. I only heard people talk about it. Naturally the stories grew in proportion to the news articles. The people talking about the murder thought they knew more about Randall, because they knew more about his background.

Crying when I went into Aunt Lucy's to get some things, I was hoping she might get the message. If she perceived my reluctance to go with him, she might do something about it after we were gone. He wouldn't let me out of his sight, so I couldn't tell her. But he couldn't stop my tears. I tied to give her indications with my eyes, but that didn't work either.

The first night on the way to Denver, Colorado, we stopped and stayed the night with the same family in Amboy that Randall had told me about. "How are they going to take us staying at their place?" I asked Randall.

"They'll take it just fine," he answered. "I've got some clothes there I need to pick up."

They did take it just fine: they seemed to even welcome us. They offered us a beer. I spilt mine on my dress—the same blue satin dress I'd worn earlier, because I hadn't taken the time to change. *Was he lying about killing the man? Why would they welcome such a man into their home?* I asked myself.

Later that night I asked him similar questions while lying in bed with him. This seemed like an odd situation all the way around: them accepting us so readily and now I was here in bed with him, moments away from making love. It was as if I had no power of my own. I was being washed away onto some deserted island by a giant wave and feeling just as helpless.

The next day we were on our way again. Sleeplessness brought him discomfort in the hours ahead. He hated to go to sleep and leave me unguarded. "I can drive," I told him. "You have to get some sleep. I don't have a license, but it hasn't bothered you in breaking many other laws, so why not?"

He briefly warned me of the weather conditions: "You could hit a patch of black ice at any moment. Be careful!" He also warned me, "Not even I know what I will do, if I wake up and find us somewhere different from what I expect."

A few things crossed my mind on how I could get myself out of the mess I'd gotten myself into after he'd drifted off to sleep. We were out in the middle of nowhere with miles and miles of nothing. Very few cars passed. I wasn't even sure of where I was. *This isn't the right time to make a move*, I reasoned. *Might as well ride the wave.*

The weather seemed nice: the sun registered its bright existence in the ten o'clock position of the eastern sky—the direction in which we were traveling. I rolled down the window about half way to check out the temperature. *It's fairly cold, but warm enough not to cause any problems,* I thought. So I increased my speed. Just over the next hill I hit a patch of black ice. The car spun around several times and ended up facing the opposite direction. Randall woke up but just sat quietly observing while I got the car back under control. He calmly reminded me not to hit the brakes. "It's a good thing there hasn't been much traffic. We would've had a wreck," I told him.

As we pulled into Denver, the snow was three or four feet deep along the sides of the road. The road had been scraped, but it was still a solid sheet of ice. Randall was driving. He'd taken over when I almost wrecked. He knew exactly where he was going, pointing out different structures—the place where he use to work was one of them. We pulled into a horseshoe type motel. He didn't have any money, and I knew it.

"How are we going to afford a motel room with no money?" I inquired.

"I'll take care of it," he said. "I know the owners here. They'll let us stay and pay later. I'll go to work tomorrow and get a draw by the end of the week."

"Yeah, but motels are really expensive. Are you sure you can afford it?" I wanted to know.

"Everything will be alright," he reassured me.

Once we settled in, Randall wanted to go out. He didn't say why, and he didn't want to take me with him. "If you want to go somewhere after I get back, we will," he said, wanting to please. "Right now, I've got some business to take care of."

When he returned he had a roll of bills as big as his fist. "Now, how did you get that?" I asked.

"There's plenty of people around here willing to help me out. I get what I want in this town," he answered.

"What about paying them back later?" I continued.

"I don't want you to worry your pretty little head about anything as long as I'm around," he said, smiling and reaching to hold me in his arms.

I was still on that giant wave, being washed to who knows where. Randall was extremely intelligent. He had an I-Q of a genius level. I had seen what the wrong reaction to a situation with him could bring. It was better to ride the wave gracefully than to go down fighting.

The next day he went to work, just like he said he would. Over the next few days he taught me how to cook better and treated me like I was his queen. He was going to work for awhile there in Denver until he built up his funds a little, and then he was going to take me to Florida. His mother owned a large grocery store there. We would manage it.

The trouble didn't start until I made some attempts at getting away. He came home in the middle of the day and caught me hanging out of the bathroom window. I'd placed a kitchen chair under the window to climb upon. The window was small, even for me to climb out. It was the only window at the backside of the motel unit, which offered the least detection of getting caught. I knew he knew the owners, and they would notify him at work if I attempted to get away through the front. The snow was almost as high as I was, but I'd worry about getting over that stumbling block when I got to it. Why he just happen to walk through the door at that time and catch me trying to escape, I don't know. His six-sense was working much better than mine was.

We got into a fight. Somehow I got my arms locked around his neck in a position to where he couldn't get loose. I started laughing. "All this time I've been afraid of you," I admitted. "But you're easier to whip than I thought."

The fire then came out of his eyes. He looked wicked. I knew then what I was really afraid of, the evilness inside him. His eyes ejected power; so much power I backed away. He threatened using the diamond ring, which he'd used to cut others with, to slice my face all to pieces. "If I can't have you, then nobody else will want you," he retorted. He managed to get in one blow on the right side of my face before I fell across the bed, using my feet to kick off his blows. After some time he mellowed out like a helpless kitten, or at least like a compassionate person. "I thought you were happy," he said almost in tears. "I wanted so much to make you happy. What went wrong?"

"I don't know. Maybe it was because I didn't have enough time. Maybe it was because of our age difference. Maybe it was because of the force used to bring me here in the first place. Or maybe it was all those reasons combined."

"Do you think we can work it out in time?" he urged.

"I don't know," I solemnly answered.

"You know I won't let you leave," he pointed out. The motel owner—calling him by name—"told me you were over there yesterday trying to sell his wife your record player to get enough money to leave on. Maybe that's why I showed up today in good time."

"And he told you?" I astounded. "I explained to his wife I just wanted to go home. I didn't think you'd find out. I asked them not to tell."

"Now you know that didn't work," he said, leaving to go back to work. "I have to go now. I'm already two and a half hours late."

I was starting to have some good feelings toward Randall. He had shown he didn't really want to hurt me. He treated me with utmost respect and love as long as I wasn't trying to get away from him. The next couple weeks I wondered what it would be like to be married to him. By this time I knew I had to be pregnant. My conclusion was I really wanted to go back home.

It looked like I needed to change my strategy. So I sat down to write a long letter to Lucy. Randall would get the incoming mail, but he wouldn't get the outgoing mail. I asked her specific questions so she would answer with a reply that would possibly encourage Randall to let me go. Nothing else had worked, and I believed that if something fails, try something different. It worked. The letter from Lucy came back through the motel owner's hands, which I expected. He gave the letter to Randall instead of me. She wrote back saying the man I'd worked for would be happy to send me the money to come home. She understood my feelings and wondered why I'd left in the first place.

Bringing the opened letter to me almost in tears made me wish I hadn't done it. I didn't know he cared so much. "If you want to go home that bad," he said, "I'll let you go." He'd been caught up with the feelings of being rejected and the feelings of loving me. No one thought he could ever love anybody. "I love you enough to let you go now. If you don't change your mind by tomorrow, we'll go to the bus depot to get you a ticket." He wanted to come back with me, if that was what I wanted. I couldn't see myself living my life out with him either. I wanted to see what else my life had in store. Even if it was bad, at least it would be a surprise, and it would be different.

The next day he took me to the bus station, kissing me goodbye before he left. "If I don't go now, I might change my mind," he said. Turning around and walking away, he never looked back.

After coming home I went to work in Portland, Oregon, at Coleman Camping Equipment, quilting sleeping bags. Within three weeks I was doing their specialties and within six weeks my production had reached almost to the level of a person with ten years experience.

I visited Mom on the weekends, doing as much for her as I could. She first suspected I was pregnant at six months, because my boobs were becoming so large. She asked Lucy about it, and she told her the truth. By the end of my pregnancy, my breast had increased so much in size that I wore my mother's bras, a 42-C, seaming them to make them fit my small frame. Otherwise, I could still zip my pants and weighed only 104 pounds.

With a little over a month left, I became so stiff I couldn't work. When I came home, I got into a fight with Net Suller*, the girlfriend I had when I first entered high school and the one's future I'd predicted years ago. I remembered I would lose the fight, because I felt so stiff. Now I knew why. I was pregnant. The doctor told me I had the tightest stomach muscles he ever saw. My stomach was holding the baby in so well that one couldn't tell I was pregnant. Net thought I had gone out with her husband, Paul B, while she was in the hospital. Actually, we were just close friends. The friendship had started when he took the coat off his back and gave it to me in High Point, North Carolina. I'd slept in a car with no windows in freezing weather then, because Mom had run me off.

I quit working in Portland and went back to Longview. I'd left a beautiful pair of earrings at Norm's place before I left Washington. Using that for an excuse, I went to see him after I got back. We started living together shortly afterwards. It was a weak time in my life, being pregnant and all, so apparently Norm felt enough security with himself to ask me to marry him. Sherry was born September 7, 1964. It was Labor Day. Norm and I were married November 4 of that year. Shortly after, he adopted her. During the time we lived in Norm's studio apartment, Sherry slept on a couch pillow along side the hide-away bed that Norm and I slept on. We didn't have enough room in the small apartment for the baby bed that Norm had bought her. I washed her clothes in the bathtub and dried them on the back of a chair, which was set in front of an electric heater. I also washed our clothes the same way, because I felt uneasy about using Norm's money. It must have been just part of my personality to be that way. I didn't figure his money was mine to use.

I felt like someone else besides me had planned my life. Oh, I could do little things to make it better, but the important parts left me riding the wave to who knows where. *I'd like to be in control,* I told myself. *What other choices do I have?* Something deep inside says, *Ride it out!*

Chapter 16

Words of Hope

Norm worked at Weyerhaeuser Paper Mill when I married him. He also started to work as a carpenter, helping build the four-plex right next to the first house we bought on North First Avenue in Kelso. Both jobs were full time. We bought some printing equipment and put it in the one car garage next to our house. With this equipment, I started a printing business; even though, I was pregnant again with my second child.

My mother said the lithographic equipment looked like it belonged in a garbage dump, replacing the word equipment with "garbage." It was old, but it did the job when somebody knowledgeable, such as Norm, operated it, and it cost only $2,000.

Months and months of tears—every day and almost every minute of my waking hours—they flowed like water from the time I got up at 6 a.m. until I went to bed at midnight. Norm even started a joke: "You don't have anything to do in between midnight and 6. We'll have to get you another job."

His words weren't very funny. To me, they were barbed and cutting, tearing out more anger and pain. He didn't have the least inkling as to how I felt. Still, it was only a joke, and I had to hold onto every ounce of focusing.

My baby, "MySher"—my adorable little girl—sometimes I thought I cried for her. With my efforts so focused on immediate accomplishments, she would definitely be lacking for attention.

My unborn child, I could still carry him around with me…in my belly. My eating habits of catching a few bites on the run would possibly have some effect on him, to say nothing about how I felt. One thought that brought me closer to accepting the situation, without trying to change it, was that God fed a multitude of people on a very small amount of food. Maybe what I did eat would suffice.

Tommy had taught me: "Trying is not good enough. You have to do it." These words still rang in my brain like a giant bell. *There's no giving up…not today…not tomorrow. I just hope God will help me. A little prayer never hurts*, my mind concluded. So, I repeated one. No one knows how difficult it is to learn some jobs the hard way until they've tried it themselves. With Norm working two jobs, he had little more than enough time to tell me where the "off" and "on" switches were. A bare minimum of the basics was offered for the rest.

The phone rang; I answer it in tears. I knew it had to be Norm. He was calling from work to ask how was I doing.

"Okay, I guess. The floor is two feet deep in papers. Papers are flying every which way."

"Why are papers flying every which way?" He asked with a patina of calmness in his voice. He could remain calm through an earthquake.

"I don't know. I just put the paper in. I adjust the printing press. I flip the switch on, and papers fly all over the place. That's not all: Sometimes the print is light, and sometimes there's black streaks all across the page. Everything is wrong. I don't know how to work this…thing. I don't know how to take the negatives, either." In the lithographic process of offset printing, one had to put the copy into a large camera, adjusting it according to focus and size. Photographs, taken much like x-rays, were then put on an offset plate to burn imagines on it. The plate was then put on the press, picking up imagines where the bright lights had burned though the lighter parts of the negative.

"That's not hard to figure out," he tried not to sound too knowledgeable. "Black streaks across the page means you have too much ink."

"Oh, yeah," I butted in. "It's easy for you to say. You don't have to do it."

"Light copy means you have too much water solution," he continued in a calm voice. "Slow down, take one step at a time and try to reach a happy medium. Go back and re-adjust your paper intake," he further advised.

"It sounds ridiculous, but I'm not really sure what a paper intake is. Do you mean where the paper goes into the press."

"Yes, that's it. You'll need to adjust it, so the press will accept only one sheet of paper at a time."

"I've already done that for about the thousandth time," I screamed out in frustration.

"Try it one more time, but this time take each step more slowly. Make sure you have it right before going to the next," he calmly persuaded. During the five to ten minute phone call, he further explained the differences in paper weight and the process of adjusting the paper intake.

Once he hung up, I started talking to myself: "He sounds like Tommy now; forever pushing…pushing me to do better. He does have more patience though. And Tommy wouldn't be that nice about it," my mind concluded out loud. "Back to the drawing board for about the thousandth time; if that doesn't work, it'll be one thousand and one. I better get to it, if I ever want to get done with this job in time." *I'm not only talking to myself but answering myself as well. I've heard that it's okay to talk to yourself, but when you start answering yourself too, you're losing it. Oh well, I've got to get some answers somehow.* "If I can get through this job, maybe I'll learn a little more for the next."

Just a few months old, Sherry soon became a handful. Like other children I suppose, she got into everything and climbed even to the top of the kitchen cupboards. She seemed more like a monkey than a human being when it came to climbing. I couldn't even turn my back on her. She would be out in the middle of the street naked in two minutes flat and screaming to the top of her lungs following a bath. I didn't have enough time to pull the plug of the kitchen sink, where I gave her baths. Every week her room had to be redone because she emptied all the drawers, scattering her clothes all over the floor. Thinking back: *This was the same thing that Tommy's girlfriend, Nancy*, did.* It was a definite indication she needed more attention. Now it helped me understand Nancy more, instead of judging her. My thoughts slipped back into judging: *She was an adult and should have known better, and Sherry is only a child.* Nancy had never grown up. She still needed attention and acceptance from others. I really didn't have the time to reason it out. My first obligation should've been to give my daughter the attention she needed. Instead, the job at hand took priority over it.

If only Sherry would lighten up, I would have more time to give her; the thought briefly intermingled with the others. Too busy to think to any extent, I rushed on toward acquiring what I thought to be my own family's security. I even prayed a prayer for God to help me be able to support my family.

Nothing was safe…not even Sherry herself. The first week in business, she smeared several pounds of black ink all over her body. She looked like a little "tar baby" for weeks, because it was too hard to remove. I thought she was just expressing her personality.

It wasn't long before Norm decided to buy a small newspaper in the nearby town of Kalama. I was eight months pregnant with Myron when we purchased it. Norm started his persuasion to encourage me to take the next step in business. "No time like the present for doing something. Otherwise, things are often put off for a life-time by saying 'not now.'" So we bought the Kalama Bulletin, a small town newspaper founded in 1889.

A stairway of words, leading to perfection, would be next on the agenda. A backward girl from North Carolina with very little education, how was I going to accomplish all the responsibilities that went along with owning a newspaper, even if it was a small one? I'd already learned how to operate equipment I'd never seen before. Now, I would have to learn much more, without even a high school diploma. I reached ahead, toward the ladder of words as if they were stars, desperately grabbing with all my might: Respect, discipline, dependability, reliability, honesty, work, effort, patience, persistence, love, honor, belief, endurance, strength. With every constant effort, I pulled myself higher and higher onto each rung of self-taught realism. Yes, the words I knew, but to put them into a real life situation of accomplishments…was like reaching for the stars. I seemed to fall short. As one effort accounts for only one star in the sky, too numerous to mention even a tiny portion, so are my endeavors.

Since I already had Sherry and was eight months along with Myron, Norm thought some help would be beneficial. Don Mowry, Norm's coworker at Weyerhaeuser, and his wife, Mae, ventured into this phase of the business with us. Norm and Don decided Mae should be the one to operate the linotype, since she had seven years experience in a bank. With only three months of typing at Lower Columbia College, a local college, it was obvious I'd take whatever was left over—in this case, the proofreading. My spelling was just as lousy as my typing. They handed me the dictionary. "How am I expected to find a word, if I don't know how to spell it?" I asked. "You'll learn," Norm said.

It was January 18, 1966, when I walked into the Monticello Stationers, a stationery store in Longview, to get supplies with a new dress on. Lucy had an old skirt that she was going to pitch in the garbage. I told her I wanted it to make a smock. I added one of my old blouses to it; reshaping it here and there and cutting it off to make it shorter, I ended up with a beautiful pink smock. It had a high waist and three-quarter sleeves. Unlike the normal style with a bow in front, I wanted it to have a bow in back to show off my pregnancy. The owner of the stationery store looked at me with surprise as I walked through the door. "I never knew you were pregnant," she said. "You've been coming here once a week for some time now. I never would have guessed you were pregnant, if you hadn't been wearing that dress. When are you due?" She added. "Almost anytime now. The doctor says it will be February 5th; I say it will be the 3rd."

Myron was born February 3rd. When I went in the hospital, they started to send me home after checking me over, but the doctor showed up in time to take me back. The nurse said I looked like I couldn't be over two months at the most. The doctor told the nurse, "Don't you know everyone is different?"

I actually didn't like Myron for a name, but those nurses at the hospital kept bugging me for a name. Apparently, they didn't know how tired I was. I would have told them anything to get them to shut up. I went through three days of hard labor to the point of sweat popping out on me as big as my little finger. One nurse held up the sheet and rung it out in a container, as if it had been dipped in water. They gave me three hypos, which seemed more like aspirin. Even the nurse in the delivery room cried. I looked up at the nurse and said, "These men, they just don't understand." Then I looked up toward heaven and told God, "If you're ever going to help me, you'd better help me now." The doctor called me every name in the book. He later said he did that to make me fight to stay alive. He said if the baby had weighed seven pounds, we would have both died. He didn't get to the hospital in time to take him cesarean. Myron was already in the birth canal. He weighed six pounds, seven ounces. I went back to work the same day I got out of the hospital.

Myron was a very unusual child. He would cry more when I picked him up than when I left him lying in his crib. I had less time to spend with him than I had with Sherry. Besides, Sherry demanded every free moment that I could possibly spare.

He was continually getting pneumonia and was hospitalized several times, staying in the hospital up to five days. I asked Norm if I could visit him, and he told me, "You have work to do. He won't even know you're there. He's only a baby."

All the more reason to see him, I thought, *I will know.* "He needs to feel wanted," I said. "Babies feel, don't they?"

"He'll be totally unaware that you're there," he said.

"I want to go anyway," I told him.

"We can't get all this work done without you," he said. "You'll just be wasting your time." Even though I believed that men were the king of their household, that they were the boss, I obeyed, but I started turning against him after that.

Myron would no more than get out the hospital and he would get pneumonia again, even before he finished a bottle of medicine. The doctor told me in his fancy language that I wasn't giving him his medicine. I didn't say anything to the doctor, but underneath I was boiling mad. When I got home, I told Norm what the doctor had said and decided to do something on my own. He was only ten months old when I took him off his bottle. I got up in the middle of the night to feed him or give him juice, water, or anything, except milk. I don't know how I learned that milk was bad for someone with pneumonia; I just knew I had to do something. Taking him off the bottle was the right thing to do. He has never had pneumonia since.

A little more than six months into the business, Don's doctor told him he would either have to get out or have a nervous breakdown.

The wife of the previous owner was the only replacement for Mae. Not very many people had ever seen letter press equipment dated back to the late 1800's. The Kalama Bulletin, its equipment, and the equipment I'd started out with all had something in common: they were the first to enter Cowlitz County. (Many years later, Norm donated some of the equipment to the Cowlitz County Museum.)

When a correction for a mistake took more space than the mistake itself, like a word being left out, the rest of the paragraph would have to be retyped. Because of this reason—the type being set in lead on a Linotype—I generally had to work all night on Tuesdays, our deadline. Norm sometimes worked up to forty-two hours without any sleep. I worked up to thirty-eight. Often I would fall asleep on a cold, hardwood floor from being exhausted.

It didn't take long to figure out, "Maybe I can do a better job of this by making fewer mistakes." I had about three-quarters of the paper to retype anyway. It all had to be redone on the last day of publication, which gave me very little time. Within three weeks I doubled Mae's production with fewer mistakes.

I felt pushed all the time. One day I was doing job orders such as printing envelopes or forms for local businesses, the next day it was bookkeeping, the day after it was reporting, and so on. After the newspapers were addressed I threw two eighty pounds sacks full, one across each shoulder, and carried them a block to the post office.

At the beginning I cried a lot, as before, because I felt more and more burdened. I faced each day with a multitude of new things to learn. I dried my tears to answer the doorbell; then when the customer left I returned to the crying state. I dreaded to even answer the telephone. People called for all kinds of reasons: to hopefully get some free legal advice, to give us advice, to dictate legals or news items that needed every word precisely stated, or just to chat. I developed my own style of shorthand, but felt I didn't have time for idle chatter.

No one knew how I felt. *Am I too shy to do such a simple task as answer the phone or am I afraid of failure?* I remembered some past experiences: A friend used to drop by after work to see me before I married Norm. I went into the bedroom, closing the door behind me and turning on the record player. I left Mom in the kitchen to talk to him. Another incident when I was staying with Aunt Ruth in Atlanta: It was the first time in my life I'd ever seen a telephone, much less answer one. "Is that how a person feels every time they have something new to learn?" I asked myself. *Those feelings have passed and these will pass too.*

Four months later an elderly lady—probably in her early 60's—stepped through the doorway. Introducing herself as Emma Long, she announced she was going to work for us as a bookkeeper. She didn't ask for the job; she commanded it.

While she was inside talking to me, Norm was outside placing a sign above the office door. With his hands reaching high to nail the sign in place, his shirt went up and his pants went down, so one could see his crack. It was embarrassing. Two older ladies passed by about that time. That was even more embarrassing. "Norm, pay attention to what you're doing; your butt's showing," I pointed out, while briefly opening the door to hear one say to the other, "Well…I never."

"That phrase is as old as the equipment I have to work with," I told the lady in front of me. With their eyes bugged and their mouths open, we could see them mumbling though the glass front as they walked down the street.

Norm just smiled and took it light heartily, as he did with most other things. The lady in front of me did the same. Although she was commanding in her attitude, she was calm and easy-going. She had matured very gracefully with respect for everyone.

I admired her boldness; silently wishing I could be more like her. I told her, "We really can't afford to have a bookkeeper."

"You can't afford not to have one," she replied. "I won't charge you very much. I can also help with the walk-in customers."

Great! Maybe she's an answer to my prayer for help, I thought. I just didn't know how we were going to come up with the money to pay her. "Okay! We'll give it a try. We may have to cut back every now and then. As long as you understand that, we should make it work eventually." I felt like I was being forced to accept her help. *Maybe this is God's way of saying I'm supposed to have faith that it will be taken care of without knowing how.*

A very observing personality, Emma read me like a book almost immediately, as if she knew what I was thinking. Identical to my own senses: This had always been one of my traits. We seemed to be reading each other. To meet someone who could surpass me was quite exciting. *I like her,* my mind concluded. We chatted sporadically. I found out she had the same birthday as me. "Martha, you worry a lot about your mistakes, don't you?" She asked during one of our conversations. Her words sounded more like a statement than a question.

"Yes," I answered. "Aren't you suppose to? Norm doesn't seem to care. Did you see the double page add he put together last week? Here, look!" I showed her the center page grocery add that read "Stake" across the top of the page in 72 point lettering. "I don't think it could've been much bigger." It was obvious the add should have read "Steak." I don't have time to proof read all his work," I explained.

She laughed, "It sure got lots of attention…You'll have more time now." I laughed too, the first time in months, an indication that she'd relieved some of the burdens I was feeling.

"If you don't make any mistakes, you don't do anything to make them." She offered her words of wisdom, just like Tommy had done so often. These were words I needed to hear. Even if they were in a forceful tone like his, I gathered she cared. It was just her way.

As this lady appeared in my life, so did my self-confidence. My tears vanished. She offered a lifeline in this horrifying world with her acts of goodness—just a few kind words of understanding and encouragement.

We moved into a better building. I moved into a better frame of mind. I helped Norm move the equipment and three-phase motors, some of the motors weighing more than 300 pounds. My time for sadness had passed. Emma was just what I needed to move to a higher star in the sky. We hired a few other employees. New growth had begun.

Norm and I became involved with most community activities and organizations. I advanced to the other side of my personality like a flip of a coin. I told a Jayceette, Junior Chamber of Commerce Auxiliary, member how shy I was when I first came to Kalama. Relating the story about me going into the bedroom to get away from the friend that came to see me when I first came to Washington, I added, "I even dreaded to answer the telephone when I first came to Kalama."

She didn't believe me and expressed, "I was afraid of you when we first met." Her answer to "why?" was: "It was your eyes. You looked at me as if you could see right through me. I thought you could even read my thoughts." That's how Emma looked at me, but I wasn't afraid of her.

I didn't want people to be afraid of me. So I began to blink more often or look away somewhat. I never wanted to lose the power, strength, and control they portrayed. I just wanted to conceal it a little to avoid making people feel afraid or intimidated.

Norm, president of the local Chamber, became sick the same day of the installation. With him home—sick and in bed, as well as both kids—I went to work alone. Arriving there at 6:30 a.m., the entire south end of town was flooded. I called our employees, telling them not to come in because of the situation. Knee-deep in ice cold water, on our publishing day, I began making plans to clean up the mess and prepare for the Chamber banquet.

Roy Trull, a long-time friend of Tommy's and mine, owned a truck. I knew he would be willing to help. Roy and I moved two truckloads of floating paper from the premises before I stopped to think about the next step.

After preparing each phase of the Chamber agenda and printing it as well, very little time was left to complete the newspaper. Our publishing day would have to be delayed.

Returning home and stepping into "Cinderella" shoes, I dressed in a purple and white gown for the installation and awards banquet. Norm wasn't able to attend. On his behalf I accepted his awards. My awards were my accomplishments to make it to this point. I felt grateful.

I learned to take things in order of priority and try not to expect any more, or any less, than I was able to give for a brief period of my life. All the words of self-improvement, I'd learned from Tommy. Accepting myself as I truly was, I learned from Emma Long. Starting at that point, I could learn to improve.

"Expecting too much from ourselves causes frustration," she later commented. "It works like a scale: Self-expectation is on one end and preparation for a task is on the other. Our expectation outweighs our preparation, causing the scale to be out of balance. This can be corrected when our preparation (our education) for the task catches up, which will relieve our anxieties. To have faith that everything will turn out okay is important too." Emma was well educated in book learning as well as having a higher form of wisdom. These things, reinforced in my mind by Emma, swung me to the next rung on the star-stepping ladder of words, leading me into the future. They eventually became a way of life and were embedded into my spirit. I hung on like glue. *Maybe—just maybe I could make it one step higher than the half-way point.*

The self-expectations later came back because of the drilled words that Tommy had taught me while growing up, molding me into a perfectionist. The kind of person I was had already been established. It was hard to expect less of myself than I was able to give when I'd been taught: "You have to do it, or die trying."

The stars, as bright as a supernova twirling in space and depicted here symbolically, represent words of hope. In another way they are unlike the supernova; their brightness will last forever. Because of them and the people in my life, I will go on making one step after another through a sky of brightness, losing more fear with each step I take.

Chapter 17

Ups and Downs

For the most part, Norm and I didn't have much time for friends the first ten years of our marriage. We went to work together and come home together, except during some of his travels to a Washington State Jaycee (Junior Chamber of Commerce) convention or some other related function. Sometimes I went with him. He was the P.R. (public relations) man in business, and I was the doer. Shortly after the move into a better building on Main Street in Kalama, he became the editor/publisher of the Washington State Jaycee magazine, a monthly publication for the Junior Chamber of Commerce, and attended many of the organization's functions. Later he also became editor/ publisher of the Oregon and Idaho State publications as well.

I felt like we even went to the bathroom together. He would shave while I took a bath, or one of us would use the commode, while the other took a shower. If I went to the bathroom without him, he would say, "What're ya doing?" (Today's answer to that one would be "I'm down loading.") Even some of our employees at work began to notice the closeness and commented on it. "I don't see how you can spend so much time together," our secretary, Margaret Moore, stated one afternoon. "My husband and I would be at each other throats if we spent that much time together."

"Let's do something special tonight when we get home—something that doesn't involve work." I told him while driving home. "The house is in a mess. I haven't stayed home long enough to clean it up. How can we clean it up and do something special too? Back to work again. That involves work," I said with a slight laugh of a sarcastic tone in my voice. "It's got to be clean before I can feel anything special."

"I'll help you do it," he promised. "It won't be all that bad. You'll see. How about a French dinner with candlelight?"

"Sounds great…but that's a mighty big chore. Do you think we can pull it off before daybreak? It's already 7 o'clock."

"Yes…of course we can," was his answer. He was always optimistic about everything, and I felt like I could do anything by his side. Together, we were good in business, and we were best friends. His calm, easy-going personality fitted well with my high-strung, caring nature.

When we arrived home both the kids, Sherry and Myron, were in bed. Our babysitter was in bed too with her boyfriend. Very few things made Norm angry, but this did. "Get dressed!" he demanded. Anger flushed his face. Encouraging him to calm down a little was like trying to slow down a fast moving freight train with nothing to do it with except your bare hands. Lifting both of them off the floor by the seat of their pants, he pitched them out the door. She was near six feet tall and not skinny by no means, and her boyfriend was as big as she was—an incredible task even for a big man.

"Well, that took a little bit of time. Are you sure you still want to continue with our plans?" I asked.

"Yes," he answered. "I'm not going to let a little thing like that stop me."

What a man? What a man? "It wasn't so little, or at least, I didn't think it was. How did you do that?"

"Just do it," he now answered with a smile in a calm, easy mannered way, much like his usual self.

At the stroke of midnight the table was ready with candlelight, and the fire in the fireplace was burning brightly. He carried to the table a burning platter. When the flames died down, he bent over to kiss me.

What a surprise? I was astounded. He'd done all the cooking, while I did all the cleaning. "I didn't know you could cook like this," I told him.

"You know I can cook," he said. Together we'd prepared banquets for as many as three hundred people.

Norm's best friend, Ken Watson, was just as active in the organizations as Norm was and helped us prepare those dinners. I'd stood up at one of the formal banquets and called them "the odd couple." That was the biggest laugh of the evening. We briefly recalled the incident while eating dinner.

Norm went all out during those times, making matching placemats and menus in the foreign language they represented as well as the interpretation in English. His books never failed him. He could find anything he wanted to know in them—even to cooking an international dinner and making it fit for a king.

"I knew you could cook, but this is a little extravagant, don't you think? It's beautiful. It's everything I don't have words for. And I didn't think you'd have enough time…It's perfect."

After dinner we undressed, sat in the middle of the floor naked holding hands, and performed a séance. This evening was the little something I needed to add some variety.

Our lives together were never boring. There were plenty of down times too. Sometimes we laughed, sometimes we cried, sometimes we loved, and sometimes we fought. Our secretary didn't think we fought at all, but she didn't know everything.

Norm's brother, Walter, who was a deaf mute, started living with us. Tired after a hard day, I came home from work in a bitchy mood more often than not. While cooking dinner and washing dishes at the same time, Walter generally sat on the couch, watching TV. He actually had the nerve to ask me to make him a pie. Since Walter was his brother, I felt it was his responsibility to tell him to help me.

My bitchiness escalated to the point where Norm got tired of it. He bent my arm back while I was standing over the sink washing the dishes. I told him to turn my arm loose at least three times, but he didn't. With the other hand, I picked up the hot coffee setting to the left of the sink and pitched it in his face. He came unglued, but he didn't hit me. He turned around bringing his arm down over the opened oven door and demolished it. Then he turned and hit the kitchen table. It buckled.

There was no stopping: I continued with my bitchiness. The argument was later staged in the bedroom, where he pushed me against the headboard, cutting my head. I should have gone to the hospital to get stitches. Instead I lie down on the bed, next to a large circle of blood, too exhausted to move. "Okay, you win this time. Next time I'm going to whip your ass." He snickered at my words. "Go ahead and laugh. Your time a coming, buddy. I mean what I say. I'm too tired to do it right now, but next time I'm going to whip you."

The next time came and I knew it would. We'd gone out that night. Afterwards we picked up the kids at the babysitter's who was Norm's half sister. I was wearing a royal blue suit with a fur collar. Not wanting to argue with him, I thought it would be better just to go out, sit in the truck, and wait for him while we both cooled off. Because he thought I was going to leave him, he reached and grabbed me, yanking my top from my body in front of everyone. They were having a card game and their house was full. It's a good thing I was wearing a slip. I continued walking toward the truck, with him grabbing at me, because I didn't want to cause a scene. "No, you're not going to leave," he demanded, grabbing me and holding me back. I took off my high heel shoe and beat him with it until I got tired. While he was bending back the forefinger of my left hand, I managed to reach an empty quart beer bottle laying in their yard and picked it up. "Turn my finger loose," I told him, "or go to the hospital for about four months." He not only turned my finger loose, but he started crying. The fight then ended. Everyone in town laughed at him for weeks. Both his eyes were black and blue. He had scratch marks, some more than a foot-long all over him, which I didn't remember doing. People in Kalama asked him, "You let that little girl whip you?" Naturally his only reply was "Yes," with a shy grin on his face.

Some time later, Margaret did have the opportunity to see us fighting. I'd been selling fair princess tickets all day. My goal was to reach one hundred dollars. I'd taken the fair princess candidate out to the businesses in Woodland and Kalama selling the tickets at one dollar each. Since we owned the newspaper in Kalama, most of the business owners in both towns knew me. Most of them knew Norm too, for he had brought the Kalama Fair from a dying state to a pretty good size fair and was very active in many organizations around town. The manager of the grain elevator in Kalama bought the first ticket and asked all of his employees to line up. We sold quite a few there. By the end of the day, I needed to sell only six more tickets to reach my goal. The local Jaycees and Jayceettes (the women's auxiliary) met at a Woodland bar to celebrate. From time to time during the evening I excused myself, so I could sell the other six. Norm reached under the table and pinched me on the leg. It was like having a pair of pliers grab my tight skin and twist it. Tears came to my eyes and dripped from my face faster than I could wipe them away. In the dim lighting, I thought I could conceal them, but Margaret was the first to notice something wrong. "Norm got jealous, because I was talking to some people," I explained to the group—it now being too late to hide my tears any longer. "I just wanted to sell a hundred dollars in tickets before the day was out. He pinched me under the table. I don't understand why, because I was talking to older people and couples. I wasn't talking to any young guys." His explanation was I should've let the other girls sell them. I had sold enough, and they weren't doing anything. The people there thought that wasn't a very nice way to handle the situation, and neither did I. It didn't fit into Norm's personality either. Nobody's perfect, but this was carrying things a little too far, plus doing it the wrong way. "This was my goal, not theirs," I told him. "They can set goals of their own." Since the night was ruined anyway we decided to go home. The fighting continued out in the street. By that time I was no longer tying to cover it up from anyone.

After that Margaret, as well as the general public, viewed another fight. At a Jaycee crab feed Norm heaped his plate to measure a foot or more in crabs. It was embarrassing. He didn't seem to care. "With your plate heaped that high, people are going to think you haven't eaten in a month," I said, and tried to walk away from him again. As before, he grabbed me. I turned around and slap him as hard as I could, knocking his beer out of his hand. How he managed to hang on to the plate of crabs was beyond me, but he did. The beer went all over the barmaid's new, white dress. She was angry. "Norm, since you're the cause of it, give her the money to have it cleaned," I said and tried to walk off again, but this time justifying my actions, "I'm just going over there to sit down."

The pinch on the leg, as well as the way I felt about him not wanting me to visit Myron in the hospital when he was a baby, were straws that helped break the camel's back. As time went on, other straws finished breaking it. One of them happened on New Years Eve. Except for some kind of Jaycee deal, which I didn't consider recreation, we didn't go out much—maybe twice a year when some of Norm's relatives came down from Seattle.

Our daughter, Sherry, had now grown up and was living in Seattle. She sent her son, Brandon, down to visit with us for a few days. We had kept Brandon a major portion of his life, since she'd had him when she was only fifteen. This New Years Eve was the only time I ever needed a babysitter for him. Most of the time girls would line up to do the job, totally free of charge and insisted on having it that way. He was such an adorable little boy. I told Norm that a simple dinner out and a movie would be enough since we had to take care of Brandon. He was only seven. Norm not only approved, he thought it was a good idea.

One of my friends came by at four o'clock in the afternoon. Apparently Norm got restless. He used this as an excuse to get out of the house. "I'm going to visit Tom (a friend of his) for awhile," he said. "You girls can talk better if I'm out of the way." She mentioned she would be leaving shortly. He insisted on going anyway. When she left I called Tom and he said that Norm hadn't showed up.

I stayed home with Brandon alone. Norm came in about three in the morning, so drunk he couldn't even hit the wall unless he staggered against it. He'd lost about three hundred dollars gambling. I thought to myself, *no wonder*. He was an excellent pan player and seldom lost at it. Once he got involved in a game of stud poker, then came the losses, and as drunk as he was "no wonder."

After we had discussed and he had promised both Brandon and I that we'd have a fun night together, this would make anybody mad, I thought.

I stopped bitching after that and started doing something. I wanted a divorce, but he wouldn't let me go. After I tried to get rid of him in every way I could think of, I started going out without him. Most of the time when he asked to go with me I simply said, "No, you're not going." Sometimes I went out with a boyfriend. I went with one for three years and another for about the same length of time. I even went to see an old boyfriend I fell in love with when I was seventeen and first came to Washington. His name was Hugh Temple*. I went out with Hugh only once and Norm knew it. Whenever he asked where I'd been I told him the truth. He asked how mud got on the bumper of my new Cougar, and I told him I'd went to see an old boyfriend. That was Hugh. Norm just dropped the subject. Most of the time I went out with an elderly couple who had moved into a house across the street, Faye and John Longbrake.

One night when I was out driving alone I saw three young girls, slightly younger than Sherry, hitchhiking. No way would I want my own daughter out there on the road, so I picked them up and took them about a hundred miles out of my way. Because I'd taken the time to go in their place of residence and talk to their foster parents, I got back home at seven o'clock the next morning. I told Norm the truth about this too. Who's to say whether he believed me or not—he didn't say.

It looked like the table had turned. At the beginning of our marriage, Norm sometimes went out with the boys and stayed until nine o'clock the next morning. He said he'd been playing pool all night, and used his public relations with the group as an excuse. Even though it sounded unbelievable, I'm sure this was at least partially the truth. Norm wasn't the type to go out on me.

Most people were like Margaret. They never saw the hidden parts of our marriage. Except for the two incidents, they saw mostly the things I did against him, because I didn't hide much. Norm's friend, Ken, condemned me for going out on Norm. I figured he had a right. He wouldn't even speak to me for years. Finally when I told his daughter some of the details and how I felt about what Norm had done to me, especially his gambling, he began to speak to me somewhat. I suppose he came to the conclusion that there're two sides to every story.

I told Norm I loved him, but I wasn't in love with him. I thought that I would eventually fall in love with him, but I never did. He asked, "What's the difference?"

"The best way to describe it would be to tell you a little story: It wasn't too long ago an acquaintance at church approached me. He said he'd been going out with a girl that said she loved him, but she wasn't in love with him. He asked the same question you're asking now. It was Easter. Walking through the churchyard, a man was holding a little three-year-old girl's hand. He was looking down at her with a smile on his face talking to her. Anyone could see he loved her. I pointed toward them saying, 'There's an example. He loves her, you can tell. But he's not in love with her. He doesn't have any physical attraction toward her.'" Then I added, "I love Jeanie (a neighbor), down the street, but I'm not in love with her." He still refused to see the difference. He saw only what he wanted to see, possibly because his need wouldn't let him see otherwise. He knew he was going to die, and he didn't want to die alone. Maybe I was in love with him when we first married, because there was some physical attraction then. Now, it had died altogether. I not only slept in a different bedroom, but I slept on a different floor, in Sherry's old bedroom.

There aren't any perfect people—everyone knows that. There's just happy mediums or semi-happy mediums. A relationship works much like a checking account: When your minuses exceed your pluses, you become overdrawn. For each bad incident, a couple goes one more step into the red, the distance between each other getting wider with each step. It may seem strange, but we have to go through all the bad steps to get back to the good. Then, and only then can our love for each other grow.

Chapter 18

Friends and Neighbors

Both Faye and John Longbrake were friendly, heavy-set people. They moved into a little house across the street. I thought of them as being jolly. Welcoming Faye's friendly attitude, I gave her a front row seat in my theater of worldly dramas.

A long time had passed since my first friendships in Washington. Mamie Cochran had taken that place. Now living in Alabama, Mamie came back to see me only once in a great while. Sue Parker, a cousin, and Shirley Parker, who married Uncle Fred, came next. Sue got married and moved away. Shirley must have been in her early thirties when she died. She got a divorce from Fred and remarried. Her second husband killed her. Linda Mosteller, who later became Linda Carter, was one friend I kept fairly close contact with from the very beginning.

Faye and I visited each other at least once or twice a week. Sometimes we walked to the little store on North Pacific, talking all the way. Naturally, we told each other about different parts of our life.

As it so often does in Washington, it was slightly raining one day on the way to the store. A neighbor's little three-year-old girl and her older sister of about six were outside just walking up and down the street in the sprinkling rain. I wouldn't have noticed it so readily if the weather had been suitable.

"Their mother should pay closer attention to those kids," I told Faye. "I should go in and talk to her. They're going to get killed by a car or something bad is going to happen."

"They're always in the street," Faye responded. "She never looks after them."

"Yeah, but I feel uneasy this time," I said. Walking back to their home to tell their mother, I stopped, asking Faye and also asking myself, "How am I going to tell her she should keep a closer eye on her children? She'll probably just get mad and tell me it's none of my business."

"They'll be alright," Faye contended. "They've been doing that for as long as I've lived here."

On the way back from the store, the little girl was lying in the street, totally helpless. "Oh no," I said. "I should have talked to their mother."

"She wouldn't have listened to you anyway," Faye said.

"It looks like one of her ears are missing," I noticed, as we crossed the street to go into my house. "I never wanted anything bad to happen to her kids, but it's a little late for that now." The little girl was dead on arrival at the hospital.

Faye came into the house to visit with me for awhile. I didn't drink very much, but I generally kept a bottle of Black Velvet, her favorite, on hand. I offered her a drink and she accepted. She generally drank about half a fifth each time she came.

A few days later I went to her place to visit. She wanted me to tell her fortune almost every time I went to her place. As we sat down at the kitchen table, she greeted me in the usual fashion, "How about us going halves on a pint of whiskey?" John went after the bottle.

"How long am I going to live?" she asked, as I dealt out the cards. "Will I live longer than John?"

"You know Faye, you shouldn't ask those kinds of questions. You might not like the answer for one thing," I advised, "and especially now. It's been only a few days since the little girl died in the street." Most of the time I was bold and straight-forward with my comments.

"How did you know something was going to happen to her?" Faye solemnly asked.

"I just have a feeling. I don't know where it come from. It's something inside me. When I don't want to know the answer, I block those feelings. They should come through naturally. If I block them, you may not get the right answer anyway."

"I want to know how long am I going to live," she insisted, and continued bugging me.

She seemed healthy enough, although she was nearing her sixties. Both Faye and John were quite a bit older than I was. John was a retired timber faller.

I didn't want to lie to her by telling her something she wanted to hear. I wanted to tell her the truth. Instead, I told her a story about a guy at work. He had kept on me to tell him his fortune when I didn't want to. "He wouldn't shut up until I gave in and told him his wife was going to leave him. He not only didn't believe me, but he got mad."

"Did it ever happen?" She asked.

"I saw him much later with another guy I used to work with. We sat down and talked over old times. He told me his fortune was right on. They had been separated for years."

Faye continued with her request. Just to get her to shut up, I told her she would live to be an old woman and outlive John, exactly the opposite of what I thought.

After having a couple drinks and finishing her fortune I went home. On the way, it crossed my mind that I'd been holding back the truth as I'd done earlier in regards to the children. This time, it wasn't going to hurt anyone by not knowing the truth, just as it would have helped my co-worker not to know. Sometimes it was hard for me to know what was against my neighbor and what wasn't. This time, I felt sure I wasn't doing anything against Faye by telling her a lie.

It also crossed my mind that maybe I wasn't such a good fortune-teller after all. Maybe it was just a good observation. The man I worked with was somewhat like another person I knew, who was too afraid to give. He didn't seem to be the type that deposited enough to a relationship. As for Faye, she was a smoker and a fairly heavy drinker. The little girl was in the street most of the time, just like Faye said. In all cases, it could have been a logical assumption.

I looked forward to going out with Faye and John. Most of my life consisted of work otherwise. The Riverview in Rainier, Oregon, was a favorite spot. The last time Norm and I had gone with them, John's drink was too weak, he thought. He mentioned it to the waitress. She told him, "They use a dispenser here." He came back in a husky voice, "Yeah, it dispensed it so fast it missed my glass." After the waitress returned to her station John said, "Let's get out of here."

Afterwards we went to their place and played strip poker for several hours. Hiding portions of our nakedness under the kitchen tablecloth, Faye lost all of her clothes, and I lost most of mine. She wasn't necessarily the modest type, she just thought of herself as having equal rights to men. I lost most of my inhibitions by being around her.

She brought up the subject of her lampshade. Norm had gotten drunk some time ago, falling against her lampshade and braking it when we started to go home. Thinking that I should do something to repay her, I'd made a scrape-work quilt, worth several times over what a lampshade would cost, and gave it to her. I specifically stated that that was the reason for giving it to her. It was my way of accepting responsibility for him. I believed if you're married to someone, or even living with them, you should be responsible for them. I hadn't seen many men that were responsible for themselves. A few months had past since then, but now she brought up the subject again. "Faye, I told you when I first gave you the quilt that that was to pay you back for Norm breaking your lampshade. I also told you that the quilt was worth a lot more than your lampshade."

"Yeah, but I can't get a matching lampshade," she said.

"In that case, buy two. You'll still come out ahead —quite a bit."

To put it bluntly, she was too stingy to buy even one lampshade. I had seen her ask her stepdaughter to pay her back a quarter she'd borrowed to play penny-ante poker. Faye still wanted me to buy her some lampshades and brought the subject up more than once. "Well, I'm not going to. I've already paid you back with more than enough."

Faye came to visit me a few days later. "What's that hanging out of the window across the street?" I asked her, as she stepped through the front door. We both went out to catch a better look. "No one would believe this. It's a little boy's bare butt," I answered my own question. "He's going potty out the window."

Faye filled in the details. "They don't have a toilet," she said.

"Why," I asked.

"It got plugged up, so they just took the toilet out and started 'pooping' down the hole."

I was flabbergasted. "Couldn't they call the landlord to get him to fix it?"

Faye didn't seem to be all that concerned. The neighbors had seen it before, she explained. "Yeah, they could…if they didn't care about the landlord seeing their nasty house."

"I knew she was nasty, but this takes the cake. Every time I've gone over there they've had a blanket covering the door to the kitchen. That must have been why."

"She recently visited a relative. While she was gone, her boyfriend hauled three truckloads to the dump out of the kitchen alone, and it still looks like shit. They used a shovel to scrape the filth off the floor," Faye continued.

"You said 'they.' Did he have help?" I asked.

"Yes, he needed it," she responded.

"We should call the city or do something about it," I told her.

"It won't do any good. They know it. The Welfare sent a person out to teach her how to clean her house, but that didn't do any good either."

The little boy that had his butt sticking out the window was the brother that went to marshal arts with Brandon, our grandson, twice a week. Brandon stayed with us most of the time. He wanted someone his own age to go with, so I paid his friend's way for six months. I was heavily involved with work and other domestic chores. I asked his mother to take the boys once a week. I wanted her to split the responsibility of taking them. She never took them even once. I told Faye about it, and added, "The one that plays with Brandon is a little older and a very intelligent little fellow. How did he get to be that smart with his mother being so lazy?"

"She's much better with her kids," Faye said. "She sits around all day on the couch, sometimes reading to them."

"That's a plus, but that doesn't make up for this type of situation," I noted.

"She thinks it does. I think she just does what she wants to do," Faye conjectured.

Faye lived on the same side of the street and closer to her than I did. She didn't work outside the home either. She should know more about it. Later I made a point to see for myself just how bad her house was. It was pretty bad. All that Faye said was true.

"Mom came to see me once when I was working a lot of hours. She said my kids should've been taken away from me. My house has never come no where near what that one is," I told Faye, in a later conversation. "If my house had been anywhere near what that one is, my mother would have told me I might as well not have been born. And I believe she would've been right.

"The little boy that went potty out the window didn't know any better. Why don't they take her kids away?"

"She feeds them and sends them off to school. I suppose they think that's enough."

"I don't know about that either," I told Faye. "Every time her son has come over here, he acts like he hasn't eaten in a week. I felt sorry for them and took her some green beans out of my garden. They were already strung and ready to cook, but they stayed in the kitchen and rotted.

"Oh well, that's not much better than some other renters. I've paid as high as $8,000 to get one place back in shape after one moved out. I've had everything imaginable thrown at me, even to snot boogers on the wall that looked like they'd been deliberately placed there. They say that four out of five people are sick. It looks like if they're not sick in one way, they're sick in another. Can you figure out why? I can't."

Some time later I went to the Blue Ox (or Smoke Shop, one place with two names) with Faye and John. Faye ordered tomato juice with her beer, using only half of it. I used the other half in mine. She told me I would have to buy her another tomato juice. For a while I just sat silently, thinking over what she'd said. "Is something wrong?" She began.

I didn't answer for several minutes, thinking if I did, I'd probably choke her. Getting up from the table, I said, "Yes, there's something definitely wrong. I'm here where I don't belong. Faye, with friends like you I don't need enemies." With them calling me back, I walked out the door.

The tavern was several blocks from home, but I could walk it. Making long strides as I walked home, I thought of all the things I'd done for her and she'd given me so little in return. I not only kept a bottle for her in my home, but I'd taken her out and paid her way all night more than once. If I borrowed money from her and John, I repaid them with interest, sometimes taking them out to a nice dinner. "How is it possible to be so self-centered," I said to myself.

I also needed to judge myself and make some changes to start regaining some of my own self-respect. It would be so easy to have a warped mind in this world of constant incongruousness.

I wasn't mad at John so I continued to go fishing with him occasionally. He wanted me to forgive Faye. He said she was like that because she'd had a life of poverty. "That's no excuse," I told him. "I've had one too." We caught more than our limits of fish, which we hid under the front of the boat and made plans to go again.

He called me at five o'clock in the morning for our next fishing trip. I answered the phone while still half asleep. Dreaming about a boyfriend calling me, I told him to never call me again. It was a long time after that before John forgave me, even though I explained why.

Faye called me later to ask forgiveness for herself. "I'll never do that again," she said, Words of forgiveness were said, but after that we remained distant to each other.

I had spent some time having fun. Now, it was time to work again. I worked so many hours I became totally exhausted. Staying home from work on a Tuesday, the publishing day of the newspaper, I felt if I didn't get some rest I would drop in my tracks.

Another neighbor lady showed up at my door. I went outside to talk to the older lady. She wanted me to do something about our rabbits getting out of their pens and eating up her garden. I told her I couldn't do anything about it, because I was sick. She said, "You don't look sick."

I responded, "I am. I wouldn't have stayed home from work, especially on a Tuesday, if I wasn't."

She wouldn't let the subject rest and kept talking. Being polite, I just stood there and listened for as long as I could. After awhile I said, "I'm sorry. I got-a go." Turning around, I took one step and fainted. Trying to bring me out of it, they put smelling salts under my nose. I would no more than come to, and I would go out again. I couldn't even sit up. It scared almost everyone in the neighborhood out of their wits. They thought I was having an epileptic fit, because I was shivering so badly. Barely conscious, I told them I was cold. They wrapped me in several quilts, and I was still shivering. They called Norm at work and he told them to call an ambulance. The doctor called it a virus and said all I needed was two weeks of rest.

For the next three days I couldn't even lift a spoon to feed myself. Mom took care of me at her place. The images on TV multiplied several times whenever I tried to watch it. Large black splotches showed up in mid air or on the wall, which looked weird. Other than this abnormality and being extremely tired, to the point of being weak, I was normal. After one week, I went back to work.

The lady who had come to see me about the rabbits never approached me after that. Maybe she was afraid she'd start the same thing over again. We never did catch the rabbits; even though, I reminded Norm plenty of times to do it. Being responsible for him had to take a back seat, because I felt like I was killing myself taking care of so many responsibilities. Apparently the rabbits never multiplied to destroy her garden the following year. I didn't see any. They probably died that winter.

A few years later, Faye got cancer and died in her early sixties. As for John, we're still friends, but we don't go out together anymore. Once in a great while, I take him out to breakfast. We don't have anything in common, so we don't have very much to talk about. He's still one of the best friends I've ever known and a nice person to have as a neighbor. It's too bad other friends and neighbors couldn't be more like him.

Martha Harris

Chapter 19

I Was Once There

Twenty some years passed before I arranged to see Hugh Temple* again. The meeting was arranged through his brother. His brother opened a bottle of champagne, which he'd had for years. "I knew a special occasion would come around someday," he said, as he opened it for us. We went to Morton Lake and parked, facing the lake and a full moon. We held each other tight. We kissed. The feelings were still there. Time didn't do a thing for making them go away.

He was married and had three children, but not to the girl he first married. I was married too by that time, to Norm, and had two children of my own. He had become a minister. I asked him why he consented to go out with me, considering the circumstances. He answered, "I'm human too." I thought maybe that his real reason might have been curiosity.

"You've taken me home innocent lots of times," I told him. "This time I'll take you home innocent; at least, innocent to some extent."

I first met Hugh before I met Norm. Some say love at first sight is infatuation. If you don't have much to talk about, it's just a physical attraction. Norm and I had plenty to talk about; we were buddies. I've been a buddy with others; neither of us ran out of words to say to each other. None of those guys put that special feeling in my heart, like Hugh did. With some, I felt only disgust when they touched me. *This can't be love either.* "Mature love is open and honest; it grows stronger, not weaker. It's sure. It makes you want to charge out into the world to do something big; it doesn't keep you cooped up, daydreaming about one person." All this I've heard, and I believe it to a certain extent. Some people also say, with time an infatuation will die. When I met my "puppy love" I knew it was just that, even though it lasted five years. I do believe in love at first sight. I listened to society tell me what they thought love was; I followed their advice, thinking that everybody can't be wrong. Because of this and because of my religious beliefs, I stayed in a marriage to Norm, which was everything this definition gives, for twenty-five years, but it didn't have physical attraction. Many friends, such as Faye Longbrake and Linda Carter, told me that the physical attraction would grow —but it didn't, even after twenty-five years. It got to be less and less. I've been separated from Hugh—my true love—more than forty years now, and it lives just as strong today as it lived then. The only difference now is I deal with differently: I accept reality as it really is.

It still burns brightly inside my heart. I'd like to shake it loose, if I could. I wonder if it will ever die. Probably not, not in this lifetime. Some say there is somebody for everyone. I think I missed mine. I think he missed his too. Maybe he realizes it, or maybe he doesn't. All the words in the world can't change the way things were. All the hoping and praying can't either. With our religious beliefs the way they are, he has to belong to someone else now. *Will love ever come back for me? No, not in this lifetime,* I thought, answering my own question. *I have to accept things the way they are, not the way they were. I can only improve on now. I can't improve on yesterday.*

I loved Norm more than my own father—and in the same way. I eventually got a divorce from Norm and married again. I loved my second husband, Wayne, in a way that was strictly sexual. It lasted for awhile, then it died for me. In the end, I divorced Wayne and went back to Norm. The love Wayne carried for me must have lasted for a lifetime, because even his new wife told me he talked about me all the time. It's strange, he did so many things to make me think he didn't. Looking back, I now know he was just one of those types that needs more than one lifetime to make it work. His spiritual development was much too slow to acquire anything of value in this life.

There's no way to describe the love I have for Hugh, except undying—one that can never be replaced by someone else. It covers all the earthly loves that one could ever imagine and maybe by now it has grown into a godly love. It will not only last a lifetime…but will continue through infinite time. Remaining on the same level I had for my father, the love I had for Norm will also continue through infinite time.

I told Linda Carter, my long-time friend, how Hugh and I met, while we sat in the Rib Eye Steak House, outside of Chehalis on I-5 one afternoon. At this very same place I'd fallen in love with Hugh over forty years ago. By now the little restaurant had been torn down and the Rib Eye put in its place. Something there remained the same: They still had stuffed animals. Linda wanted one when we came in, just like Shirley had done the night Hugh and I met. I also told her about going back to see him after twenty some years. After telling her the story I bought her one of the stuffed animals. A small part of the memory had circled in time. I wondered if the other parts would ever circle in time. *Probably not in this lifetime,* my mind concluded. "As for all the other memories, I'm willing to forget," I resolved.

In the Garden of Eden, God created Adam and then took one rib from him to make Eve. There could be additional lifetimes—I don't know that either. Occasionally I ask myself, *whose rib do I belong to.* I'm not taking about somebody you can live with or someone you can make it work with—the kind that says I used to love him and dies with time. I'm talking about the kind that lives on; it lasts forever—from the moment you see them till the moment you die, and your heart and mind are telling you it will go on beyond, maybe even beyond the stars in the sky. To love someone this much makes one think that this is what forever is for. Until we can make it work, life's journey will not be complete—not in my mind. I'll always love Norm too, but not in the same way. There's too many things that can't be resolved. We are still only half-way there. Additional lifetimes, we need them—to make it work for ourselves, to make it work for others, and most importantly to make it work for God. At least, some of us do, and all for different reasons. I can daydream about that Garden of Eden and say I was once "there." That's been a long time ago.

Chapter 20

The Storm

Eight inches of snow lay on the ground. Our place in the country generally gave an intense aesthetic pleasure with soothing comfort. Situations of the immediate past had caused altered changes. The changes had come about because of Wayne's drinking and gambling. He was my second husband.

I first married Wayne following a divorce from Norm, while he was still living. Later I went back to Norm, right before his death. Then after Norm's death I went back to Wayne.

Wayne sat around on the couch, watching TV until I left for work at 2 p.m. when I was working swing shift. Then he went to the Brass Rail, a cocktail lounge in Kelso. It was his "home away from home." He couldn't stand to be alone, even for one minute. Even when I was there with him he had to have the TV going night and day. It seemed like he needed something to cover up the restless undercurrents of something deep within his mind. Apparently he was running from his own thoughts, thinking they would go away if ignored. He needed friends. Since his best friend, Clancey, had died at age 39, he'd started going downhill. Clancey's death was long past. I figured he should have gotten over it by now.

Our relationship reached heights above "Cloud 9" in the beginning. Lately it had been like a roller coaster with its extreme ups and downs. We were consistently breaking up and getting back together again. Each time we broke up I went back to Norm. Apparently I needed someone who cared about me. It took me long enough to realize that. This time, the separation between Wayne and me had lasted one whole day.

With all the snow on the ground, he wouldn't be able to get out without a four-wheel drive. So he took me to work in my truck. I was on day shift that week. Naturally he didn't like getting up so early in the morning, but he hated staying home alone even worse. Our conversations touched only on surface items, making me well aware that another storm was just beyond the hills—a different kind of storm.

I chose to bate him to see what the outcome would be: "There's $80 in the glove box. We need some milk. Would you stop and get some today? You can use some of the money, but be conservative about it. We're not out of the woods yet," I reminded him. He'd been staying at a motel while we were separated and living on a credit card, a card he'd gotten under his dead father's name. I didn't want to see him get into trouble, so I paid the $850 balance on it.

He agreed that spending too lavishly now wouldn't be wise. "Okay," he said softly. Yet, a hint of puzzlement was in his tone of voice.

I should have noticed some other signs, which I chose to ignore. He'd taken me to work several times before when I was on day shift, and he should have known what time I would get off. This time he asked specifically again, as if he needed to know the exact time.

"It won't hurt you to wait on me a few minutes? Will it?" It was obvious he wanted to stay out drinking longer than 2:30 in the afternoon.

A taxi showed up in front of my work place when I went out to go home. While waiting for Wayne to arrive, I wondered why it was there. The driver finally got out and came inside. He asked, "Are you Martha Harris?"

I answered, "Yes."

"Your husband told me to pick you up and take you over to the Brass Rail," he said.

"Why?" I asked astonishingly. "Why didn't he come to pick me up?" *Stupid question,* I told myself a few moments later. *He wants to do exactly what he's been doing more than he wants to be with me.*

"I don't know," the driver remarked with a common, courteous answer. "I suppose he had something else he wanted to do."

Wayne came out of the Brass Rail when we arrived and paid the man with my money. He'd already spent most of the $80. Needless to say, he didn't have any milk either.

The conversation in the bar kept repeating itself, between Wayne, another friend, Sid, and the bartender, Helen. I kept extremely quiet and soft mannered throughout it all. Wayne had said over and over again to Sid that he had to pick me up. Apparently he'd repeated it so many times that Sid got tired of hearing it and told him to get me a taxi. "If you're dreading to pick her up that bad, why don't you just call a taxi to pick her up?"

Oh boy! His way out! And he could blame someone else for the decision, as well as getting a little humor out of it and doing what he wanted to do. His basic nature of continually choosing a humorous note found its outlet. Sid joined in on the rationalizing fun he gave himself. Helen didn't see any humor in it. She would have been extremely mad if he'd done something like that to her, and she told him so.

"You did what you felt like doing," I told him. "If you hadn't wanted to do it, you wouldn't have done it." I kept concealed all the hurt and anger inside, like a great poker player, and tried to make him feel better about himself for doing something he was apparently beginning to feel guilty about. *If only he could acknowledge his actions as being cruel and apologize, it would help him change for the better,* I thought. *It takes more than feeling guilty about a situation to change. Guilt, without change, can only do more harm.*

Finally, after all the rationalizing to himself and to Sid and Helen, his guilt became overwhelming. He turned to me, saying, "If you can't see anything humorous in this, then you and I are through."

Still, I remained good natured and calm on the outside. Underneath, the storm had already begun, and he didn't have a four-wheel drive to get himself out of this mess.

We went home, acting like very little had changed. I told him we could discuss it further at a later time when we weren't drinking. I knew I could weather the storm and overcome. I wasn't so sure about him. These were just thoughts that I kept to myself.

The next day he took me to work, as he'd done the day before. Snow was still on the ground, and it was growing in inches. I couldn't get what he'd done off my mind. Even though, I was determined to handle the situation diplomatically.

When he came to pick me up at work, I started casually. "You know that subject we were talking about yesterday?"

He butted in, as if he expected something more than he could handle to happen. "Before you say anything."

"No, before you say anything," I rebutted. "I've been thinking about it all day. Remember you saying that if I couldn't find anything funny in it, that you and I were through. Well, I've thought about it all day, and I can't find anything funny about it to save me."

He hit the ceiling. His guilt was still very active. No apology came. No remorse came. No acknowledgement of any kind, except he believed he'd done the right thing. It wasn't his fault, he said. Sid had suggested it. All he could see was the humor. Humor was supposed to make everyone happy, so he thought.

This reminded me of another incident: My friend, Dawn Smith, her boyfriend, Lanny Nelson, and I had recently went to Portland to the dog races. We passed by a handicapped boy who had short, deformed arms. Not meaning to and totally unaware of his surroundings, Lanny began laughing hysterically at something Dawn had done or said. The boy had seen him laughing. One could see the feelings in his eyes, in his entire expressions. After we passed him I hit Lanny on the shoulder several times. "Don't laugh at me. Don't laugh at me," I repeated to get him to acknowledge what he was doing. "Didn't you see that boy and how he looked?" Apparently he hadn't noticed. I felt sure the scares would be burned into the boy's mind for a long time to come. We probably should have gone back so Lanny could have apologized, explained that he didn't see him, and told the boy what he was really laughing about. It was more important for us to continue with our fun. *Besides, going back to talk to him might make things worse,* I thought. It was totally unintentional in his case; yet the damage had been done. So laughter isn't always the best medicine for everyone. Some times, more often than we realize, sadness and tears makes the heart grow stronger.

My mind came back to the subject at hand. "It looks like you and I are through. I'll take you wherever you want to go. Then I'm going home."

"You're going to call it quits just because of a simple thing like that?" he asked. "I can't see why."

"First of all, it wasn't that simple. Next, you just laughed. Because you didn't acknowledge what you did as wrong, you received no growth. You've received every opportunity to change, but you haven't done so. I'm not doing you any favors by keeping you around. Maybe someone else can help you grow. I can't."

I felt like I'd tried everything in my power to keep our love alive and provide growth in our lives. Remembering what I'd asked God for before I met him came to mind: I'd asked for someone to help me make it through the next phase of my life. I was feeling like a prisoner in my own home, and every attempt I'd made to get away from Norm, my first husband, had failed. Maybe the real reason I married Wayne in the first place was to get away from Norm. Legally, I was now married to Wayne, but not morally. Norm was still living. Our vows said, "till death do us part." This acknowledgement told me I was totally free, morally. I'd thought like this before, but the feelings of wanting to be loved physically kept me hanging on. I wanted to be touched—more often than when I was growing up and more often than when I was with Norm. I wanted companionship and the feeling of knowing when I had to be away working that my husband was home doing what he could to improve the structure of our relationship, instead of drinking, gambling, and playing. Now, the reinforcement of accepting life as it was offered—not how I wanted it—was staring me in the face, forcing me to take another leap into the future. I had been rationalizing too, believing something Wayne told me. He said that whenever a love dies, that represented the death in one's vows, not the person themselves. I had believed him. I didn't want to lose the physical side of love that I had with him, but I knew it was now time to end the ride. His acceptance price was much too high. He wanted me to accept him, regardless of what he did.

Several years later, I saw Wayne without his new wife, the sixth one, at the Brass Rail. I just stopped by for a casual drink. His eyes lit up like candles when I walked through the door. Arms outstretched, he stood up. "I need a friend," he said. I hugged him and sat down for some casual conversation. His wife was across the bridge, drinking at Kellon's in West Kelso. He'd chosen to go to his home away from home, and she'd chosen to go to hers. Their marriage had deteriorated like all the others before. A comment—one of his—came to mind: *"It takes two." Yeah, when one excludes themselves, you no longer have two.*

I bought him a drink. He'd gotten paid that past Friday, and now it was only Sunday afternoon. His take-home pay for one week was $920 plus. He'd spent it all on booze and pull-tabs and didn't have a cent left.

"You know?" He changed the subject. "Every time I make love to that woman (talking about his wife), I have to fantasize she's you."

"You asked for that situation," I told him.

"No, I didn't," he said. "You're the one that run me off."

"Yes Wayne, you asked for it—with your actions as well as your comments."

"No, I didn't," he insisted. Odd to say the least, this reminded me of my vegetable garden. Apparently, he still hadn't learned what he was suppose to learn to provide himself with the growth he needed. *People are very much like vegetables,* I concluded. *When they don't allow themselves to be picked, they die on the vine.*

A short time later I heard he had two kinds of cancer—bone and lung cancer. He was in his mid fifties and looked like he was in his eighties. The people who knew him said they had a hard time recognizing him. He was no longer that good-looking man he used to be.

I wondered if he'd ever come to terms about himself. That phase of my life was over. The storm had subsided and melted away. I had endured and over-come this phase of it. *Our relationship was meant to last only a little while, to "help me make it through the night." God apparently didn't want me to suffer through another "Dead and Buried,"* I told myself. *It's too bad he died during the storm.*

Chapter 21

Angel on Her Shoulder

Linda Carter was my closest friend since I moved to Washington State…and also a friend of Tommy's. I hadn't seen Tommy in several years. He was somewhere in Georgia working for a firm that made under ground storage for a backup gas supply. As my daughter, Sherry, grew older, her jealousy of Linda also grew, thinking I gave her more attention. The truth was I needed a friend separate from my own family, as Fannie and I had apparently needed each other so many years before.

As the years past and the responsibilities of owning our own business subsided, Linda and I started going out together. We often exchanged thoughts and feelings. She came over often, bringing her two children and a boyfriend with her, to play cards. We still lived on North First in Kelso, the first place that Norm and I had bought when we first married. After dinner we played pinochle to the early morning hours. She was the one who taught me how to play it. I loved those visits. The visits started as far back as when her children were small and needed to be wrapped in blankets prior to taking them out in the cold morning air. She sometimes wrapped them in my handmade, scrape-work quilts, never thinking to bring them back. Some time later I'd find them at her house spread over a chair or couch, practically torn to shreds. When I mentioned it, she'd say, "Oh, is that yours? You can have it back if you want it." I told her "No, it's too late now. It's already torn to pieces. It would take too much work to repair it."

Her two kids, Jennifer and Raymond, are grown now too, the same as my two kids, Sherry and Myron. Linda still visits occasionally. She stopped by today just to visit, she said. I could tell she needed more, someone to listen to her. Her best friend had just died, leaving an empty feeling in her heart. I became silent, listening to her every word.

"I'm glad you've forgiven me for going out with Wayne," she began. "You had already gotten a divorce. I thought you didn't love him anymore."

"To me it's a moral code that a friend doesn't go out with another's ex-husband or ex-lover. That's all past now. We should get started on the future. It's easy to forgive once you understand the other's feelings," I told her.

She noticed I was putting together some information about Tommy so I could finish my book. All my life—from the time I was four years old—I thought of one day writing a book. I started out with one page in 1995 about a ghost; then I added another page and made corrections to it. After that, it just grew. One page at a time, it grew and grew. I kept going over it, reading parts of it to friends, and making corrections until I thought it made a good story. Then, I figured if I made one good story, I could also make two and so on. The stories just came out of my mind. What I didn't remember, I interviewed people—Tommy, my daughter Sherry, Mom, Linda, and many others—to find out additional information. Lately, I had been interviewing Tommy a lot. He lived close by in one of my apartments and made himself available.

"You know Tommy was a good friend of mine until he tried to rape me," she said.

"Oh, when did that happen? I really didn't think Tommy was capable of raping his first cousin."

"He came over one day when my first husband was at work. You know where I lived then on First Street in West Kelso."

"If he'd truly wanted to rape you, he would have succeeded. He told me how it could be done. The girl would be held in the same way that one of my past boyfriends held me the night we got into a fight.

"Tommy dated one girl for three years once after gang-raping her with a bunch of his friends. But I never thought he would rape his first cousin.

"Oh, what am I talking about? I know Tommy like the back of my hand. First off, he didn't believe you were his first cousin. You know what your mother used to say, you weren't Fred's daughter (Fred was Dad's brother); you belonged to someone else. Secondly, boys from back home were raised to give it their best try. If you gave in, then it was your fault." Fred was married to Eulah, Linda's mother, before he married Shirley.

"A friend of mine married a man that raped her. Later he raped me. When she went into the hospital with her first child, she needed someone to take care of her for awhile. Not having the least idea what would happen, I stayed with her as a friend and helped her out. My kind services were repaid with his madness. Furthermore, they thought of it as normal. The female species were just supposed to accept the males as just being boys. It was commonplace unless it happened to you. If it did happen to you, you were in the wrong place at the wrong time; they figured you shouldn't have been there in the first place. Apparently that wasn't the case with you; you were in your own home. The real effort comes from trying to live with all the pain without becoming so bitter you could kill. A deep understanding, along with God's help, is the only way to overcome such feelings; for another matter, it's the only way to overcome any bad happening. I know it's not right, but we could lose our minds if we dwell on it too much. Tommy's not like that anymore. Try to forgive him. It was a way he learned, but he has overcome that bad part of his character.

"We all have our secrets. The failures, the mistakes, the betrayals—some we keep locked up in our cupboard of memories and others we talk about. There are other such incidents locked up in my cupboard of memories, just as shameful and painful as this one. Just because it happened to me doesn't make it okay for it to happen to someone else. I wish things could have been different. That was then. This is now. I can only believe that those memories won't hurt me. There're just memories now.

"I'm glad you told me. You came here to talk to me, and here I am doing all the talking. I'll shut up now so you can say whatever you came here to tell me."

"Yeah, I come here to tell you about Jim," she said. Then she began:

Comforting Hands—"I love you," written on a balloon touches the white ceiling of the hospital room where her dear love prepares to meet his angel of death. Linda's heart is broken. She is devastated. Their closest and most intimate moments—a time of becoming "one"—was shared in words and in spirit. This precious time was about to run out.

The life support system beside his bed indicates he is dead. Linda returns to a standing position, reaches for the balloon and walks out of the room and down the long hall, but not alone. Jim's spirit is right beside her. He reaches to touch her hand, trying to console her with a mere touch. It feels very satisfying. Their peaceful, quite walk to the hospital yard filled her body with loving contentment.

In the hospital yard, she turns her tear-stained face toward Jim, thinking this will be the last time. She lifts the balloon toward heaven and turns it loose, softly saying to him, "Jim, you can go to heaven too."

This wasn't the last time for Jim's spirit to visit her with loving comfort. "My angel just comes to me ever since Jim passed away. He returns to me when I need him...sometimes at night when I feel like things are becoming unbearable."

For years she'd wanted a Great Dane. Jim and Linda had gone shopping for one several times before his death, but they were never able to find the fawn colored Dane she was looking for.

He knew how much she loved animals—to the extent that whenever she died she wanted to become a zookeeper in heaven. She had goats, pigs, peacocks, horses, and all kinds of animals on the farm, which he left to her in his will.

Even though Jim had four children from a previous marriage whose mother had died before him and Linda got together, Jim left everything he owned to Linda. Their love had grown to unconditional proportions, poring out to each other in continuous emotion. It had gone through the four seasons of a relationship and survived beautifully. They considered each other first, before all other people.

One Sunday afternoon while she was having an early dinner at Sheri's Restaurant in Vancouver, Washington, with me, a complete stranger drove into the parking area and parked directly in front of the window where we were sitting. Two Great Danes were in the back seat of the stranger's car. They were exactly what she'd been looking for, for so long. She cut her dinner short and immediately went out to look at the Danes. Three puppies accompanied the pair.

"Would you like to have one of the puppies?" the stranger happily asked.

"Oh no," Linda commented while showing her admiration for the dogs. "I can't afford to buy one."

"They aren't for sale," the stranger said. "You can have your choice."

Jim was the only one who knew exactly what she had wanted for so long and how much she'd wanted it. She hadn't even told me, her best friend, until now. This puppy, she called "Duke", was a gift from heaven—a gift for no other reason than a replacement to help her cope with Jim's death—so she accepted with sheer delight.

The stranger was never seen again.

Coincidence? Maybe! Who's to say? "Coincidence is God's way of performing a miracle anonymously," someone once wrote.

She believed Jim had become her guardian angel. "For he shall give his angels charge over thee, to keep thee in all thy ways."—PS. 91:11.

Many times Linda herself has reached death's door, but apparently God isn't ready for her yet. She has cancer which has come out of remission three times, went into a coma from taking a wrong combination of drug treatment, and more recently she had a heart attack at age forty-five. Each time she feels a warm touch on both shoulders as if Jim had walked up behind her. So many times before his death he offered those comforting hands.

She was driving north on I-5, near the Vader, Washington, turnoff when her heart attack occurred. Thinking she had to get help and if she stopped she would die, she continued under the wheel to finish the trip home. Yet, the hands of her angel were on her shoulders as she doubled in pain. With one hand on the steering wheel and the other on her chest, she remained in a state of semi-consciousness to reach home in her 1995 Dodge Ram truck which was left in cruise control until she reached the turnoff. Maybe she somehow took it out of cruise control, but she doesn't remember doing so. She felt as if her angel took over the driving, continuing the trip home, which is located a few miles southeast of the Mossyrock exit, a total of eleven miles.

In the hospital her thoughts turned to the people she loved, acknowledging how much she was going to miss them for the first time in her life.

When she went into a coma for two weeks the soft touch of the comforting hands brought her out of it again. On her mother's request, the hospital released Linda to go home with her mother to die. "Out of the blue, a letter from God suddenly appeared." A warm spirit directed her eyes toward the coffee table where it lay. Everyone in the house asked questions about how it got there, but nothing could be confirmed.

Alfred, Lord Tennyson of *The Ancient Sage*, I: 66 states: "For nothing worth proving can be proven; nor yet disproven: wherefore thou be wise, cleave ever to the sunnier side of doubt."

The letter she found on the coffee table, she handed it to me. "Here it is. Read it!" She said.

A Love Letter

I love you!
I shed my own blood for you to make you clean.
You are new so believe it is true!
You are lovely in my eyes, and I created you just as you are.
Do not criticize yourself or get down for not being perfect in your own eyes.
This leads only to frustration.
I want you to TRUST ME, one step, one day at a time.
Dwell in my power and my love.
    And be free—be yourself!
        Don't allow other people to run you.
I will guide you if you'll let me.

Be aware of my presence in everything.
I give you patience, joy, peace.
    Look to me for answers.
        I am your Shepherd and I will lead you.

Follow Me Only

Do not ever forget this. Listen and I will tell you my will. I love you! I love you!
Let flow from you—spill over to all you touch.
    Be not concerned with yourself—you are my responsibility.
    I will change you without you hardly knowing it.
    You are to love yourself and love others simply because I love you.
Take your eyes off yourself! Look only at Me!
    I lead, I change, I make, but not when you are trying.
    I won't fight your efforts.
    You are mine. Let me have the joy of making you like Christ. Let me love you!
    Let me give you joy, peace and kindness. No one else can! Don't you see?
You are not your own. You have been bought with blood and now you belong to me.
    It is really none of your business how I deal with you.
        Your only command is to look to me and me only!
            Never to yourself and never to others.
                I love you.
                Do not struggle but relax in my love.
                I know what is best and will do it in you.
                How I want freedom to love you freely!
Stop trying to be and let me make you what I want.
    My will is perfect! My love is sufficient! I will supply all your needs!
Look to me! I love you.

Your Heavenly Father

Job 12:2—"No doubt but ye are the people, and wisdom shall die with you." In my own mind, this has come to mean if we have doubts, wisdom will die with us. To keep an open mind is like growing to become as beautiful as the Sea of Galilee, far from being like the stagnated waters of the Dead Sea, which is nearby and its only difference is free flowing water.

Linda's mother, Eulah, died nine months after Jim. This time her comfort came in the form of a dream. "Linda, Linda, Linda," her mother called repeatedly from the yard, waving her hand to get Linda's attention. "I love you and I will always love you," Eulah told her. In the dream her mother was slender and beautiful as she had been as a young woman. Eulah had been fat for years, and she hadn't walked the last three years before her death. In the dream, Linda was a child of about ten or twelve watching her mother walk across the lawn.

More recently Linda and I went to Reno, Nevada, where something very strange happened. Linda said her angel advised her to go with me instead of someone else. Her plans to go with someone else in the beginning fell through. While there, someone stole her billfold, which is not strange at all, but what happened afterwards was. The I.D., with billfold, mailed from Reno, was home when we returned. An apology accompanied it saying, "I'm sorry. I'll send the money back to you as soon as I can." It was signed "Russel." Three or four days later she received the money back in the mail with a Vancouver, Washington, postmark.

We—both Linda and I—have had a change of heart since she went out with my ex-husband, and we have become better people because of our experiences shared with one another. Linda thought this trip to Reno would be a time of real sharing. She believed her angel requested that she go with me. We could renew our broken friendship of several years.

I have not been so fortunate as to have an angel on my shoulder. Maybe I've had a different kind of help. I've always thought of myself as being very self-reliant, helping others instead of them helping me; giving instead of receiving. A person is nothing unless God makes them better. If an angel is "an idea of God," then I have plenty of angels, leading me on to a better way of thinking.

That better way of thinking includes forgiving Linda for going out with my ex-husband. It seemed to me that a real friend didn't go out with someone else's ex; or at least, a real friend didn't make it so obvious. At the time of our broken friendship it mattered. Now it doesn't. Just like aged wine, our friendship has grown better with time, through wisdom and understanding. We have also weathered through the cold seasons…and now it is spring again.

The letter from God had said he would change us without us hardly noticing it. This time, we noticed it.

"Come on!" I said. "Let's go out and listen to some music. We need a night out."

A Place Called There

Play on music, oh sweet food of love.
   Sound into the valleys…
      Across the hills…
         And over the planes…
Come back to rest where the mountains are high,
   And echo your sound into the valleys above our sky.

Never so near, never so far.
   Too far away to touch; yet, your love lingers here.
      So far into the past—we hear.

Your touch, your smile reappears.
      Rest on my shoulder and stay awhile, dear.
But now, let it be me…and let it last.
   Meet me in the morning while the dew is still on the grass.
      And in the afternoon, when the sun shines upon man.
         In twilight, let me touch the golden daffodils
            And feel the sand with my feet and hands.
Bring your sound to life over the land.

All your happiness be mine. And all my happiness be yours.
   We all are one in a resting-place. It's made for you and me; may we find?
      A beauty we can share, can't we?
         A sound, sweet to the ears, a caring beyond compare!
         A calmness no one has ever before shared.

Play on sweet music! We hear what you say!
   I'm sure God will be there!
   Where are we going…My friend and I?
      Back home…to play! To a place called there.

   I hate to spoil a good story, especially if it's my own: I later found out the "Love Letter" came from FISH, a non-profit organization that helps the needy by feeding, clothing, and helping pay some household utilities, such as lights and water. It was stored in one of their food boxes, which they distributed to the public. We were back home again—and down to Planet Earth, another example of being only "half-way there." To be over the half-way point, I realized that it really didn't matter where the letter came from: It only matters that we accept it through faith, and love the goodness it brings.

Chapter 22

I Want to Believe in Cinderella

My friend and accepted cousin, Linda, went back to North Carolina to compile some of the family tree, while I decided to compile just a little bit of the history. Fred Parker, my uncle, was Linda's accepted father. His brother, Roy Parker, was my father. Staying closer to my immediate family and covering only certain issues, I started with my brother, Jimmy. I wanted to know each family member better by knowing what kind of people they really were. Jimmy and I had been enemies for a long time. We wouldn't speak to each other for years. After I left High Point, North Carolina, I never wanted to see him again. He'd done too many things wrong for me to ever want to continue our relationship. Often, I looked back on the beating he gave me when I first went to High Point and remembered the hurt over and over again. I no longer needed him for any reason. It was harder to forgive him than Thelma, because Jimmy was my brother.

Then in the late summer of 1992, when I went back on vacation to Hayesville, I visited with him one night. We sat at the kitchen table, talking practically all night. The conversation started off casually. He was the first to bring up the subject of that earlier incident and apologize for what he'd done. He apologized more with actions than with words. Tears came to his eyes. I never thought the day would ever come to see that. He wasn't the type.

More recently on one of my vacation back there, I took some fancy dresses and modeled them at Mom's place. The house was full. June, my half-sister, and her three daughters helped me model them. Jimmy and his wife, Barbara, were visiting Mom at the time. He said I looked like a "five and dime store bought whore." This really didn't sound like a person who had changed totally. The old tendencies were still there. At least, some of them were. I just ignored him and kept on modeling the clothes.

Myron, my son, was with me. He was helping Mom in the kitchen. Mom had recently had a heart attack. When Jimmy saw this, he said to Myron, "Where's your skirt, boy? Where's your skirt?" This is a learned pattern: Most people there still believe that men shouldn't do any kind of housework. Myron says he will remember this as long as he lives.

During my time spent there I got to know Jimmy's oldest son, Jimmy Randall Parker, very well. He is extremely handsome, like Jimmy was when he was young, but somewhat taller. Jimmy looked an awful lot like Grandma Kitchen, Mom's mother. Apparently "Randall" had some qualities of his mother, Thelma, too. For he has those great big, brown eyes, just like her. Thelma had done something right: She had Randall and had raised him properly. With one of the best personalities that anyone could want, Randall has grown in his love for God and bears fruit of the most gorgeous kind. Nothing like his father, except in his looks, he apparently got enough of his mother in him to out-weigh the effects of his father. Since both his parents were very good looking, it stands to reason he would be very handsome. More importantly, he has something special in him that very people ever acquire. His kindness is unsurpassed, and he's married to a lady that is every bit as good looking and as kind and sweet as he is. Her name is Lisa.

Randall wanted a beautiful house located at the very end of Eagle Fork Road, a side road off Old Route 64 in North Carolina, close by the area where we all were raised. Wondering how he was going to buy the house with the circumstances the way they were—very little credit, young, and without a good paying job—he prayed to God.

I didn't know anything about this secret wish of his until much later. It just happened that I went to see this same house, and upon first sight of the exterior decided to buy it. I was still working in Washington and had no immediate plans for retirement. The $100,000 ranch home, located at the edge of national forest land, was like walking into a candy store and asking for a nickel's worth of candy, except I didn't have the available cash. It didn't matter. I knew I wanted it. With my credit rating and income, it didn't seem to be a big deal. So I purchased it, not having the least idea about what would happen next. I never asked myself once who was I going to get to live there and take care of the place. Using no logic, I just let everything happen as if some supernatural power was guiding me…and maybe it was. I felt sure that it was the right decision, with absolutely no reason why that I could see.

On a turn of the page, Randall and his family became the occupants of the house. I'd made a wise decision. The house that I bought was the same one Randall had wanted. When I went back home on future vacations I always made it a point to stay with his family at least one night. We sometimes stayed up all night long, sometimes going to bed after six in the morning, even when he had to work that day. When I was home in Washington, Randall and I talked for hours over the phone.

Through Randall, my brother's firstborn son, I learned a different side of my brother, Jimmy. Even though I'd grown up with Jimmy, I'd never seen this side before, except for the one incident in High Point, North Carolina.

Tommy, who now lived close by in one of my rentals, had told me very little about Jimmy until now. Jimmy was home very little when we were growing up. Norm and I had purchased twelve rentals before he died. The last one we acquired after our divorce was final. I paid the down payment of $3,000 on it. Norm thought the more property we owned, the more he would be able to hold me. Even though, I still let him have all the property while he lived. He never gave up the hope of getting me back, and it eventually paid off.

The story, which follows, gives a general description of Jimmy's personality as seen by his oldest son, Randall. He gives the description in fairy tale form and I record it, as it is given except for a few added changes:

Three sisters lived on a tobacco farm with their parents and two brothers in our small part of the world —Hayesville, North Carolina. The girls—Blonde, Ormae, and Thelma—were known as the Ledford girls and were very happy living in the valley of rolling hills and beautiful green pastures. Like stair steps in size with Blonde being the tallest, as well as the oldest, and Ormae being the smallest and the youngest, all three girls had long, jet-black hair with beautiful dark eyes and outstanding figures.

Their chores were many during that time—the '50's. Each day after school they helped their parents with their large garden and a seven-acre tobacco field. Following a full breakfast in the early morning they helped their mother, Elizabeth, clean the house, milk the cow, and churn the milk to make butter and buttermilk. On weekends they helped her with canning and preparation of food for the winter. On Sundays they all attended church. Any type of church outing or a simple trip to town was a big event for them.

Making themselves look even prettier, they made beautiful dresses with full skirts out of feed sacks of various patterns and colors. The dresses were then starched and iron to perfection. Since money was scarce for all families of that area during that time, starch was made with flour and water. Prince Albert tobacco cans were cut into long stripes and wrapped with cloth to roll their hair.

One particular night, their mother wanted to go to a tent revival. Thelma was to meet a handsome, young prince there. Even though she didn't know how the true story would unfold, there was always hope to fulfill the dreams she carried from earlier times of reading fairy tales of handsome princes. They immediately noticed each other when Thelma arrived. When she saw Jimmy, she thought he was the best looking man she'd ever seen. He had dark hair, dark eyes, and dark skin—just like hers. Young men often went to religious functions to meet girls, but some of them seldom went inside. The sides of the tent were left open, allowing a cool, summer breeze to blow through. The young man flirted with her and motioned for her to come outside. For he thought she was the prettiest girl in the world. Throughout the meeting, she went out to talk to him.

After that night he walked from the head of Shooting Creek to Hayesville where she lived, about ten to twelve miles, several times a week just to talk to her. They often sat on the front porch swing and talked to each other for hours, sometimes until dawn softly touched the eastern mountains. This went on for about three years. Thelma fell deeply in love with him. She knew he was the man she wanted to wed.

They were married in the spring of 1959. For the first seven years they lived in High Point, North Carolina, a few hundred miles from their hometown. The first year was wonderful and beautiful in every respect. She thought she'd found the man of her dreams.

Their first anniversary was only twenty-eight days away when the first signs of the darkness within him began to appear. She caught him with another woman. How much peace and happiness would be shattered during the coming years? He swore that it would never happen again. She believed him. In all innocence of the farm girl that she possessed, she had no idea of what the future might bring. She just hoped everything would work out for the better. With all the love she carried for him, she tried to understand and stayed with him.

Four years into the marriage, she was often left home alone. Nine months pregnant with her first child, she became uneasy because Jimmy was away. *He should've been home hours ago,* she thought. A few miscarriages had preceded this almost full term. Her worries persisted. Except for a bicycle, there was no transportation to get to the hospital or to go anywhere.

She reasoned, w*ith the situation the way it is I need to try to find him.* Deciding to ride the bicycle into town to find him took several hours of debating with herself. Arriving at a filling station in downtown High Point, she spotted him with a woman. Riding the bike over to him where he was sitting in a car with the strange woman, he saw her and rolled down the window. His anger came out: "Get your ass back home, now!" Cussing at her, he jumped out of the car and slapped her. Pushing her, he told her to get back on the bike and go home. He stayed with the other woman. She cried all the way home.

She knew she'd be safe back home in Hayesville with her parents. Often she daydreamed about the farm of rolling hills and beautiful pastureland, which she had forsaken because of love. The fairy tale of finding a wonderful prince she'd read and dreamed about when she was just a young girl took on its own reality. The reality spread its wings into her mind and heart, gathering less and less of the love she needed and wanted so badly. Building false hopes on mountains of empty promises, self-deception became a way of life with no foreseeable way out.

No money and pregnant—and so far from home—she felt she had no other choice but to stay. The baby, weighing nine pounds and eight ounces was born. He was named Jimmy, after his father. Their first child—this should have been a happy time.

She worked to help pay the bills even though the child needed her during the early part of his life. Jimmy kept her broke, as well as himself, on partying and hanging out with friends and women on the weekends. Southern men used to say they kept their women under their control by keeping them barefoot and pregnant. The man of her dreams—the love of her life—disappeared into the man-made darkness of their worlds. It brought no candle to light the way, just deception and mounting unhappiness.

She lost weight, down to ninety pounds. A neighbor lady wrote her parents, telling them if they didn't come to get her she would die. The lady checked on her daily, because she'd become seriously ill from all the stress. Still she carried on, as the responsibilities mounted. Stressful events became a regular occurrence.

As time passed she became pregnant again. Having no idea as to how she would ever get back to the protective nest of her parents, she prayed. Her prayers were finally answered when Jimmy was picked up on a probation violation and sent to prison. Her mother sent her a bus ticket. Seven years had past and finally she was on her way back home—pregnant again.

Jimmy somehow managed to get transferred to a prison in Franklin, closer to Hayesville, where prisoners were building a road in the Highlands territory. He sent word for Thelma to come to visit him there. She washed clothes and baby-sat to earn enough money for gas to make the trip. With her mother accompanying her, she drove the old farm car over the mountain to see him. A little sparkle of hope still existed.

He apparently convinced her he loved her with that first visit. For thereafter, she visited him every two weeks. At times she even siphoned gas out of her father's old pick-up truck.

Six months passed. He was released from prison. They moved into a little trailer on her parents' land. At least, this time she was closer to home—the security of her parents and the land closest to her heart.

The dark side of him only surfaced when any of his friends came around. He usually left with them to party with women to all hours, coming home whenever he got ready. There were never any happy mediums, just extremes of swaying from one side to the other between good and bad.

A third child was born. They moved into a little, white house below town.

He tried to straighten up for several years, but periodically he still hung on to the one-night stands, which he had been so accustomed to. He made big money, and he still had his great looks. Thelma looked her best then too—in the 70's and 80's.

There was never a dull moment whenever he was around. The family became involved with wagon trains, horse shows and camping. They bought a pair of matching black horses. Remembrance of her racing with him in the early morning breeze brought tears to Randall's eyes, as he portrayed the picture to me. Their oldest son had been named Jimmy too, but he went by his middle name, Randall. Even though hurt clouded his mind, he continued with his story:

Jimmy started running around with a couple of men from Hiawassee, Georgia, in the early 80's. Major fights occurred whenever he wanted to go out partying with them. They became more frequent as time passed and continued throughout their marriage. Starting with something as simple as him not liking supper, it always ended up with black eyes…sometimes even worse.

"He lost control when he became angry. This reminds me of one incident in particular," Randall recalled. "Jerry Ledford (Lillie's youngest son) lined up two women for the two to go out on a double date together. He threw all the food setting on the table across the room, smashing it against the kitchen cabinets. The fight escalated. He poured all the drinks over Mitchell's, Bobby's and my head. Mom stepped in and they ended up on the floor. He choked her. I grabbed the broom and repeatedly hit him on his back and on the back of his head. She became almost lifeless. Ormae felt something was terribly wrong and called at that time. When Jimmy jumped up to answer the phone, we all ran out the door and hid in a culvert for about three hours. Jimmy went up and down the road searching for us. When he finally gave up, we crawled out and went to a neighbor's house where we called Ormae to come after us. We stayed at Ma and Granddad's about a week."

Trying to make the best out of an impossible dream, Thelma took her three sons back home, only to face the reoccurring events of the past once again. They became worse. Jimmy stayed out for weeks without telling anyone where he was going or when he'd be back. Three to five hour quarrels occurred regularly so he wouldn't have to explain where he'd been. Then they became physical. For several hours straight he beat Thelma. Turning his anger toward the boys, he used a belt buckle on them, or he stomped them with his cowboy boots.

A year of this extreme discomfort passed. It was Christmas—no tree, no presents. Emptiness filled the air as well as the hearts of her three sons. A house full of drunks staged the scene of what should have been a beautiful Christmas Eve. Thelma looked at her sons and said, "This will be the last year we have to spend like this."

Jimmy continued running around with the men from Hiawassee. He was seldom home anymore—maybe one week out of a month. He came in one night after some time out with them, his temperament as usual. The boys had developed a skill of staring at the TV instead of listening to him. He called Thelma every name in the book but a white woman, while she said nothing.

Randall confronted him, "How can you come back home after being gone for two weeks straight and call my mother all these names? We know where she was at."

Jimmy took his boot off. With it, he hit Randall on the head and all over his body. Bobby, the youngest at age 14, charged at him, shoving him away from Randall into the kitchen. Then Jimmy got Bobby down and started beating him with his fist. Randall looked down at the cowboy boot that his father had used on him. With his eyes closed, he picked it up and hit Jimmy on the head. He fell to the floor, almost unconscious.

Thelma told the boys to get out of the house—fast. Too tired and confused, they sat down on the grass in the yard to rest for awhile.

"I wonder what's going to happen next," Mitchell commented. Then out of the corner of his eyes, he noticed Jimmy crossing the lawn with a pair of scissors.

"I'm going to kill every damn one of you," he charged. After chasing them for some time with the scissors Jimmy got a pitchfork. One of the boys distracted him while the others rested, making changes whenever necessary. Finally Jimmy became too tired and went into the house. He locked all the windows and doors behind him.

Upon returning to their home after spending a couple weeks at their grandparents' place, they found Jimmy had put the house up for sell. A couple looked at the house and decided to buy it, even though Thelma told them it wasn't for sell. They said Jimmy told them she would say that and to look at it anyway. They wanted to start taking the doublewide apart the following Tuesday. The family had bought the mobile home since their move from the little, white house below town. It had been the first without renting, and she hated to give it up.

The movers came on Tuesday, like they said, and took half. They came back the next day, taking the other half. Thelma and her sons were left in the yard with nothing except their clothes and a television set. In hopelessness and desperation, they just sat there in silence. With tears flowing down Thelma's face, she turned to her boys and said, "I don't know what we're going to do now."

Returning to Thelma's parents for a place to stay until she could manage to get a house of their own, she eventually found a trailer down in Georgia on Nicely Road. She didn't see Jimmy for at least six months. She heard he'd gone to work on a cattle ranch out west. Then one day he showed up in a Lincoln, pulling a friend's Corvette behind it. Just a brief visit, described as "Hello, goodbye, and go with me," he flaunted his status without Thelma.

The family didn't see him again until he was broke. He wanted Thelma back. By that time, she couldn't stand to spend another night with him because of what he'd put her through.

Apparently, he couldn't stand her rejection. In his mind, it was too close to the rejection he felt as a young boy when Mom left. It was like hell opened up, showing its ugly teeth for six more years. Fights occurred weekly. He tapped the phone, hired people to watch them and sometime watch them himself, cut eight sets of tires, threw their pump down the well, cut insulation off water pipes, and locked the car down by pouring syrup in the gas tank. He came back weekly, telling them they had only so long to live. He said he was going to blow up the house with dynamite, while they were still sleeping; or, he was going to turn a copper head snake loose in the house. He told her it would be setting on her belly when she woke up.

Pissing in their water, he told them he had aids. His threats became more serious when he disconnected the pipes of the gas line, causing detriment to his entire family.

"If I can't have you, nobody else can," he screamed out at Thelma. Fighting all the way through the house, she slipped away from him for a brief moment. He came at her with a knife. Lying on her back under the blade, she tried kicking to push him away. She grabbed his wrist and managed to take the knife away from her throat. She could feel he had already sliced the left side of it.

Mitchell came home finding his mother in a bloody mess with her blouse torn open. He went straight to his room to get a rifle. His anger boiled beyond control. He put the rifle between his father's eyes and told him to get out. With resistance, Jimmy left.

While lying flat on the floor, thinking Jimmy would surely kill her, Thelma's mind snapped. For six months straight, she didn't do much more than go from the bed to the bathroom. Hallucinations and a total state of panic consumed her every thought. Worrying for six years about whether she would make it through the next day, as well as worrying about her sons' lives had finally taken its toll. She was insane. It progressed to the point of having so much fear that someone was going to come inside the house to kill them, she started staying in the car. She got out of the car only to use the bathroom or to get the bare necessities of life, just surviving. No one could reason with her.

Realizing he couldn't let her remain in this condition, Randall went to the police department and had her committed to a mental institution. She stayed in the institution for about a week only, but her condition has never been the same.

"Since then, she reverts back into that state of mind when any major event occurs in her life," Randall concluded his story. "We get shadows of the woman she used to be, but she's not the same. A woman of her strength has been reduced to a shattered person. From now on—as long as she lives—she'll go through these mental instabilities. The terrible choice of going down the road with what she thought was the man of her dreams—a prince charming—left indescribable anguish and pain that can't be eliminated in one lifetime." Her memory, never to be recalled again, had been blocked out by too much pain.

"Mom used to say you never really know a person until you live with them. I lived with Jimmy. He's my brother. I didn't have the least idea he was that bad.

"Tommy's told me some pretty mean things he's done, and I've seen enough to make me think I didn't want any part of it.

"I didn't turn out that bad and I was younger than both of them. I think I went through a lot more than they did, because they always left when the going got ruff. Tony and I were left home to endure. Tony didn't turn out that bad either, and he was the youngest. Actually, Tony turned out to be the most successful of all of us monetary wise. He came out to Washington and went to work when he was just barely eighteen and stayed with that same company until he died. Tony was strict with his kids, but he didn't beat them or his wife. He was basically a good person; he just needed some growth in the spiritual department.

"You didn't turn out that bad," I told Randall. "You're very good…and Jimmy was your father. He put you through a lot more than he had to go through himself. What is it that makes some people so mean and cruel?" I asked.

Randall seemed to think it was the pain and anguish, apparently carried over from his childhood. "His mother had left him to survive on his own." Both Randall and I tried very hard to understand why.

"Yeah, but he's not the only one that's ever been left to survive on their own," I added. "There comes a time when everyone should grow up and accept responsibilities for themselves, regardless of whose to blame and regardless of the circumstances. Besides, Dad should have been responsible too, but he wasn't. In my mind, the man should be the stronger one. According to the way we were raised, he's the head of the household. How did men ever get to be head by wanting all the benefits, yet refusing to pay the price?" Neither Randall, nor I could manage to see the logic in all this.

"Jimmy's moved on now. He's with another woman and he doesn't treat her that bad. Maybe that's because he knows she'd whip him." I told Randall, trying to reason some sense into the situation. "He hasn't corrected his spiritual self yet. The evil's still there, lying dormant. It's just not visible to the naked eye. He needs to see his real self. He's changed to some degree, but he still has a long way to go.

"As for Tommy, he's changed for the better. He still doesn't trust people, which is probably good in a way. Forgiveness for others comes slow for him.

"We are all different. Our darkness or weakness—whichever way you want to put it—lies in different areas, making it hard for us to understand another's motives or the real reason behind a reaction. We all still have a ways to go to heal the many wounds of yesterday's past. I wonder if God gives us additional lifetimes to get there. We need them.

"There are truly no Cinderella stories in this life, none that I can see anyway. They're only in the movies. I wish the stories did exist somewhere in the future. I want to believe in Cinderella."

It's apparent that "Satan is" definitely "alive and well and living on Planet Earth." One has to believe that good will eventually overcome the evil within us—or the evil upon this earth.

I know that part of overcoming must be to know that the bad memories of the past will never hurt us unless we let them. They're only memories, just passing thoughts with no substance. It's time we change what we can for the better and accept the things we can't. We can't change a memory. It's just there. We can change today for a better tomorrow though.

The deeds we did yesterday, we will pay for today; and the deeds we do today, we will pay for tomorrow. What doesn't catch up with us in this life will catch up with us in the life after. I'm just hoping that we'll have more than one lifetime to correct our mistakes and pay for our sins, before we reach judgment. There're so many of us that need the extra time. But again, maybe some of us wouldn't ever change for the better, or maybe we would change only a small amount— much too little to make much of a difference.

All the talking in the world won't change the past. The only gain seems to be: We could certainly see the ungodly misdeeds of the past and decide for ourselves that nothing is worth the price we'll have to pay in the end.

Tommy added this to the story about Jimmy:
"I'm not afraid of Jimmy as long as I'm facing him. If he has something against you, you're liable to go to sleep at night and never wake up, because he's burned your house down and you in it. He won't do you any harm as long as you're facing him…but he will behind your back. That's what I call 'a snake in the grass.'

"He got drunk and stayed out of work three or four days once. Because the company, which he was hauling logs for, hired another person, Jimmy got mad. He sharpened horseshoes and threw them on the tracks of the road so the new comer would run over them, causing him to have flat tires.

"He cut Marsh Kitchen's tires up when he was in the fourth grade." Marsh was the principal of the school, and apparently he got mad at him for some reason.

"As for cutting Thelma's tires and upholstery, he replaced them. Thelma told him she was going to take him to court if he didn't.

"Jimmy didn't learn these traits from anyone in our family or the Parker side," Tommy concluded.

According to my memory, Dad was a good man while Mom was home. His meanness had only lasted through his younger days. Apparently he had changed sometime during the earlier part of their marriage. He was a good man even after she left, other than his drinking.

Additional thoughts later came to help me reason things out. I needed to receive as much benefit from it as I possibly could. It would add growth. By understanding Jimmy, I would also reach a higher level of understanding myself. Randall was a good friend and counselor. No words could ever say how sorry I felt for the way things happened. If everything happens for a reason, I wonder why in regards to most of them.

The reason as to why Dad was so mean when he was young and why some of his children were mean during a certain portion of our lives all had one thing in common. We were searching for approval from other people in the wrong way. We had experienced rejection. If we had measured up to the standards we'd set for ourselves, maybe we wouldn't have needed so much approval from others. Maybe the people around us did give their approval in some ways, but we didn't feel it enough. This left hurt which caused us to fight back in the only way we knew how. The hurt I had eventually went away after Norm accepted me no matter what. He was a good man and good for me; I needed him. The same goes for Tommy; his girlfriend, Carol, is good for him. Upon my advice, Carol no longer puts up with beatings from Tommy. I told her to get an equalizer. She wanted to know what an equalizer was, and I replaced the word with weapon. She got the point. Maybe Jimmy has changed to some extent too; his condition wasn't just camouflaged, like I thought. When he got with the other woman, he felt she expected less of him. According to his mind, he didn't have to measure up to anything then. Barbara, Jimmy's new wife, is good for him. One reason we accept them is because they accept us. Jimmy has changed somewhat for the better because of this reason. He also "line-dances" now; she keeps him in line and he dances. Furthermore, he's older, fatter, and uglier. As Jimmy grew older and uglier, he probably felt that Thelma wouldn't continue to accept him. If you've never felt love, you're always testing it to get a reaction. If the acceptance is still there after the testing, the love feels more real. If the acceptance isn't there, then we feel like we did the right thing in the first place by testing it: it really wasn't real, so we continue testing each other. Back when Jimmy was good looking, he needed another way to test its reality and apparently chose the wrong method; now, he tests its reality with his looks, every day. When Norm accepted me no matter what, I finally realized there was no further need for testing. Thelma was too good for Jimmy, and he knew it. He didn't measure up to that expectation of himself. It's really too bad we can't see things more clearly and know the best way to measure up is to do better, rather than choose the wrong method to test one another. If we gave without expecting to receive, there would be no need to test.

If we don't have enough love in our hearts without expecting something in return, we are less likely to see the better side of others or the love they have to offer. I'm ashamed to admit that once upon a time I knew how to hurt others and did. Besides hurting my husband Norm, I hurt my mother, my step-dad, and Thelma too. Now, one reason I can love them is because I don't expect them to love me. It's not necessary for either of them to love me, because I love myself. The reason I love myself is I now try to make corrections within me, instead of trying to force a correction in someone else. In other words, I try to measure up to my own expectations, leaving others to do the same. Neither is it necessary for me to have the approval of my brother, my father, or my mother. I can easily over-look what Jimmy sometimes says and his actions, saying to myself, "Ah, that's just Jimmy." I don't want to be part of "the walking dead"— the kind of people who know how to take and how to hurt. They aren't giving anything back to this world or to the people in it. I know I am loved by God; that is enough. Through this realization, I'll go on making choices to change for the better. Whenever we are cruel, regardless of the reason, it would be to our benefit to look around and notice something in our own lives, which we aren't measuring up to. We should give our best effort to change that something for the better.

In real life, Cinderella's glass slipper has been shattered. No one can put the pieces together again. In this age where people admit partial truths years after the damage has been done, I can only surmise that a new pair of shoes is needed.

If we're not afraid to face our past, we can reason our way to success, regardless of how deep the hole is. "Believe it or not!" There is always something to be gained if and when we realize it. Then we can lay claim to it. Realization is the first step in making changes. Even in today's world, there is hope for change. *Hope has a place.*

Where do we look? Our experiences—especially the bad ones—in the past will tell us. We learn more from our mistakes or failures than from the things we do right. We can not learn from our future; we have not crossed that bridge yet. If we look at our past in the right light and with the right heart condition, it will show us how to build a better bridge to the future. The only way I know how to build a better bridge to the future is with a better heart condition through God. Real love has no boundaries. May it be the only thing we take from this world into the next.

Chapter 23

When I Think of Tony

When I think of Tony, my youngest brother, I remember him leaning his head up against a tree in the yard and crying for days. That was when Mom left. He was seven then. How was a little boy of seven supposed to think about his mother who had petted him all his life and all of sudden one day he heard her tell his father, "I'm leaving you and your damn kids with you?"

I think of the times when I worried about providing for his well being after she left, mainly a way to attain food for his next meal. The time when I couldn't put him out of my mind was most vivid when I ran away. I wasn't there to take care of him then. I returned home to find Dad stone sober for the first time since Mom left. Dad was sitting in a chair on the porch, crying. Concern for Dad took second place. I couldn't wait to find out about Tony. Questions about him poured from my mouth like water bubbling from a spring. Tony took priority. Dad had made his own bed, but Tony hadn't. He was only a child. Dad's deep concern for himself showed through in facial expressions of surprise when I continued asking about him. Or maybe he was surprised that I cared so much.

I think of the time after Dad died when I went with Jimmy to Mom's, later returning to his school to find him in rags and worn-out shoes. Somehow, I managed to buy him a pair of shoes later. It was hard to get into town, much less get the money for them. I was only thirteen. The only kind of work I could do to earn the money then was babysit or clean house, but I was very capable of that. It took me about a month to earn the money; then another week to get a ride into town. When I went into the store, across from the front entrance of the courthouse in Hayesville, to buy the shoes the owner asked me, "How much do you want to spend?" I told him, "I want the best pair of shoes you've got." He asked, "Are they for you?" "No," I answered. "They are for my brother." "What size does he wear?" he continued questioning. "I don't know," I said. "I'll have to get them as close to his size as I can just by looking at them." "What if they don't fit?" he asked. "If they don't fit, maybe he can find a way to come down to exchange them. You see my brother is staying with my uncle, and I'm staying with my grandparents. I happened to run into him at Shooting Creek School the other day on my way to Hayesville School. The bus stopped there for a few minutes, so I got off and looked for him. His shoes looked really bad. I have to get him a pair of shoes." I said, trying hard to force back the tears. The owner then asked, "Why didn't you ask his size then?" I didn't want to tell him everything: When I found Tony some boys were trying to ruff him up. They knew me. Immediately backing down, they scattered when I jumped in to take his part. He wouldn't speak to me, possibly because he thought I'd run off and left him willingly, like Mom had done. He told the boys he didn't need anyone to take up for him. I just told the owner of the store, "I didn't have time. The bus had to leave before I had a chance to." They cost $28, the most expensive shoes for boys he had in the store. I didn't have a way to take them to him in person, and it was too far to walk. Running into a first cousin, I asked her to take the shoes to Tony, since she lived close by. Many years later when I asked him had he received the shoes he said, "No." They were boy shoes: I didn't think she would wear them herself. I still don't know what happened to those shoes.

It's strange he couldn't keep himself clean. He was only a child then. I was young too, and I managed. I wondered why Uncle James and his wife couldn't do something to improve his appearance. *I would have done more for a dog,* I thought, even then. Yet, I had to find the strength and ability to forgive, as well as not judging. It was obvious nobody cared then, except me.

I remember the time he later came out here to Washington and came to see me the first time in years. He leaned up against my new sewing machine, which I'd just paid $650 for, and cut notches out in the cabinet without realizing what he was doing. I never said a word about it. I knew the circumstances of his life.

All of us were between three and four years apart, Tony being the youngest and Tommy being the oldest. I was next to the youngest, and Jimmy was next to the oldest. As for material value, Tony turned out to be the best of us.

Occasionally Norm, my husband, had asked Tony to borrow money when he had spent too much on gambling. Norm always asked him to keep it a secret from me, and he obliged, at least for awhile. When the time for pay back elapsed into months, Tony then called me, asking me to pay the debt. Naturally, it made me mad, but I paid him back anyway, plus a large percentage in interest.

Tony changed the oil in my car once and charged me the same as he charged others for the same service. He didn't offer anything free to anyone, not even Tommy. Hearsay was that he used Tommy, and Tommy wasn't the one that said it. Some people, who were closely related to Tony, suspected that Tommy got little or no pay for working in Tony's garage. Tony earned additional income by working on cars in a garage that he and Tommy built. To get things more accurate, I asked Tommy himself. He said he did do some work for Tony without pay, but Tony let him use his garage to work on his own vehicles. That was payment enough. Tommy was more like me; he would give anyone the shirt off his back if someone needed it. It's sad, but people seem to take advantage of others who give so freely. Tommy didn't feel like he was being taken advantage of. He was more willing to give freely than anyone I've ever seen, including me. He said he worked on his own cars most of the time. The main thing to learn from this is not to get offended by what people say. This world is on a good and bad balance check basis.

Humbleness, Tony didn't have. In fact, he was much of a chauvinist. Very seldom did I spend much time around him or his immediate family. Years earlier, I'd made one trip back to North Carolina with him and his wife, Joyce. I hated to close my eyes, because every time I did something happened. Near daylight the first night, he ran over a hole in a construction area in the suburbs of Salt Lake City, which caused considerable damage to the car and delayed the trip twenty-four hours. The next time I closed my eyes briefly, we were in a cornfield that paralleled with the freeway. Joyce was driving then. Both Tony and Joyce were young. I thought I could trust Joyce, because she was more mature. She did have a lot of qualities that Tony didn't have, such as maturity and humbleness. She was also more refined. Later on during the trip, we got lost due to a slight difficulty in knowing the right turn-off near Chattanooga, Tennessee. Since then, I've gone back home many times, at times riding through traffic of eight lanes going in one direction so thick that one could practically walk on cars as far as one could see. Every time I've made the trip, I've run into the same problem at the same place. Chattanooga must be one of the fastest growing towns in the United States. They don't even have time to change the road signs. It's really a screwed up mess. First, you're going south, then north. After that, the road has a split, one fork going northwest and the other fork going northeast—believe it or not, but one should take the northwest turn to the left. A short distance from there, a right turn to the east is necessary to get on Route 64 going into North Carolina. You get the feeling you're making a figure eight, and sometimes you are, depending on how much construction is going on. Compound all this with no updated signs, it is worse than L.A. during a busy time of day. Joyce and I stayed in the car when we stopped to get directions. I wanted to get out of the car and go closer to the guy giving Tony instructions, so I could hear what he was saying. Joyce said Tony wouldn't like it. Going four hundred miles out of our way could possibly have been avoided, if I had.

I'm sure Tony's immediate family loved him dearly and many others loved him too, including me. I felt he didn't love me. It was something I couldn't put my finger on, just a feeling. Once when I was at his house, I was talking to Mom in a bold way—nothing serious, just a little more than calm chatting. He came in from the shop, looked at me as if I'd done something drastically wrong and said, "Toots, we don't need anything you've got around here." I looked at him as if he were crazy and said, "Where are you coming from?" Maybe it was the time when I left him and went with Jimmy to Mom. He'd lost Mom, but still he felt enough compassion to forgive her, without her justifying her actions by telling him why. He had never found out why I left either. Even though many years had passed, I had never told him. I wanted to tell him plenty of times, but his disposition never made things like that very easy. Even though he didn't know it, he didn't have to justify his actions to be loved by me. *So, why should I have to justify my actions to him?* The old ways of never talking about anything continued to some extent. It was just another one of those half-way points. It just didn't happen.

It was an observation: I thought he was greedy and self-centered. Maybe it was caused by earlier childhood poverty of needing so much. His childhood had made him completely opposite of what I was and what Tommy was. He was excessive in attaining material wealth. It was his way of life. He wanted to show people he could do it. According to what people told me, I was too free with my own material goods. Maybe I expected him to be more like me.

I never did learn the lesson of "tough love" either. Even though my kids have told me I didn't give them enough affection, there's no way to describe the love I had for them. There didn't seem to be any limits to what I gave…and what I forgave, especially when it came to my kids. Now, I look back on it and think they must have been testing me, as they're testing me now; just like Jimmy had tested Thelma, and I had tested Norm. I often wonder when will they come to the conclusion that my love is as real as it's going to get. No amount of telling them seems to work. There's no way to describe the love I had for Tony either. Maybe, he was testing me too. The love he showed to his kids varied from the love that I showed mine. He was very strict with them and made his kids earn their own way. His way has proven more right than mine has in this area. For his children have learned to make themselves successful monetary wise, while mine still have a long way to go; even though, they are older. Mine have come to depend on me too much. Because I offered everything too freely, they have come to expect it. Giving very little appreciation in return, they even say I haven't given them enough.

Tony overcame a good portion of his past. He acquired all the material goods he wanted. I don't think he ever overcame the scars left on his soul made from a conditioned life, though. I don't think he ever acquired the ability to grow spiritually either, not to any extent. His life ended tragically when a fire burned ninety-seven percent of his body to a crisp.

The day before the accident he was in my back yard with Tommy. They were looking at the 1950 Ford truck, which Tommy had restored. It entered my mind then to go out and have a serious talk with Tony. We hadn't gone through a conversation like this in an entire lifetime. *Why should something be talking to me now, trying to persuade me to get him started on his spiritual growth?* I told myself. *He wouldn't listen.* "He would even think I was crazy and wonder what I was talking about."

Linda Carter, almost a life-long friend and a first cousin, heard about Tony's tragic accident and came by a few days afterwards to offer her condolences.

We'd previously discussed a prediction. It concerned Tommy's death. In an earlier conversation, she'd said she didn't want me to finish my book. When I asked her why she said, "Tommy will die when you finish it." I thought along those same lines too, so there was no surprise when she said it.

"Now, I think it must have been Tony," she added. "When I went up to his house the other day I saw a calico cat. Joyce offered me the cat." Jennifer, Linda's daughter, wanted the cat, but she wouldn't let her have it. This was the first time Linda turned down the gift of an animal. Rita, Linda's sister, gave her a calico cat prior to a mysterious accident. Fred Parker, Linda's father, who'd had another mysterious accident, gave her one too. Rita had died from fatal wounds when the center, metal piece of a windshield pierced through her body, caused from her husband running over an elk on Interstate 5. The elk went through the windshield. It happened near Castle Rock, Washington, right at Exit 46, which is Headquarters Road leading to Tony's house. Fred had died from a broken neck, caused by an ostrich. According to

Linda, he was probably disoriented from a heart attack the previous night. The ostrich had got out of its pen and came into Linda's yard. While Linda was away the next day, he tried to put the ostrich back into its pen. It was a time during the large bird's mating season. The third death in the family, all considered mysterious accidents, involved a calico cat. First, Rita, my first cousin; then Fred, my uncle; and now, Tony, my brother. Strange! We both thought so. The accidents were all weird, very unusual to say the least.

Alternately, she listened to me recapture some of my feelings about Tony and his past, while telling me this story. "And get this!" Linda emphasized. "The elk accident was the first to occur in thirty years on Interstate 5. It was very unlikely that a large buck would go so close to a major highway. The ostrich accident was the first to occur in the United States. I found that out by reading the newspapers."

They had both mysteriously died from animals. Another mystery is the "warning" of a calico cat. As much as Linda loved animals, it made it somewhat easier to see, just possibly the cat had a different message to bring: Maybe the cat accidentally tipped over something in the shop, causing the fire in the first place. No one knows for sure just how the cat is related to the accident, except as a warning to Linda that another death was on its way.

With a brief interruption of puzzlement, I continued telling Linda about the day before Tony died. "All the while, I gave myself excuses for not going out to talk to him that day," while my thoughts reverted to the past, captioning some of its highlights. "'He will laugh at me,' I kept repeating 'and call me crazy.' I kept having this conversation with myself out loud. A voice inside my mind was talking to me. It kept nudging, but I thought I'd have more than one day to do it. That makes the third time this has happened to me. This same voice told me to talk to two guys at work. I talk to one of them. I never saw either one of them again. They both died. The voice said something would happen to Tony, which would be so drastic he wouldn't have time to listen. The next day it happened. I never had the chance to talk to him again."

Mom, Jimmy, and his wife, Barbara, and June, our half-sister, came out to Washington from North Carolina. A lot of other people came to the Burn Center in Portland, Oregon, to offer their sympathy, but very few wanted to see him. He was covered from head to toe in bandages, excluding his mouth, eyes and the tip of his nose. Barbara saw him once without the bandages. She said it was as bad as any horror movie that she'd ever seen. He didn't have a nose. Because of eye protection, his eyes were saved.

I prayed for his soul, but I didn't pray for his life. At 53 years old, he died after two weeks of complete unconsciousness. It was April 26, 2000. Doctors had "lost him" and brought him back several times through artificial respiration before taking him off machines totally. His immediate family had a hard time in giving their final consent to take him off the machines, but I didn't. At that point, it was better for everyone, including and especially for Tony.

A short time before Rita died I sat in Linda's living room, across from Rita, and had a similar conversation with the same little voice inside me about her. The voice said I would never see her again. I didn't. It also said that she was a very unhappy person and didn't know how to get out of the situation. I've learned since then that that was true and that some of the happenings after her death would have made her more unhappy. She deserved more. She went to a better place.

Tony collected old cars and restored them. He learned how to restore them to perfection from Tommy. Tommy could completely redo a car into mint condition from a little more than an old rusted shell. When he finished with it, it would be ready for any show room floor. Tommy had collected old cars long before Tony started. Tony followed suit. It was said that there were only three left in the world like one of Tony's cars. It was a 1957 powder blue Thunderbird. The reason it was so unique was it had factory air conditioning and a rumble seat, along with factory electric windows and the more modern extras that cars of that age didn't have. It also had a continental kit. Tommy noted, "Very few of those cars had a rumble seat and a continental kit. They were very unusual. The few that were made came from Canada. I believe Tony's car was made there." In excellent condition, it burned in a previous fire. A 1955 Thunderbird was also destroyed. According to the fire department, an over-heated freezer caused the first fire.

Tony had bought another '57 Thunderbird. He and Tommy had plans to restore it to look just like the first. They were going to put all the fine details of the first T-Bird into the second. The second car was destroyed in the second fire, which killed Tony. He'd just purchased a 1929 Model A Ford. It was completely destroyed too, along with another T-Bird and a '57 Chev.

The only cars saved were a 1957 Chevy Convertible and 1931 Chevy Coup. His son occasionally drives the '31 Coup.

No one knows for sure how the fire started. Tommy thinks he was grinding on something. Since he was a millwright, the accident should not have occurred. He called Weyerhaeuser, the place where he'd worked since he was eighteen, that day to ask how to weld on gas tanks. Tommy said he was very careful about not having any gas in the shop. The major mistake he made was he didn't have anyone with him at the time. It appeared he was trying to put out one fire when an explosion occurred from behind, lighting him in flames. Still enveloped in total flames, he ran out of the large shop, where a neighbor sprayed him with water until the rescue helicopter arrived. During that time he told the people there to hook up the motor home to his tractor and pull it to safety. The motor home was also saved. He was still conscious when the helicopter arrived and didn't slip into an unconscious state until the neighbor stopped spraying him with water.

Tommy was later working on a project when a similar accident occurred to him. He thought it was going to be a repeat of what happened to Tony. A friend, doing some work for Tommy, was welding in his garage near the gas tank of Tommy's 1950 Ford truck when gas fumes ignited. Apparently the gas tank had a tiny leak in it. Three men were there to help put out the fire, which possibly prevented a similar accident from occurring to Tommy and his friend.

Carrying on the family tradition, I became involve in collecting old cars too. Just today I bought a 1949 Ford. Tommy came over to tell me about it and later came back to say, "Toots, if you find you don't want the car, I'll trade you straight across for my Cadillac, or I'll buy it, if you'll let me make payments. It's a man's car, the kind you tinker with. So, you may not want it."

"I've already thought about that," I told him. "If I don't want it, I'll give it to you. I don't want your Cadillac." *It would make a nice companion to "Little Red,"* the name I'd given his 1950 truck, I thought.

Other than a paint job and new upholstery, it's in pretty good shape. None of us like the color purple. It runs well, and it has only 53,000 original miles. If Tony were alive, he'd probably be in my back yard, again today, admiring it and giving me a few pointers to make it better, if he talked to me at all. Tommy is back there today showing it off to a few neighbors and another relative who has a classic of his own. Tommy is still "leading the pack." I'm sure our cousin, Jerry Crabtree, started collecting old cars for the same reason that Tony and I started—because of Tommy. Later, I did give the car to Tommy. He was tickled pink.

It's sometimes puzzling why certain patterns are maintained throughout life. It's also puzzling why some of us remain unable to see ourselves as we truly are, something that might change us to a more desired state. I sometimes wonder how many lifetimes will it take to get to *A Place Called There*? Or, will we just go without making those corrections? Will *Half-way There* be enough? How will Tony ever learn how to grow spiritually without another life? Maybe we sometimes carry something major, such as this, to the next. How could he ever have learned what he needed to learn without such a serious accident? I still say he wouldn't have listened.

Chapter 24

"Poppy"

Grandpa Fred Hogsed—we called him "Poppy." This family's history would not be complete without him. He was Mom's dad. I lived with him and Grandma during my teens, off and on for a short while. A small man about 130 pounds, he stood about five feet, six inches tall. Unlike the "Grandpa" we'd all like to remember—if he ever showed any feelings of compassion or love, very little was remembered. Everyone wanted to forget. He never told any of his eleven children he loved them, not even the one he loved the most.

My grandfather's eyes were colder than steal; not fiery red-hot steal, as some might think evil should look and associated with the color of red. Not white, the color of white is associated with purity; but light gray and colder than ice. It's cold enough to burn you. When he got mad, his eyes would turn glassy like a snake's eyes. Even the milkiness of a snake's eyes tinged his. The coldness in them looked like they could burn you with one slight glance. It was something one could see in the movies but never believed it to be real.

No one knew what went on in Grandpa's mind, except God, himself, and maybe Grandma, later on in years. The details of his actions were never adequately explained. He hardly spoke to his offspring, except to discipline them. The look generally always came first, before any disciplinary action. I've seen him very few times with looks of understanding and mercifulness when words were on his mind. Then, he had Grandma beside him encouraging him to go softly. Most of the time he was commanding and forceful. Probably the only things that kept him from killing someone were God and the law that threatened his freedom or his life.

Tommy and I both had a softer form of this look in our eyes. We don't have it anymore. Neither do we still have the ability to control anyone anymore with a mere glance. I don't know if it's true or not, but I've heard as many as thirty-five men back down from Tommy once. That's probably stretching the truth, but I could see where half that many would have backed away. The look held power that transcends from the soul, the kind of look Hitler must have had. Drastic results occur unless this kind of power is channeled in the right direction. I've seen a picture of Hitler with the lines of a pitchfork in his face. Still, there must have been some good things about him. I think back and wonder what would I have been capable of if I hadn't have had this little voice inside me leading me on to a better way of thinking. I tend to think that that little voice is in all of us, just waiting for us to accept its message, even Hitler. It showed up a few times in Grandpa.

It has something to do with what we learned but not much. For what we learned, we came out of it into a better light. I believe we inherited it through Grandpa. He passed on the power in his eyes and his soul to Tommy and me through his genes. I'm sure he passed on this same power to some others in the family as well, but it wasn't so evident. Tommy and I have learned this is not the right power to deal with. I hope before their time is over, the others will have learned this lesson too.

To channel that power in the right direction, we should use it to endure and overcome. The good brings us closer to the half-way point, and sometimes above, while the bad takes us back. If we try to gain connection and love through control, we lose it. If we get a negative response of any kind, it brings what we think to be significance in the wrong way. It really takes us back. The camouflaged significance never lasts—somewhat like a mirage we might see after a long, dry spell in the desert. We can at least maintain our position and hope to go forward through accomplishments of the right things. If we can't take some good from it, then we should pray it be taken away totally.

To know our enemy we gain power—the right kind of power attained by the right method: I suppose that means I should get to know my Grandpa, even if it is a little late.

William, Grandpa's father before him, taught all twelve grades in a one-room schoolhouse. He was also the Clay County treasurer and a state legislator. A lieutenant in the Army, he fought in the front lines along side his captain who was killed. He was then promoted to captain and survived the war to become heavily decorated with honors.

So Poppy grew up well educated. Serving as a poor model, he never reached even a small portion of his potential because of his laziness. Hatred was well demonstrated up until just before his death. The responsible children who were still alive had dreaded the time when he would become helpless and would need their care. Aunt Marie took him to a Gainesville, Georgia, hospital following a stroke, then a massive stroke. He died about a week later.

"At age 82, he finally became as meek as a lamb. He must have had the stroke in the part of his brain that made him passive. God apparently chose this method to bring him down," Aunt Lucy said.

The beatings my mother gave Tommy when he was growing up were like child's play compared to how Poppy beat his children. He didn't have to take any one of them by the hand. Often just a look would change the rowdiness of the boys into a perfect calmness. One could hear a pin drop following his cold stare. If he said, "That's enough," that was usually all it took. If that wasn't enough, the boys were then sent to the crib to shuck corn.

Of all the bad traits Poppy possessed, some good ones came to the foreground. He could be trusted. People were considered to be as good as their word… and Poppy's word was good. He also possessed the quality of cleanliness. His favorite child, Margaret, made sure he had plenty of hot water to clean up with when he came home. Water was boiled in kettles on a wood stove.

Grandma inherited a home from her father who also passed down 364 acres. Her family was "well to do." Her father was a history professor. She could talk for days on that subject, giving anyone the entire details of its contents. Whatever she learned never left her mind. She remembered it up until her death, in the fall of 1979 at the age of 83. She was a mischievous woman. Playing practical jokes on people and scaring them out of their wits were just part of her personality. It was her way of having fun.

It's easy to understand how the saying "A long row to hoe" got started. Corn became their livelihood. It furnished cornmeal as their bread; it fed the chickens, cows, hogs, and beef, if they had any. Poppy frequently took the children to the cornfields and paced off the area he wanted them to complete before the day's end. Sometimes they traveled for miles just to reach a cornfield where they worked from sun up to sun down in the scorching heat. One day when they were out in the cornfield the house burned down, and they didn't even see the smoke. Since they had no tractors, it was a back-breaking job to be done by hand with the only tool they possessed, the hoe.

Although Grandma stayed home most of the time, she worked as hard as the children did. She cooked the meals, tended the large garden, canned and preserved their winter food, and did all the cleaning.

In the early part of their marriage, Poppy caught a ride with the star mail carrier from Shooting Creek to Hayesville in the early morning and returned with him in the afternoon. The mail was locked in mail sacks and placed in the back of the car, allowing room for passengers. This was their only means of travel, other than horseback. The courthouse square was a gathering place for men to "chew the fat" and gossip. Poppy was often a part of this group of men.

"No wonder I grew up thinking all men were lazy. My grandpa, my father, my brothers, my two husbands, and all the other men I have ever known have given me that impression." I shared similar feelings with Aunt Lucille, who was filling in the blank spaces about Poppy. "A resentment, which nearly turned to hate, I still have to fight against this impact of transgression. Thinking things over thoroughly, I truly believe that most men are unaware of it. Their focus is straight ahead when it should be all around. Even when they are aware, their behavior of thousands of years has given them an excuse not to change. It's been taken for granted too long that women are the servers and the doers."

Aunt Lucy viewed Poppy the same as I did. She uncovered the story about him, as she perceived it. "Following school once, I stopped off at my brother Robert's where Madene (Robert's wife) offered me some peanut butter and jelly with biscuit. I arrived home at 4 o'clock after walking a mile. School was let out at 3. Poppy wouldn't accept my reason for being late. He beat me until my high-top shoes overflowed with blood. It's hard to say what he would have done, but he got tired and stopped," she remembered. Her dress clung to her body in shreds, soaked in blood.

"Grandma Kitchen, Grandma Hogsed's mother, was there. A nice woman, she hugged me and told me, 'Don't you ever make your dad mad again. He'll kill you,'" Lucy continued.

Later she passed by a group of boys and girls at a swimming hole during a trip to the store. They encouraged her to come close to the bank. When she did, they pulled her in the creek. Two hours late when it should have taken her only forty-five minutes to return home, Poppy came after her. He calmly stated, "You know what I'm going to have to do…Don't you?" As he broke a peach tree branch in the front yard, she passed out. "If it scares you that bad, we'll just let it go," he said, and walked off. The truth was she was no longer coherent enough to realize the pain; he wanted her to feel it.

Lucille grew up saying, "No man will ever control me again." She married six times to five different men. She married one of them—Roy Trull, Tommy's best friend—twice. She never did let any other man control her. She lives alone now and probably will for the rest of her days. She's independent. Her dreams were never fulfilled, although she says she's happy with the circumstances and doesn't have any regrets. Knowing my aunt, she has come to accept that part of her life as reality. Her priorities have stood firm on the words she said as a young girl.

David, next to the youngest son, perceived his father to be quite differently. Apparently Poppy changed during the later part of his marriage to Grandma, probably due to Grandma's brothers, Henry and Gorman Kitchen. They didn't like Poppy beating Grandma. He would break chairs over her head, knock her down with a poker, or pull her hair out by the handfuls. Hitting her with objects showed his cowardliness. We believed she would have whipped him otherwise.

Henry told Poppy, "If you ever lay a hand on her again, I'll come back and destroy you personally." They apparently fought somewhat like "The Hatfields and the McCoys." I often wondered how could they stand up to him. The strength he portrayed through his eyes was over-powering.

Poppy took Grandma away to his side of the family. He continued to flout over his brothers and sisters like he'd done in earlier years. Grandma started seeing the better side of him.

He started to work peeling tanning bark. The juice of the bark was used to preserve leather. Later Poppy went out west to Washington, Oregon and California where he mainly worked as foreman of the Carringer Ranch. Lucy thought it was the same Carringer Ranch, shown on the TV show "Diansty," but she didn't know for sure. He was trusted to pay the employees directly from the safe.

Unmerciful to all except Grandma when he came home, his son Robert lay unable to move for six months because of Poppy's beatings. Dr. Paul Killian was called in to tend him. Being just a country doctor, he didn't do anything except check him.

Uncle David said Robert hemmed in a neighbor's cows, making them go across a creek. Robert grabbed the last cow by the tail, following behind. The sheriff and the owner of the cows came out to Poppy's house and insisted that he beat Robert until they said it was enough. A teenager of about 15 or 16, Robert learned the strictness of his father, as well as the strictness of the people in that area.

David perceived his father as being very strict. He remembered a night when he'd been out all night drinking: "I was as high as a 'Georgia pine.' Those Georgia pines get mighty high," David recalled. "When you get that high, you're high." Grandma fixed him and Jimmy, my brother, who ran around with David at the time, breakfast. Poppy was talking to Grandma when David butted in and told him to shut up. Poppy hit the floor, grabbed a chair and told him "Don't you ever tell me to shut up in my home." David became stone sober and apologized.

Most of his children, four boys and seven girls, died early, some from violent deaths. Doctors practically lived at the Hogsed residence during those times.

Margaret, a favorite of Grandpa, died from gangrene at the age of seven. She jumped from a barn loft, causing an obstruction of her bowel movements. Her pain was so great that she ground out her teeth. She lay in Poppy's arms, handing him her teeth, one by one. Softly, he reminded her of the times when she would come to meet him after work, even if it was after dark. Poppy doted over her. This was the closest any of his children came to seeing feelings of compassion from him.

Margaret was described as a gorgeous doll. She had jet-black, curly hair with green eyes. Poppy paid a photographer to come in and photograph her after she was dead. The photographer was ordered to make her picture look like she was still alive, with her eyes open and with her teeth put back in. Swelling, caused by poisons in her body, made her look like she was fat. The background of the casket wasn't shown.

Novalee had heart trouble, caused by rheumatic fever, and died when she was nine. She was sleeping with Mom at the time. When Mom awoke early the next morning, Novalee's body had already become cold and stiff. Mom was too afraid to wake Poppy to tell him. Water had poured out from broken skin on her legs prior to her death. She was buried in the fetal position because rigormortis had already taken place.

"Robert died from an aneurysm. He was driving home from work one day and exploded," Lucy said.

"Exploded? What do you mean?" I curiously asked.

"His eyes popped out of his head and blood was oozing from all cavities," she explained.

"He wanted to retire and redo the old home place," Lucy changed the subject, without realizing her intent, or maybe she did realize it. Lucy was the type that didn't like remembering the past. It brought back too much pain. "His wife (Madene) carried out his wishes."

David added to the story, "He had two guys helping him remodel his house. Robert got drunk one night and showed them a large sum of money. They came back that night and hit him in the head with a blunt object, robbing him of $5,000. He was still knocked out when they found him on the floor. He was taken to the hospital with a fractured skull. He didn't die until much later, but that incident could have caused the aneurysm."

Next to the oldest, Gilmer possessed one of their highest qualities: honesty. He worked on a "CCC" Camp, a division of the WPA for young, unmarried men, for twenty-five cents an hour and sent money back home for the family. At age twenty-four, he died with Hodgkin's disease at an Atlanta hospital. Treated at every major medical facility between California and Georgia for the disease, it was described as "a spider web" and got into his vital organs. They said he was a good man, meaning honesty was at the top of their list. Honesty to them not only meant a person who didn't tell lies, but a person who didn't steal or cheat either. Secondly, he was neat and clean.

Grandma protected Johnny, the youngest, from Poppy's evil temper. Lucy and I thought she also protected David. David was her favorite and resembled her in looks, so she thought. Now, many years later, David's a perfect image of Poppy in looks. His over-all character is much better than Poppy's was though. She was no longer alive to see this transformation.

Johnny was found dead in a railroad boxcar. Not even his own brother, David, recognized him. I probed David for more details about how he looked:

David just said, "He wasn't the Johnny we knew. He was completely different."

"Different in what way?" I asked.

"He was no longer neat and clean like he used to be. He looked like a bum. He'd been traveling like a bum across the United States following a long span in prison, nineteen years. He didn't look anything like himself. They had to identify him by his teeth."

He was a good person up until he went into prison. He was blamed for someone else's crime—grand larceny. The torture in prison—sometimes staying in the "hole," complete darkness, for as long as nineteen months—held its toll on him. For after entering prison, he killed one of his fellow cons for ratting on him. David said Johnny sliced his fellow inmate's head off with a metal tray while standing in a food line. The others gathered around the victim lying on the floor, hiding the incident. They never gave up the true information that would have led to a life-sentence, which officials wanted to give him. It was hearsay that he killed another, but this one was never verified.

David took Johnny's only son, first named Robby Marshal and later changed to John David Hogsed, to raise as his own. He was eight months old when David and his wife, Lenore, got him. He was born September 28, 1971.

By the time David and Johnny came along, Poppy lost control. He was afraid of the two boys. Basically they did anything they wanted to. Johnny wouldn't acknowledge Poppy and talked back. This was something he wasn't accustomed to. Johnny just ignored him and David followed.

Johnny's sentence started as Tommy's had, with a small amount of time in comparison to what he eventually got. The five to seven year sentence was placed on him for burglary when he started running around with the same men as Tommy had run around with when he got into trouble.

David said, "Johnny was unjustly sentenced, and this was the reason he started striking back. His fellow con ratted on him, causing him to go to the hole for thirty days. While the others gathered around hiding what actually happened, Johnny picked up a tray in a food line and killed him. He sliced his head off with the metal tray, displaying absolutely no remorse. They wanted to give him life for this, but they couldn't prove anything. It happened so quickly, and there was a lot of commotion.

"Johnny was different from all the rest. Being a blue baby (a blue, gray, or dark purple discoloration of the skin, caused by inadequate oxygen in the bloodstream, which may point to a congenital heart defect) probably didn't have anything to do with him not feeling any remorse," David related.

They sent him to Ivy Bluff, the worst prison in North Carolina. Guards out-numbered the prisoners there two to one. He was later transferred to Ogden Farm after one breakout. Then they closed Ivy Bluff.

"I remember a time when Johnny went out with someone's wife," I added to Lucy's and David's recollections. "He came home one night with his jaw laying on his shoulder." Lucy was there. She remembered it. Two guys had held him, while another had taken a double-bitted ax to his face. "He was extremely good looking prior to that. He probably felt his entire life was unjust and he'd given up hope." In my way of thinking, this was extreme punishment. I panicked, running to a neighbor's house asking them for help. It was all in vain, because they did absolutely nothing. I just returned home to Grandma's, crying.

Ruth—nicknamed "Cutie" who looked an awful lot like me, according to my aunts and uncles—died at 29 with heart trouble. She was admitted to an Atlanta hospital for surgery to repair two holes in her heart. Her blood was circulating the wrong way, causing her to become exhausted just from walking across the street. The operation went okay. When it looked like she was going to pull through, a turn for the worse took place. Her death came on Christmas Eve, the same day as my father's but two years later. I was staying there at the time. I'd just turned 15 the previous month on November 9. Cutie expected her house to remain spotless, and I measured up to her expectations.

The Three Wise men, a movie starring John Wayne, was shown on TV that morning. I hated to let the movie take priority over washing the breakfast dishes, but something inside me kept nudging: *You've got to see this movie*. So during each commercial, I cleaned a little more of the kitchen. By the time the movie ended I completed the last choir in the kitchen—wiping off the stove. The movie was sad and I cried a few tears through it. While I was still wiping off the stove, tears started to roll off my cheeks and drip from my chin onto the range. *Cutie is dying*, I heard something inside me say. *She is starting that journey now.* I turned around and told the people in the sitting room this. David was one of them. Her oldest daughter, Joyce, 7, and her husband, Jerry Simpson, were also in the sitting room. Her baby daughter, who was only six months old, was still taking an early morning nap in her crib in one of the bedrooms.

"You feel that way because of the movie," David calmly stated. The movie had depicted a similar event during Christmas: A mother had died and left her child to be taken care of by the three men. In this real-life picture there were two children Cutie was going to leave behind. I turned to the picture of the three wise men, which I'd painted on her living-room window a couple of weeks earlier. Looking through the open spaces of it, out into the streets of Atlanta, the tears were still flowing.

"No," I said. "It's not just the movie. Cutie is dying…now." My confirmation on this was so strong they had to believe me. The people there began to scatter in a restless fashion, each wondering what they could do about what I'd said.

"Nothing," I told them. "It's her time to go." I felt like I could sense each sensation of her departure as she came closer and closer to the final step of walking through death's door. She didn't want to leave her children behind, but God's calling was strong and persistent. Then, all of a sudden, I felt good. In my mind, she had entered God's presence at that moment. Wiping the last of the tears from my face, I put my hand on Joyce's shoulder and softly said, "Go! Go tell Cutie's friend that she is dead," and pointed to the house across the street.

Joyce came back after telling them, asking me how did I know? Apparently Cutie's friend wanted to know: had I heard something from the hospital?

"No," I answered. "Go," I started to explain but stopped. "Wait, don't tell them anything. They won't understand. I'll tell them myself."

Walking across the street, my emotions still hadn't completely subsided. Not having heard any word from the hospital, I knew they wouldn't believe me, "Call the hospital and you'll know for sure," I told her friend's family. The phone call didn't confirm the information, but I still knew I was right. A hospital representative called back within minutes, finalizing the confirmation of her death.

Her friend wanted to know how I knew. "I just felt it," I told her.

"How could you just feel it and be so sure that it happened?" She asked.

"That's all I can tell you," and repeated, "I just felt it."

Now, David admitted he felt it too. I think in his case, he was drawing a logical conclusion. He remembered, "About six months before she died I caught her praying to God several times. She asked him to let her live until her baby was older."

Many years later Marie committed suicide at the age of 46, it was said. She took an overdose of drugs. The church told her she was living in adultery with Arb, her husband. She'd been married before. Even though she'd moved out into a trailer, she apparently didn't want to live with the impact of this sin in her consciousness…or maybe the acknowledgment of living alone drove her insane. Others believed her medication somehow got switched. Still, others thought she was incoherent because of being sick and took the wrong medicine by accident. Some accepted one reason for her death, while others refused to believe she would kill herself, as Lucy did. She was a very religious person and a very kind one. The contradiction remains, because some people accepted one belief while others accepted another.

Poppy forbade my mother to speak to my dad when they were married. He had his reasons: Dad was a drinker and didn't give up his booze until years later. When the couple first met Mom was keeping house for Fred Moore, a storekeeper, on Route 64. Unlike her parents, she'd finished the third grade only. Slave labor was all she knew from working in the cornfields and gardens, and helping around the house. Mom and Dad "snuck" off to get married. Even though Poppy disowned her, they moved into a house about a mile away from them.

Mom said she made six dollars a month while working for Fred Moore. "That was enough. I could buy a dress for fifty cents or a pair of shoes for a dollar." Some of that money was given to the family for support. They worked hard and made everything they ate except for a few staples.

Dad beat Mom all the way through her pregnancy with Tommy and afterwards. One Sunday evening when they were out sightseeing they got into a fight. "Your mom and dad could whip seven to ten men any day," Lucy interjected. Mom was holding Tommy, her firstborn, in her arms when Dad peeled the six-week-old baby's forehead with his fist. He'd wanted to hit her but hit Tommy instead. Both of them bleeding, Mom insisted that Dad drop her off at Grandma and Poppy's. Grandma told her she could come inside. Lucy was there, peeling apples underneath an apple tree.

After letting Mom get out of the car, Dad "pealed off" in the big Packard but suddenly stopped in the middle of the road. Leaving it parked there, he got out and started walking back. Poppy always wore bibbed overalls and quiet frequently he would put an arm in the bib. He pulled out a gun and lowered it to Dad's head. He shot him in the lower right check. Only minutes away from being dead, the bullet had lodged below the shoulder blade in his back. A slightly different story of how Poppy shot Dad was beginning to unfold…but I just listened.

After shooting him, Poppy walked out into the yard and kicked Dad over. "If I knew you weren't dead, I'd shoot you again," Poppy dominated with his words. He exercised no restraint.

"Poppy is mean and cruel. He's unrelentless (meaning unrelenting in her comments)," Mom said behind his back. "I married Roy to get away from home and it brought tragedy." She placed her hand over the bullet wound to keep the blood from gushing out.

I thought that this story was true; it included more of the details, which made it sound different from what I'd heard through the years. Dad had come back to get his wife, telling Poppy, "I've come here to get my wife." Poppy told him, "Don't come one step closer." Dad said, "No son-of-a-bitch is going to tell me what I can't do," and kept on walking.

Poppy later realized that he'd almost killed him. "This incident came close to sending him over the deep end," Lucy recalled. By that time, people there were beginning to feel that murder or attempted murder was wrong, regardless of the reason. To show his remorse, he visited Dad in the hospital and begged him for forgiveness. There was never any friendship between them. They just respected each other afterwards.

By the time I was old enough to see the picture for myself my mother's and father's rolls had changed. There was little doubt about who was the dominant one in their relationship. Mom would sometimes down him with a stick of stove wood. I believe she did anything she wanted to then, and he took it. He failed to build the relationship in its early stages. Later it became too late.

Lillie is the oldest one still living. She's in her nineties now. The main thing I remember about her family is that she married into a poor family. She is poor spiritually as well. She has had ample time to learn some things she never got around to learning. It's too bad that most of us don't grow enough spiritually and will probably never make it to the half-way point in this lifetime.

Yes, families really did "bow their head to pray." Religious beliefs were held rigidly. Not even dancing or wearing any kind of pants to the table were allowed willfully. Churches taught sex outside of marriage was "hell-sent." Even thoughts of sex were repressed for fantasy was considered as sinful as the act itself. Anything—exposure of the skin, as well as dancing or talking about the wrong things—created tremendous burdens of guilt when young libidos began to bud. Such fantasies were kept under unnatural rigid control.

Sometimes the control produced twin compulsions, such as sexual desire and spending. It may even have encouraged split personalities, as it seemed to do with my mother. There were many things she couldn't admit to doing. I remember once I told her what she'd done to me in High Point, telling her word by word. She said, "No, I didn't." Again I pointed out, "Mom, R.L. is sitting right there. He knows you did. Lucy's another person who knows. How can you deny it?" She repeated, "I didn't do it." Big tears rolled down her checks. Knowing it was only a defense mechanism, I dropped the subject. I thought I wanted her to acknowledge the truth. Now I look back and think there might have been another reason as well: Some bitterness prevailed because of the way she'd treated Tommy and me.

I became very shy, reserved, and instinctively obedient because of such control. Later developing a mind of my own, rebellion entered the picture when I told Poppy I didn't tell him how to wear his overalls; so just lay off me. The feelings were still so deeply embedded, I have trouble facing the millenium in the same fashion others do. I still find myself accepting some of the earlier teachings. Some of them, especially the ones concerning honesty and cleanliness, has prevailed in my mind and always will. They are the ones that should prevail.

It was almost as if girls had to kill all eagerness for affection any way they could. Most of the time marrying the wrong person—usually the first one who asked them—helped keep their emotions under control. Girls, more often than not, married to get away from home, while others sometimes married because they didn't want to be passed from man to man like a dollar bill is from hand to hand. Bernelle Mosteller (maiden name), a close friend of mine from North Carolina who has lived here in Washington for about as long as I have, put it this way: "We didn't do anything unless we were monitored."

I realized I would have been closely monitored too if Mom hadn't left. Even though it was considered wrong for her to leave, I probably turned out better because of it. In many ways, the people I met along the way have been a part in shaping the things I do. That was enough.

People faced their responsibilities with stout resolve. Bernelle remembered how little her family had. Even though we grew up together, it took her many years to open up and tell me just a few things. "I remember when we didn't even know what a Kotex was. I washed out old ragged sheets after using them. Then I put them in a bucket of cold water to soak for awhile, washed them some more, and put them in the wringer washing machine. After that I boiled them in a big, old, black pot for twenty to thirty minutes. Finally, they were rinsed in cold water and hung on the line to dry. They came out as white as snow. I didn't know what a Kotex was until I was in my twenties," Bernelle related. I remembered that she had told me about using old torn up sheets, but she had left out all the details until now.

Sometimes, lovers really did "fall in love to stay and stand by each other, come what may." I felt in love with Hugh Temple* to stay. My father also fell in love with my mother to stay. In his case, he wasn't strong enough to handle it when he lost her. Both Marie and Lucille had too many husbands to say this was true in all cases. Their strong religious beliefs sometimes kept them knitted together, as my beliefs had kept me tied to Norm for twenty-five years. Sometimes people were never faced with opportunities to get a divorce. Under the circumstances that Johnny went through when he got his jaw sliced off with a double-bided ax didn't leave much of a chance for opportunity.

The situation boiled down to the point of men wanting authority, power and control to say what is right and what is wrong. Time has proved that some of their beliefs held a stronger foundation, while other beliefs went beyond limits and weren't properly understood because of lacking in education.

"Look how people today are so reluctant in making commitments? With the women not wanting to hold relationships together anymore, the wholeness is being destroyed even more so. Awareness and communication are important keys. We have so much interference in our lives we don't even want to stop to think about it. Many are afraid to face anything that would improve our awareness. It would jeopardize the comfort zone.

"Part of the reason I made it so long with Norm is because I was so open. I didn't feel threatened or exposed, and I did feel accepted no matter what." Acceptance is another important key. It supports our need for significance. Rejection can sometimes be detrimental toward growth, if we don't recognize it for what it is and do something constructive to be accepted. Maturity should come sometime. It shouldn't be necessary to be accepted by others to make us better people. We should be better people to be accepted.

Promises were really kept, not just something the people of that place and time would say, and then forget. They believed they were as good as their word. They generally kept it.

These people, my ancestors, all represented some good and some bad. Some of them told me a little more about becoming successful and a lot about understanding. It would add to my growth. As I see things now, understanding is among the long list of words that one needs to be successful.

With her life, Marie has told me that money wasn't "where it's at." She had plenty. She used to take her money to the bank in twenty-five pound flour sacks or cigar boxes. A time when someone tried to rob her, while her husband, Arb, was away, briefly crossed my mind: While the robbers were trying to tare off the screen their son, Aaron, ran to get Dad to help them. Taking a gun with him, Dad made it to her place just in time. Marie and Arb owned a small grocery store. Arb was good at making money, and even winning when he gambled. She was still unhappy.

Lucille has told me with her actions that I didn't want to be alone for the rest of my days. So often our happiness depends on other people's happiness. Her unwillingness to change has caused her to be alone. By seeing only the good, such as thinking you're happy, doesn't necessarily make it true. It just camouflages it. I'd like to face the undercurrents and know the truth. Then I might be able to do something to change to make things better.

Poppy has taught me control is not "where it's at" either. He has also taught me something much deeper than that: If I can't get some good from it—whatever it may be—leave it alone. I don't believe that Poppy was all that bad. He was just bound and determined to have his own way. Instead of carrying his love with him, he was carrying his sins with him.

Martha Harris

Chapter 25

What Keeps It Alive?

A vining plant sets by my kitchen window, partially screened from sunlight as other objects and plants take precedence. It asks for very little—very little water, very little sunlight, and very little soil.

Pointing to its tiny heart-shaped leaves, I said to Linda Carter, my best friend, who had just walked through the house without knocking, "Norm got me that plant. It's lived for about eight years now in less than an inch of soil. No body takes care of it. But it doesn't die. Any other plant would've been dead a long time ago. All my other plants are. The others here are all new. What keeps it alive?"

"You know that saying, 'If someone gives you a plant and it dies,' it means their love for you has also died. If it lives, then their love for you also lives," Linda gestures her feelings of respect. "That old superstition must be true. He must have loved you beyond his promise, 'till death do us part.'"

She sat down at the table. "I've come to get you to type up a letter. But I can see you're not in the mood for that."

"No, I'm not. But I sure could use someone to talk to. It's already late in the day. Just leave the information, and I'll get around to doing it tomorrow," I told her.

"I still cry almost every day. Most of the time it's on the way to and from work. But sometimes I sat on this big couch or look out those big windows just crying, praying, and thinking about what I did to Norm."

"Don't torture yourself," she butts in. "It wasn't your fault."

"Both Sherry and Myron blame me for his death.

"Stay a little while," I begged. "I don't ask much, but I need someone to listen to me today." I'd listened to her many times before; now, I needed a friend to listen to me.

"You know I went back and forth between Wayne and Norm many times—as many as a dozen times or more. Norm told me he would accept me back, even if it were a hundred times. Wayne always accepted me back too, but he always bitched about it. Norm never bitched; he just endured.

"I wasn't the type to do that. I felt I had no choice. I wouldn't have left him in the first place, but I started having some bad dreams. They reoccurred so often I thought I was losing my mind, three or four times a week.

"In one dream, Norm would come to me in the middle of the night while I was sleeping and suck out enough of my blood to live on. He never would kill me because he loved me too much. An emptiness of spirit and drainage of energy always followed.

"In another dream, I was a fly caught in a spider web. Norm's big, blue eyes were in the spider. They were fixed on me. I dreaded each step it took, because I knew I was there to be hopelessly devoured. All the feelings of a helpless fly flooded my body. The spider, with its abnormal power, would eat me a little at a time, and I couldn't do a thing to help myself. I was over-powered. Regardless of my beliefs, I had to make those dreams go away.

"Norm wouldn't permit me to leave him. He permitted me going out on him…but never to leave him. I moved out quite a few times, trying to get him to accept the idea. I couldn't even discuss a separation. He refused to listen. I told him about the dreams and what they represented to me. I told him the truth about everything. Once he even stated he didn't want to hear the details. I didn't want to hurt him. I just wanted to tell him the truth and to get rid of those feelings.

"When someone loses something that means their whole life, as he did, they die in their hearts. Now, do you see how I could've killed him? I remember how much I loved Hugh Temple*, an old boyfriend of mine I had when I was seventeen—I told you about him the day I bought you that stuffed rabbit. I still do, but somehow I've made it to this point. I think maybe I was put in Norm's life to help him make it through a big phase of his life. Why do some people need others so badly? I've always had to overcome. Why can't they overcome?"

"He was sick. He would have died anyway," she tried to soothe me.

"Yeah, but I just made it a little sooner. There's got to be another reason for things happening the way they did. I don't feel like a bad person. But I can't stop crying…And I can't stop thinking.

"Remember when I moved out into an apartment on Minor Road in Kelso. Sherry went to see Norm then. She was fixing to drive off after the visit when he insisted she move over. 'You're going to tell me where she is,' he told her. 'And you don't have a choice. I'll stay here with you until you do.'

"He barged into my apartment to stay, leaving an empty ten-room house, which I'd left him. He bought me flowers and set them on the dining-room table. It was during the Christmas season. A boyfriend bought me a live Christmas tree. Norm pissed on it, and it died. The love of that boyfriend, if there was any, also died. He quit coming to see me. Norm made sure of that. When he came to see me Norm sat at the table looking like a scolded cat. Even I felt sorry for him. But I knew I had to follow through, if I ever wanted to get rid of those dreams.

"He employed whatever technique that worked at the time to keep me under his control. Two effective ingredients were my sympathy and my compassion. I went back home then. I felt there was no way out.

"I also moved into one of your places to get away from him." Linda had three rentals of her own, which she had acquired from a divorce. "That didn't work either. He would be at my apartment waiting for me to get off work. When I opened the door to go inside he'd stick his big foot in the door and wouldn't budge until I let him in. Again, I moved back home. But this time I decided to go out on him. The other ways weren't working; maybe this one would. I even prayed to God to meet someone who would help me make it through the next phase of my life.

"That's when I met Wayne. He was the only one that didn't give up, even though Norm tried plenty of ways to get rid of him too. And I was passionately attracted to him.

"It does seem like a higher power planned it that way. Maybe God planned it for another reason."

"God never plans anything bad," Linda added, while listening intently.

"I know. That's what I've heard. The picture is so complex. We're supposed to have the power of changing our lives without going against God's wishes. Why can't I win in this battle? If I go against God, I can't win. And if I go against myself, I'll go crazy. This is 'a lose, lose' situation."

An old phase popped into my mind: There can't be a penny with one side, a top without a bottom, a front without a back, or me without you.

"Norm didn't believe in a God. He believed in people. I was his god.

"I had to break free of his hold on me. I felt imprisoned in my own home when I was with him. Another side of me belonged to him. We had become 'one' during the twenty-five years together. I didn't believe in divorce, and I wanted to do the right thing. So part of me went with Wayne and part of me stayed home with Norm. I suppose if I hadn't done something about it, I would have developed a split personality. Maybe I was on my way to that anyway.

"I was living with Wayne on 46th Street, behind Henri's Restaurant in Longview. It was my birthday. I asked him to go out by himself that night. I didn't feel like he loved me as much as I wanted him to. So I'd started to withdraw. Perhaps I had developed the need to be needed from my dad and carried that same feeling into the relationship with Norm, which Wayne didn't offer. He needed friends, beer, and pull-tabs.

"For eight hours straight I cried and prayed. I'd gotten a divorce from Norm and married Wayne while Norm was still living. Norm hadn't given me any moral grounds for it. I was still living in sin. I wanted to make things right, so I could have a win situation.

"All the trapped feelings disappeared that night. By then, the dreams had gone, but the trapped feelings were still there until then. Even though, I was no longer with Norm, he would still call me occasionally, asking me to come over to accept a gift or to tell me something about Sherry and Myron," who were no longer children.

A few times I made payments on the rentals we owned, because he'd gambled too much. The judge awarded him a 'living estate,' where he was to keep the property, taking care of it and paying the taxes as long as he lived. He was to receive all the income from it too. After his death, it would revert back to me.

"Twenty-five years is too long to stay in the position that Norm put me in. If only he'd looked at me like that old saying, 'if you love something, set it free. If it comes back, then it belongs to you. If it doesn't, it never did.' I wanted him to set me free; yet, accept me back after I had time to think, time to become my own person.

"The over-powering feeling I had that made me leave so many times and come back again and again was gone. Norm had finally let go, allowing me to make a free choice. I could feel he'd finally placed me in my proper perspective and had placed God in his. I didn't have to call to ask; I just knew. The heavy, almost unbearable, burden I felt had disappeared.

"Could I be rationalizing or could I have stumbled on the truth?" I asked her, without waiting for an answer. It seemed like a beautiful thought. So I accepted it. "By me doing what I did, Norm transferred his faith to the proper God. Maybe this was the only way to change him. I believe it was. But how can this be? I've heard all my life that 'two wrongs don't make a right.'" *At least I can live with this now. So stop trying to put another wrong into it,* I told myself. *If one searches long enough and hard enough for the right doorway, they'll always find it.*

"I told myself that night—the night of my birthday —'If Norm will have me back, I'll go back and be able to stay this time for good. I'll take care of him until he reaches a hundred years old, if he lives to be that old.'

"Boy, am I in a talkative mood today? I need to get this out of my system. You don't mind? Do you?" I rambled on, unyieldingly, hoping I could fit everything I wanted to say into one visit.

A new phase of my life was born. Wayne was there to help me make it to that point.

"I went back to Norm November 16. A lot of important events happened under the Scorpion sign while he lived. His birthday was November 1; our wedding anniversary, Nov. 4; my birthday, Nov. 9; our divorce, Nov. 18; back to together again, Nov. 16; and just past the end of that sign, finalizing that part of the picture, he died Nov. 26. It was as if the picture knew when to stop drawing itself." The California king-size waterbed, which both of us hand crafted and carved a beautiful mountain scenery into the headboard, held the deadly scorpion on its circled mirror. It represented our years together and our trials apart.

"Before he went into the hospital the last time we sat up all night long talking. One thing he said to me, which I'll always remember, 'You know Dr. Bourne (one of his pet names for me), you know how I used to get better when you came home?' I told him 'yes.' 'It's not going to work this time,' he said.

"'Yes, I know,'" I told him with tears in my eyes and knowing what he was going to say before he said it. "I recalled all those times I could just walk into his room and his eyes would light up like candles glowing in the dark. He would raise up and walk, even when he was near death. The power of love conquers so much and sometimes even defies death. I have seen it many times.

"He showed me these love notes after I returned home," I said, pointing to a box full. They were dated but never mailed. They started, "To My Baby," "To My Love," "To My One Love," and "To My Dearest Darling." He mentioned he would correct his weaknesses and listed them one by one: "1. No parking tickets. 2. Stop wasting money. 3. No bad checks. 4. Pay bills on time. 5. Love you like never before. And they ended "I must work on my character because I failed at the one thing that meant the most to me: you."

He apologized for bringing so much sorrow into my life. He didn't mention his gambling in the notes, but by that time his health had deteriorated too much to do any gambling.

"We said good-byes early. He had suffered enough. I'd been there and seen most of it. He didn't want me to see anymore." His lung disease eventually put too much strain on his heart.

Wayne and I got back together again shortly after Norm's death. We spent a total of six years together, an incomplete number. Wayne and I had first married before Norm's death. We never got remarried afterwards, so it was inevitable that we eventually divorce.

"You've been so blessed," Linda said, softly touching the leaves of the heart-shaped plant. "Norm definitely went to his grave loving you. This plant lets you know his love lives on, beyond death."

"Yeah, I can still feel it.

"Now that I've seen the good in this for the second time, I should be able to stop crying. He finally put God in his proper perspective and me in mine." I was no longer his god, and that was good. "Eight years have passed and I still can't sing his favorite song, *He Stopped Loving Her Today*. I get all choked up.

"He said more than once that he would take me to the grave with him. He said a few mean things: One of my schoolmates was killed by her husband when she asked him for a divorce. After killing her, he turned around and killed himself. Norm told me I'd better be careful or the same thing would happen to me. I knew him better than that. He didn't mean it that way. He just meant that his love would live on, in his spirit, as it has in this plant. He wasn't the kind of person to mean anything else.

"Now I think Wayne did too, even though he later married someone else. Wayne always said the only way to get over a woman was another woman. But it didn't work, not this time." Two of his girlfriends and even his wife told me he never got me out of his mind. Linda was one of those girlfriends. Later he died too and his love with him. I got just what I prayed for, someone to help me make through the next phase of my life. There were times I thought I would never make it another month without losing my mind when Norm was living, much less a whole lifetime. I felt like every thing inside me—even my breath and my blood—was slowly being depleted and absolutely nothing was replacing it. Under these circumstances, it was only natural to pray for an out. My way out was Wayne's love.

Both Norm and Wayne loved in their own ways. And I loved in mine. The rest is yet to come. Life goes on. I'll just have to cross the bridges to the future, one by one, when I get there. By no means can I cross them before. I'm not there yet. The little plant in the window, which refuses to die, lives on. It represents the hearts I carry with me to *That Place Called There*. The one heart that nourishes the plant through time with a built-up reservoir of love and keeps it alive no matter what is called Norm.

What we do with our lives is our gift to ourselves... and to God. The people we meet along the way can make it better. Norm Bourne, he was special. He helped me make it through. And I helped him. We were soulmates in every sense of the word.

MySher

*The stage curtain gently closes
and reopens on a new face—
the face of my daughter.
It's real for the moment.
Sunshine and grace
announce their presence with her beauty.
It's all around.
The world keeps on turning,
and she's going with it.
To wherever it goes, nobody knows.*

Martha Harris

My adorable firstborn, she's 27 today.
My heart reaches out to catch her, as my arms did
When she was a little girl.

Martha Harris

I Will Always Love You

Half-way There

Martha Harris

Half-way There

Chapter 26

MySher

MySher, my beautiful first-born, I will always love you baby—as much as any mother could love her child. She's twenty-seven today. She's grown up so fast; seems like it was only yesterday she was headed out across the street naked after a bath. She was only two years old then. Where has all the time gone? She looks a lot like Tommy. He was a first-born too. Her beautiful smile shows teeth as white as snow, just like Tommy's. Her flawless face, every bit as beautiful as one could ever imagine Snow White's to be, holds a charm almost anyone could follow to their utmost limits. Long curly strains of golden blond hair often covers or partially covers her soft blue-green eyes that never seem to lose a glimmer of goodness in a strong, brave, and kindly way. Even at her weakest moments, somehow a kind of inbred strength comes from within to help her get through. She's learned the hard way after leaving home—the street way. And she's paying the price…much more than even I know.

I mailed her birthday present, which she should receive today. The box is empty. I mailed it to Los Angeles where she lives in a nine-bedroom home with her husband whom she married in June of this year. She'll understand and forgive me once she reads the letter within. It was the best present I could think of sending.

Norm, the only father she has ever known, spoiled her rotten and never allowed any spankings. Talking to her was her main form of discipline and that wasn't enough. I don't think he would ever agree to this form of discipline either, if he were alive. But he's dead now. He died November 26 of last year—1990. A time of year to be thankful, it was Thanksgiving or very close to that day. I'm thankful he's out of his pain and misery, misery I help put him through.

The shoulders of this gentle, kind man was a little too easy for Sherry to lean on. His strength came mainly from me—the source of his great love. He stood six feet, two and one-half inches tall and weighed 248 pounds at one time. Before his death he weighed only 160 or less, a person of skin and bones for his height and built. Weakness had overcome his frail body from vomiting up chunks of his lungs. He developed a lung disease from working in wheat without a mask when he was just a young man. Doctors said a person could live on twenty percent of their lungs, but he developed heart failure caused by the stress put on his body. His heart wasn't pumping the body fluids as much as it should, leaving his feet and legs to swell and his outer limbs to look smutty-grayish, like parts of him were already dead. He became exhausted just to walk across the street. Often he slept in a chair, which enabled him to breathe better.

Even with these difficulties, he never became too tired to help me with a project, such as sitting on a bar stool and instructing me on how to wire in some indirect lighting for our kitchen…or to talk to me. Projects that were even too hard for local companies to accomplish were child's play with Norm's instructions. He should have been a teacher…or perhaps the President. The country would have looked on him with great smiles if he'd been the President; all his friends did. He was a teacher in a way, another one of God's angels sent to help me make it to the next phase of my life. His patience, forgiveness, and love were all unsurpassed.

Before he ever left high school Boeings in Seattle offered him a job drawing blue prints for planes. He turned them down because he said he could make more money elsewhere than what the starting pay offered and he was too impatient then to wait for the raises.

He was very mischievous in school, doing such things as buying everyone in the classroom a pen to write with, including the teacher and deliberately excluding himself, when she scolded him for not having one of his own. Although his mischievous nature caused members of his school to vote him to be the "most likely to fail," the superintendent of that same school later worked for us in the field of journalism after his retirement.

Some Weyerhaeuser millwrights needed plans drawn up, which enabled them to make twenty-eight cents an hour more for the rest of their employment with the company. Norm drew their plans, charging them one hundred dollars each. He also drew Tony's plans, which he charged him only twenty dollars, the price of the materials to start the project. Tony was a millwright at Weyerhaeuser lumber mill in Longview. Norm was also a millwright and a carpenter.

The help Norm gave me was unlimited. I never did finish high school or get a G.E.D., but I had to take a test to get into junior college. I went back periodically and took everything from journalism to basic shop skills. Secretarial science, astrology, handwriting analysis, psychology, electronics, and structural engineering were just a few subjects taken over the years. In electronics, I finished with an eighty-seven average because of Norm's help. A large percentage of the electricians quit before the class was finished. There was only one instructor in the whole college whom I encountered knew what I was talking about in engineering, much less help me with it. Yet Norm, even though he had finished the eleventh grade only, could do my work like a whiz. He always said, "You don't have to know everything, just know where to find the answers." When I brought something home from school, he would first look at it. Then he would look for a book to help him find the answers. Books and papers were never completely organized in our home, but it took him only minutes to find what he needed.

His writing was horrible, worse than any doctor's I've ever seen. He failed a lot of tests because of this. At least in one case, they allowed him to come back to take the test orally; he passed with flying colors.

As people sometimes say, "A good mechanic never owns a good-running car," or "A good plumber always has the worst plumbing fixtures." Norm wasn't any different in lots of ways. He had plenty of problems with his immediate family, mainly the two girls in his life—his daughter, Sherry, whom I have lovingly given the name MySher, and me. He made his share of mistakes, like everyone else. In his case, most of his problems were caused by being too lenient…too kind …and too easy going. Or, was that really a problem? He helped me change for the better.

There's one thing for sure: I believe he left this world loving me, loving his kids, and even loving his enemies with the highest quality of love that any person has ever bestowed upon another. I know that God surely must be very loving and forgiving toward him because Norm's love and forgiveness was unmatched in human form. Everyone benefited in some way by his presence. He carried me through!

Johan Lindblad, Sherry's husband, is seven years younger than she is. A Swede with long hair, even longer than Sherry's, he's involved in hard rock music. Johan's father bought the house they live in. His son has plenty of space in the big house to invite band members to live there as well. It also has a large soundproof music studio, with every kind of musical instrument one would want, including three grand pianos. A maid's house, a swimming pool, a kitchen that looks like it belongs in a restaurant and a large utility suitable for a Laundromat grace the premises. Just the dinning and living rooms alone are bigger than a lot of houses. It sets on five acres in Los Angeles. Actually it's too much for Sherry to handle.

Johan hasn't gotten a good start on his career yet. The hard rock band, "Sin City" they call themselves, made at least one tape. They recorded one original on it, which was dedicated to Sherry and played it in her honor at her wedding. The band was doing great but they weren't doing well enough to afford the up-keep of such a big house. Somehow Sherry must have felt responsible because when they couldn't make ends meet she went into exotic dancing. The electric bill alone for the big place was around a thousand dollars per month. So she needed the money. The money was good but the profession held its perils. She developed acting skills that made everybody happy except herself. I suppose that's why she collected

Marilyn Monroe pictures. The pictures hung on the walls throughout their large home. She must have felt associated with her in so many ways. And she could deliver the presence of her ardor as well.

Still, her father by adoption had left an emptiness in her heart from his death. Her cup needed to be filled and she didn't have the answers to deal with the problems she faced. So she got into heavy drugs—heroin.

Apparently Sherry needed some extra help after Norm's death. So God sent another angel to help her get through. Or maybe it was just a time in her life when the apron strings had to be cut. And He sent someone else to carry on the good will Norm had done for so many years.

It's really sad that sometimes when help does arrive, it comes too late. Or, are we to believe it never comes too late? Just another experience in life that comes to teach us something, or just maybe it happens for the benefit of someone else. As she told me, "If my getting involved in drugs helps my kids stay free of them, then it was worth it." By this, I know she still held a kind heart buried deep within her, often too deep to touch. Even though, she still hung on to the old ways.

So while dancing one night she met this old gentleman. He sat down with her in between shows and became the angel in human form where Norm had left off. His words, he gave:

"Keep a kind heart to all.
Give more than you take.
Never judge those who fall.
Hold in your soul the warmth of the sun.
It will fill all the sadness of those to you that come.

"Be strong and bold in a positive way.
Never back down from those who have negative energy thrown your way.
Believe in your dreams.
Wish upon stars.
Go with your instincts and you'll go far.

"Two angels from heaven will walk by your side;
You may not even see one…
The other won't hide!
You'll come to know this one as a friend
Bonded by God above…for you, through thick and thin to eternal end."

He was old and gray; his words were those of wisdom. She realized he was the angel, standing on one side because he'd come her way to give her comfort in a time of great need. "You are the angel you're talking about," she acknowledged. And added with her mind, *my heart, my thoughts, my soul does not doubt.*

As her mother, I'm willing to bet Norm is on the other side. At least, I hope!

That night she looked toward the heavens and smiled at the universe. Her lips softly murmured a prayer. "I open my heart to God above and thank Him generously for smiling on me enough to send my angels of heaven from a distance, especially the one that I can see, the one I'll never doubt. He will forever be my friend…from past to present…and to all eternity."

Reminding herself to listen to his words of wisdom: "The day will come, as it has to me, when The Old Man will leave the skies. With his heart and soul, he'll lift up the world and all its burdens will go away. For The Old Man, Norm, or any other human being, who has goodness in their hearts, are all intertwined with God because they are His ideas—His will. And if the bad happens for a good reason: to make us see something we would otherwise pass up, or if it happens for the good of someone else, then it should be somewhat easier to endure. When we are at our lowest, He's not too proud to sit at our side—regardless of the situation —and be our friend, sometimes silently looking on and sometimes softly speaking to our minds."

She opened the package and found it was empty. Crying at the top of her lungs, she called from L.A. saying, "Mom, Mom…where's my present? There's nothing in the package. Even the postman examined it. He found nothing! Nothing Mom! What's happened to my present?"

"Nothing, Sherry! Nothing's happened to your present. Have you read your letter yet? Go back and read the letter! Then you'll understand what the present is."

"Mom, do you understand? Do you hear me?" She became almost hysterical. "There's nothing in it."

"Yes Sherry, I understand. Just read the letter…and then call me back."

She hung up and called me back within minutes because she lacked patience: "What letter Mom? I never got a…" She seemed almost desperate, as a child searching for something that would solve all her problems. And by now, I was sure she expected the letter to be on the outside of the package. But the letter was the gift; so I had decided it should go inside.

Thinking I had to make her understand quickly, I butted in. "The letter is in the box Sherry. Just hang up, read it—all of it—then call me back."

"What's so important about a letter?" She concluded.

"You'll see, Sherry. You'll see."

She opened the package after hanging up for the second time. The letter read:

Dear Sherry, I know this is a very hard time for you, but I still felt this was the best gift I have to offer. I have carefully wrapped this box so it will look pretty in your bedroom. Set it on a table near your bed. When you feel lonely, lost, afraid, or unloved just reach inside the slot on top of the box. Close your eyes and say to yourself all the things you want to hear. "I'm getting all the love I want or need" should give you the idea. Bring your closed fist back to your chest and release that love inside of you. Believe Sherry! Believe! The angel sitting on the other side—the one you can't see is there beside you to comfort and guide you, if you'll just listen. Have faith, Sherry! What's inside the box is truly inside of you. The gift it offers is faith and belief in yourself. It says only the truth Sherry, because I do love you with all my heart and always will, unconditionally. I can't always be there to show you or to hold you up when things get bad. You just need to stop and listen to the softly spoken words of your better self, inside your heart. Feel what the words have to say. And be the best you can be.

At that time I had no idea of The Old Man, so apparently He was softly speaking to my mind.

I thought this was a good way to wean her, to break the apron strings. I wanted to be the one she needed and I offered my best. If I truly had the wisdom of The Old Man, I would have also told her to look to the Good Lord for true faith. Ask Him! And your cup will truly be filled to the brim. Return to Him again and again, every time you feel the need. It's the only way to overcome the many obstacles that stand in your way.

*He'll stand by our side in angel form and
in the ideas of human mind.
He'll place beauty all around and beneath our feet.*

*The day will come when the Old Man will
leave the skies.
With his heart and soul, he'll lift up the world and
all its burdens will go away.*

Martha Harris

Chapter 27

The Presence of Good and Evil

Exhausted from so many hours of working, I drove into the parking spot at my new home in the country. It was August 2, 1991. The mobile home, located at the very end of Jackson Road off Eufaula Heights, was old but well kept and looked more like a newer house. *With a large deck in back, it would have a perfect place for a hot tub at the end. One could look up and see the stars at night while relaxing in it*; I thought when I bought it. A short distance from the yard, it had a lower dip in the landscaping where I could build the fishpond I always wanted. It even had some underground springs bubbling up in the right places. There was a big fir tree right beside it, where I planned to bury Norm's ashes. He would be right where he wanted to be—near water, near a big tree, and near me. Deer and whole herds of elk often wandered into the yard. One could practically feed them out of their hand. The Columbia River was at a distance below, but the trees blocked its view. It didn't matter. The place had great possibilities. *I can just see it*, I visualized. I would build a cedar fence and make steps over the rolling hill in back that led out into the woods.

This beautiful picture—I should be happy, but I wasn't. "I must be overly tired," I told myself. "That must be the reason I'm crying. I've worked too many hours."

My daughter, Sherry, had gotten married in June. I'd taken off a week from work to go down to Los Angeles to cater it myself. Huge bouquets of flowers, some as tall as I was, were distributed through out her father-in-law's home, where it took place. A life-size, man-made swan was tied off on the swimming pool. Its real feathers made it look lifelike. Seats were set up in the back yard in front of a gazebo, adorned in dark pink roses. I made hors d'oeuvres, representing countries from all over the world and dressed the food table in real silver. All of it looked like it came out of a picture magazine. Her gown was shown on the cover of one. *Any Hollywood star should have been pleased.* I was.

I'd spent too much money, though. Finding myself short $5,000 for the down payment on the place I'd bought, I'd signed a short term note saying I'd pay the money back within ninety days. A large amount of money to have to pay back on top of my regular bills, but I was determined I was going to make it. I'd made the decision to make Sherry's wedding as memorable as possible. Now I'd have to live with that decision.

I'd already worked six doubles that week at the paper mill and scheduled four for the upcoming week. On top of that, I had to clean the house I was moving out of to get it ready to rent. That would be extra income and I needed it to pay the bills. Even the grooves of the window seals of the place I moved out of were cleaned. For weeks I got by on three to three and a-half hours of sleep. I hired someone else to do the painting.

Thinking I might drop in my tracks any minute, with tears streaming down my face, I got the last bit of clothes from the old place on North First in Kelso from the back seat of the car. The first thing I pulled out was Norm's Jaycee vest. As tired as I was, how could I notice anything? Hesitating, I just stood there for several minutes looking at the vest that was still on its hanger, as if something wanted me to notice something special about it. A little pen on the upper left side caught my attention. It read "Let's Press On." I stood there a few minutes longer looking at those words. All choked up, I cried and laughed at the same time. "How did Norm know—or how did anyone know for that matter, except God—how much I needed strength right now?" That's what it offered. I felt as if Norm was right beside me, carrying part of my burdens. It was a very strong sensation, which I appreciated tremendously. I appreciated it so much that I then cried with joy. "Let's Press On," I said to myself while walking into the house carrying an armload of clothes. The tension, weariness, and feelings of apathy smoothed out. Even the tiredness didn't seem to be so drastic. Nothing was going to hold me back. *I'm going to make it.* A smile came to my face, as the tears dried on my checks. *I will keep this vest for as long as I live,* my mind disclosed, as I hung the one piece of clothing up in the closet and leaving the rest on the bed.

As I came in, I'd noticed my beautiful plants were still out in the hot sun. My Angel Wing had grown to the ceiling at the old place and was retracing its journey back down to its roots again. Everyone that saw it said that was the first time in their lives they'd ever seen an Angel Wing bloom. Tiny clusters of flowers, formed into huge blooms bigger than my two fists, hung oblong, downward on the branches. The Rubber Tree had grown to be almost as high as I was. Instead of having just single limbs grow out from the roots of the Boston Fern, it had limbs growing out from the limbs. My whole porch looked like a jungle at the old place. Some rattan furniture had set among the plants where I often sat and looked out of the full-length windows. My plants were the only reason I hated to move out here in the country. I didn't want to upset their growth. It almost turned my stomach to see them there in the hot sun. It had been a scorching day. From them being there all day they would surely die. I rushed back to the porch to get them out of the sun. Thinking my efforts might be in vain, I still had to try to save some if I could.

Out of the corner of my eye I saw Myron, my son, lying on the couch asleep as I brought the first plants inside. He'd been there watching TV and sleeping all day after a drunk, while my plants were dying and he didn't even give a damn. "Myron," I stammered, "Why didn't you think to bring in my plants? I'm exhausted. Don't you realize son that I've got almost more than I can handle? Give me a hand!" He started clapping his hands.

"I didn't mean that kind of hand. Come on now! So I can get some rest before I have to go back to work again."

The jobs were dwindling down. The payments on the loan were coming along fine. I did have some priorities left. One of my apartments had roaches. The exterminator was scheduled to come tomorrow, and if things weren't ready he'd charge me anyway. The bill reached high proportions as it was—almost $700.

I went to the door of the last one on the list in the triplex whom I wanted to remind and make sure things were in order. The door was wide open. She wasn't home. Her small son—much too little to be left alone—was in front of the closed screen door. It was unlatched, so I went in. I'd previously notified her to get things ready for the exterminator, but she hadn't done a thing. I knew it was wrong to go in her apartment, but *someone in this world has to be responsible. It's a dirty job, but someone has to do it,* my mind concluded. "It's good she doesn't have too much to get ready," I said to myself as I started emptying her cupboards out onto the table to cover with plastic. "Besides, she's the reason I have to do this in the first place. I don't think she even owns a broom," I continued mumbling to myself aloud as I finished the job. She returned just when I finished and started walking back through the house to go outside to write her a note. Before she entered my presence I thought *surely, she'll be back in a little while. Maybe I should ask a neighbor to watch her child until she returns.*

"What are you doing in my house?" She screamed out, when she saw me.

"I told you several days ago to get things ready for this. The exterminator's going to be here tomorrow," I answered. "I just did the job for you. You know you're supposed to stay out of the house for at least eight hours? Don't you?"

"You have no right being here. My husband is gone. I don't know when he'll be back. That's where I was when you came; I was trying to find him. Can't you come back later?" She rambled on, almost in hysterics. "Get out of my house."

"The work is already done now," I said calmly. "I don't have time to come back. All that's left is for you guys to be gone from eight in the morning 'till eight tomorrow night."

Leaving the door open, she started to leave again, without her son.

"Aren't you going to take him with you?" I asked.

With a snarling disposition and mumbling something to herself that I couldn't understand, she came back and grabbed her child. After getting a short distance away she came back again. I was preparing a note to put on the door, in case she hadn't heard me correctly. She seemed too rattled to listen.

Much calmer now, she said, "We don't have a place to go…And I have to find my husband."

"Don't you have any relatives you could stay with for one day?"

"No, we don't have anybody," she said shaking her head.

"Okay," I said. "Find your husband and see what he has to say. If you still can't find a place to stay, give me a call. Try calling to let me know as soon as possible. I'll be leaving to go back to work at ten."

I just barely got back home—a thirty-minute drive —and she called, telling me they still needed a place.

"Okay, be ready when I come to pick you up. You can stay at my place. I'll arrange to have someone take you home tomorrow, since I'll be at work."

On the way back home after picking them up I found out they hadn't eaten. With very little food in my house, I stopped to pick up groceries. I was planning on getting a couple hours of rest. I had another double planned that night. *It's 6:30. I won't be able to do that,* I silently told myself. Something quick and easy was steak and baked potatoes with vegetables. The bill was thirty some dollars. After getting home I ended up cooking it because she seemed too helpless to do it herself.

I explained how to work the TV and the hot tub, in case they wanted to use it, and offered my bed before leaving for work.

The next day when I got home the house was in a mess and the dishes were still dirty. So I cleaned it up. The bad part of dealing with that family was over, so I thought.

In the meantime I had another project to take care of. Going through every process available—attorney and court, the whole bit—to get this one guy out of my apartment, it still didn't seem to be enough. I was sure he was demon possessed. Getting up in his face, I looked him square in the eyes and told him I wasn't afraid of him. His eyes looked wild and scary, even worse than his appearance. He would have been fairly good looking if he'd kept himself neat and clean. I probably should've been afraid of him. This disheveled, young man had no intentions of backing down. Realizing I was only making things worse, I relaxed and stepped back. "I know who you are," I said. "You're the Devil."

He agreed and seemed pleased to be associated with Satan.

That's when I knew I'd "hit the nail on the head." I walked off, telling him I had already won the battle in court and to get everything off my property by the following day.

The following day he was gone. He was thrown in jail for some reason I don't know. Maybe it was God's way of making sure he was gone.

A trailer with two guys in it was still parked on my property. I was mad. Knocking on the door, they opened it. "You guys were supposed to be gone. I'll give you just two hours. If you're not gone by that time, I'll hook up your trailer and pull it out into the street with you in it."

They mumbled some excuse about John saying they could stay there. "I don't give a damn what John told you," I almost screamed. "Don't you know he was evicted? I've already gone to court and won. I've paid over $1,000 to get to this point. I've had enough. You have your orders, and I'll guarantee I'll follow through with my threats when I return."

I shouldn't have had to go to such extreme measures. The day before I'd called the sheriff's office five times and waited a half a day. They never did show. "The system's just set up to collect money," I said to a neighbor, my anger still boiling over. "The people working in it doesn't care about earning it."

The two men obliged. When I came back they were gone.

The place was in shambles and I didn't feel like cleaning it up. So I hired someone else to do it. Going through the apartment, I explained to the two men I'd hired what I wanted done—cleaning, painting, repair this or that—pointing to the objects I wanted repaired.

Just before I got to the bedroom closet, I stopped dead in my tracks. "Don't touch the closet," I said. The feelings I got were overwhelming. It's hard to describe them in detail, but even the hair on my arms stood up. Tremendous fear spread over me, as water would have if I'd jumped in a pool. Evil was all around. It wasn't hot; it was cold, as if no amount of heat would raise it to the right temperature. I felt as if the hair on my head was standing straight up. Thoughts occurred to me, *if I died this particular moment I might be taken with it.* An over-powering need for air was present. I felt myself gasping for breath. I couldn't ask the handymen to paint it, if I couldn't do it myself. I forced myself to take a few more steps toward the closet to test my feelings in relation to it. The closer to the closet, the stronger the feelings became. Its power seemed more like a brick wall—without the bricks. I backed off. With each step further away from the closet, the feelings lessened. There was something in that closet I wasn't supposed to see. "Okay," I said to myself. "I'm not going to live here. With the renters I've had, they probably deserve it." When I got outside and thought about the situation more logically, without fear, I knew then there was something strange about the place. I thought the real reason I didn't want to do the job myself was because I was tired and lazy. There was another reason besides that. I didn't know exactly what it was, and I was too afraid to put any more force against the power than I already had to find out.

Because of having a hard time renting it after the work was done, I accepted two other disheveled men, which I didn't want. They planned on having a third guy stay there too. I said, "Okay," since I didn't want to fool with it any longer. I still didn't want to find out what the reason was behind those feelings. *Maybe others didn't feel it. They had to or it wouldn't be this hard to rent*, I thought.

While the guy paid me $650, without looking at it, was still standing in the yard, I told him, "I've got to do one last thing before you move in." I took the Holy Bible in, which I had intentions of putting on the shelf in the closet. Just before I got to the closet I said a prayer—the Lord's Prayer or the 23rd Psalms, or both, I don't remember. I have a little prayer on the inside of the front cover of my personal Bible. I'm not sure whether I said it or not, because all the fear I felt seemed to take priority. I didn't have it to refer to, but I must have wanted to say it. I think I did. It reads: "I am a believer and not a doubter. I choose to live by faith and walk by faith. My faith cometh by hearing, and hearing by the Word of God, Jesus is the Author and Developer of my faith." I placed the Bible on the shelf. Not wanting to look around in the closet, especially to the left where the feelings were strongest, I hurried out. "Don't take the Bible from the shelf," I told the new renter. "Leave it there…and make sure you tell the other guys to leave it there too."

The men had slept on a pallet on the living room floor that first night there. I noticed it when I returned. A neighbor called and said they were gone. "I don't think they even spent the night," the neighbor said. Some of their belongings were still there. They didn't come back for them or to ask for a refund. Still, I was reluctant to see what the problem was. *The Bible's still there*, I thought. *It will give the next renters the protection they need.*

A couple from California needed a place, so they rented it next. In a short time I had a little house become vacant. They ask to rent it instead, saying they wanted a bigger place, which left the apartment vacant again.

"It's time I see what the problem is," I told my handyman. "I'd like to know why it's so hard to rent." Some major work had been done and some nice, little curtains had been put up, plus mini-blinds.

"I know what the problem is," he said.

"What?" I asked in amazement. "You know, and you haven't told me."

"It's that picture of the Devil in the bedroom closet," he answered.

"Uh! I've been in that closet and I didn't see any pictures."

"It's just as you walk through the door to the left," he said. "You can't see it unless you turn around after you enter. Its eyes look like they're following you."

I then tried to get the handyman to get rid of picture for me because I knew it had to be done and I didn't feel like I had enough strength to do it. He wouldn't. "The Bible's still in there, isn't it?

"No, no Bible. It's gone."

"You mean to say they took the Bible?"

"Yes, it's gone."

First, I had to somehow get rid of that picture. Saying another prayer, but still feeling the fear, I hoped Jesus would protect me. An appropriate prayer here should have been "Satan be gone, for it is written. I stand behind the cross of Jesus Christ. His blood is my armor." Approaching slowly, with caution, I entered the closet. Turning to the left, there it was. It was different from all the other pictures I'd ever seen of the Devil. The face was more human-like, except for the eyes; but it was easily recognizable as Satan. It even resembled John, the guy I had to evict. Mom had told me more than once that the Devil didn't look like pictures portrayed by artists. "He's a good looking man," she'd said. "He looks like that to deceive you." I added to her beliefs: *He's also dirty and has fierce-looking eyes, the kind that can scare you to death with just one glance. I hate to even think it, but that's the same way I've seen my grandfather look plenty of times when I was young.*

Sure enough, the Bible was gone. The guys had apparently taken it. I couldn't see the couple taking it. I took the picture off the wall, feeling like I was afraid of it. I knew I must stand behind the victory of the cross and have a healthy respect for what I saw. Afraid to tare it up, I put it in the garbage.

Later I asked a neighbor to come down and perform an exorcism. He asked another person from the church to help him. They went through the apartment, saying Bible verses and anointing it with oil.

I don't remember the verses they read. Standing behind them at what I hoped was a safe distance, most of what they said I didn't hear. But this seems to fit: Christ said, "Behold, I give unto you power to tread on serpents and scorpions, and over all the power of the enemy; and nothing shall by any means hurt you. Notwithstanding, in this rejoice not, that the spirits are subject unto you; but rather rejoice, because your names are written in heaven" (Luke 10:19-20).

A neighbor lady and I walked through the place to the closet, checking to feel for evil presence afterwards. The main spirit seemed to be gone. We sensed there were still some evil present, but to a much lesser degree. We concluded there must be a demon in the closet. For some reason, it felt more like a ghost with some evil tendencies.

My handyman said he would get rid of it. The evil had been reduced to the point to where he thought he could. He planned on putting a pallet on the floor; his pillow would be inside the closet, the other part of his body would extend out into the bedroom. I told him he could get into serious trouble. He said he had some ancient Indian knowledge that would work. I didn't think he was right for it because of his beliefs. I doubted his methods, but I thought I'd let him try. Afterwards he drew a picture of what he saw that first night. Even the picture he drew felt evil, so I threw it away…And it's strange, but I don't remember one thing about what this picture looked like.

It was surely a mistake to let him try to get rid of it. *Maybe it was another deception*, I thought. I think the demon went inside him. For afterwards he started doing mean things. He "Mickey Moused" the work he did for me, and later I had to have someone else do the job right. His accomplishments were jilts, although he was overly paid. He stole my checks right off the coffee table, while they were still in the box, forged my name and cashed them all over town. I suspected something wrong when he brought up the subject one day about what other people had done to me, as if he was trying to rationalize with himself: If they did it, it was okay for him. I had to evict him too. He lived there several months free while cleaning, painting, and repairing it. The job should have taken only a week at the most. He had help. He told some neighbors, whom he was friends with, he knew he was doing wrong all along. He did it anyway because he thought I owed him. He explained to the neighbors that he and a couple of his friends had done a painting job for me, which he never got properly paid for. I remembered the incident he was talking about: It seemed to me I was the one who got ripped off on that job, as well as all the others. I explained to the neighbors my side of the story: "It rained almost every day during the time they were supposed to do the painting. He called me up daily wanting to get paid. I took an hour out of every day to drive into town to pay his co-workers fifty bucks. He wasn't there very much because he was sick. I think his girlfriend and her brother, who were his co-workers, were there just to collect the money. Very little work was done, and I had to hire someone else to finish it. Fifty bucks isn't much, but when you multiply it several times it keeps getting bigger. Considering the amount of work that was done, he was overly paid for the job—drastically over paid," I finished explaining, almost in a snarl from so much anger.

The neighbors said he had to pay his girlfriend's brother another three hundred and some dollars for the job.

"Well, that was his fault. They didn't do the amount of work I paid them for, much less getting paid extra," I told them. "Besides getting ripped off is not a good reason for stealing. If that was the case, I should have been the biggest thief ever was." I don't know whether it's true or not, but I heard later that his girlfriend had a drug habit, which he supported. I thought, *maybe he had one too. How many drug addicts have I supported? They've stolen enough from me to make themselves rich, if they'd just quit the stuff.*

"A little 'slap on the hand' was all he got. It amounted to ninety days total, with thirty suspended and another thirty on community service. He spent only thirty days in jail. In my opinion it should have been a year.

"Maybe I've brought all this on myself," I told a neighbor. "Some years ago I thought I could satisfy my curiosities with the occult and still believe in Jesus. I studied and practiced a little bit of everything: fortune telling, tarot cards, horoscopes, palm reading, ouija boards, and even touched a little on voodoo and witchcraft. My coworkers were even calling me up at home to ask how to conjure up magic to do their bid. It wasn't unusual for me to take a little pouch of herbs to work with me, or even make a little doll out of bread dough and make my wish about a certain person, saying some particular chant to go along with it. I don't think I was ever possessed because I did believe in Jesus Christ. I thought I was doing it just for the fun of it. Now I know there is only one victory over demons and that is Jesus Christ. When the Devil gets through using you for his purposes, he'll destroy you…Or better yet, he'll help you destroy yourself. Apparently I had to learn this the hard way."

The renters that had the roaches came back to haunt me. I wanted them to move out, so I wouldn't fix the ceiling in their place. A leak in the roof caused some damage. I fixed the roof, but asked them to get out so I could fix the inside. That was just a reason I thought I could use to get rid of them. It was my place. Why couldn't I do whatever I wanted to? Others had done the same thing, but apparently there were no kids involved or the people had moved without fighting it. They called the city officials on me, who in turn called me to force me to fix it. I told them they had been evicted and I was waiting for them to get out so I could. That didn't work.

While I was driving over to their apartment to take care of it, I started feeling sorry for myself. With big tears rolling off my checks, I asked myself why did I bother to do so much for these people who treated me like shit and didn't even care about themselves. A few times I'd even hired the man in that apartment to come out to do a few chores for me, paying him well and even coming into town to pick him up when he was desperate for money. I think he used the money to buy booze, instead of buying something that was needed for his family. Maybe by that time I was losing it. The whole scene was much bigger. This was only a part of it. *I've been through enough,* I told myself. Feeling sorry for myself came naturally. This feeling wouldn't accomplish a thing. With big tears rolling down my face, while driving through town, I began to pray. I didn't know what else to do. I was talking to God as if He sat right in the truck beside me, but I felt like He was still in Heaven. I told Him my troubles, my thoughts, my feelings. Just after I said, "God, I've done so much for these people and they don't even care enough about themselves to take a bath. You know everything that's happened to me. Why do I have to try so hard to build these people a better home? I thought by being good to them was being good to you."

Suddenly, I felt this powerful presence. It answered me in words more clearly than my own imagination, "Yes Martha, but I'm building a better place for you." *This can't be real. I can't be in the presence of God.* Yet, it was so real I looked on the seat beside me to see if there was an indention of where He sat. I really couldn't tell. I almost stopped the truck to have a closer look. Then something seemed to say "That part doesn't matter. It only matters that you feel My presence." It felt like the past and future had touched with the presence to make it one. Nothing else mattered except that moment. My thoughts and feelings colored the surroundings pearl blue. It appeared to be mixed with royal blue, marbled with white silver. Tiny bits of lights—billions of them, which didn't obstruct my view of driving in the least—showed up everywhere. The stars in the sky became brighter. They came closer to light the way, as I thought of the Star of Bethlehem. *Was my mind playing tricks on me, or did this really happen?* I asked myself. Again, the voice seemed to answer, "That part really doesn't matter. It only matters that you think it, feel it, and believe it."

I dried my tears and felt a little ashamed for lacking faith; yet, grateful. "Dear God, thank you for Your Presence." It felt so good. Now that I had gone through the presence of the darker side, I was able to appreciate the good feelings more.

A soothing, peaceful feeling over-powered the surroundings. No pain! No hurt! No despair! No trouble! I felt like I was floating on a pink cloud in the midst of the blue surroundings. Nothing else mattered. I wanted it to last forever. *It would be so wonderful to have this feeling all the time.* I smiled—again.

These trials must be for my benefit. They'll make me a better and a stronger person, if I don't break in the meantime. I think I realized then that we shouldn't necessarily be good to evil—take a slap on the check—at least, not all the time. We should stand up, put on the armor of God, and take up the sword of the Spirit, which is the Word of God. "Help me to speak boldly, as I ought to speak. Above all, grace be with us that love the Lord Jesus Christ in sincerity." In this case: He is considered first and above all, as it should be. His presence will reign forever when everything else has failed.

A presence such as this will always prevail to help me endure and overcome. When the going gets rough, I should think of God and let Him light the way. He is the only "pink cloud" I'll ever need. Thank you God for Your Presence.

Martha Harris

Chapter 28

Evasive Goodbye

"Sometimes I'm so happy; and then, sometimes I'm so sad. I'm always around a lot of people; yet, I'm all alone. I have a lot of secrets, all of them my own. I like it when you're here with me, talking all the time; always taking care of problems, whether they be yours or mine. If you think I don't care, you are very, very wrong, because I don't know what I'm going to do when you're gone."

Words that echoed in the night, she whispered them to herself while Tim, her lover, lie beside her stoned on heroin. His trips to Sheva were becoming more frequent, more frequent than hers. He would soon be lost, if not already, in the drowning pool of the "Black Tar" heroin that smelt like vinegar.

Tim had replaced Johan, MySher's husband. A few years had passed since her residence in Los Angeles. She had moved to Kelso with Johan and lived in one of my rentals for awhile. Right under my nose, and I didn't see the changes that were taking place. Maybe I didn't want to see them, because it hurt so badly to see something so wonderful and beautiful die while still on the vine, like a dried up, wilted flower.

Johan was living in Sweden now. The band Sin City, which he was a member of, broke up because of the death of the keyboard player, Jan Svensson. The day before he died Jan, Sherry, and a few others were standing on a balcony above a pool in Hollywood talking about what would happen to a person if he fell off. One pointed to several objects below, saying they would hit there, possibly over there, then there. The next evening they were having a party at which Jan was walking on his hands and accidentally toppled over the balcony to his death. Coming over here to the United States, they thought they would fulfill all their dreams and have a happy life. Something went wrong, as it did with my youngest brother, Tony, and so many others throughout the world. Both of my children, Sherry and Myron, were in that group of people where "something went wrong." Even I can relate to that group.

MySher apparently became involved with the ways of the world. Searching for stimulation in all the wrong ways, her spirit and her beauty slowly dissolved over time, leading her toward hell. She couldn't stand the smell or the sight of the narcotic powder, called Sheva. But she loved its power to cover up what she couldn't face. Disgust for it had always been there. The need for love was her vulnerable point; it held a power over her too. She couldn't stand the needle either. The whole process of preparing it by heating it up in a spoon made her sick to her stomach. She had relied on Tim to take care of it and shoot it up in her veins so she wouldn't have to face the undercurrents of its demons. All in the name of love, she let her lover get her hooked on heroin. "Where did she get such a distorted view of love?" I whispered to myself, while reading the words in her diary, which she had given me.

My whole self seemed to shatter as I read the diary of my beautiful daughter. Not even one piece of existence stared back at me. "Why? Why?" My soul cried out with tears and despair.

She hated me for not loving her, a conclusion she'd found all on her own. The bad information still rang in her brain. Just like a computer filled with bugs, her brain didn't function right anymore, no matter what one might do. "You mother, dear, have fucked with my brain. You've made me the way I am. You turned me into a monster, both inside and out." I continued with the reading of her words.

"Oh God, I don't have the least idea what I did wrong." Last Sunday the minister spoke on the subject of making decisions, and I tried to recall his message. I chose this method of thinking of something good—anything good to replace the overwhelming hurt inside me. He started his sermon by asking us, "What do you know about making decisions?"

Even though I hadn't read the Sunday school lesson, I spoke out: "An airplane pilot is more apt to make a better decision than his co-pilot because he has more experience." This didn't relate entirely, but it made good sense.

One guy in the group believed God made all the decisions for us. He argued his point. It was brought out that we have the free right to make our own decisions. To rely on God to help us is another decision that is up to us.

Turning around and facing the church member, I said, "Even Shakespeare said it: 'To be or not to be.'"

Returning my eyes to the print on the diary, I continued reading. She says Tim doesn't make sense anymore. She doesn't realize it, but most of the time she doesn't make sense either. The sweet little girl when she is doped up and the demon when she comes down, distinctively two different personalities—one representing God and the other representing the Devil. This is what my precious, MySher, has turned into?

"I hate drugs…with a passion!" I whispered to myself. Looking up from the words in front of me I hear a song on TV. This is "Martin Luther King's Day," I realized. "Before I be a slave I'll be buried in my grave" is the sound of music coming from the TV. "A good comment? Maybe! But I'd rather be a slave than hooked on drugs, a fate worse than death…much worse."

Sometimes she whispered in the night when she wasn't too high on Sheva herself: "Please God, please bring him back to me, the way he (Tim) used to be. I don't want him to die. I love him. Please! I'll quit everything too. So we may be friends again…and have fun…and live together happily. Please God, help!"

My hope and faith return for a moment: "Maybe by seeing a loving man destroyed, along with a mother's prayers, will bring her out of it. At least, she's asking for help. That's a beginning. For now, she's drowning in self-pity, blame, and self-destruction. This roller coaster is headed downhill toward Hell at a speed beyond her control.

"Oh God, where are you? What am I suppose to learn from all this? The torture is already so bad I feel like praying for the rocks to fall on me and hide me now. You said you would never put us through more than we are able to bear. At this point, I can't learn anymore. The pain is too great." I look on the wall and see a cross of Jesus Christ through tears, thinking to myself; *at least, your suffering had some dignity to it.*

"I can't even use the bathroom because she (Sherry) spends a great deal of her time there. When I ask her to let me in, I need to go potty, she gets angry, hollering and screaming about all the things I've done to her and what an evil bitch I am. Even when I say something good she becomes outrageously cruel. She blames me for Norm's death, the way she is and the way her brother is." These words I silently whisper to myself while watching the tribute to Martin Luther King on TV.

Her brother is in the halfway house in Kelso now, released from a thirty-one month sentence of prison. To me, his crime didn't seem to be that bad. I did pray for him to change for the better; maybe that's how God chose to deal with him. He got drunk, stole my truck while I was at work, and wrecked it causing $6,000 in damages. He was involved in a three-car accident. Charged with a hit and run, he was also driving on a suspended license.

My mind reverted back to Sherry's diary: "She hates the drug so bad she has to have a friend or a lover deliver the stuff into her veins." My heart cries out, all in vain, "What have I done to make her this way?"

The only thing I can think of is I worked a lot of hours, leaving Sherry and her brother, Myron, with a babysitter all their lives. I thought I had to work to help pay the bills, to keep the water and electricity from being turned off. I recalled a scene out of the past when they were just babies: All the utilities were turned off. We didn't have a home phone at the time because we spent so many hours at work, and our watts line there covered three states; so there wasn't much need for one. I must have been sick because I seldom spent any time at home without needing rest very badly. Myron was just a baby, a couple of months old. I wrapped him up in a blanket, carrying him with one arm to the nearest phone booth. I held onto Sherry with the other hand. She was less than two years old and needed the control.

"Both the water and electric have been shut off. I have to clean bottles, fix formula, and take care of these kids. I was right in the middle of doing that when it happened," I told my husband, Norm, at the other end of the line. "It's extremely hard to hold on to Sherry when she's trying to get away from me, hold Myron in my arms, and make this phone call too. You shouldn't put me through so much. Why do you? I'll give you just twenty minutes to get up here and pay those bills. That means you'll have to hurry." I reminded him of the fifteen-minute drive between our work place in Kalama and our residence in Kelso. He knew I was plenty angry so he'd follow through. Shortly after I got back home, I expected the utitlities to be turned back on.

Normally my anger lasted only a few minutes, but I was still boiling when I returned home. I busted every cup in the house except one big, fat mug, which would not break no matter what I did. Everything I threw it at broke, but not the mug. It would have taken a sledgehammer to bust it. After the anger subsided I thought, *What have I done? Just destroy a lot. Norm's so easy going; he'll just pay the bills and help me clean up the mess. It wouldn't even make him mad. Why did he have to carry things so far?*

I could certainly see now that Sherry was part of me. She hadn't been as lucky. No man would ever stick with her like Norm had stuck with me. She had pushed her husband, Johan, out the door. Now a lover had taken his place. Norm wasn't that easy to get rid of; he wouldn't leave regardless. When I left him he would follow me and not give up until I accepted him back. He would even wait until I got off work and put his big foot in the door, blocking its closure. Sleeping on the couch, he would stay in my apartment, until I decided to move back home. Apparently I needed that kind of clinging. It showed he needed me as my father had. It served its purpose at the time. Not even I could ever find another one like him. I could search the world over and never find one. His love might have been clinging, but it was the best he had to offer.

Maybe I shouldn't have acted that way, especially in front of Sherry. She was probably just as impressionable as I was when I was young. I had carried that same need for my father into my marriage with Norm. He had withstood the pressures of time and stayed with me regardless. Sherry had the same need, which she had carried into her marriage with Johan. She needed to be needed, as we all do, but both of us had carried that need to extremes. Choosing different ways, we both had tested our husbands. In my situation Norm had passed all the tests, loving me regardless, but in Sherry's situation, Johan had failed. With all her efforts to get rid of him, she'd succeeded. Apparently she wanted Johan to prove his need for her by sticking it out. That wasn't the case with Johan. He was gone now.

Trying to think of something I'd done wrong, I continued with my thoughts: *During the time of my pregnancy with Sherry I was extremely depressed. Could that have caused her to be so depressed now? She says she's off the drugs now. But she's lied so much I can't trust her anymore.*

I went to the bathroom where Sherry lay in the bathtub crying from either depression or withdrawal symptoms. She took lengthy baths often. Most of the time she was grouchy, but her moods slipped from one to another within minutes, possibly even seconds. I didn't know what to do, except pray. I lay my hand on her head and began to pray with everything I had inside of me. The tears came so easily from both of us. *Tears are supposed to release pain,* I thought. The hurt still lingered.

Lost for words, I began, "Jesus, when you were here on this earth you taught us to pray like this" and repeated the Lord's Prayer. The situation seemed to need more, so I added, "You say you will go into the belly of Hell to get out one of your children. Dear God, Sherry is one of your children too. I'm asking you to go there and bring her out. Please God, bring her peace. She needs You. You say whatever we ask in your Son's name will be granted. I ask with every thing that's in me. Please! Please help! Give her faith back. When she doubts, even for a moment, reach down and take her hand as you did with Peter when he doubted and began to sink into the water as he was walking toward you. Have mercy, oh Lord. Please don't forsake her. She needs you to calm her, give her peace, happiness, and joy. Deliver Your mercy and grace… Your understanding, Your forgiveness, and Your love. Always in Jesus' name, I pray. Amen!"

She said my words had power. And I believe they did. Jesus also said that we would be able to accomplish more than Him (John 14:12). I wonder what He meant by that. Could it be that we could be seen, felt, and heard after he descended into heaven? We have to make a difference. If one candle is lit, it makes the world a little brighter. We have seen so much darkness. It's time for us to light that candle and show the world we really care…to give our love in "something that we do."

We dried our tears. She opened up even more, the first time in her life. "For a long time I carried a needle around in my purse, along with enough heroin to kill myself. But I was too chicken." Then she placed her journal on my lap. The first page of the journal opened to this poem:

Evasive Goodbye

"Mother Dear,
Hear my cry.
Let me prepare you for an evasive goodbye.
These words to you…I do not speak.
Holding them in my heart…Silently I keep.

"Wondering mind, building to madness that I
find too hard to hold.
Selfish pity I ride side by side.
Hurting…only to you I can't confide.
Tears of sadness overwhelm as a whole…inside
of me, throughout my heart and soul.

"No more words, no more hellos.
No more hugs as a child.
These evasive feelings I withhold.
Feeling abandoned, as I grow old.

"No more hugs to a child, I've lost;
Maybe, never to hold.
Of bare necessities
I just barely hang on.

"A betrayal goodbye
Tomorrow I may die."

I didn't know if these words belonged to a poet, or if they actually belonged to her. They were distorted and misarranged. I changed them somewhat to bring out her true feelings of communication.

A lot of the pages were missing from both the journal and the diary. "Some of the times were so bad my boyfriend didn't want anyone to know the secrets in those pages," MySher explained. We will change if we clearly see just how bad things really are. *Could it be that evil sometimes presses in our direction so much that it destroys our only means to look back on its direct reality.*

She cared a lot for friendships, people to fill a cup that was always empty. "All I ever wanted was to be loved," she said.

Surely I had offered that love, but reality told me I'd fallen short—terribly short. A few memories came out of the past to light my way. I used to cross my legs, place her on one foot and bounce her up and down, saying over and over again, "I love you, I love you." I didn't know what else to say to a small child. So many times I repeated that sentence that by the time she was eight months she repeated the entire sentence: "I love you." Not Mommy, not Daddy; but "I love you."

Sherry always was a very smart child. So tiny, she got up in the middle of the night, all alone, even when there were no lights turned on, to go to the bathroom. I felt very proud of her. She had potty trained herself before she reached a year old. She'd done it the hard way, boosting herself upon the toilet seat by the bathtub. Most of the time I was too tired to give her much help. She broke herself from the bottle about the same time. All this made me think she was going to be an exceptional adult.

Now her beautiful face was left with deeply imbedded scares caused from drugs. A plastic surgeon had told me MySher needed a face peal. Even though, I was twenty years older than she was I didn't need one. She couldn't seem to shake her drug addiction before it destroyed everything of value.

What could I conclude from all this? Elvis Presley had what seemed to be everything a person could desire and died at 42. His real condition was truly denied. Pictures of Marilyn Monroe, the one MySher closely related to possibly because they were both beautiful, which now hung on her apartment walls, furthered the idea that no matter how good we are, we are still lacking at this point and time. No matter how much it hurt, I could only conclude that we are only half-way there.

"Sherry, if you think I don't care, you are very, very wrong. There is no one quite like you. Don't try to hide what makes you different. When you are true to that person inside you and accept that person as you truly are, you'll have something to offer yourself...and the world. Our imperfections are hard to accept...but we have to. I want you to accept whatever you've done wrong with everything that's inside me. To become a better person we have to accept ourselves, regardless of what has happened or what we've done; then make the necessary changes to improve. If we fail to see ourselves as we truly are at a particular point in time, it's just like coming out of the woods with a broken arm that heals before it's set in place. The arm will be healed wrong. So are our minds: It jumps over the one correction that's needed to heal properly.

"Maybe this sounds cruel, but I do know what I'm going to do once you're gone. Although I'd give my life in a split second to give your life back to you: I'm going to pick up the pieces and try to make a half-way journey complete."

Methamphetamine

My name is Methamphetamine—they call me "Crank" for short.
I entered the country without a passport.
Ever since then I've made lots of scum rich.
Some have been murdered and found in a ditch.
I'm more valued than diamonds, more treasured than gold.
Use me once and you'll be sold.

I'll make a schoolboy forget his books.
I'll make a beauty queen forget her looks.
I'll make a renowned speaker a bore.
I'll take your mother and make her a whore.
I'll make a preacher not want to preach.
I'll make a schoolteacher forget to teach.

I'll take your rent money, and you'll be evicted.
Murder your babies, or they'll be born addicted.
I'll make you rob, steal, and kill.
When in my power you have no will.
Remember my friend, my name is the big "C".
Try me once, you'll never be free.

I conquer actors, politicians, and many a hero.
Decrease bank accounts from millions to less than zero.
I'll make shootings and stabbings a common affair.
Once I take charge, you won't have a prayer.

Now that you know me, what will you do?
You must decide. It's all up to you.
The day you agree to sit in my saddle,
The decision is one you'll have to straddle.

Listen to me, and please listen well.
When you ride with Methamphetamine,
You're headed downhill, toward H E L L.

You used me...until you were all used up.
Now you're cranked down...
And all FUCKED UP.

You're all spun out and all up tight...
Don't you know...you're just not right?
For you have now—begun to see...
That you have gone through "HELL JUST FOR ME."

Ronnie Monroe & Sherry Lindblad

Chapter 29

Live in Hell and Die and Go To Hell

He was here today. After being on a long-haul trip for two weeks strait, Doug was pretty keyed up. I was on my long weekend, well rested, and ready for some variety to stimulate my senses.

It's Monday, September 7, MySher's birthday. Another year has passed, I thought as I arose that morning. She was born on Labor Day. While Doug lay in bed watching TV, I decided to call MySher to wish her a happy birthday.

She first told me she was leaving. "I've got some things I want you to have," she said. "What you don't want you can put in storage. There's a TV and some other items I like to go to Brandon."

"How about if Doug* and I come up to get them? I'll ask him and see what he has to say." To me, it sounded like a perfect outing for this holiday. After all, it was her birthday, and I wanted to see her. It had been a long time since we'd even talked. We'd got into a fight during one of her visits to Kelso.

I remembered it distinctively:

She wanted to take every thing she thought belonged to her out of my house. First, she took all pictures of her and the boys off the walls. Next was Norm's picture. That made me mad. I tried to get it back, but couldn't. She cut the phone wires so I couldn't call the police, and she tried to choke me. Then she took the Elvis Presley telephone, which she'd given to me as a present. A figure of Elvis, standing a top the phone, would dance to *Jail House Rock* every time someone called. I took the phone away from her while she kept fighting to keep it. After awhile, I just threw the phone on the sidewalk and busted it all to pieces. "Here, take it!" I angrily fought back, throwing the phone as hard as I could. "You've taken every thing else." I couldn't believe my eyes when she reached for my Bible. It had been a gift from Norm before he died. Gold letters across the front cover said: "To My Love, Martha." *This takes the cake!* I thought. "Now, the old devil's even trying to take my Bible away from me. You're not going to get that," I said, grabbing it. After holding the Bible in my hands a few moments I handed it back to her. "Here, you need it worse than I do. I hope you get some good out of it." In my mind, I started hoping and praying she would get some good from it. Eventually, I gave up quarreling with her and went to the little store on Pacific Avenue to call the police. I bailed her out after a night in jail. I thought twenty-four hours in jail would do her some good…but it didn't. She pulled out of her parking spot, giving me the finger as she drove by. While she was in jail, I'd given Brandon almost $500 to get her car out of the garage. She'd run over something on the Kelso Bridge causing some damage to it, according to what she said. Then it cost me $1200 to bail her out of jail. *After all the things I've done for her and she still gives me the finger. That's real appreciation,* I sarcastically thought of her actions. The fight had apparently started because of her guilt. She'd been nothing but a bitch from the moment I walked through the door. Later I found a hypodermic needle in my bathroom. She must have used it to shoot up with drugs. Already the cravings had grown so strong she no longer needed someone to administer the shots. I'd returned from her place in Seattle after having same-day surgery in Tacoma. She wanted it that way. She said she could take care of me for a couple days while I recuperated. While I was still there in her home in Seattle she insisted she come down to my place and clean it up before I got home. That was another lie. I found out later that she stole some important records of mine so she could apply for credit cards under my name. She had previously stolen some old checks of mine, which I didn't know about either. I'd written her a check for $10,000 to open a business earlier this year. The door to that business was never opened. I thought she might get her life together if she could do something constructive to earn a living. Wrong! Then a little later, I'd given her another $2,000 so she could move closer to Jeffery's school. With her not having to take her youngest son back and forth to school, she'd have more time to do those constructive things. Again: wrong! I found out later: at the same time I gave her the last check she had several two and three thousand dollar checks go through the bank which I felt responsible for and stood good for. *Someone has to be responsible for their actions. The banks didn't have her; I did.* It's always been fairly easy for me to forgive, especially her—too easy—seventy times seventy-seven seemed like a drop in the bucket. Still, I was thankful God put that forgiveness in my heart.

"Doug," I said after hanging up the phone, "how about a little drive to Seattle? Come on! Get out of bed and get dressed. It's already late in the day. We have to hurry, if we're going to go."

Boy, did the "shit ever hit the fan?" It was a constant quarrel, all the way to Seattle and the rest of the day. I told him before we started, all he had to do was say no, he didn't want to go. But he didn't. On the way there, I asked him several times if he wanted me to turn around and come back home. He finally said, "No, we've come too far now." We got stuck in a traffic jam, which made things worse. "I told you this is what it would be like, didn't I? I drive all the time. The least thing I would like on one of my days off is this."

"I thought you would be happy just being with me. I'm happy being with you," I said. Apparently nothing I said eased his mind. He was stuck in a feminine way and I was stuck in a masculine way. No amount of listening or ducking his words meant anything. *What's wrong with you,* I thought. *You sound a lot like Sherry. You've got your bottle of whiskey. What more do you want? That must be it. You've been drinking. Why can't some men handle their booze?* Then I tried drowning it out by singing to music on the radio. That didn't work either.

Doug had known me long enough to know Sherry had been on drugs. He knew only part of what she'd put me through. *Now he's putting me through a bunch of his shit.* He was my fiancé. In slightly less than three months we'd become engaged. He'd written me some beautiful notes and letters—the only love letters I'd ever received from a boyfriend during my entire life. Almost all of them started with "Hi, Angel." (He always spelled angel with an "le" on the end, rather than an "el.") I adored their wording. Every time I read them, it was like foreplay to our making love, which made me think that our ears must be one of our "turn on" or "turn off" spots. He was terrific when he wasn't drinking, and he generally drank only on his first day home, to relieve the stress of his job, he said. This was a holiday, another reason for drinking. I hoped he wouldn't be like all the other alcoholics: add another excuse daily. He'd bought me a $3,000 engagement ring, but we hadn't set the date yet. I was waiting for his true personality to show through before I made the final decision. And here it was. Even though, I went a little further to drown out his bitching by remembering the letters. They were sweet.

More than once, Doug had mentioned all the letters he'd written to me but never received any from me. "And you're the writer," he reminded me. They were truly something I could appreciate. So I'd written him an eight-page letter.

Now that everything was going great, the devil showed his teeth—again. *Why does life have so many ups and downs? I thought men pleased themselves by making their mates happy.* Yet, he was miserable. *Was he trying to sabotage the relationship because he didn't feel worthy of it? Who knows?* But he meant to succeed before the day was out.

In the letter, I'd told Doug we should listen to the bad, as well as to the good, and use those negatives as gauges to tell us something is wrong. But not to use that "shit" in our lives to make things worse. We needed to be morally right with our actions, so we could be sure we'd made the right decision.

During the process of loading the truck at Sherry's, Doug kept reminding me, "I told you it would be like this." Sherry was having troubles with a boyfriend. She was going through one of her down periods. Between her crying and hollering on the phone with her boyfriend and Doug's dissentious nature, it became more than I could stand. My thoughts were, *He's supposed to be my helpmate. I'd like a mate going in the same direction that I'm going; one that lifts me up and supports me, not one that pulls me down.* I put my hand on Sherry's knee and patted it to console her. *Now what does Doug want?* I asked myself. It didn't feel very good to be between two addicts—one hooked on drugs and the other hooked on alcohol. I asked him, "Please pick another time for this." Needless to say, he didn't listen. I felt he was acting like another over-grown brat, but I didn't say it. After listening for some time I took off the ring and handed it back. That made him madder than ever.

That night, back in Kelso, we made up. On the condition that Doug try to curb his temper, I accepted his ring back. I agreed I wouldn't make him feel obligated to do something he didn't want to do in the future.

The following night we went out, hoping to spark some excitement. We did that. I sang some karaoke. He didn't sing, and he wouldn't dance. So I danced with someone else. The guy I danced with I'd known for a long time. He was a contractor who'd sold me a place in the country. I'd had breakfast with him once but didn't feel any interest. Like lighting a match to an already fueled fire, he came up to me shortly after the dance and asked to talk to me privately. I told him, "Whatever you have to say, you'll have to say it in front of Doug." Doug seemed to be too angry to hear even those words. With the help of two men, I managed to somewhat quieten Doug down. We had two cars there because I'd worked swing shift. After I went home, he got into a fight. I don't know if it was with the same guy or a different one. From the answers he gave me after he got home, he didn't know either. He blamed me for it. "The real truth is you just wanted to fight, and it really didn't matter about the reason." From that comment, we got into a fight. Putting me down on the couch, he put his right knee on the left side of my chest and used that leg to hold my left arm behind my back. He placed his left hand on my right arm to hold it down. I still managed to get an empty ashtray on the coffee table with my right hand. I repeatedly hit his elbow with it. I couldn't hit it as hard as I wanted to because of him holding my arm. My thoughts were *you'll have to let me up sometime.* When he finally let me up I hit him across the face as hard as I could with the ashtray. Blood splattered everywhere. My couch was a mess; blood smeared all over it, with us wresting in the mess.

I gave his ring back again; told him he knew where the door was at and to get out.

Then it started again. During this whole mess of fighting Doug stopped right in the middle of it and started praying, an unusual gesture to say the least. Apparently his temper was back under control. Or maybe an angel of the Lord intervened. He picked me up in his arms and carried me off to bed as if all the fight had left him.

I told Doug I might let a woman whip me, but I wasn't going to let a man do it. He asked, "Why?" Apparently that didn't seem logical to him.

"Because I've seen too many women beaten up by men," I answered. "They seem to do it just because they can.

"I could have easily broken your neck," he said.

"You'll have to kill me before I give up. My brother, Jimmy, and my dad found out that a long time ago. They'd finally give up and sit down in a corner. I've been solid blue from the neck up, and still I didn't give up. They told me to 'go to it. I can't do anything with you.'"

I must have been tired and needed some rest. So I went to sleep. When I awoke in the middle of the night, I crawled out of bed and went to the couch to sleep the remaining part of the night.

The next day before I went to work on swing shift not one word was spoken. When I came home Doug was gone. Two days later, he called me on the phone to ask what made me so mad.

"My chest has a large bruise on it; my hand is still black; a knot on my jaw; and some bruises on my neck and arm. Isn't that enough? You should have some counseling. Now, if you don't mind, I'd like to go."

Several days passed. Apparently Doug had gone back on the road again. I wrote him another letter and took it to a married couple, Jan* and Leon*, who were good friends of his. I told Jan to read it before giving it to him. "There's a lot of insight in it, which he probably won't understand," I told her as I handed it to her at the Chinese Garden's, a cocktail restaurant where they went every Friday. "I'm hoping you can explain it to him." Apparently she didn't understand it either like I hoped she would—at least, not at that time. I found out later from her that they both said it sounded like a book. The main thing he noticed was that it wasn't signed with "Love."

Several months passed. I saw Doug in Kim Bowl's, a place where I go to sing karaoke. He was with his friends. We still hadn't lost our feelings for each other. He bought me a bouquet of flowers and held me off the floor in his arms while we danced slow waltzes.

One more time—when was I ever going to learn? Shortly afterwards Doug and I went out to Kim Bowl's again. Lou* was there and I hugged her neck on the way to the restroom. Both Doug and Leon were dead-set against having anything to do with her. They said she was really a man. She looked like a girl to me. Besides, what she did with her life was none of my business. After I came out of the restroom and sat down beside Doug he moved over as if he didn't want to touch me and repeated in a snotty way, "Where's your husband? Where's your husband?" I thought to myself, *this is not going to work out.* It didn't! I drove off smiling and left him standing in the middle of the parking area calling me names— names I'd prefer not to mention.

"Breaking up is hard to do." Whoever first said those words must have known it would become an old cliche, I thought on the way home.

Dawn and Lanny, my friends, must have thought Doug and I still loved each other because we wouldn't have anything to do with someone else and were unhappy being alone. They brought him over to the house some time later. Dawn was hoping Doug would go into the bedroom to talk to me. Instead, he stayed out in the living room with them and got drunk. I could hear him talking to himself most of the night over my karaoke mike, even after they'd left. He must have thought he was singing—making up words as he went. Then about daylight he came into my room and tried to crawl in bed with me. I kicked him out. This didn't set too well. He threw microwave popcorn all over my living room floor. When I got up I told him to clean it up. When he didn't, I told him to leave.

A long time after that, I saw Doug's friends at Kim Bowl's. I was so happy to see them I hugged their necks and danced a few dances with Leon. Jan had finally seen through Doug and understood why I broke up with him. She mentioned "Doug's new girl friend just puts up with it. You wouldn't."

"There was a time when I put up with his mental cruelty too. You have to get sick of it before you can manage to change."

I remembered what I'd said long ago to my father: "Live in hell and die and go to Hell." He'd slapped me. That's the only time during my growing up period my nose ever bled.

I had gone through hell—one more time. This time I was ready to get out of the hole. The top of the hill was in sight. I visualized the green, rolling pastures beyond. Yellow golden daffodils on both sides of the path led me into the valley of Truth. The sun tilted its spout to pour out more beauty of its radiant color, on and on as far as one could see. I was a child again—all new and free of life's empty shell of wanting to be filled, especially by a man with no substance. A smile lit up my face, and I was skipping again.

Back home in my apartment, a picture of Doug still hung on the wall. Another part of me—the worldly part —reached out to touch his chest, the part where his heart should have been. I touched it with my forefinger. "You don't know what you've missed. You could have come along too."

Chapter 30

My Prayers

Frequently, I weep and pray to God for Him to send me someone to help me make it through the night. The pain, the depression, the loneliness seems unbearable.

I continue to give so I may receive some kind of consolation to deaden the pain. Nothing comes. My cup has not even one drop left; then I borrow to give more to this demon within me who has an unquenchable thirst. He must be a lot like the demon inside My Sher…or the demon inside all of us. He comes in different forms—in the form of addictions or obsessions. He has no appreciation for what he gets… and he gets plenty, even my soul. He keeps me paying the price. Is it possible for God to help me? My mind, what mind that's left, says I'm too far gone. Or, are these words coming from the demon within?

Out of the mist of the night another begotten voice is heard. Is it my brother Tommy's…or is it God's? "You forgot to give…to laugh…to cry…and to love," it says. "The person behind the mask you try to present to the public isn't you. You are numb."

"Wait just a minute," I told myself: "I've cried, and I've loved. The only thing I haven't done is laugh. Where are these thoughts and feelings coming from?"

I'd trade in my own mother for another fix and the results get worse each time. All of a sudden, I realize, not all of these words are my own. *I wouldn't lower my values to this point.* But all the feelings seem to be my own. "Some are My Sher's," I now realize. I was experiencing her feelings, as well as my own, from a distance.

I must continue, I thought, hoping these feelings wouldn't disintegrate. For I needed to know more. *Each fix never lasts as long as I want it to. And I feel there is no tomorrow without them.* "How do I satisfy this voyeuristic craving, even for a little while, to numb the constant gnawing of an already raw interior?"

My own feelings interrupt and mingle with hers, making me think possibly the situation actually started generations ago: *I can relate to this demon.* Once it stood before me. It showed its face in a fiery display in the middle of the night. I couldn't sleep. I couldn't eat. If someone had stuck me in the belly with a knife and twisted it, it wouldn't have hurt any worse. *Is that what it feels like to grow up?* I was only seventeen then…I stood my ground then. I prayed a lot.

Did I acquire this inculcated fear, anxiety, and torment from my father? Did my continuous paying slot machine start with the rivers of puke I cleaned as a girl? Or, did it start earlier when I competed with my mother for any attention I might grab? What father? I was his parent, even as a child. He didn't fulfill my emotional needs and apparently he never fulfilled my mother's emotional needs either. No wonder I love, yet despise men. I have a right to be angry. My step-dad was a weakling too. He was an alcoholic and a pill popper. A multitude of other men in my life have also been weaklings. Even Norm—he couldn't stand on his own two feet without using me as his crutch.

A dream repeatedly comes back in my memory to picture my feelings in three-dimensional, full color: I'm invited to a feast. When I get there the food is already gone…Nothing! I'm starved. No one cared enough to leave even a small portion; and I require only a small portion. I'm left with hunger pains. Still, I wipe the crumbs from the table and clean it off for their next meal. I'm left empty.

I call MySher, who is now living in Seattle, on the phone. *I hope it won't end in disaster as before.* She'd hung up on me so many times, leaving me in distress. I wanted to help her. My mind spilled out a picture of her as a little girl. My whole heart reached out to catch her, as my arms did in my mind.

The conversation started off casually. She asked me about the boys. Her seventeen-year-old son, Brandon, was already living here in Kelso, directly above me in one of my apartments. He chose to accept the responsibility of raising his twelve-year-old brother, Jeffery, even before he finished school. He had recently graduated from high school.

I told her the boys were doing fine. "I have prepared meals plenty of times and invited them to join me," I said, trying to ease her mind. "I told them if they needed anything, just ask. Brandon's asked a few times. I bought Jeffery his eyeglasses. Brandon's very competent for a seventeen-year-old."

"Yes," she said. "I just wanted Jeffery to have a father figure."

I didn't tell her that I knew what she was thinking, that I sensed it. "You did the right thing," I consoled her. "It will teach them how to stand alone."

She asked me what had I done with her belongings. A few weeks ago, I had went to Seattle to bring a truckload of her things back with me. She'd said then that she was going to California, then to Texas, and on to Florida. She didn't want her things lost because of her leaving.

I told her I had went through the stuff and carefully separated it; threw some away, gave some away, and the rest was in storage.

"If I'd known you were going to get rid of it, Mom, I wouldn't have let you have it," she said in an upset tone. "That was my most cherished possessions. You don't know how much they meant to me." Crying, she became ill and had to go to the bathroom.

She couldn't care that much about a few belongings? I thought. Her want of a few material things covered up the real spiritual concerns. As a headache is a symptom—and not the real source of a problem—so were her actions, which distracted from the true source.

After waiting about fifteen minutes I called back. Instead of trying to explain, I listened attentively, telling her she had a right to feel that way.

Since she'd never had a husband or boyfriend listen to her, I felt she'd never get better if I didn't show her now that I accepted her just as she was. This was a passing thought, which I didn't relate. I just listened.

"Sherry," I started, after she quieten down somewhat, write a letter to God, telling him how you feel; then write yourself a letter saying all the things you would like God to say to you. I did that once and it made me feel better."

I read the letter of long ago—the one I wanted God to write to me:

A Letter From God

Martha, You are my most prized and precious possession. I will always be there for you and with you. To pick you up when you fall, to hold you in My arms when no one else can or will. You are after my own heart. I'll be there for you through eternity.

I'll help you with your kids, lift them up and talk to them when you're not around. And when you are around, I'll put the right things to say and do in your heart—continuously, never letting go.

I accept you just as you are. I'll help you to understand yourself and others. I'll help you reach the highest planes of wisdom and spiritual development because I appreciate you.

I wanted you to try hard, in all of life's endeavors, for this purpose: so you could grow with me. Tommy wanted you to grow to higher levels too. That's the reason he was so hard on you. He loved you too, you know. And your mother, she had so much healing of her own. Your father needed to be healed too. I wanted you to see that you could make mistakes with your children too.

I wanted you to write a book, one of the greatest books the world has ever known. To be able to write it, you must live it. It's your destiny to do this—for me… and for all the people of this world. So remember when you go through something, there is always a good reason for it. Don't give up little one. I'm on your side and my love last forever. I'll give you strength and wisdom to see it through.

My little one, I love you. Tommy, your mother, and your step-dad also love you. Even your father, who now stands in another dimension, he watches over you as one of my angels.

With Continuous Everlasting Love,
Your Heavenly Father

"I wanted to hear God say this to me," I told her. "I imagined it so."

Her burdens seemed to disappear. It didn't seem so important to read to her the letter I had written to God. Her life was different than mine. *Her letter to God should reflect her own feelings,* I thought.

After hanging up I read the letter I had written to God to myself. It brought back memories, as well as tears.

A Letter to God

Dear God,

I've always tried so hard to please You and my own family. I had family after family to try for again and again.

I feel sad because of so little attention, so little love. I know I'm told that You love me just as I am, but I felt I had to earn it. Please accept and love me just as I am. Then maybe I can change to please You more. Or, maybe You can help me change.

My anger goes deep because I've tried so hard and it seems, no matter what I do, it still isn't enough.

Lois and I used to drown cats because we were forced to. Our hearts cried out every time. I told her we had to follow through. We couldn't lie by telling her parents we did when we didn't. That would be dishonoring her parents. To this day, Lois still keeps some cats around, possibly trying to make up for what she did then. I never thought animals were more important than people. Now I feel less than those cats. I don't want You to forsake me because of my deeds, to leave me, or to help animals before helping me. I need to feel significant too. I fear that with so much contradiction and imperfection in this world, I'll never meet Your standards.

I'm sorry, oh Lord. Please forgive me for the wrongs, which weigh down my shoulders so much. Please understand the deepest reasons in my soul for doing the things I do, such as neglecting my children to earn a living. I thought it was important to put a roof over their heads, to provide food, and to pay the bills. It's important to earn a living. This is why I blamed Norm: I felt he should have earned the living while I took care of the home and the children. I'm sorry I was too tired to do both well. And I'm angry with You because You didn't give me enough strength, enough knowledge, and enough ability to do both well. You didn't give me a mate able to help me in this endeavor either and understand my feelings.

Please forgive me. I want desperately to get all the garbage out of my life, to heal my heart, and grow to be a more loving, compassionate person. I don't want to go through the hell over and over again by offering my love in all the wrong places—where it's unappreciated and undeserved. I don't want to become bitter either.

It's my fault I had to learn the hard way, because I didn't listen to your words.

Thank You for these cigarettes I smoke, one right after the other, to deaden the pain. It was an addiction with the least side effects, so I thought. I didn't want to face the past for fear of refueling the pain.

Thank You for helping me face all the pain inside of me now, so I may be healed properly, instead of covered with scars.

Don't desert me oh Lord. I need You...Your strength, Your wisdom, Your understanding, Your healing, Your acceptance, Your love. Be there for me, totally in all ways forever and ever.

Loving You Unconditionally and Hoping You Love Me Too,
Martha

I needed to accept my imperfections—to love me. Now my daughter needed the same. She needed my acceptance...as well as her own. Maybe with time she would eventually pull out of the demon's clutches.

So I prayed for her—again:

"We are mighty warriors in the authority, power, and strength of the living and the loving God. We wrestle not against flesh and blood, but against principalities, against powers, against the rulers of darkness of this world, against spiritual wickedness in high places. May we stand steadfast, established in the armor of God's light to fight against lies, tricks, schemes, and plans of the devil. And may we forever be in Your arms...MySher and I."

Chapter 31

Father and Daughter

The anger of "wanting to kill" had passed away. It had taken a good part of a lifetime for her to overcome.

Sherry had taken some success tapes from our house in Kelso. Surely they would help her in some small way. While listening to the tapes in the bathtub her thoughts sailed into a restful state, which took her away from the constant pressures of daily life in Seattle.

Asking herself why was she like she was, it dawned on her that something must have happened to her while she was in the womb. "How did I feel when I was pregnant with my two kids?" She asked herself. Her conclusion was that her kids displayed the same personalities as she felt when she was pregnant with them. "Did my mother get beat up by Randall when she was pregnant? What happened?" She continued to ponder. With no definite answers, she decided to talk to me about it later.

Sherry came to Kelso, went by and purchased $250 of drugs, which she later resold in Seattle for $1,000. Excitedly, she stopped by the house afterwards to talk to me. "Mom, I've figured it out," she happily informed me. "I want to tell you about it."

Totally unaware of her purchase, I didn't want to disregard her happy mood; I just wanted her to know the truth—the whole truth. Before she could utter another word I butted in. "I need to tell you something," I told her. "It's been bothering me lately." I didn't realize it at the time, but what I wanted to tell her was exactly what she wanted to talk about. Obviously, I answered her question even before she asked it.

She was overly anxious and didn't want to wait for me to finish. "What is it Mom? What is it?" She repeated.

"I don't know how else to tell you except blurt it out. You don't wanna wait for me to choose the right wording."

"Okay," Sherry said. "I'll wait. What is it?"

"You've been trying to reach back into the past to find something that contributed to the way you are."

"Yeah, I know that, but how did you know?" She asked.

"I just know. A mother just knows some things. Often what they don't know they are refusing to admit." I really didn't realize how much of a truth that was.

"Your life has been good. You couldn't have received more love from your parents. But what I did when I was carrying you must have caused it or contributed in some way." She became more still and less fidgety, waiting for the answer. Then I blurted it out: "I tried to abort you."

"You mean, evil bitch," Sherry's disposition changed to match her wording.

"I'm sorry for doing it, but I did. Now I have to accept that truth, face the consequences, and ask for your forgiveness."

Sherry acted like she didn't even hear a word of it and grabbed me by the throat. Her whole body was trembling with hate, like I used to be. She wanted to kill me. Naturally I tried to protect myself. She might have had the strength, but she didn't have the willpower. She left angry.

My own thoughts were punishment enough. Actually I wasn't cold and uncaring, as she thought. I was depressed—a depression carried over into years and ran into decades. I felt ashamed of what I'd done. At that time I thought my life was so bad that it would have been better if I never had any kids. I didn't want them to see the hell I'd been through. *It's obvious I didn't have the guts to carry it out,* I thought. The none-caring attitude Sherry perceived was a feeling of hopelessness. A yearning or hunger, the only thing I had left, filled my heart, partially because I couldn't get her to understand. I can still feel it: Nothingness!

Emptiness! Loneliness! I cared too much. I loved too much. I couldn't get what I needed from my husband, Norm. He loved me dearly; I knew that. Sometimes I would cry and beg him to help me. There was no way for him to take away the agonizing pain. It was just there, and I somehow had to live with it. It would be gone after my death, but I couldn't kill myself. I'd already tried that, and it didn't work. Somehow the deeper, spiritual side of me had to work it out. Any happiness I managed to grasp was like a melting snowflake, which disintegrated the moment I touched it from the warmth of my hands. When I reached for another snowflake, it did the same over and over again. It seemed like a hopeless effort. *I've lived with such hollowness all my life*, I reflected. *I'm tired. Why can't they understand?* I never stopped to think that my feelings could possibly be embedded into both my children. They would suffer too. Suffer, they did. I'm sure now that no woman should have a baby unless she is happy. It's her husband's duty to listen to her, talk to her, see a councilor with her, or do whatever is necessary to make her happy before she becomes pregnant, not wait until it's too late. I did the right thing by telling Sherry, but it was a little late in coming. "It's okay to get the truth out in the open, no matter what the consequences," I reasoned. *The suffering will only be released when I take out the bad, look at it, and think about what I was feeling at the time it happened. This is the purpose of the past—to set us free without scars. After it has served its purpose, then I can choose to throw it away. Otherwise, it seems to hang on like glue in one form or another.* We seem to be averse to writing bad things about ourselves. We want others to know only the good in us. We sometimes hide the truth from ourselves when we really mean to hide it only from others. That's one more way to deny it exists, and we go on with pretentious shadows in the back of our minds, appearing normal when actually we're suffering from a disorder.

Later Sherry began to understand somewhat. We started talking again. Norm helped her a great deal, she said. "If it wasn't for Dad what would have happened?" She recalled.

Thinking back, Norm must have helped me too. His undying love stopped clinging after twenty-five years. He offered it freely in his own way no matter what. I learned to love him more than anybody in the entire world because he loved me unconditionally. No matter what I did, he was always there in my many times of need. Sometimes he became stubborn and wouldn't listen to me or accept my ideas, but he was always there. In the end, I felt the same as he did because he eventually gave me my wings—even though he didn't want to—and loved me anyway.

"How did you over-come those bad feelings of your past?" I asked Sherry.

"You think a lot about it. You moan. You scream. You ask that little boy or little girl inside of you questions. You tell that little boy or little girl to come here: tell her everything she wants to hear. Then maybe you'll find the answers for peace, for healing after you go through it."

Our lives are somewhat like a waterfall—a continuous succession of present moments—except when you take water from a waterfall, it doesn't matter. The difference in our lives—all of it—bears some kind of significance. If we try to block it out, our discomfort takes on a different form to cover it up with calluses, scars, and sores. We are told to forget the past, but I say remember it until it serves its purpose. It's there for a reason and for a season. We are told not to be uneasy or impatient with the present. This is all in good taste and will do wonders for the soul, if we can manage it. If you can't, lie back and relax, become perfectly still with no sounds in the background and listen to your higher self point the way. This is the day for acknowledgment and learning wisdom. Sometimes it's impossible for us to accept ourselves the way we are and still be happy. When this happen, let us reconnect with our souls with quiet times to learn what the necessary changes might be. We are told not to worry about the future; it will take care of itself. When we become the person we want to be—and should be—then it will take care of itself. It's using our common sense to want to be constructive, doing what we love to do. To be more successful at anything, we should put things in order of priority and group things together in order to save time. For example, if we have a bunch of phone calls to make and a lot of letters to write, we should group them together, instead of switching back and forth between them. Again—that's common sense. Then the journey becomes a downhill process of stimulation, instead of the constant struggle of an uphill climb. At this point, I gather we will be five-eighths there. Know that from each bad there must come some good. It's called growth. I wanted to tell Sherry all this, but I didn't. Sometimes, it was difficult to get her to shut her mouth long enough to get my two cents in.

I also wanted to tell Sherry the complete story of how I met Norm, her adopted father, and Randall, her biological father. It didn't happen. I'd previously told her Randall was her real father. As for now, I told her, "I'd left a beautiful pair of earrings at Norm's place before I left Washington to go to Denver, Colorado, with Randall. Using that for an excuse, I went to see Norm after I got back to Longview. We started living together shortly afterwards. It was a weak time in my life, being pregnant with you. It gave Norm the opportunity to ask me to marry him, since he was shy, and it gave me a reason to accept. I wanted to provide you with a father."

Finishing, I told her, "You were born on Labor Day, Sherry, (September 7). Shortly after you were born, Norm and I were married, November 4th. Shortly after that, he adopted you."

I took her back to visit Randall several years later. He was aesthetic to see us, even though he was married to another woman, a redhead, and had a nine-year-old, redheaded daughter. He seemed especially happy to see me. Wanda Gay McClure (maiden name), my first cousin, and her daughter took Sherry and me to their house in Hayesville. Accompanied by Wanda's daughter, Sherry knocked on their door and introduced herself. Randall asked was I waiting in the car. Apparently he saw Wanda and me sitting in the car. Dim outside lights provided some visibility in the dark. When Sherry told him who we were, he insisted that I come in. He told Sherry to tell me he would come outside and carry me in if I didn't. So we went in. I knew he meant what he said. He still hadn't changed in that respect. We had one beer with him and his family. He offered every kind of hospitality imaginable, according to his capabilities. One could definitely see that he wanted to please. When we left, he wanted to carry me across the lawn since I was wearing heels, which made it hard to walk on the grass. I refused to let him carry me across the grass and got away with that.

A few years afterwards, he died. Sherry didn't like it because I didn't tell her. I couldn't understand this because Randall had no part in raising her. Now, I can understand somewhat why anyone would care that much about their real father.

As I look back to try to understand and heal myself, it seems like I was on a giant wave going nowhere, making everyone else happy except myself, just like Sherry had been most of her life. It just happened, and I don't think I could've done much to change it. Possibly, I passed all the unhappiness that I felt onto Sherry. I tried to break the chain, but I didn't know how. Maybe it'll happen sometime in the future. I hope so.

Martha Harris

Chapter 32

Under "L" for Heart Doctor

Each day I come home from work and look out these giant windows over looking the Columbia River. Most of the trees are cut down now. I look mainly toward the sky, thinking about the space between God and this world. A beautiful picture, if only my mind would welcome it. Instead, my brain wraps around the worldly displays of today and yesterday.

My tears start again, as they did on the way home today, and as they have done almost every day now for months on end. I hardly have time to get into the truck before the weeping starts. *Where did so many tears come from?* I ask myself. The circumstances of the past press hard against my heart, never letting me see much peace. I have to admit that I chose to do some things that are responsible for this pain.

This place is too big for me and too far out in the country, I submit with a long sigh. Wayne is gone now. I no longer have his company…or his troubles. *I'm too much alone here with so many moments of emptiness to face. I'll be glad when I sell it.*

Sometimes, I sing karaoke. Today, I sing "From a Distance," a song that reflects my feelings, over these hills while I continue to look out over the vastness of the sky. The song awakens me to what's inside. *I'm not in a singing mood today. My mind is too full.* To move on, I feel I have to think it through. *My mind can hold only one thought at a time.* I believe that one thought should be as realistic as possible; learn something beneficial from it; then move on in a positive way. In this way, I will reach a higher rung on the ladder. Eventually, maybe it will happen.

Sherry isn't living here now. So why am I crying so much? Is it because I feel what she's going through again, as I have in the past. Or is it because of all the guilt I still have inside me from treating Norm so badly before his death?

MySher did come down from Seattle to spread Norm's ashes under a big old fir tree on a lower part of the property. My eyes lowered toward the spot where they were spread. My bedroom had become cold. I'd stored them in an urn on a shelf in my huge closet. I wanted to take them back to North Carolina. I'd bought some property back there, but my thoughts said it wasn't the right place. I wanted to let my nephew, Randall, have that place. Norm wanted his ashes spread near water, under a tree, and near me. I no longer wanted to stay here. The place where his ashes were spread didn't have much water; it just had some underground springs. To build a fish pond down there was something I'd planned if I continued to stay. Something inside my brain keeps saying I will buy the beautiful place right below Randall's. It has a creek on both sides of it. But I can't see how it's possible. That place was up for sale a little over a year ago. At that time I didn't have the money to buy it, because I'd spent all my money on buying Randall's. *Too much time has past. My bedroom keeps getting colder. I have to make a decision now. Who knows for sure when I'll purchase the other piece of property*, I thought the day Sherry and a few friends attended the burial ceremony. Patience was lacking. Faith too. Ken Olsen, a co-worker of mine, officiated. I'd hung on to his ashes for years like they were gold waiting for the right opportunity to put them in the right place and also put them where I wanted them to be. I couldn't wait any longer. My bedroom had been the hottest room in the house because it was so close to the furnace. Now, for some reason it had become the coldest. *Maybe I'd kept Norm's ashes too long.* By this, I believed he was telling me it was time.

While MySher and some friends went down to the big fir tree for the ceremony, I stayed in the house—just thinking. Accidentally I came across an old letter written by Norm. It was neatly typed and double-spaced. A host of misspelled words and the grammar wasn't exactly right, according to my viewpoint, but its meaning ran clear to the soul. I couldn't help but notice the title—again. It sounded strange. I'd read it a long time ago when Norm first gave it to me—and several times after that. Now, I decided to read it again. There was a message in it that I was suppose to get.

Look Under "L" for Heart Doctor

All things are blurry as I open my eyes. Everything is gray, no black; the walls, the floors, the furniture; and yes, even the people. Where is this place? Why am I here? What have I done? Am I dead? These questions and a host of others flashed in my brain like a giant neon sign in downtown Vegas.

All of a sudden a tall, black capped person came over to my side shouting. "You're in mid air. Oh yes, the air! Can't you see how gray it is here?" And he added, in a bellowing tone, "What are you here for?"

Shaking I answered, "I don't know. I was in bed at home crying over a lost love when I got this sharp, funny, numbing feeling in my upper stomach."

"Broken heart, broken heart, broken heart," someone went screaming down a long, narrow, dark passage. I could faintly see them—about six or eight, maybe ten—coming nearer and nearer at a quick pace. They grabbed me, spun me around and around and then flipped me end over end several times. Stopping short, they moved off to a huddle, like a football team of Darth Vaders. They broke and came running back, screaming "Broken heart, broken heart!" Like a flash of bright, white light, they shoved me through two large, dark-colored doors that were marked with the letters "N-L" in small letters. Under them were the words: "need love."

I thought to myself, *Oh, if only they could?*

Now in a cotton candy pink room, the ceiling must have went on forever. It looked as though it was covered with large, fluffy, white clouds. The walls were covered with large, gold letters outlined with silver descriptions. Among the many, there were the letters "A" for affectionate love; "C", crazy love; "E", everlasting love; and "X", extra special love.

I was in deep wonderment. "Oh, if only I could possess one of those many hearts?" I whispered.

As I tried to take it all in, they quickly moved to the letter "L", marked "heart doctor" and pushed it six times.

One shouted, "Broken heart! Bad case, bad case!" The file cabinet, marked "L", flew open. A half-dozen, small men that looked like fingers about the size of a quart Mason jar floated out toward me. They were dressed in white doctor type jackets and had small mustaches with cigars in their mouths like Groucho Marks.

I tried to pull back but was unable to. Something was holding me there in mid air—a sky-hook, maybe, from out of nowhere. They seemed to be examining me from head to toe.

Then in high, shrill voices, all together they screamed "Broken heart, broken heart! Bad case, bad case!"

I lay there, shrunken in my skin, not able to move or speak.

All at once, they seemed to enter my body, and as quickly reappeared with my broken heart. Red drops, like tears, felled to the floor. The heart was in so many pieces that one could not have counted them. It quivered, as if in its last moment of life. Flying to the end of the room, they dumped the crying, broken pieces into a large, red can, marked "broken hearts only." From the can, I could hear the sobs of many hearts, broken and discarded by other thoughtless lovers. It over-flowed with red tears making a huge lake. I could not bear to look any longer. Turning away, I saw the little doctors hovering over the letter "N" for "new hearts." Pushing the letter, the drawer slid open and out popped a new, shining heart. It was not red, but bright green—a very shiny, wet, glossy green.

I squirmed and wiggled to get their attention, but they paid me no mind.

In a high voice, once more, they screamed "New heart, new heart! Good case, good case!" Once again they disappeared into my body. Seconds later they reappeared, smiling as if they'd fixed the problems of the whole world.

Suddenly I was able to move to a sitting position. My head was light; my chest—no, my heart felt a warm glowing feeling. Then a vision, not a thing, far off moved toward where I was sitting. Closer and closer it came until I could make out its shape. It appeared to be a large, foil-wrapped, chocolate kiss. Only, it was a dull green. Its pointed head—if it was a head—had two large, green eyes like that of the family cow, and lips—lips that looked like they were right off an orangutan. But guess what, believe it or not I was in love. The closer it came the warmer my heart felt. I shook my head, pinched myself, and repeated over and over again, "Wake up." As this lovely creature moved closer, I no longer wanted to wake up or ever part from her side. Her sensuous, dull green body moved me deep inside. "But wait, what is this? What am I doing?" As a last effort for sanity, I pulled my wallet from my back pocket and pulled out a picture of my lost love. As I stared at the photo, tears came to my eyes. But now they were green tears. Then slowly, ever so slowly, my old love's picture changed to look just like my new love. I couldn't remember the faintest thing of my love from the past—her looks, talk, or smile. Nothing! My new life's companion and I seemed to slip away to what was to be our new home. It appeared to be everything one would ever need. Everything was green—green carpets, green walls, green tinted windows—but I didn't seem to mind. I thought I would be happy forever. "God bless those little doctors who did it." I was happy.

It was about the third week, as the green sun rose over the green hills, my dull-green love cooked a breakfast that wasn't the normal. It wasn't green eggs and ham as usual but something special. This morning she fixed southern biscuits and gravy. When the smell of this breakfast grabbed my nose, my eyes watered, my heart begin to beat so fast. It wouldn't have beat any faster if I'd run a foot race. Without thought or feelings, the green tears started. I could not stop. They flowed for many days. The floor was covered with pools of green tears. She took my hand. She knew. We sailed back to the dark waiting room.

Quickly, the "Black Vader" type men hustled the green beauty off, hurling me through the doors marked "N-L" for "needs love." They hollered "New heart broken!" In the pink room, once again, they pushed "L" for "heart doctor" and the little ones flew swiftly to my aide—once again.

Green tears were still running like rivers of Gatorade. Words came from my lips, which didn't move, "My old heart, my old heart."

They quickly moved to the can marked "broken hearts," still over-flowing with red tears. Sobbing with pain, pieces started flying ever which way. They screamed "Old broken heart." Like the king's men trying to put Humpty Dumpty back together again, they scrambled throwing out extra pieces and picking up others. Finally they sang out, "Broken heart together; back together again."

As they came back and slipped it into my body, I could feel the green tears stopping and the vision of the one I'd loved for so long was returning. I took her picture from my back pocket and sure enough there she was. Her medium brown, long hair, her beautiful eyes, her lips—I felt I could reach out and touch her soft, lovely skin.

But wait! What is this? No! No! The tears, the real tears, were back. The pain in the old broken heart, it's there too. I long to hold and caress my love. I need her near me to tell her of my love, my plans, and my dreams. But she's not here. The tears will never stop. The hurt in the old heart will never leave. But I'd rather have this old, broken heart with tears for my love than to find a new love and someday wake up in a puddle of green tears.

This was signed "With Love to My One and Only." It was written in October of 1987 by Norman Raymond Bourne, my first husband, and given to me prior to my birthday in November of 1990, the year of his death. I've read it many times. Until today, I didn't get its true meaning. Today, when I read it, I cried again; then laughed and cried at the same time. The first tears were for sadness and the second tears were for joy. I can truly say I've been loved. And for the first time in my entire life, I can truly say I loved him too. That battle is over. "Oh, God how did You ever come to the conclusion I was worthy of making it this far?"

Chapter 33

Dreams

Acting as hostess at the bed and breakfast, right next to where she was living in Seattle, MySher was dressed in a floor-length gown. It was light green with a touch of blue; the two colors sort of blended together, much like a rainbow overlapping in colors but the blue faintly stood out in form of lightening bolts. It clung to her every curve. Her grace and poise were absolutely magnificent. Her demeanor and attitude were very dramatic and sophisticated. Over-hanging tree limbs bowed to her very presence.

The three of them—two older ladies and Sherry—walked through the backyard, live with flowers, shrubs, and ivy. There were others engaged in light conversation—I believe I counted four. Dim lights hung from tree branches over the elegantly draped tables.

One could tell it was almost dark, only some dim gray still hung in the sky—the opened part where one could see through the branches. Some shadows outlined the area where they were walking.

MySher was happy. Her mouth broadened in a restful smile, showing her teeth. I was standing on the sidelines as if suspended in mid-air. I felt like an angel. I was happy that she was happy.

Then I woke up with the thought of "Seven Spanish Angels come to take another angel home." The mental image was so striking that I even said it out-loud.

The people there were waiting for something to take place. It seemed that I was there for the same reason, which I didn't know.

I wondered what does this have to do with Armageddon? The question I'd asked God to give me the answer to before I went to sleep last night. My curiosity had always run high, sometimes getting me into trouble. But I still desired a higher sagacity. I wanted to know.

As I wrote, "take another angel home," that morning, it occurred to me that this dream represented Sherry's death…or, at least, a serious change in her personality: the death of her old self and the birth of a new one. That this was the shadow among all the other beauty. It also represented peace, contentment, and joy in the air, the kind not often experienced in this life on earth and possibly the kind MySher had never experienced before. *She is so young,* I thought. *How could she die without killing herself? If she were to kill herself, this contentment couldn't prevail.* And it seemed to have no relation at all to Armageddon. The time of day meant there wasn't much time left according to our standards. As for me being an angel, I couldn't see that either: only by the grace of God that I could be an angel, and especially in human form. In my mind the blue represented truth, but I didn't have the least idea about what the color green meant; maybe, it meant earthly. I think that we were waiting for some decision from Sherry. Maybe I would put the pieces together later. I would go to sleep and dream again. Additional parts would possibly be revealed in other dreams.

I awoke from the second and third dreams. In them, chaos had befallen on the earth. Rats were scampering for their lives. So were the people. They were screaming in the dark. The whole world was dark, with the exception of scattered fires bursting forth from molten rock. I realized I was not a part of this. My body no longer held the form it was so attached to while among the living; in fact, it held no form at all. I felt sorrow for the people below me. There was so much Hell it was incomprehensible and unbelievable. Molten rivers of fire begin to form and widespread throughout the land. I didn't want to believe any of this.

"Was my son, Myron, among those left behind?" I wondered. He had been so busy feeling sorry for himself and thinking the world owed him a living. Does this picture depict the world paying him back for his discontentment, for his lack of endurance? Out of the dark sky I heard a powerful, yet soft and peaceful, voice from a distance say, "It's too late to ponder about those questions now."

I felt my daughter, MySher, had been saved. The first dream had given me that indication. Yet, I didn't see her anywhere in the near heavens, as I turned around to look at the vast universe. I had awakened from the first dream before an answer was given. A deeper feeling inside of me said, "She's okay." Was this feeling something I wanted to believe or was it really true? "I hope it's true and I hope I meet her somewhere in the sky," I whispered to myself, looking around at the vastness.

With that note, I ascended further and further into the universe, leaving all the screaming voices behind. They faded into very low tones, then nothing at all.

Later only fragments—small pieces of wonderment, such as one word left an impression following sleep. They must have been pieces I was supposed to fit together later. One such word I totally forgot because it seemed so unimportant.

One three-dimensional picture hung in my mind I do remember: It depicted war. An old-fashioned cannon, probably dated back to the sixteen hundreds, set in the foreground. The cannon seemed useless; it was just there. No person was in sight to operate it or for no other reason.

I was closer to the ground in this dream than the other dreams. Dressed in a long-flowing, white gown, I occasionally touched the ground with my bare feet. It felt neither hot nor cold, like normal dirt which seemed unusual for barren soil. There was no vegetation in sight. The gown's many-layered nylon-type skirt had uneven edges.

A large kitchen knife, hanging in mid-air with no one to hold it there, was above and in front of the cannon. Much larger was its presents, representing major significance. It was upside-down. It never occurred to me before, but I've always pictured a blade downward, toward the earth. This blade's sharp edge was facing upward, toward the heavens in a horizontal position. Its sharpness and shininess were noticed, even in the dim light of flashing fires; one in particular, just over a small hill situated at a distance behind the cannon. The brightness of the knife reflected colors. The fire must have caused it. Along the sharp edge, it reflected the lightest yellow. A darker yellow, in the middle, gradually became even darker. A bright orange, a bright orange-red, then the darkest of orange-blood-red neared the none-cutting edge. The flashing fire in the background must have caused the colors to change. Then it was of the lightest lavender blue on the sharp edge, which pointed toward the heavens. The same as before, the colors became darker—a light blue, a deep royal blue, purple, then black.

Just normal dreams occurred later. The two different kinds of dreams were distinctly different from each other. They were unusual to say the least.

I showed Ken Olsen, a twelve-year friend of mine, my dreams after they were written down. He works at the same paper mill as I do. We both agreed they were bazaar. An interpretation was something else.

"You know how dreams are—very symbolic. And they're made of what we think and do throughout the day. People who have had dreams in the Bible prayed for an interpretation. But most likely it's just a wild imagination," gently patting me on the head, inferring I was one of those people. "I'll help you pray," he said.

Over the next few days I was left with brief, fleeting indications but nothing really definite. I prayed some more.

That night my dreams handed me a ream of the best quality paper that money can buy and a pencil also extended in mid-air. It seemed to have come right out of the clouds but no one was holding it—as if to say: "Here, write it!" These words were loud, over-powering sensations that seemed to come through by mind transference only. The paper and pencil were man-made products. The pencil was pointed upward. Just above its point was a bright light, which made me think of the Star of Bethlehem. The fact that it was pointed upward, suspended in mid-air with no one holding it inferred to me we already have all the right information we're going to get—in our minds, in our books, in occurrences that happen throughout the day, in our reasoning powers, and in the Bible.

My mind went back to this incident:

It wasn't too long ago I'd gone to Tacoma to sit in on a jury of a federal trial. I knew right from the very beginning I would be chosen. It was meant for me to be there. The judge gave precise instructions at the end of the trial on how to make our decision. He also said if we had any questions, we were to send them to him in writing. A couple times we wrote questions to him. He didn't answer them in the way we wanted him to. In other words: he wanted us to read the instructions. We already had all the right information we were going to get—in the instructions. We had to read many pages, parts of which we read more than once to help us gain a clear understanding. Even then, I'm still not sure all of us "got it." We wanted it made easy.

Another aspect of it was different people have different opinions. In this case, we all were right to certain degrees; they were just different.

We are meant to come up with our own interpretations—through the Bible, through books, and through our own search of the mind that provides reasoning. If two people, or if a hundred people, go to New York and are asked to give a description of it, we'd have as many different descriptions as there are people. Some may be similar, but they'll all be varied somewhat. Most likely, they'd all be true, because they would all apply to the person giving the interpretation.

Nothing is as easy as it looks and nothing is as hard as it looks. It's up to us to find our own answers. Hopefully we will find the right ones. You've heard that God helps those who help themselves. I feel comfortably sure that He's not going to come down here to mow our lawns for us.

It's a definite fact that some people come up with the wrong answers to life…and to death. Or, we wouldn't have so much violence—stealing, raping, murdering, drugs, and sadistic and other related behaviors. We even have drugs to help us eat more…or less. We need help! Where one is right in one area, he/she may be wrong in another. This leads me to think that sometimes we should let others be right for the gratification of their own significance, or at least consider different aspects pertaining to such a large picture. Neither should we be offended in any way when others state their opinions. Who's to say that anyone of us is right except God? A picture doesn't have just one item to look at; it has many. It's hard to make decisions without the interference of ego, personal belief, or the inner desire to control. We love power. As long as we do the best we can and for the good of all, rather than just ourselves, we are headed in the right direction. If we can't be part of the solution, then don't be a part of the problem. In a way, that was what Bill Gates, a brilliant mind of modern technology, meant when he said, "Lead, follow, or get out of the way." Some people have expressed disbelief in this statement. Those people just didn't understand completely what he was saying.

God didn't create all men equal. We'd like to believe He did. If you don't believe that just line up about twenty-five men naked and you'll get the point. This doesn't always apply to physical either. In many other countries, people are born into different rights. We are lucky to have "free choice," if there is such a thing. Even our own government has taken away some of our rights. It seems the less we have the more we have to do to get to the same point. Or, is it that some things should be less important? They're important to us. We need to learn to let go, especially of control. It takes a very humble person to do this. Maybe those losses are there for further testing—testing of bigger and better things to come. When we learn—if we can learn without becoming bitter and resorting to resentment or becoming defensive—maybe then, we'll be rewarded whatever is earned.

Sometimes I believe in reincarnation. In my mind, I don't think the Bible rules it out. Maybe it rules it in. If He knew us before we were in our mother's womb, did we have life then? Did we exist then in a different form…in a different person? Why are we born with certain talents? My son, for example, has had electrical abilities as far back as a small child without training. When he was just a kid, he wired in lights with no training at all. The electrician later came to check it out. He told us the average adult would have been electrocuted. It's a fact that some of us need more than one life to "get the point." And there are an unlimited number of "points" to get.

People seem to be learning more by asking the right questions. Yet, the other end of the scale is fighting hard too. Let's off balance that scale by reaching out with kindness and love to the best of our abilities. If we don't measure up, maybe God will let us have another shot at it. Our job is to endure and overcome. All of us are lazy and any words mentioning hardships are "put on the back burner" and ignored. It's easier to believe in positive things, rather than accept reality and work toward a positive change.

We should keep the pen or pencil pointed toward the heavens, writing about things that direct us to higher levels.

The knife's sharp edge pointed upward represents we are cutting away all that is pure and good with our earthly deeds. We should reverse the blade of the knife toward the earth, cutting off all that is evil.

The position of the colors will continue in the same state. Brighter, prettier colors will remain upward; that is where the good is. Darker colors represent earthly or unholy material objects: "Be, however, nearer toward the light," someone once said. (I don't remember where I got that exact wording. If someone didn't say it before, they should have.)

We are the products of what we put into our own minds. It runs the full scale from shadow to light—from the darkest of Hell to the brightest of Heaven. The concept of Armageddon, the place where the final battle will be fought between the forces of good and evil, has been here since Adam and Eve. When they ate of the forbidden fruit, from the Tree of Knowledge of Good and Evil, the battle began in our minds. Right then, it opened the door to evil. Before that, it didn't exist for us.

The actual battle on earth will take place in the Valley of Megiddo, located in Northern Israel, for the possession of the Chosen City of Jerusalem. This will be the climax. The fight will be over beliefs and power. Striving for the same thing—the grace of God and the Chosen City—will be the reason behind this devastation.

When I say "Chosen City" I think of Heaven, not a place here on earth. The climax, whether it be fought by man or by God's holy angels, is left unknown to me. God doesn't want us to kill our neighbor because they believe differently than us. He said to "Love thy neighbor as thy self" and to love thy enemies. This goes back to "The Ten Commandments" and "The Golden Rule." In my reasoning, we should "butt out."

Armageddon is to reestablish God's right to rule—His sovereignty. One word that comes to the foreground on how it relates to the dream I had earlier is the *waiting*. God is waiting for the world to make changes and accept Him as our Divine Master—if we will. Somehow, I also get an impression of the number seven being of great significance. But I don't know where this piece of the puzzle belongs. It's apparently not over yet. Our concerns, right now, should be to correct our own actions as people and make the best possible decisions we can, according to our Holy Father's will. We are on his side.

This dark and gloomy picture shows only part of one side of the coin, a "far cry" from the whole picture, because it's only one person's viewpoint. In my mind, the other side looks very promising. I'm tempted to think that the New World be of our own making. Whatever decisions we make now will determine the outcome. Everything under the sun of value to people is on its way. The hell or evil we've experienced in the past and will experience sometime in the not too distant future will push us into a better way of thinking, changing everything. Even now, we know and understand there are unlimited possibilities if we stop to think about it. The comments: "A house divided against itself will not stand," and "United we stand" gives a good beginning. "There's a time for everything under the sun." I'd like to think the time of our testing is almost over. It's lasted for thousands of years. The future holds a brand new philosophy to begin that New World. Our hope stands in today's soil.

Does this mean we will be over the half-way point to reach that *Place called There*?

Ken told me I was crazy. I'm tempted to believe he's not far off. Even I don't realize where I got some of this material. It just happened in my mind. Who's to say who or what put it there? I do think I was meant to write this book. I haven't been able to find someone to just be able to do the typing or even number the pages and print it out. It shouldn't be that complicated. One example is when I was in Washington: I'd just come back from Seattle after interviewing Sherry. While there, I wrote three chapters in long hand. Thinking that I could get done a lot quicker if I got someone to type it, I called up the local college and advertised for a typist. Two women came over. The first seemed totally uninterested, and the second one briefly looked at the material and said she wanted to take a chapter home to read before she made a decision. Later, she came back, telling me she didn't want the job. I wanted to know: "You mind telling me why?" She said, "I can't handle it. It's too sad." From time to time, I've had others try to do corrections or renumber pages for me. Every time, I've had nothing but chaos to handle later. A good portion of these pages have been almost completely destroyed five or six times. (The most trouble I've had was in the beginning of the book) Type would sometimes appear in computer language, some parts would be totally blocked out and not retrievable, or the last line on a page sometimes didn't justify. You name it—I've had all kinds of trouble. Then, when I tried to get help from people who knew the Bible well, they either couldn't help me with the information at all or were afraid to. They were afraid that they might distort the Word of God in this chapter. I'm actually afraid of that too, but I write these words as the dream directed me to. I studied the best I could and I prayed for the words to come out right—according to the Holy Father. The little voice inside my mind still says, *seek for yourself and the answer will be given*.

Martha Harris

Chapter 34

My Religion of Reality

MySher's love of wantonness grows stronger with passion, only to eventually die in ashes of desire. With constant hunger—greatly intensified and never satisfied—she becomes sad and wonders about her purpose. This passion, the seed of love in earthly form, was never fed enough. The yearning keeps growing stronger…and stronger still, until she forgets who she is. It's pacified only for a moment. Then she slips back into the dreaded, distant past. It leaves this sole embedded aching—over and over again.

Looking for new faces, new passions to somewhat ease the pain, she turns to new addictions forever in vain. The direction of where she goes is left uncertain. The numbing spirit dulls the constant gnawing. Passing thoughts—thoughts she finds too hard to face—are left behind in a hurrying race. She has eaten a forbidden fruit. The price weighs heavy. Sometimes I think it's too much.

The more enlightened I become, the more I realize I don't want to know. There are many kinds of fruit, as there are many kinds of knowledge. One fruit—I don't know what one would call it and it's too hard to describe—is totally out of Sherry's reach…and possibly mine too. I, too, have a ways to go. For every time we reach for it, it slips right through our fingers.

Some people who eat of this fruit go insane. Some die from trying to reach the lofty heights. While others dull their true senses with drugs trying to reach a higher rung of passion, like she has done. One step forward, two steps back; then she falls in her own mess—a mess she doesn't have the strength to get out of.

I remain beside MySher in this savagely cruel and harsh way. My thoughts then drift away to solving her problems and mine too—but only in my imagination. As this is the only way I can hold her near and make her feel dear.

Tiny pieces of puzzles put together will eventually make one giant picture. As for now, the picture is broken apart. When we can't get a piece to fit, maybe with one slight turn of the piece, it will slip right in. Or maybe, we should not worry about the pieces that don't fit—not at this time—and just accept things the way they are. Walk away! Leave it alone! Rest awhile! Think it over! Then come back again some other time —on a clear day when I can see better. I'm too tired to fix it now. Maybe we can solve our problems when things aren't so pushed in the wrong direction. Something keeps saying anything can be realized with time.

I don't have a bunch of lifetimes to become perfect. Or, at least, I don't remember the past lifetimes—if I had any—so I may add all the accumulated knowledge and put it all into the present.

Most of us hold a clouded future in the palms of our hands—we hope those clouds will slip by, unnoticed. My Aunt Lucy says you can have everything today and lose it all tomorrow. I'm sure she's right. She had everything she wanted at one time, but I think she feels the emptiness that I feel now.

We are the people, with pride and ego that stem to the sky. "Our destiny is our own," we say. "We make our own future." We want to believe we control our own destinies with our own decisions. Otherwise, hope is lost, we think. We like to think that we are logical people; yet, we are emotional and rationalize our way to what we think is logic. I feel I made the best possible decisions I could, in most cases, under the circumstances. Yet, my life is far from being perfect, or what I want it to be. And no one can tell me a baby born "two months early, hooked on crack," is the result of their own decisions. *Oh, that's only part of a song I haven't learned to sing yet. That doesn't apply to MySher…or to me.* Just as no one can tell me all of my past is the result of my own decisions. There's a fine line to what should or shouldn't be our own fault. My mother used to say, "It's not a sin to get the lice, but it's a sin to keep them." This comment held a double meaning for me—and for her too. The most important meaning, the one I had to read on my own, was a person was not always responsible for what happened to them, but they were responsible if they chose not do anything about it. In other words, we don't have to wallow in a pigsty that might already be there. Neither do we have to leave it dirty. We don't have to hold in our hearts the ungodliness of jealousy, lack of forgiveness, and a multitude of other things that wrap around our souls and place limits on us.

With effort, stamina, morals, and a long list of other words, may we gain enough strength to overcome. John 14:12—"Verily, verily, I say unto you, He that believeth on me, the works that I do shall he do also; and greater works than these shall he do, because I go unto my Father." Also in John 14:14—"If ye shall ask anything in my name, I will do it." And in Ps. 68:11—"The Lord gave the word; great was the company of those who publish it." All words of hope have power. May we continue to add to the list of words that put endurance in our souls and help us prevail in the long, hard struggles of a conditioned life. May we never give up hope for the best. May we conquer and overcome our clouded future.

I am told "People who see ghost usually have very powerful beliefs, which may alter their views of what might actually be happening." One of my co-workers made an experiment to help me understand how our perception is altered. He rolled up a piece of paper. "An eight and a-half by eleven will work," he explained. Then he instructed, "Using your right hand, hold up this roll of paper to look through with one eye. Hold up your left hand about halfway down. Have both eyes open. With your left hand open, touch the paper with the side of your hand. You can see a hole through your left hand. You know there's no hole in your hand, yet you can see one."

People who have taken hallucinogentics claim they have seen through posts. The drug produces an uncontrollable, mind-altering state, reducing clarity. Shock or anything traumatic can also create an altered state. A euphoric state—an exaggerated state of well being, having no basis in truth and reality—can occur in the brain from our bodies' own induced chemicals.

This is a real gray area because of lack of proof. Maybe it's not time for us to understand and be able to explain the additional knowledge sometimes presented our way. We have aroused our minds to know more and more. Maybe it happens to help the people who are nearly ready to understand.

Our perception of reality is based on what we see, hear, feel, and think. Our senses can sometimes dull the picture, making things so fragile they can fall apart. Distortions play a big part in not being able to believe or find proof in what is real and what isn't. Our minds can alter the view without drugs, in so many ways it's unbelievable. Whose to say what it takes to bring the gigantic puzzle together. With time and patience, I believe we'll find out enough to overcome our inadequacies. I need to remember when I don't understand something: think of the song "Father Alone." Part of its wording says, "Father alone will know all about it. Father alone will understand why. Cheer up my brother; live in the sunshine. We'll understand it all by and by." Patience is probably the last thing on the list or at least one of the last things on the list…and the hardest to learn. In the end, I have faith the pieces will all come together. In the meantime, our search continues. For now, we are only halfway there, waiting at a depot for a train leading to the beyond. I just hope that my spiritual growth is enough to present myself to God with dignity.

We can't say we just woke up. Our perception diminishes with time. It's a continual struggle to live with constant clarity and make it flow as evenly and as beautiful as a waterfall.

Some of us will never make it past the half-way point. This additional part, which I have been trying to describe, may die while still on the vine. Even the person who has hope may still have "a long row to hoe."

When God made man and put him in the Garden of Eden He soon realized that to make him happy, He would need to make woman. God also wanted to please man. So he took a rib from Adam while he was sleeping, molded her and breathed life into her body. Woman became part of man; they were "one." They would forever after need each other.

We read that Eve made the horrible mistake of being deceived. Sometimes I wonder why do we have to suffer because of her. Then I realize, I've been deceived a thousand times or more—by the people who worked for me, by my own children whom I extended life to, by a husband who worshiped me, and even by friends. How can I blame someone else for doing something I have done so many times?

The two being one, Adam was soon to follow. She had followed him in her existence. Now he would follow her in life. Did you ever stop to think that maybe God, the All Powerful, the All Mighty, knew all alone what He was doing? Maybe He planned it that way.

One theory about the Devil is "God knew He would strengthen good if we exercised in the battle against evil. So He called upon his angels to volunteer for the job of spreading evil throughout the land. The Devil volunteered." We've had a belly full of exercise ever since.

Endurance and overcoming are strongly recommended in Revelations. How? Two sticks, separately, doesn't have a great deal of strength. By laminating them together they become stronger. I believe that's part of why God made man and woman. They were supposed to be helpmates and share the load of the difficult road ahead. Have you ever wondered how much strength we would have if all the people of the world bonded together? Don't you think that that's what God wants us to do? Why are we all so different, having qualities in certain areas and extremely lacking in others? Where one is lacking, another makes up the difference. From what I've seen in this lifetime, it's going to take more than one to make the journey. We are too superficial to persevere to see beyond self-wantonness. I hope my darling—MySher—will see beyond herself to stop taking from her mother, especially without consent.

MySher interrupts my thinking with a visit. It seems nice. A smile comes to my face. She has a girl friend with her, whom she introduces to me as her assistant. Her friend, or assistant, seems like the innocent type. My higher self tells me there is much more to this girl than meets the eye. I don't have time to stop and listen to my enter-self now. My thought process has lasted too long, or maybe I didn't have enough time to start with. I need to get some things done before I have to go back to work. So I leave the two alone in my house while I go run some errands.

Much later to my surprise, I find out this girl stole my records to set up a scam of embezzling. I lost $50,000 due to that visit. Both MySher and she knew exactly when I sold the house and when it would be beneficial, monetary wise, for them to go to work. I was now tired of living out in the country and wanted to move back into town. Sherry thought it was okay for her to take from me since she was my daughter. She thought whatever belonged to me also belonged to her. She didn't work for it. How could she possibly see it that way? I went though months of "hell" trying to straighten out the mess. For a long time I worked with the Seattle Police Department. Eventually they caught the girl (who is unnamed here to protect her privacy). She got one year in prison for this crime and many other similar ones, which she admitted to.

Shortly afterwards, my handyman stole my checks off the coffee table, probably while I was in the kitchen fixing him a cup of coffee. They were still in the box. I should have known what was up when he mentioned that Sherry and others had done so many bad things against me. He was giving himself a way out, thinking *they did it. If I don't do it, somebody else will. How can we ever expect to get past the half-way point thinking like this?*

It's extremely funny that even the more innocent type of people can't even stop for one drink after work without being thrown in jail and burdened with so many fines it takes years to undo while these people get a mere slap on the hand. Some might say I deserved it by letting it happen. Those people will laugh about the situation, maybe because they have never had anything like that happen to them. Maybe they never had it to start with; you can't take nothing from nothing. If you do, you'll end up with a minus. Here's where "one step forward, two steps back" comes in. And the long journey becomes longer.

Our success—if we are to call it success—leads out in many different directions. When will people ever learn that it takes work to steal? It even takes more work to steal than it takes to earn it because it leads back to that saying—again: "one step forward, two steps back." Often we end up in jail. The worst thing we do is not to others, but to ourselves. Whatever we do for or against others, we also do for or against ourselves.

From the tip of the roots of a tree, it grows to be "one" in the trunk. Then it extends separately into branches representing the roads of our lives here. The blossoms on the end of the branch show the beauty of true successes, through giving and receiving. It's not always monetary. We would truly overcome if we could see that tree as the people of this world, somehow being hooked together as the tree, branches, and blossoms are.

Sherry has learned that many of her so-called friends are not really friends at all. They are just there to use her. "Mom," she says, "I'll never steal from you again." Later, I found out that that wasn't entirely true. Recently I uncovered some of her expenses, which were listed on my credit card statement again.

My love for MySher is so great I can feel her pain. Yet, I sit back, waiting and praying for more changes to come. We—the Good Lord, the angels, and I—are still waiting for her to make those changes. The blossoms she carries are full and beautiful in places. Yet, other parts are sparse and colorless, dulling the picture considerably making it look bare and ugly in places.

I sometimes wonder if one missing piece of the puzzles lies in the word energy. The dictionary gives the meaning of energy as available power—a feeling of tension caused or seeming to be caused by an excess of such power. An old friend, whom I took some clothes from once, revealed some possible beneficial knowledge. She changed her name to Joanie*, once she became a harlot. She said that the Georgia State College football coach told his students to go to the whorehouse to relieve their pent-up emotions. She also mentioned that he recommended a vigorous workout to relieve their tensions. Can a few minutes of such fulfillment satisfy, when we're looking for a whole universe? There are so many variables.

Success courses teach us—or tries to teach us—how to overcome and become successful. Flowing in a three-step method, their teachings say we should first get a "leverage"—a motivation. Then they advise us to replace it with an interruption—to change our thinking process. The more elaborate the replacement the more effective it will be. This is why some firms that help us quit smoking use tiny electric shocks every time we take a puff. It changes the thought process to associate it with something bad, instead of something good. I suppose similar reasoning is behind the treatment of people who are put under electric shock for mental disorders. The third and last step is a more permanent replacement. This is supposed to be the lasting step; if not included, the old cravings come back. The old pattern will regain its strength and come back after a certain amount of time, especially if triggered by some type of interference such as the wrong thought or reaction. This is why hypnosis works for only a short time. Sometimes our replacements tend to be other drugs, alcohol, food, sex—you name it. Just what is strong enough to help us overcome? Are we forever to remain at this half-way depot, impatiently waiting for a train to complete the journey?

Let there be hope for us.

"For there is hope for a tree,
if it be cut down,
that it will sprout again."

Chapter 35

"Beasty" and "Big Red"

All packed up and ready to go, I started out to Montana in "Big Red." It was my vacation—away from all the stresses of home. I wanted to give the sheep up there a little competition.

Also chasing an old dream, I didn't want to leave anything out. The dream included a little log cabin nestled back against a mountain. Dark-green grass carpeted the slightly rolling landscape foreground. An area, about half the size of a football field in the lower right corner, took priority. I was standing in the middle of this fenced off area shoveling manure, which was up to my knees. The manure covered the entire fenced off area. No way was I permitted to go outside the fence and return to the comfort and security of the little log cabin, until I finished the job of cleaning up that mess. It seemed like an impossible chore. But I couldn't let up. It had to be done. The log cabin was so beautiful. Rest would only come with completion of the task. I suspected it to be in Montana, and I was going there to find out.

A couple friends, Dawn Smith and Danny Whalon*, trailed along behind me in "Beasty," Dawn's old Plymouth Duster. It was mostly a rusty color. Dawn had started painting the top white but never finished. The grill was missing, and I think a few other things must have been missing too. The old car, made sometime in the mid '60's, had a difficult time getting up the hills. She spurred the old jalopy up and around every corner, as it sputtered to move onward.

"I'm afraid Big Red's going to catch a cold or something from Beasty. Do you think we could leave him behind in Butte and check him into a hospital? We don't want to stop every few minutes for Beasty to catch his breath again or to replace another hose. My vacation will be gone, if we keep this up."

In Butte, we stopped at a restaurant and ordered breakfast. The waitress asked Danny, "How do like your eggs?"

He answered, "Side by side."

She looked at him as if he was crazy. Dawn looked up at the waitress and confirmed her thoughts: "He's crazy!" she said. We laughed.

"According to some doctors, we're all crazy, just to different degrees and in different areas," I added.

We fooled around in town for awhile, just having fun. I picked up a little bell from one of the gift shops.

On the way out of town Big Red, a name I'd given my four-wheel drive pickup truck, was like a great stallion raring to go. A guy in a black Corvette must have sensed it. He pulled up along side us, spurring his motor, wanting to race. Big Red was "a looker." Dawn said I might as well put a red light on top of it. It attracted all the young guys…and apparently the cops too. A cop ignored him, taking out after me. This time Big Red had attracted too much attention—the wrong kind. He gave me a D.U.I. since I had three drinks during the times we'd stopped for various reasons, mainly to give Beasty a rest. We got out of that mess and continued onward. Dawn took the first turn driving.

"Remember that movie about every time a bell rings an angel get their wings?" I said, attaching the little bell to Big Red's center mirror. "Well, there's going to be a lot of angels get their wings today. If I have to run into so many bad things, somebody somewhere is going to run into something good."

From Butte, we went up the center of the state to a place called Buffalo Hot Springs, which wasn't too bad. The owner of a restaurant let us park in his lot all night without charging us. Dawn and Danny went into a little tavern while I slept. I figured I had enough excitement for one day. The owner gave them a nice big steak dinner free. Naturally, I had to miss anything good. It wasn't in the cards.

The next day we bask in the sun and I got a sunburn. We ate lunch outside the restaurant in a picnic area. An older gentleman, named Darrell, told Dawn he was waiting for her to get into the pool. "It will be the most excitement we've had up here in months," he said. He wasn't lowbred about his comment. It was just obvious he'd noticed her big boobs. The pool furnished with water from the hot springs was soothing to the sunburn.

We didn't meet any Montana cowboys there, just older people and one very foxy, young girl who told us a story. A few days earlier she had gone to a place where they let her do a strip tease act. She had gotten about four hundred dollars for dancing but lost it all. "I have no idea as to how I lost it," Cecellia* explained. "I needed some money. To get up enough nerve to do it, I had to get really drunk. Some time later I went to change my clothes, and it was all gone. I suppose it just dribbled out along the way and I was too drunk to notice. Too bad, I needed that money too," she ended her story.

Danny wanted to visit his mother in the northeastern corner. So heading Big Red in that direction, we pulled out. "Dull, dull, dull—the horizon meets the sky all day. I can certainly see why people call this place 'The land of the big sky.' If they have to say something good or nothing at all, the sky would have to be it."

We got there, in Plentywood, where Danny's mother, Lee*, lived. She was the oddest woman I've ever met. "And that's putting it mildly," Dawn also implied.

Lee seemed terrified just because I dressed up to go out. "People up here don't understand that type of dress," she said. "They won't know how to treat you. You'll be out of place. People here just dress in old blue jeans and shirts." She kept repeating herself, getting more nervous by the minute.

"Well, this is how I dress," I said. Apparently, it wasn't too bad. I got all kinds of attention and didn't have to pay for a single drink…or my dinner. Even the bartender bought me one. *What's wrong with this woman? Is she just jealous…or just plain crazy, somewhat like her son?* I asked myself.

She was totally the opposite of what I'd seen from the other people living there. She didn't offer either one of us—her son, his girlfriend, Dawn, or me—anything, except a cup of coffee. I even had to ask for the cream to go in it.

That night Dawn and Danny had to take her home early because she got too drunk. They left me downtown with a stranger and didn't call or come back to see how I was. It was a place I wasn't very familiar with. I'd been to her place only once and I wasn't too sure about how to get back. The only security I had was Big Red and the stranger. He was a nice fellow. He didn't make any passes, and he directed me where to go to get back to her place. Apparently he'd known her for a long time.

I went back to her place and parked on the street in front, after dropping him off at his place. Without changing my clothes, I crawled in the backseat and went to sleep.

Danny came out to get me the following day. He was smiling as usual. I was mad. "What are you smiling about?" I scowled.

"I've furnished you and Dawn with a place to live totally free for over a year. And you do this to me. What's wrong with you people anyway? Are you afraid to give someone just a few minutes of your time? I'm not just someone, either." My thoughts added to the situation: *I'm somebody—somebody you've been using for several months. The somebody that's paid your way up here in the first place…or mainly paid your way.*

"If you're going to talk to me like that," Danny started, but never finished. Then he ran for cover. Apparently he meant he didn't have to stand there and listen to it.

As he started to leave the room I said, "Wait here just a minute. You not only deserve what I've said, but you deserve more."

Still not out of my hearing distance, he went down-stairs where he had to listen to Dawn's comments too. "Danny, get your ass back up there and face it," she said.

"This is an example of the way I treat people when they come to my house: My first cousin brought a friend of hers from North Carolina to my place for a week's vacation. I asked one of the restaurant owners downtown to start them a charge account, which I would take care of. They could charge any amount of food or drinks they wanted. Not only that, but my brother, Tommy, furnished them with a car to drive while they were here. The only thing I've been offered since I got here was a cup of coffee. And I used your bathroom to take a shower and clean up. To top it off, you guys took me downtown, tried to get me lost, and treated me like shit. Even after you've treated me this way, I'd still treat you like a guest and with respect if you came to my house," I told Lee after Danny had left the room.

"From the weakness I've seen here today, you people don't even come close to the half-way point. It would be a miracle if you touched the bottom rung." I continued, but realized I'd opened another can of worms.

Danny's grandmother, Doreen*, was the only person there who realized what I was talking about. She later cornered both Dawn and Danny in the bathroom telling them, "Wait just minute, you should be ashamed of yourselves for taking your friend downtown and leaving her there by herself."

It was actually Doreen's place. Lee was supposedly staying there, taking care of her mother. Both Dawn and I thought it should've been the other way around. Doreen was more capable.

Lee didn't know what I was talking about. How could she? She hadn't realized a thing since we arrived. Her previous pattern of nervousness had showed up again last night, even when I ordered a drink. "They won't know how to fix that kind of drink here," she said. "This is not the place to order those fancy drinks," she rambled on, but I ignored her.

I decided to "shut up and drive" away from that place. Dawn was downstairs trying to explain it to Danny. They'd get ready in a hurry if they wanted to go.

I could understand somewhat why Danny was like he was. His mother had nurtured his fun-loving character, while at the same time she'd given him nothing to handle any kind of problems he was likely to have in daily life. He'd learned from her to run from them, ignore them completely, or get nervous and fall apart. Without some serious changing in him, I didn't see how it was possible that him and Dawn were going to make it together. He had too many traits that had been left behind by the feminine world long ago.

I could understand a little more why Jesus said, "Forgive them Father, for they know not what they do." Lee didn't realize a thing she'd done wrong. Or maybe, the over-powering urge she had for alcohol camouflaged the matrix of her mind.

As we crossed "The land of the big sky"—again, Dawn contemplated the perfect murder. She was just bitching at Danny for the fun of it. This time we headed back westward toward Glacier National Park. The desolation of the countryside brought to her mind the ease for which the task could be accomplished. We saw only one car for what seemed like hundreds of miles. Apparently repulsiveness showed up in my face. She noticed and pointed it out. "Oh, I'm just mad at Danny. And this is my way of getting it out of my system," she explained.

"Skip it! You'd have to kill me too. You can't leave any witnesses," jokingly, I told her.

"Tommy has previously described to me what he thought would be a perfect murder," I said, connecting it to the subject. So I revealed the story: "Get the person out in deep water. Act like you are trying to save them. Put your arms around them tightly. Naturally, there'll be some scratch marks on your face. But, just tell the police you were trying to save them and they panicked. Apparently, he's thought about it a few times, but to my knowledge he's never carried it out." We all laughed—a happy feeling after the earlier incident.

"Come on now! Let's change the subject," Dawn delightfully corrected our conversation. "Just look at that beautiful lake down there."

The park, in the northwestern corner, was the prettiest place in Montana. It was beautiful there and worth returning to again, sometime in the future. I didn't find the little log cabin I was searching for. But I'd certainly found the pasture of shit.

It was obvious I, too, needed to climb a few more rungs before approaching the half-way point. All this beauty, like finding a Garden of Eden in the middle of a desert, could certainly make the journey of improvement more accessible. As we approached a rainbow over a waterfall, it occurred to me that colors could also do wonders. "The smell of fresh greenery: that makes me happy. A lengthy bath—something I'd like right now—I'll take tonight. I need to look for things that make me happy."

We met a couple in a cocktail lounge of a large restaurant and resort area. They invited us to spend the night with them, as they had already rented a three-bedroom house for the night. We accepted—just talking, drinking and having fun most of the night. It's amazing how some strangers can be so trusting.

After returning home Dawn told Tommy the story about what happened. He told her and Danny he would have left them there with his mother.

"One of these days I'm going to get rid of all the shit that lay beneath my feet by cleaning it up. I'm going to go through that fence and only come back to that spot when I've got something good to plant in the richest soil in the world. With all that manure, it's bound to be the richest soil.

"Let's see if I can get there with my mind," I told Dawn, after returning home. She had gone out with a guy prior to going out with Danny who had taught us the exercise. He said one could tell what a person was like by giving them this little exercise:

I reclined on a big chair taking myself through it, one step at a time. In my mind, I took myself back through the exercise: I went down a road—it was gravel, but smooth. I came to a body of water, like he had instructed. It was a deep inlet. On the right side, overhanging trees cast some shadow over the deep, clear water. An opening, of twenty feet or more, provided space to go close to it. I went close to the water's edge, viewing its beauty, and noticed a larger body of water at its mouth, maybe a hundred yards or more from where I stood. The larger body of water was slightly choppy, unlike the smooth surface of the inlet. It was a gorgeous place to take a swim, but I chose to go further down the road. I came to a fence on the left side. It was made of three rungs of split logs; very easy to crawl through, but I kept walking. On the other side of the fence there was a small hill and a few rocks—not very encouraging. All of a sudden the fence ended—just stopped. I walked around the end post just to see how it would feel. No big deal! Then I walked back to the road and continued. Next, I came to a huge bowl in the middle of the road and wondered why it wasn't off to the side. It was an old-fashioned, translucent bowl, light blue in color. Whatever was in the bowl I had to see. A ladder materialized out of no where. I climbed twenty or thirty rungs—this was a huge bowl. Inside was a clear liquid, bubbling like boiling water. "Boy, whatever this is I have a lot of," I said to myself. "It's almost full." The liquid came fairly close to the top. I climbed down, surrounded the bowl and continued on my way. Next, I came to a little log cabin, just like the one I thought I might find in Montana. A compost pile was in the extreme lower right corner, surrounded by a fence. It was a small area; nothing compared to the size of the manure I had to shovel in the dream. The other fence was gone. All the manure was cleaned up. There were no weeds, just rich soil ready for planting. A light was on in the little log cabin. It seemed to beckon me welcome. I walked up the steps, across the porch, and entered the cabin. No one was at home. Then I realized this was my home. It had been waiting for me. Everything was in order, even the wood for the fireplace. I built a fire and watched the burning flames take me into a comfort zone. *This is where I belong,* I thought. *Everything else along the way is just an adventure.*

The interpretation of this exercise was the road of life. The body of water represented my sex life. Since I walked past it without going for a swim meant I didn't jump into sexual affairs, but I wasn't afraid to go close. The still waters, running deep and connecting to the larger body of water, pointed out that my feelings of a lasting relationship went right along with my sexual desires. The fence was the trouble I've had, mainly with my kids. What trouble I had could be overcome, since the fence did end abruptly. That's how it would probably end, once I made the decision. The bowl represented my spiritual self. A bubbly spirit I did not want to overcome. It was there for whenever I needed it. So, it remained in the middle of the road—or in the middle of my life. I had cleaned up all the garden spot, leaving nothing but fertile soil. Past experiences of facing responsibilities and developing my mind the best I could was the task, which was now completed. I could rest now and grow in other areas. I was a good person. But I couldn't do anything to make other people good too, except be myself. *The year 2000 will bring many good changes and bring them abundantly.* I can feel it!

Martha Harris

Chapter 36

"Honey, I'm Home"

Walking through the front door and making an immediate right turn, one might see a guy with his lower lip protruded so far they felt like stepping on it to spring themselves over to their work station. Every time I walked through the door and saw him, I felt like playing this weird, abstract trampoline game in my mind.

Returning to work from vacation felt like a warm welcome. I was happy to be there.

Or, one might see a small version of Santa Claus, without the big belly that Mr. Claus is visualized to have, in the middle of May. Just a small tummy, as he would describe as "love handles," will suffice in his case. "Mini-Claus" is a virgin; he's never had a girl in his entire life. And he's nearing 60, if not already there. Yet, he's had well over 300 men last year alone…and proud of it. Once he gets to know someone, he greets them in a cheerful way. Apparently he has sex on his mind a great deal of the time though, because he grabs "off-the-wall" comments and questions about the subject. Adding a few words of advice, he tells me I need a boyfriend to relieve my frustrations.

"I've been feeling a little strange lately," I reply.

"Why?" He asks.

"Maybe it's because I haven't had any for the last six months," I add, teasingly.

He laughs. "You know, a friend of mine kept track of my experiences between the first of September to the end of last year. He found I had eighty some men during that time. Almost all of them were married. I've discovered the best places to pick up men are down in Portland in front of an adult book store or in front of a massage parlor. The police picks up women prostitutes, but leaves the men alone. And I have a ball," he adds.

"Yeah Harry* (I call him by name, instead of Mini-Claus), but you're a whore. I'd like to have a lasting relationship. My last boyfriend used to argue with his friend across a table who was going to be the biggest 'ass-hole.' If all the guys I meet have to be ass-holes, then I don't want any. His picture still hangs on my living-room wall to remind me of the 'ass-hole.' I know: everybody has one. The trouble I have is the men I meet have a bigger one."

A guy, whom I'll call "Gampa," sits at his workstation, right next to Mr. Mini-Claus. He greets me with a salute, "Hi, you old bag."

Laughing slightly, I look over to the left and see a sign, which covers half the building. It reads, "Martha is 49 today."

"Now, who put that up. I don't want everybody to know how old I am."

"Charlotte did it," an answer came back.

"Why didn't she bring me a cake? Was the bakery closed?" I don't think they heard that comment. There was too much noise.

Shifting our attention in a different direction, Charlotte comments, "One of the machines is down today. We don't have any steam. It's cold in here."

My co-worker, Hong Lim, wants me to help him move a portable gas heater closer to our workstation. So he motions for me to come, in a demanding Cambodian fashion that fits his personality. "Here, help me," he demands, motioning for me to come and holding his body trying to stay warm.

Harry, being close by says, "Martha, you're going to have to take him over there and warm him up."

"I wore two pairs of long-johns today. I'm okay. He can take care of himself."

Even though, I butted up against one of the "hot headers" to get warmer. The 350-degree piece of equipment disintegrated my new, nylon pants. It left a heart-shaped hole, right where my butt was. I stuck it out so they could take a picture of it. They talked about framing the pants and putting them in the entrance hall for a conversation piece. (The pants had a lining.)

Harry laughs, "Hong should get a thrill out of picking the pieces of fabric out of your butt."

Others added their comments of teasing, and laughed. I laughed too.

On the way to the restroom Kimber says, "I see skinny is getting skinnier. How do you maintain your bra size?"

"It's easy. I cheat: push ups and pads," I respond.

Some weird things have happened to me since I came over here from the sawmill. A spider came down from the ceiling and landed right in my eye one day. After that, I was surprised they didn't start calling me "Spider Woman." This was probably one of the few times I ever observed the signs and walked where I was supposed to.

I like it here though, I thought. *It's nothing like the sawmill I first started to work at twenty-two years ago.* Most of the women in that department condemned me before I ever started on the job because of my size. I remember one woman at Mill B who must have been three to four times my size. I thought she was a man for the longest time.

At the planer I felt as if I had to walk on eggshells, which I did for years before deciding to take action. Going to the superintendent, I told him he should do something about the situation. The friction between the head lumber racker, Shelly Newland*, and me would eventually lead to something worse. With one eyebrow raised, resembling my father's expressions, I told him that I was fed up, clear to the brim. "Someone's going to get hurt, and it's not going to be me." I opened the door and started to leave.

"Martha, if you think it's bad now, you ought-a have been here several years ago," the foreman said, while I was still standing in the doorway.

Holding the door open, I turned around. "Don't you think it's about time it stopped?" I rebutted. Then I walked out.

I decided it was a lot easier working with the men, straightening and pulling lumber instead of racking it. I didn't have to go through all the daily tension. My muscles developed beyond expectation.

They changed the process from tying the lumber into bundles of four to stacking it directly into loads. Most of the "old bitties" were moved to the opposite end of the mill to do different jobs. One, in particular, stayed to send the lumber out to us. She worked with a couple of nice girls, whom I liked. Since she made my job harder than what it should've been, I approached her when the right opportunity arose. Explaining in a nice way, I told her she could make our jobs easier by changing her procedure just a little.

"Well Martha," she said, in an obnoxious, conceited tone, "It's their job." It was obvious she didn't care enough to change.

Women can be "ass-holes" too, sometimes even more so than men. I walked away; thinking, *it can also be your job.*

In time we made a complete switch. She took my job and I took hers. I rotated with the two women she previously worked with, stamping grades on lumber, stacking it, and pulling it off onto another belt which sent it out to her to straighten.

The stamping was too fast for most employees to handle because it required more changes than a person had hands for. The girls, Linda Chisom and Claudia Whitner*, took me under their wings and taught me how to be more efficient. We became good enough to eliminate the middle job. Every fifteen minutes we rotated breaks.

I still had time to pull any miss-graded lumber off so it could be re-graded later. This gave our machine one hundred percent accuracy. The grader supervisor often stopped by to talk to me. When he was there, I placed the bad board on top of the others, continually moving it back until he re-graded it. He wondered how I did my job and graded the lumber too, while at the same time I talked to him. By that time it was easy: I'd looked at enough boards. Claudia told one grader I would have a "field day" with his work. He learned to appreciate me, I think, for correcting his work because only ten-percent tolerance was allowed. And our machine put out more lumber than any of the other planers.

I told Linda and Claudia what had happened with Sue*: the one I'd exchanged places with. The girls decided to give her some rough treatment to pay her back the same way she'd treated me for years. Sue didn't last a week without going to the boss. Another girl tried it and went home after a few hours. They revamped her station, making it easier for her to handle.

The boss later talked to me about a couple of jobs since I'd been on one of them the longest. I told him we deliberately made it hard on her and why, mentioning the time I'd talked to Sue and what she'd said. We both agreed she was getting what she deserved.

Linda and I occasionally partied together. She told me she'd heard about me being able to make wishes, which came true. During those outings she tested my skills, requesting I get rid of her hiccups. I looked straight into her eyes and pointed my finger at her, saying, "They're gone." Sure enough, it worked.

The story which she'd heard was true. Norm, my deceased husband, had showed his disbelief in my comments by repeatedly saying, "Auh, hum bug." One day when we were going to work at the Kalama Bulletin, I'd told him something and he said it again. I told him, "If I tell you a wish, an impossible one, and it comes true, then will you believe me? Will you then stop saying 'hum bug'." He said, "Yes…if it comes true."

"Okay…just off the top of my head, I wish we will get $50,000. You know that's impossible. Don't you?" He answered, "yes." "It has to be within two and any number of zeros to be my wish. I mean 20 cents, 200, or 2,000. It can be two with any number of zeros above $50,000 or below, but I have a feeling it will be below. If it's not within this range, it will not be my wish. You know that's impossible, but I'm going one step further to make it even harder and let you know I mean business. Let's jump a state, and say it has to come from California. You can't expect it to come true over-night. Just give it a little time." I told about 30 people this wish, so I would have plenty of witnesses.

Sometime later our editor met me at the door of the Bulletin, smiling, "Your wish came true today," he said.

"Oh," I said, shaking my head, thinking it wasn't time yet.

"We received $6,000 from the Bon Marche of Seattle today."

Still shaking my head, I told him, "No, that's not my wish," and repeated the information: "It's has to be within $50,000 by the number two and any number of zeros, and it has to come from California. That's not my wish. Just wait a couple of months; it'll come true."

A couple of months past, and we received a check from Union Oil of California for $48,800 and some dollars. It was within two in almost every way, even to the pennies. California was written right on the check, and it was signed by three top executives. Later, we paid a good portion of it back because it was a mistake. According to what we heard, Union Oil bought out our attorney, telling us we had to pay the money back. According to another attorney we later asked, we didn't have to pay it back. The Bon Marche of Seattle never asked for their $6,000 check back. I believe that my wish held so much power that it influenced the other check. Since I had told so many people about this wish, the word had eventually got around to Linda and a few others.

Linda became a bit lazy at work, or maybe she was just bored with the job. It was a hard job, but I'd built up lots of stamina by working with the men. She asked me to wish the machine to go down so she could rest.

At first I think I did it just to see if I could. Besides, Linda wouldn't shut up until I did. Between ten to twenty minutes later the planer would break down. Every day—or almost every day—the same thing occurred. I warned her, we'd better stop or the machine would go down for good. "A lot of people are going to be out of a job. I have a feeling that you and I will benefit, but there are others we should think about."

"I don't care," Linda remarked. "I'm tired."

It was nearing its end, I felt sure. I had done it too many times. "Okay Linda, but be prepared for the ultimate results. I think we have only one more time left to wish it before it goes down for good. Are you ready for that?"

"Yes," she said, "do it."

Our machine, Number four, was the first to go down permanently, even though it had produced more lumber than any of the other planers in both the old and new departments. It was also the only machine to carry 100 percent accuracy.

Linda and I went our separate ways. I moved over to the new planer on clean-up. Piles of lumber, as high as houses, needed to be picked up nightly. The operators didn't want to send bad boards that they thought would split through the planer, so they pitched them out onto the floor. Whenever possible, I used a forklift to pick up the boards and gradually shake them off onto a conveyer belt, which sent them to a trim saw table. One could handle the boards from only one of the planers in this fashion because of the opened space needed to operate a forklift. Sometimes even those boards were crossed so badly that the job had to be done by hand. There were three planers, as well as three end-feeds, which I cleaned nightly.

Sometimes they sent me extra help. With the help they sent me, I could've done the same amount of work with an extra thirty minutes. One guy placed his wheel-borrow about twenty paces from his work. He would fill his shovel about half full, suggesting he was there for the money only. He was working to get out of work. When I suggested he move the wheel-borrow closer to his work he got angry. After that I chose to do the job alone.

Another cutback sent a lot of women to the High Com, or Mill B, where they were "washed out" by the dozens. The foreman there called me into the office before I started. He said, "Martha, there are men that come over here who are over six feet tall and they can't handle the job. What makes you think you can?"

"If I can't handle it, then you should find a different means of doing it," I told him.

The foreman used a good portion of his time watching me. He even counted the lugs I missed and later told me about it. We had to change jobs every three weeks to prove we could handle it. Sometimes he changed me more often, apparently hoping he could "wash" me out a lot quicker. Eventually his efforts paid off. I was working on the edger. He was standing on the catwalk, where he usually positioned himself to watch me. I accidentally stepped on the wrong foot lever, causing a board to slightly brush my shoulder. So he called me in the office and told me I was laid off due to a safety factor. Some of the guys said it would never have been mentioned if I'd been a man.

My boobs were already starting to look like pears from all the chest muscles I'd developed. It was a difficult job all right. On the separator, more often than not, the lumber was stacked several feet high, crisscrossing each other, for the length of half of a football field or more. The only help in separating these boards and deciding where they should go to be re-cut into smaller sizes of lumber were pop-ups. My biceps became as hard as a rock, without flexing. Yet, the water soaked, twenty-foot lumber was beginning to take its toll on my small frame. Just one top was enough to stay warm in the "dead of winter," when cold wind was blowing through the mill. So I was happy to be laid off. I was also glad it was his decision and not mine.

Later I was called back, this time to work at the other end of the mill. That eliminated some of the jobs I didn't like anyway. About a week passed. It was extremely cold and during the time of some home improvement projects. I was in a bitchy mood. Leaving the house to go to work that early, frosty morning, I slipped and fell on a grooved board, which replaced our steps. Stopping off at the medical center, I found out that I'd fractured a finger. Both the doctor and the medical center attendants said it was okay to go back to work. I'd made enough mistakes without a broken finger, but this made things seem even clumsier. Sending a nice big log to the chipper and getting another knotty log hung up on the wrong conveyer belt was just part of the scene. The guys in the lunchroom started a joke about the foreman having to carry around a power saw on his belt to get me out of jams. Pretty soon the doctor told me I would have to take off some time, or I'd have to have a steel pen put in my finger.

Again, I went back to Mill B after the recuperation period to work the graveyard shift. They called it clean up, but it should've been called maintenance. The job entailed changing saws and knives, as well as the hog hammers, for all the equipment. The equipment was designed for people six feet tall. At times, I handled the situation by standing on big blocks of wood to raise the guard gate so I could get to some of the saws. On those trimmers, I loosened the bolts with fifteen-pound hammers and changed the eighty-pound saws with muscles and blood and skin and bones. We did some clean up, but the major portion was done with a caterpillar, both big and small.

I enjoyed the sometimes-difficult challenges and the variety it brought. One guy fell eighteen feet to his death. Another was turned into a "vegetable" because of an accident. They said he somehow got his head caught in some equipment and was "squirted out of his hat." The hard hat he was wearing was demolished.

I relied on different techniques to accomplish the jobs. Occasionally the millwrights helped me, especially at the beginning. Even the boss mentioned one method at one of our safety meetings. He started, "I've been hearing about your methods of doing things."

My first thought was *Oh my God, they'll get me on a safety issue and I won't be able to do it my way anymore.*

"The other night I decided to check it out for myself," he continued. "You didn't see me. I stood back and watched from a distance. I've never seen it done that way before but it works, doesn't it?"

"It works for me," I said.

The following night I stood back and watched two millwrights struggle to get the edger saws in place. I wanted to see how long it would take them. After about five minutes I said, "Stand back, guys." They were shocked to see me accomplish the task so easily. The reason the saws were so hard to put into place was because of an unleveled wood floor. The set of four edger saws that hung on a piece of equipment was all rolled into place at one time. What made it easier for me was that the saws were placed far enough apart for me to get my body in between them, pushing them in place just by walking forward.

There was one other girl there. She had been there for several years and never did some of the jobs. After the boss saw I could accomplish them, he told her she would have to do them also. She followed me around for days to learn my techniques. In the case of the edger saws, she was too big to get in between them. I explained the unevenness of the floor and she apparently developed her own method.

She also helped me out on another job. I told her, "I don't have it down pat yet." In changing the re-chipper knives, I needed to torque each bolt 400 pounds. There were four knives to put into place. About ten or twelve bolts for each knife had to be precisioned. A cheater bar could not be used on the torque wrench because a large post was in the way. She noticed a pipe right above the machine and suggested I grab hold of it and put my feet on the wrench to push it down with my body weight. It worked.

The hog hammers were somewhat easier for me to handle since I could get my smaller fingers down along side the hammer to lift them out. On the trim saw I struggled and eventually gave in and went to ask the guy who trained me for help. At first I asked my little brother Tony, who worked as a millwright there. He had the same results as I did but told me not to give up. "They're just waiting for any reason to get rid of you. So don't ever admit you can't do it." I'd been working through my breaks and lunch periods to accomplish this job to no avail, while Clute*, the one who'd trained me, was laughing it up having a good time, apparently thinking this would "wash me out." So I went to the lunchroom to get him. "Apparently there's something about this job you haven't told me," I said. "You're going to come with me and show me now," I told the big guy that towered over me. I showed him the tool Tony had suggested I use. "You're on the right track, but you're using the wrong tool," Clute informed me, and showed me the correct tool to use.

These jobs eventually became easier for me than they were for the men who weighed over 200 pounds. One of the union representatives brought a head safety person from Tacoma down to see me. "If you really want-a see something, come with me," he urged.

I was working on a chipper at the time. I could see them through the Plexiglas window, but ignored them because the chipper was plugged. The lumber could get as high as houses for the distance of a full street block or more in a very short time if not unplugged. The production of the mill would cease for at least a half a day, if it got in this situation. The chain saw was too big for me to start in a normal way. So I left it on the floor, putting my foot on it and pulling the cord. After the jam-up was taken care of and everything was running normal I turned to see what they wanted. I expected them to notice I didn't have on any chaps, but they didn't. Jerry* introduced him, while his eyes were still partially bugged and his mouth opened. "I've never seen men who could handle their job as well as you do," he said. "And," hesitating, then continuing, "and look at you. You're no bigger than a child."

"Yeah, that's me," I said, smiling. Then I gave them a brief tour. He was still spellbound when he left.

I spent some difficult times in other departments too. I was laid off every year except one. Whenever I wanted to go back to work after being laid for awhile I talked to Betty Phillips, the personnel manager for the woods division. She generally put me in positions all over the plant site, filling in for people on vacations.

The superintendent at the Pulp Division felt uneasy about me being able to handle the job there. When I arrived, there was a truck strike and a big snow in the mid-west. No paper was moved for two weeks during my training period. After the guy went on vacation everything broke loose, causing stacks of orders to be filled daily. The place was in a mess. Nothing was organized. I had to move as many as thirteen double loads to get to one order. Sometimes I'd try to make things faster by climbing atop a double load, which needed only a few cartons on the top load to make it complete, and handing down a carton of paper to a man below me. The guys said it weighed 165 pounds—and it probably did. At that time I was too busy to look at the fine print on labels. Even the guy below me complained about his back. *You should be in my shoes*, I figured. *I have the worst job.* The superintendent came down, apparently hoping to get me on the right track. He kept asking for the shipping schedule. I thought he should know what a shipping schedule looked like; he'd definitely been there longer than I had. So I told him "in this pile," pointing to the stack of orders. The schedule was the only one of colored paper; the orders were white. "Where's the shipping schedule?" he asked for about the third time. I rammed my arm down on the table, pulled out the bright pink paper, and said, "Here it is. Now get out of my hair so I can get something done." He got lost, and I never saw him again until I went back to my old department. He shook my hand before I left, saying, "Martha, I had my doubts at the beginning, but you're one of the best workers I've ever had."

On another occasion I was welcomed right from the beginning. I was working with two millwrights, riding around in a little car in between jobs. The men always did the driving. Apparently one day they decided to have a little fun. "We're going to let you drive today," one of the guys said.

"Okay! That's going to be fun," I approved. When I got in the driver's seat and tried to make it go it wouldn't budge.

One of the men put his hand on my hard hat and push down; then it would take off. He'd let up on the pressure, and it stopped. They took a few turns, laughing and joking, especially when it stopped. "I thought you said you could drive," one pointed out.

"I can drive. It goes only when you put your hand on my head, and it stops only when you take it off. I don't know what it is, but it has something to do with that." They continued laughing. "Okay guys, give up the secret," I said laughing. "Tell me what's wrong!"

"It's your weight; you don't have enough weight. You have to weigh at least a hundred pounds to drive this thing."

"Huh? Why did they ever make a car like this?"

"Maybe because they didn't want any kids driving it," he answered.

The refresher course of my memory had just turned pages. I was glad to be back where I belonged. The guy I call "Gampa" followed me from the Weyerhaeuser Saw Mill at Mill B to the Fine Paper Department. He was the foreman the guys had made jokes about wearing a chain saw around on his belt. Now, he greets me every day with a salute every time he sees me. "I've finally found a home," I said to myself, smiling.

On the way home—my other home—an upside-down sign of Longview greeted me on the way by. At the door my girlfriend, Dawn Smith, was in her usual, cheerful mood, that attracts people in a divine magnanimous way. "Hi, honey!" She says sprightly.

I respond, "Honey, I'm home." (No, we're not gay; just the best of friends. She is that sweet to almost everyone. I'm that sweet—sometimes.)

Chapter 37

Ravenous

The night was cold with misty rain, the coldness being felt clear to the bone. Wind howled through the creepy surroundings. A carload of girls and boys played whoopee in a Cathlamet (Washington State) graveyard. Tommy was in the group; in fact, he led the way as usual. Rowdiness blended in as foreplay. Tommy lost a shoe. From there, they carried the rowdiness to a Centralia bar where he lost the other shoe.

Tony, our youngest brother, and a friend of his, Lonny Daily, showed up later in Cathlamet that evening after the group went to Centralia. They almost got into a fight with some guys. Even though Lonny was a good fighter, he didn't want to tangle with so many. They were considerably outnumbered. "Don't you know that Tony is Tommy Parker's brother?" Lonny informed them.

This comment brought a "stand up and listen" attitude to the group. "We don't want no part of Tony if he's anything like his brother," one stammered. They backed away.

Two different men brought back the shoes Tommy lost a few months later at different times. Tommy didn't know the guys; they were complete strangers. That was the first and last time he saw either one of them. They didn't know him either, but they had heard of him. He'd built his reputation to this point in the 1950s.

His name had been so bad; while in prison his reputation went from prison to prison before he got there. It was the same on the outside. He peregrinated mentally to gain a vicarious thrill by fighting, which threatened his constitution if left unrestrained. He had known pain that was connected with joy. Anyone who knew him was afraid to touch him even while he slept. The prison guards had learned not to touch him during sleep. He had gotten to the point of staying in a rage for three to four days before he could manage to pull himself out again.

Over the years, Tommy had actually developed a taste for blood. He'd go into a fight, laughing. When somebody hit him, sometimes on the nose or mouth, and he got the taste of blood in his mouth, he went into a rage. He didn't care if someone hurt him. He enjoyed it. And he enjoyed the taste of his own blood. It was a frame of mind he put himself into by thinking repeated thoughts, which brought a high.

These rages were first noticed at a North Carolina prison. He was watching TV in a barber's chair when one of the prisoners came in and hit him so hard it bent the headrest on the chair. The husky six-foot, three-inch weight lifter, weighing 210 pounds, explained to the guards, after the commotion had ceased, that Tommy had said some bad things about him. The prison mate continued, "He came at me like a tiger. By rights, he should've been knocked out. But no matter what I did I couldn't get him off me. I've never seen anybody that fast."

Tommy also attacked five guards who finally got him under control. The cellblock was practically destroyed. They'd never seen such violence.

Nothing was done about his condition until he entered a Marion, Ill., prison. It was a federal institution replacing Alcatraz. Since it was federal instead of state, they started checking into ways to help him. At state prisons, the guards picked at him, which made the problem worse. They checked his records. The warden remembered what he'd said to Tommy when he first came to Marion from Alcatraz: "They don't send any people here with that small amount of time. The only way you get out of here is in boxes," he recalled part of his conversation. The prison was built for cons that were never going to see their freedom again.

The eighteen months Tommy had gotten at the beginning of his sentence and built into eleven years was looked at professionally. They checked out the reasons why. Their only conclusion was that something was wrong with him.

Looking back at the situation for reasons why he'd gotten the guy mad at him in the first place, he recalled something he'd said. "It was completely misunderstood. Some of the boys were talking about a man—I don't even know his name—he had sexually molested his nine-year-old stepdaughter. I added a few views of my own. The man that hit me must have thought I was the one who started that story about him. Besides, it wasn't about him; it was about somebody else."

Tommy enjoyed the once-a-week visit to the psychologist because of so little time away from his cell. The psychologist had been an Army doctor. He brought him to beneficial realizations through a different kind of treatment. Tommy disclosed some of his secrets to him. He'd never before done that.

The following week he began with telling him a little about his wife, Brenda. He had beaten her with a water hose. They were presently separated. She had gotten his car stuck on wet grass.

Brenda's sister, brother-in-law, and their two teenage children, who lived nearby, came down to Tommy and Brenda's where they took Brenda's favor in the incident. Tommy got tired of fighting all of them and went into the house for a gun. He took it outside and pointed it toward Brenda's brother-in-law, pulling the trigger all six times. The gun never fired. Then he pointed it downward toward the ground and pulled the trigger. It went off the first try. He knew then that there must be a higher power, which prevented him from killing the man.

Tommy didn't realize he liked the taste of blood, until the psychologist pointed it out. He also pointed out that it was caused by early childhood beatings. He was finally getting the help he needed. When he went into a rage, he became a different person in order to protect himself. Sometimes he could remember only bits and pieces. Other times he'd come to his senses after officials got him under control and wonder why everything was in such a mess.

Recapturing some of his past, Tommy told the psychologist some information about Dad. Dad would periodically want him to drive when he was very young. Since he was so little he couldn't reach the gas feed or brake, Dad would place him on his lap. He would then pass out from all the alcohol he'd consumed. Tommy was left with the question of how to handle the situation, while at the same time the car was speeding out of control toward a tree or some other object with the help of Dad's foot becoming heavier against the gas feed. After they wrecked Dad would wake up and turn on Tommy, giving him a beating for wrecking the car.

It's puzzling that most of the craziness that Tommy was later involved in had something to do with cars. These memories were so deeply imbedded into his subconscious. Under normal circumstances he'd forgotten about it. Then, when put into a situation involving a car, it brought back the impact of previous conditions. Dad would use an object, such as a stick of stove wood, a glass gallon jug, or any thing he could get his hands on, to hit him on the head or wherever he could.

It was later figured out that most of Dad's problems came from suspecting Mom of adultery. Sometimes he took his anger out on Tommy because he thought Tommy knew this to be a fact and wouldn't tell him the truth.

Mom was never helpful with the situation either. She actually encouraged the beatings and often times she performed them herself. On some occasions the reasons for abuse were as simple as a comment they didn't like, which he said at the dinner table.

"A twisted state of euphoria created an illusion of satisfaction from the situation," the psychologist explained. "The mind is a powerful thing. It produces chemicals of its own, which can be many times more influencing than heroin. The state of mind can extend to a heavenly high. It's brought about with obsessive thoughts that are repeated over and over again. When the deed is over the pendulum swings back to the opposite end—a hellhole of self-punishment. It's hard to climb out of the hellhole—no ladder, no means of releasing the anguish. Your condition is somewhat like the man who molested his stepdaughter, and possibly caused from a similar form of abuse, but in a different form and to a different degree."

The doctor told him the rages would come back. They did. In Harrisburg, Ill., after he got out of prison they surfaced again. He was working there, sinking shafts up to 3,000 feet for oil shell.

While working there, he parked his car too close to the job. Cars were supposed to be parked outside the fence. His superintendent hollered out, "Parker, this car ain't suppose to be here. Take it outside where it belongs." It seemed unfair to Tommy since others had parked there. The pressure had also been building from previous times. Tommy jumped in his car and tried to run over him. The superintendent jumped up on the steps to get out of the way just in time. He called him into the office afterwards and pointed out that he could fire him for that. Tommy told him, "I don't think you have the guts to fire me…or fight me. Take your pick!" He dropped the subject and never did either.

A foreman ordered him to clean the yard when he wasn't doing anything else. "Keep the big rocks out," he instructed, handing him a garden rake. The guys started teasing him, asking when was he going to plant a garden. Tommy did an excellent job of keeping it clean until then. He then threw the rake in the "muck" pile, where the rocks are dumped when they come out of the hole. The foreman wondered what happened to the rake and mentioned he would have to get him another one. "If you bring another one down here, I'll brake it over your head," Tommy scowled. The foreman pointed out he was the boss and he could make him do it. "I don't give a damn who you are or what you do. You can go over there and jump in that lake for all I care," Tommy sounded back, pointing to a nearby lake.

Later, Tommy was working on an air winch—they called it a "tugger." They were pouring concrete to make a shaft. The foreman threw some vibrators and two-by-fours in the concrete bucket, hollering out to Tommy to send him to the bottom. To go down the shaft just to see what was going on wasn't a good reason, in Tommy's opinion. He was fifty yards or so away, so he came over to the head frame so he could hear above the high noise level. The head frame was about sixty to eighty feet high. It had a pulley on top of it with a cable that goes to the bottom, which transports the bucket up and down the shaft. The signal buttons were transmitted to the hoist man from that position. The hoist man needed to receive a signal for everything he did because of lack of visibility. Horns and lights were part of the signals. The foreman hollered out again, "I said to send me to the bottom."

Tommy gave the signal: "I-da-hoe," meaning to drop the bucket. Even though, Tommy was standing over the "stop" button, the bucket fell so fast that there was one hundred feet of slack in the cable by the time he pushed it. The bucket caught on the doors to the shaft and tilted. The vibrators and two-by-fours had already gone to the bottom and the foreman was barely hanging onto the door for dear life. He knew he had to hang on or die. It was 1800 feet to the bottom. He asked Tommy politely, "Would you please put me back on top?" The bucket was still swinging. Tommy signaled the hoist man to come up slowly. When the slack got out, he gave other signals: "man in bucket," "shut the doors," "put him on top," and "put bucket on doors." The foreman walked to the office and never said one word about it.

By that time, the hoist man had a pretty good idea about what'd happened. The six men at the bottom were waiting to be taken out. Some were hurt. When they heard the falling objects, they stepped against the walls, staying as close as they could until the clanging ceased. Vibrators fell through the work deck, one and one-half inches of steel grate. The work deck hung on cables against the wall and travels downward as the men progresses. It had two stations. Calling on the intercom, the boss in the shaft sounded out, "What's going on up there?" They conversed a little while: Tommy tells him what happed. He asks him to send a bucket down to get the men and bring them out. "Some of the men might need attention," he says. A vibrator hose caught on one of the guys' raincoats and tore it off. If he'd been two inches closer, it would've killed him.

They continued drilling, and reached coal at 2100 feet after taking the men out and regrouping. By first drilling a core, they knew exactly how far they would have to go. They were relieved that all the men were safe and the project was done. The guys just teased Tommy about both incidents later, saying things like "Don't make him mad. He'll throw a rock down on you." Tommy had learned a dear lesson on his own. He knew how close he came to killing someone.

"Wade or Steve Dockery—I think it was Steve—was the foreman in the hole. Jaycee Grant—they called him 'Red'—was also one of the men down there," Tommy recalled. "Red now lives six to eight miles west of Murphy, North Carolina, on Route 64. He still calls me and that's been fifteen years ago. In fact, he just called me the other day. Most of the men that worked there are dead now. All of them got 'Black Lung' from working in the coal mines." Tommy has it also.

Even though he'd learned a good lesson, another incident still occurred. He was then living with a girlfriend, Ginny Hall*. She had two boys and a girl. Tammy, Tommy's daughter by Brenda, was there too.

During one of their arguments, Ginny's oldest son, Doug*, who was 16, drew a gun on Tommy. While he was in the process of taking the gun away from Doug, her daughter, Joyce*, hit him on the head with a hatchet.

This brought out the old rage and the taste of blood again, the prison psychologist had warned him about. He was like a crazy person—a living vampire—craving more of the iron rich substance and enjoying the taste of his own blood. It took twenty-one cops to bring him under control.

He got out of the "drunk tank" they put him in, which had no facilities at all, in a couple of days. They put him in with the other guys. One of the jail mates asked him, "Don't I know you?"

"No, you don't know me because I don't know you," Tommy apprised him.

The man left and came back with a newspaper. "This is how I know you," he said, showing Tommy a picture of himself in handcuffs on the front page.

The court dismissed the domestic violence charge against Tommy, saying that something must have happened to him when Ginny's daughter hit him on the head. It was the easy way out for all concerned. And all was forgotten.

He was worried about Tammy being left with Ginny's family. Later he found out that Dave Tatem, a friend of his, had taken care of Tammy while he was in jail. Dave and his wife had heard about the incident and checked on her. They found her hid in a closet. All the others were gone.

He'd gone back into that state of mind, which he had to pull himself out—again. First, he had to admit that the situation could get worse if left unchecked. It doesn't happen over-night. In a gradual process, it can develop into ineffable situations leading to cannibalism, serial killings, and child abuse. Some of this had already happened. He'd previously beaten his daughter, Tammy, with a wire coat hanger. He'd beaten Brenda with a water hose. And he'd beaten Nancy*, an old girl friend, with a belt buckle. The many—and there were many—others were never mentioned. I remembered a time when he'd also seriously beaten Deanna, his daughter by his first wife. She was just barely two years old at the time. I talked to him in a soft, encouraging voice and got him to stop. After that, for some reason, he never let me see him beat anyone again. And he never beat me, even though he sometimes threatened when I was younger. He'd already proven to himself and to others that he was capable of murder.

He was basically easy going until someone made him angry. The important thing was his anger needed a different kind of outlet. The only difference between the Sea of Galilee and the Dead Sea is one has an outlet and the other doesn't. The one that doesn't is stagnated and with no life, while the one that does is blossoming with growth and beauty. His acknowledgement of the situation did exist following treatment by the prison psychologist. If he was going to have a better life, he would have to find a way to get an outlet for his anger that was constructive.

It's hard to discern where and why dysfunctionalism actually begins—when the secret cry of someone's soul turns inward to devour itself. Driven by desire, it becomes a learned method for managing anger and dissipating rage. Sometimes we pamper ourselves with continual indulgences of depraved acts.

Does my heart have repressed or hidden acts of violence that can only be seen after the fact? I pondered while he was still talking, filling in some understanding of my own. "Oh God, help us measure our diminishment before it happens," I silently prayed under my breath. "I thank you for all the times Tommy meant to harm but didn't because of you."

He told Dawn Smith, our friend, he dreaded to tell me this. "There are plenty of areas I haven't told 'Sis' about in my life," he'd previously exposed to Dawn, and recounted some of the details. Apparently he wanted me to see only the good in him, not the vile and ugly—not his degeneracy of that point and time. For reasons of his own, he held the feeling of being condemned by someone he loved, and at the same time he felt it was important that I know. "Somehow, someway, I'm going to have to get up enough nerve to tell 'Sis' this story," he disclosed to Dawn. Eventually he did.

I didn't feel contemptuous of him. I understood. In fact, I've had some of that rage inside me too. It was more evident in the time when I'd returned to Mom's place in High Point to fight Thelma. If she would've fought me back, possibly I would have killed her. The strong sensation of anger needs a constructive outlet to be checked. Mom had no business telling me to "go outside," that I was in Thelma's home. She didn't realize the damage she did then and still doesn't even to this day. There is nothing that hurts any worse than rejection, especially by a parent. If we could do away with rejection, we would have one of greatest healers of the mind ever known. I've gotten over it, but I had an outlet a lot sooner than Tommy did. I got over it by saying to myself, "God forgive her for she knows not what she's done. Forgive me too for feeling the way I do." God must have been protecting both Tommy and me through all these years with his angels.

It wasn't imputed to me our father's fault and our mother's shame. He blamed himself for his unforgivable anger, once spontaneous and powerful. I didn't want to point a finger at my brother's mistakes. I had my own.

Conversation with the psychologist—the part about the hellhole—came back into his mind. It would go on and on, until he made the decision to change himself.

He reached inside his pocket and pulled out a pocketknife; slightly cutting his finger to see if the blood tasted good after the rage was over. It didn't. The pendulum had swung back to the opposite end. It was all a state of mind he'd put himself into, his mind accepted. "If it can be put into the mind, it can be taken out," he noted with authority. "Not realizing what I've done don't give me excuses for doing it."

In comparing himself to Johnny, Mom's youngest brother, Tommy decided to take a better look at himself, face some facts, and do what he could to change. He considered himself lucky. He felt grateful. Johnny had never spent time in a federal prison and he had. State prisons didn't provide the mental help needed for improvements. Marion, Ill., was that life-saving beginning for Tommy. Johnny had died at a young age in a railroad boxcar, beaten so badly he was unrecognizable even by his own brother, David. Tommy was still alive to reason his way out, whatever it may be. He thought about what the Bible said, "You live by the sword, you die by the sword." He was finally going through a healing process that possibly meant his life. It definitely meant a better quality.

"I've thought about it quite a bit," he said. "It really scares me when I lose my temper. I think I might slip back into that state again. If it should happen, I know somebody is going to jail and somebody is going to the hospital.

"I'm not giving you all this information to make you think everybody can be helped if treated right. I'm giving it to you because it pertains to me.

"Just to be in prison can help you realize that some belong there. All of us are individuals. Some of them are just plain crazy. One con, who had been in prison since he was eighteen, got twenty-five years for cutting off two people's heads and parading them around town. That was drug induced though. You could just look at some and tell they were pedophilers (pedophilias) and others you could look at and tell they didn't belong there. In most cases your judgment would be right."

"Yeah, I suppose," I said. "They say 'your eyes are a mirror to your soul.' But why some people get like that in the first place is beyond me (puzzling)."

"Distorted views in your brain. Sometimes it has to do with culture. Sometimes it has to do with survival. It could have to do with education or a multitude of other things, such as family life or even jealousy.

"I was a lot like Dad. I'll take anything for so long. But when it builds up I explode. Everything that's right goes bad. Dad was a lot like that," Tommy rationalized. "He had an easy-going personality to a certain point. But he had an evil temper. He treated people mean, even Mom in the beginning. When he flew mad he might kill anyone. He even held his own dad down and was going to chop off his head with a double-bitted axe. I sometimes believe it was inherited. It came from Grandma Maney's side of the family." (I later checked out this part of the story with Ines, Dad's sister. She said it was true and gave me a few details, which aren't added here.)

"So you're telling me that there are some things that love doesn't cure? Sherry has always said, 'All I ever wanted was love.'"

"I believe our life was a mistake. The way we believed: I had the faith to do anything I wanted to do. But that faith, along with the way we were raised, is what got me into trouble to start with."

I found myself counseling my brother in my mind, as he'd always counseled me. I knew he was still too stubborn to listen to much of my advice. Sometimes I gave it anyway—but not this time. *When I first came out here to Washington I decided to leave the fighting spirit: unpacked. My energies are going to be put into something constructive, if I have anything to do with it. Everyone has those energies and they are as capable as we are to release it in the wrong way...or the right way. It's up to us to choose "the shoal of the road" or firm soil to plant our tree. Hopefully we will do it when we are young, when we have a lot of energy left to do it.*

"The real trouble I see is when the true self is fearfully hidden deep within us," I revealed. "We don't acknowledge it, possibly because of pride. I think these people would open up more, if they didn't fear being condemned or talked about in a bad way. Doesn't that by itself teach us something? We should never do something we're ashamed of. But if it does happen, we should acknowledge it and change for the better. We can never change anything if we think it's right."

"The prison psychologist got me to notice my condition in the first place. But Angie Louddick* and her father were the wonderful people I needed to help me improve. They helped me beyond words I know how to say. I'd like to somehow get the message to her of how much I appreciated her and her family. I'd like to say 'Thank you,' but I don't know if I'll ever see her again."

She must have truly been an angel in human form, I thought. His reflections reverted back to her whenever he talked about any of his prison time.

I think God's angels must have heard his voice, with all its sincerity. Even with his development, still at the half-way point, I felt his improvement had been acknowledged. A bell rang while I was writing this chapter. Very clear was its sound, not loud and course like a church bell, but very high pitched, yet soft to the ears as if it came from Heaven. It rang only once. But once is enough for one more angel to get their wings. For one more person has come from complete disaster to reconsidering.

The holy angels must be singing praises to God, thanking Him for the many blessings: For one more person's ravenous appetite to feed voraciously did exist. Now, it doesn't.

We Thank Thee

By Martha Harris

We thank Thee, Lord, for moun-tains high, for stars that shine all through the sky, and for life in trees, and plants, and flow-ers, for rain-bows at the end of show-ers. How God cre-at-ed in a mase, our earth in six long nights and days,

We thank Thee, Lord, for friends we meet. We thank Thee, for pos-ses-sions sweet, for our house, and home, and lands so d-e-a-r, and for the feel-ing Thou art n-e-a-r. We thank Thee, Lord, for Chil-dren small, their touch, their smile, their help-less call,

Martha Harris

About the Author

From the time I was four years old—a time when I played in mud pies and hated it—I would say, "Some day I'm going to write about this." Regardless of how little education I had, the incidents kept piling up. Throughout the years I repeated, "Some day I'm going to write about this." At the time I got into a small newspaper business, I had no idea it would lead me to this point. It must have been written in the heavens because a little more experience, a little more knowledge, and a little more wisdom also kept piling up. All of a sudden one day I said to myself, "Today is the day." I stopped saying "Not now!" And today has become the day.

The gown I'm wearing on the cover of this book corresponds with one of its chapters, Dreams. The design came to me in a dream. The color was different; in the dream it was blue and green, and my daughter, Sherry Lindblad, was wearing it. I just happened to have the color purple on hand. A woman I know, Cindy Lasseter of Longview, Washington, did the sewing to make part of the dream come true. The chapter will describe the dream more in details. It can be read as a completely separate story or included as part of the book itself. It is definitely not the usual type of story. In fact, it is probably one of the most unusual types of stories you will ever read.

"It's a long row to hoe" to cover all of my life in just one book. This one covers only some of the highlights. Maybe other points will be brought out in the future. All of us have little books stored away inside us. Don't be afraid to touch it.

A great philosopher once said over eight hundred years ago: "From suffering to wisdom" summarizes our history. It's held true for me, as well as millions of others through out time.